VENUS
IN
COPPER

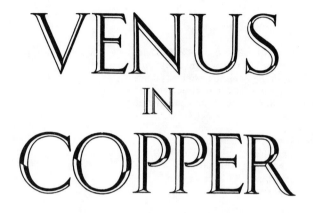

VENUS IN COPPER

A Marcus Didius Falco Novel by

LINDSEY DAVIS

CROWN PUBLISHERS, INC.
NEW YORK

Published by Crown Publishers, Inc.,
201 East 50th Street, New York, New York 10022.
Member of the Crown Publishing Group.
Originally published in Great Britain by
Hutchinson in 1991.

CROWN is a trademark of Crown Publishers, Inc.

Manufactured in the United States of America

LIBRARY OF CONGRESS
CATALOGING-IN-PUBLICATION DATA

Davis, Lindsey.
    Venus in copper : a Marcus Didius Falco novel / Lindsey Davis.
        p.   cm.
    1. Rome—History—Vespasian. 69–79—Fiction,   I. Title.
PR6054.A8925V46   1991
823'.914—dc20   91-37297
                                                         CIP

ISBN 0-517-58477-8

10 9 8 7 6 5 4 3 2 1

First American Edition

For my parents – Welcome to Kent!

Acknowledgment

Selfridges' Food Hall, for supplying the Turbot

ROME

August–September AD71

'The bigger the turbot and dish the bigger the scandal, not to mention the waste of money . . .'

Horace, Satire II,2

'For me it's "Enjoy what you have", though I can't feed my dependants on turbot . . .'

Persius, Satire 6

'I've no time for the luxury of thinking about turbots: a parrot is eating my house . . .'

Falco, Satire I,1

PRINCIPAL CHARACTERS
Friends, Enemies, & Family

M Didius Falco	An informer; trying to turn an honest denarius in a distinctly inferior job
Helena Justina	His highly superior girlfriend
Falco's Mother	(Enough said)
Maia & Junia	Two of Falco's sisters (the madcap & the refined one)
Famia & Gaius Baebius	His brothers-in-law, about whom it is best to say nothing (since there is nothing good to say)
D Camillus Verus & Julia Justa	Helena's patrician parents, who reckon Falco has much to answer for
L Petronius Longus	Falco's loyal friend; the Captain of the Aventine Watch
Smaractus	The landlord Falco is trying to lose
Lenia	Proprietress of the Eagle Laundry, who is after Falco's landlord (or after Falco's landlord's money)
Rodan & Asiacus	Falco's landlord's bullyboys; the seediest gladiators in Rome
Titus Caesar	Elder son and colleague of the Emperor Vespasian; Falco's patron, when he is allowed to be by:
Anacrites	Chief Spy at the Palace, no friend of our boy
Footsie, the Midget, & the Man on the Barrel	Members of Anacrites' staff
A prison rat	Ditto, probably

Suspects & Witnesses

Severina Zotica	A professional bride (a home-loving girl)
Severus Moscus	(The bead-threader) Her first husband (deceased)
Eprius	(The apothecary) Her second husband (deceased)
Grittius Fronto	(The wild-beast importer) Her third husband (deceased)
Chloe	Her feminist parrot
Hortensius Novus	A freedman, now big in business; Severina's betrothed (can he last?)
Hortensius Felix & *Hortensius Crepito*	Business partners to Novus (all friends together, naturally)
Sabina Pollia & *Hortensia Atilia*	Their wives; who consider that Hortensius Novus ought to be a worried man (an interest some might say was worrying)
Hyacinthus	A runabout to the Hortensii
Viridovix	A Gallic chef, reputedly a ruined prince
Anthea	A skivvy
Cossus	A letting agent Hyacinthus knows
Minnius	Purveyor of suspiciously delicious cakes
Lusius	A praetor's clerk, who is suspicious of everyone (a sharp type)
Tyche	An evasive fortune-teller
Thalia	A dancer who does curious things with snakes
A curious snake	
Scaurus	A monumental mason (with plenty of work)
Appius Priscillus	A property mogul (just another rat)
Gaius Cerinthus	Somebody the parrot knows; suspiciously absent from the scene

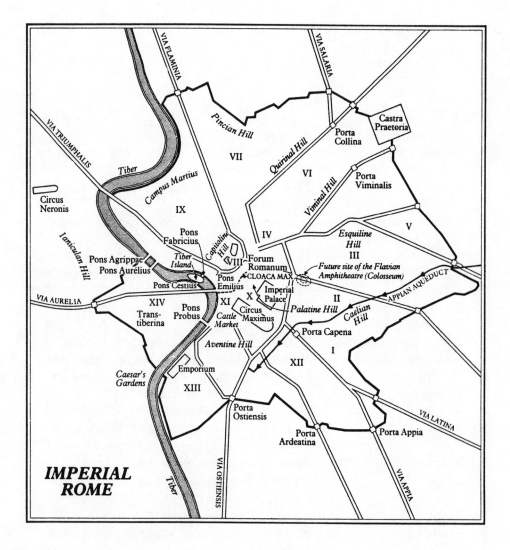

IMPERIAL
ROME

I

Rats are always bigger than you expect.

I heard him first: a sinister shuffle of some uninvited presence, too close for comfort in a cramped prison cell. I lifted my head.

My eyes had grown accustomed to near-darkness. As soon as he moved again I saw him: a dust-coloured, masculine specimen, his pink hands disturbingly like a human child's. He was as big as a buck rabbit. I could think of several casual eating shops in Rome where the cooks would not be too fussy to drop this fat scavenger into their stockpots. Smother him with garlic and who would know? At a furnace stokers' chophouse in some low quarter near the Circus Maximus, any bone with real meat on it would add welcome flavour to the broth . . .

Misery was making me ravenous; all I had to gnaw on was my anger at being here.

The rat was browsing nonchalantly in one corner amongst some rubbish, months' old debris from previous prisoners, which *I* had avoided as too disgusting to explore. He seemed to notice me as I looked up, but his concentration was not really there. I felt that if I lay still he might decide I was a pile of old rags to investigate. But if I shifted my legs defensively the motion would startle him.

Either way, the rat would run over my feet.

I was in the Lautumiae Prison, along with various petty felons who could not afford a barrister, and all the Forum pickpockets who wanted a rest from their wives. Things could be worse. It might have been the Mamertine: the short-stay political holding cell with its twelve-foot-deep dungeon, whose only exit for a man without influence was straight down into Hades. Here at least we had continual entertainment: old lags swearing hot Subura oaths, and wild swoops of disconcerting mania from hopeless drunks. In the Mamertine nothing breaks the monotony until the public strangler comes in to measure your neck.

1

There would be no rats in the Mamertine. No jailor feeds a man condemned to death, so leftovers for the rodent population are scarce. Rats learn these things. Besides, everything there must be kept neat, in case any high-flown senators with foolish friends who have offended the Emperor want to drop in and relate the Forum news. Only here in the Lautumiae among the social dregs could a prisoner enjoy the keen excitement of waiting for his whiskery cellmate to turn round and sink its teeth into his shin . . .

The Lautumiae was a rambling affair, built to house squadrons of prisoners from provinces which were restive. Being foreign was the regular qualification. But any thorn who prickled the wrong bureaucrat could end up here as I had done, watching his toenails grow and thinking harsh thoughts about the establishment. The charge against *me* – in so far as the bastard who committed me to prison had a charge at all – was typical: I had made the fundamental error of showing up the Emperor's Chief Spy. He was a vindictive manipulator called Anacrites. Earlier that summer he had been sent to Campania on a mission; when he bungled it the Emperor Vespasian despatched me to finish the job, which I smartly did. Anacrites reacted in the usual way of a mediocre official whose junior shows any tenacity: he wished me luck in public – then at the first opportunity rammed in the boot.

He had tripped me up over a minor accounting error: he claimed I stole some imperial lead – all I did was borrow the stuff to use in a disguise. I had been prepared to pay back the money I took in exchange for the metal, if anyone ever challenged me. Anacrites never gave me the chance; I was flung into the Lautumiae, and so far no one had bothered to book a magistrate to hear my defence. Soon it would be September, when most of the courts went into recess and all new cases were held over until the New Year . . .

It served me right. Once I had known better than to dabble in politics. I had been a private informer. For five years I did nothing more dangerous than seek out adultery and business fraud. A happy time: strolling about in the sunshine assisting tradesmen with their domestic tiffs. Some of my clients were women (and some of those were quite attractive). Also, private clients paid their bills. (Unlike the Palace, who quibbled over every innocent expense.) If I ever managed to regain my freedom, working for myself again was beckoning attractively.

Three days in jail had doused my happy-go-lucky nature. I was bored. I grew morose. I was suffering physically too: I had a sword-

2

cut in my side – one of those slight flesh-wounds which chooses to fester. My mother was sending in hot dinners to comfort me, but the jailor picked out all the meat for himself. Two people had tried to extricate me; both without success. One was a friendly senator who tried to raise my plight with Vespasian; he had been denied an audience due to Anacrites' baleful influence. The other was my friend Petronius Longus. Petro, who was Captain of the Aventine watch, had come to the prison with a winejar under his elbow and tried the old-pals act on the jailor – only to find himself pitched straight out in the street with his amphora: Anacrites had even poisoned our normal local loyalties. So thanks to the Chief Spy's jealousy, it now looked as if I might never be a free citizen again . . .

The door swung open. A voice grated, 'Didius Falco, somebody loves you after all! Get up off your backside and bring your boots out here – '

As I struggled to raise myself, the rat ran over my foot.

II

My troubles were over – partially.

When I stumbled out into what passed for a reception area, the jailor was closing a heavy drawstring bag, grinning as if it was his birthday. Even his grimy sidekicks seemed impressed by the size of the bribe. Blinking in the daylight, I made out a small, pinched, upright figure who greeted me with a sniff.

Rome is a fair society. There are plenty of provincial backwaters where prefects keep their felons in chains, ready to be tortured when other entertainment palls, but in Rome unless you commit a horrendous misdemeanour – or stupidly confess – every suspect has the right to find a sponsor to stand surety.

'Hello Mother!' It would have been surly to wish myself back in my cell with the rat.

Her expression accused me of being as degenerate as my father – though even my father (who ran off with a redhead and left poor ma with seven children) never landed himself in jail . . . Luckily my mother was too loyal to our family to draw this comparison in front of strangers, so she thanked the jailor for looking after me instead.

'Anacrites seems to have forgotten you, Falco!' he jeered at me.

'That was his intention, presumably.'

'He said nothing about bail before trial – '

'He said nothing about a trial, either,' I snarled. 'Holding me without a court appearance is as illegal as denying bail!'

'Well if he decides to press charges – '

'Just whistle!' I assured him. 'I'll be back in my cell looking innocent in two shakes of a bacchante's tambourine.'

'Sure, Falco?'

'Oh *sure!*' I lied pleasantly.

Outside I took a deep breath of freedom, which I instantly regretted. It was August. We were facing the Forum. Around the Rostrum the atmosphere was almost as stifling as the bowels of the Lautumiae.

4

Most of the aristocracy had dodged off to their airy summer villas, but for those of us at the rough end of society, life in Rome had slowed to a sluggish pace. Any movement in this heat was unbearable.

My mother examined her jailbird, looking unimpressed.

'Just a misunderstanding, Ma . . .' I tried to prevent my face revealing that for an informer with a tough reputation, being rescued by his *mother* was an indignity to avoid. 'Who provided the handsome ransom? Was it Helena?' I asked, referring to the unusually superior girlfriend I had managed to acquire six months ago in place of my previous string of flea-bitten circus entertainers and flower girls.

'No, I paid the surety; Helena has been seeing to your rent – ' My heart sank at this rush of support from the women in my life. I knew I would have to pay for it, even if not in cash. 'Never mind about the money.' My mother's tone indicated that with a son like me, she kept her life savings continually to hand. 'Come home with me for a good dinner – '

She must be planning to keep me firmly in her custody; *I* planned on being my footloose self.

'I need to see Helena, Ma – '

Normally it would be unwise for a bachelor who had just been redeemed by his little old mother to suggest sloping off after women. But my mother nodded. In the first place, Helena Justina was a senator's daughter so visiting such a highly placed lady counted as a privilege for the likes of me, not the usual depravity mothers rant about. Also, due partly to an accident on a staircase, Helena had just miscarried our child. All our female relations still regarded me as a reckless wastrel, but for Helena's sake most would agree that at present it was my duty to visit her at every opportunity.

'Come with me!' I urged.

'Don't be foolish!' scoffed my mother. 'It's you Helena wants to see!'

That news failed to fill me with confidence.

Ma lived near the river, behind the Emporium. We crossed the Forum slowly (to emphasise how Ma was bowed down by the troubles I caused her), then she set me loose at my favourite bathhouse, which lay behind the Temple of Castor. There I sluiced away the stench of prison, changed into a spare tunic which I had left at the gymnasium to cover emergencies, and found a barber who managed to make me look more respectable (under the blood he caused to flow).

I had come out, still feeling grey in the face after being locked up, yet much more relaxed. I was walking towards the Aventine, running my fingers through my damp curls in a vain attempt to turn myself into the kind of debonair bachelor who might rouse a woman's ardour. Then disaster struck. Too late, I noticed a pair of disreputable bruisers posing against a portico so they could show off their muscles to anyone who had to pass on their side of the street. They wore loincloths, with leather strips tied round their knees and wrists and ankles to make them look tough. Their arrogance was horribly familiar.

'Oh look – it's Falco!'

'Oh cobnuts – Rodan and Asiacus!'

Next moment one of them was behind me with his elbows clenched round my upper arms, while the other shook me charmlessly by the hand – a process which involved pulling out my wrist until my arm joints strained in their sockets like bowlines fighting their couplings on a galley in a hurricane. The smell of old sweat and recent garlic was bringing tears to my eyes. 'Oh cut it, Rodan; my reach is already long enough . . .'

To call these two 'gladiators' insulted even the clapped-out hulks who usually feature in that trade. Rodan and Asiacus trained at a barracks which was run by my landlord Smaractus, and when they were not smacking themselves silly with practice swords he sent them out to make the streets even more dangerous than usual. They never did much work in the arena; their role in public life was to intimidate the unfortunate tenants who rented homes from him. For me, being in prison had had one great advantage: avoiding my landlord, and these pet thugs of his.

Asiacus lifted me off my feet and shook me about. I let him rearrange my guts temporarily. I waited until he grew bored with it and put me back on the paving slabs – then I carried on downwards, pulled him off balance, and threw him over my head at Rodan's feet.

'Olympus! Doesn't Smaractus teach you two *anything*?' I hopped back smartly out of their reach. 'You're out of date; my rent's been paid!'

'So the rumour's true!' leered Rodan. 'We heard you're a kept man now!'

'Jealousy gives you a nasty squint, Rodan! Your mother should have warned you, it will drive away the girls!' You may have heard that gladiators trail throngs of infatuated women; Rodan and Asiacus must have been the only two in Rome whose special seediness deprived them of any following. Asiacus got up, wiping his nose. I shook my head. 'Sorry; I was forgetting: neither of you could interest a fifty-year-old fishwife with two blind eyes and no sense of discretion – '

Then Asiacus jumped me. And they both set about reminding me why I hated Smaractus so bitterly.

'That's for the *last* time your rent was overdue!' grunted Rodan, who had a long memory.

'And *that's* for the *next* time!' added Asiacus – a realistic forecaster.

We had practised this painful dance so many times that I soon twisted out of their grip. Throwing back one or two more insults, I skipped away up the street. They were too lazy to follow me.

I had been free for an hour. I was already battered and despondent. In Rome, a landlord's city, freedom brings mixed joys.

III

Helena Justina's father, the Senator Camillus Verus, lived near the Capena Gate. A desirable spot, just off the Appian Way where it emerges from the republican city wall. On the way I managed to find another bathhouse to soothe my crop of new bruises. Luckily Rodan and Asiacus always punched a victim's ribcage, so my face was unmarked; if I remembered not to wince there was no need for Helena to know. A sickly Syrian apothecary sold me a salve for the sword-wound I had already been nursing in my side, though the ointment soon produced a greasy mark on my tunic, blueish, like mould on wall plaster, which was not designed to impress the fashionable residents of the Capena Gate.

The Camillus porter knew me but as usual refused me admittance. I did not allow this fleabag to delay my entry long. I walked round the corner, borrowed a hat from a roadmender, knocked again with my back turned, then when the porter foolishly opened up for what he thought was a travelling lupinseller, I rushed indoors making sure my boot stomped down hard on his ankle as our paths crossed.

'For a *quadrans* I'd lock you out on the step! I'm *Falco*, you muttonchop! Announce me to Helena Justina, or your heirs will be quarrelling over who gets your best sandals sooner than you expect!'

Once I got inside the house he treated me with sullen respect. That is, he went back into his cubicle to finish an apple, while I searched for my princess by myself.

Helena was in a reception room, looking pale and studious with a reed pen in her hand. She was twenty-three – or perhaps twenty-four now since I had no idea when her birthday was; even after I had been to bed with their treasure, I was not invited to share the family celebrations of a senator's house. They only let me see her at all because they cringed from Helena's own wilfulness. Even before she met me she had been married but had chosen to divorce herself (for the eccentric reason that her husband never talked to her), so her parents had already realised their eldest offspring was a trial.

8

Helena Justina was a tall, stately being whose straight dark hair had been tortured with hot curling rods, though it was fighting back well. She had handsome brown eyes which no cosmetics could improve, though her maids painted them up on principle. At home she wore very little jewellery, and looked none the worse for it. In company she was shy; even alone with a close friend like me she might pass for modest until she piped up with an opinion – at which point wild dogs broke pack and ran for cover all along the street. I reckoned I could handle her – but I never pushed my luck.

I posed in the doorway with my normal disrespectful grin. Helena's sweet, unforced smile of greeting was the best thing I had seen for a week. 'Why is a beautiful girl like you sitting on her own, scribbling recipes?'

'I am translating Greek History,' Helena stated pompously. I peered over her shoulder. It was a recipe for stuffed figs.

I bent and kissed her cheek. The loss of our baby, which we both still felt, had inflicted a painful formality on us. Then our two right hands found and gripped one another with a fervour that could have got us denounced by the pompous old barristers in the Basilica Julia.

'I'm so glad to see you!' murmured Helena fiercely.

'It takes more than prison bolts to keep me away.' I uncurled her hand and laid it against my cheek. Her ladylike fingers were perfumed with an eccentric combination of rare Indian unguents and oak-apple ink – quite unlike the stagnant whiffs that hung around the floosies I had previously known. 'Oh lady, I love you,' I admitted (still buoyed up by the euphoria of my recent release). 'And it's not just because I found out that you've paid my rent!'

She slipped from her seat to kneel by me with her head hidden. A senator's daughter would hardly risk letting a house-slave find her crying in a convict's lap – but I stroked her neck soothingly, just in case. Besides, the back of Helena's neck was an attractive proposition to an idle hand.

'I don't know why you bother with me,' I commented after a while. 'I'm a wreck. I live in a pit. I have no money. Even the rat in my cell had a sneer when he looked at me. Whenever you need me I leave you on your own – '

'Stop grumbling, Falco!' Helena snorted, looking up with a mark on her cheek from my belt buckle, but otherwise her old self.

'I do a job most people wouldn't touch,' I carried on gloomily. 'My own employer throws me into jail and forgets I exist – '

'You've been released – '

'Not exactly!' I confessed.

Helena never fussed over things she believed I ought to sort out for myself. 'What are you intending to do now?'

'Work on my own again.' She said nothing; no need to ask why I was unhappy. My bright plan posed one great problem: I would earn much less independently than my notional public salary, despite the fact that Vespasian's payclerks kept me months in arrears. 'Do you think this is stupid?'

'No; you're quite right!' Helena agreed without hesitation, though she must have realised going freelance destroyed any hope of me affording marriage into the patrician rank. 'You've risked your life for the state. Vespasian took you on because he knew just what you were worth to him. But Marcus, you're too good to suffer poor rewards from a stingy employer and petty Palace jealousies – '

'Sweetheart, you know what it means – '

'I said I would wait.'

'I said I wouldn't let you.'

'Didius Falco, I never take any notice of what you say.'

I grinned, then we sat together in silence a few minutes more.

After jail, this room in her father's house was a haven of tranquillity. Here we had rag rugs and tasselled cushions to make us comfortable. Thick masonry muffled out sounds from the street, while light flowing in through high windows on the garden side lit walls which were painted as mock marble, the colour of ripened wheat. It provided a gracious impression – though a slightly faded one. Helena's father was a millionaire (this was not good detective work on my part, just the minimum qualification for the Senate); yet even he regarded himself as struggling in a city where only multimillionaires attracted election votes.

My own position was far worse. I had no money and no status. To carry off Helena on respectable terms, I would have to find four hundred thousand sesterces and then persuade the Emperor to add me to the list of pitiful nonentities who form the middle rank. Even if I ever managed it, I was for her a disreputable choice.

She read my thoughts. 'Marcus, I heard your horse won his race at the Circus Maximus.'

Life does have its compensations: the horse, who was called Little Sweetheart, had been a lucky bequest to me. I could not afford to stable him, but before he went to the horse sales I had entered him in just one race – which he won at amazing odds. 'Helena, you are right; I made some money on that race. I might invest in a more impressive apartment, to attract a better class of client.'

Her head nodded approvingly, close against my knee. She had her hair pinned up with a pantheon of ivory bodkins, all with knobs carved as strict-looking goddesses. While I mused about my lack of money I had pulled one out, so I stuck it in my belt like a hunting knife, then teasingly set about capturing the rest. Helena squirmed in mild annoyance, reaching for my wrists. Eventually she knocked my fistful of pins to the floor; I let her flail around trying to find them while I carried on methodically with my plan.

By the time I had her hair all loose, Helena had repossessed her bodkins – though I noticed she let me keep the one stuffed in my belt. I still have it: Flora, with a crown of roses which is giving her hay fever; she turns up sometimes when I burrow for lost pens in my writing-box.

I spread out Helena's shining hair the way I wanted it. 'That's better! Now you look more like a lass who might agree to being kissed – in fact you look like one who might even kiss me of her own accord . . .' I reached down and pulled her arms round my neck.

It was a long, deeply appreciative kiss. Only the fact that I knew Helena very well made me notice that my own passion was meeting unusual restraint from her.

'What's this? Gone off me, fruit?'

'Marcus, I can't – '

I understood. Her miscarriage had shaken her; she was wary of risking another. And she was probably afraid of losing me too. We both knew more than one bright spark of Roman rectitude who would automatically ditch a distressed girlfriend at a time like this.

'I'm sorry – ' She was embarrassed, and struggling to escape. But she was still my Helena. She wanted me to hold her almost as much as I wanted to. She needed to be comforted – even though for once she shrank from encouraging me.

'My darling, it's natural.' I loosened my grip. 'Everything will right itself . . .' I knew I had to be reassuring so I tried to treat her gently, though it was hard to take disappointment when it felt so physical. I was cursing, and Helena must have been aware of it.

We sat quiet and talked about family matters (a bad idea as usual), then not long afterwards I said I had to leave.

Helena took me to the door. The porter had now disappeared altogether so I undid the bolts myself. She threw her arms round me and buried her face in my neck. 'I suppose you'll run after other women!'

'Naturally!' I managed to make a joke of it too.

Her huge stricken eyes were affecting me badly. I kissed her eyelids then tormented myself, holding her tight against me while I lifted her right off her feet. 'Come and live with me!' I urged suddenly. 'The gods only know how long it will take me to earn what we need to be respectable. I'm frightened of losing you; I want to have you close. If I rent a bigger apartment – '

'Marcus, I just feel – '

'Trust me.'

Helena smiled, and pulled my ear as if she thought that was the quickest way to make our difficulties permanent. But she promised to think about what I had said.

My step lightened as I walked home to the Aventine. Even if my lady was reluctant to join me, with my winnings on Little Sweetheart there was nothing to stop me leasing a more gracious apartment anyway . . . Knowing what I was going home to, the thought of living somewhere else was bound to cheer me up.

Then I remembered that before I was hauled off to prison, my uncashed betting tokens had been swallowed by my three-year-old niece.

IV

The Eagle Laundry, Fountain Court.

Of all the groaning tenements in all the sordid city alleyways, the most degrading must be Fountain Court. It was five minutes off the great road from Ostia, one of the most vital highways in the Empire, but this ulcerous spot in the armpit of the Aventine could have been a different world. Up above, on the double crests of the hill, were the great Temples of Diana and Venus, but we lived too close to see their lofty architecture from our deep, dark warren of aimless, nameless lanes. It was cheap (for Rome). Some of us would have paid the landlord more just to have him hire a pair of competent bailiffs to evict us into the fresher air of a better street.

My apartment was high in a vast, ramshackle block. A laundry occupied all the space at street level; woollen tunics awaiting collection were the only thing in our neighbourhood that were clean. Once on, their pristine condition could be ruined by one short trip down the muddy single track that served as both our exit road and the nearest we had to a sewer, amidst the smuts from the lampblack furnace where a one-eyed stationers' supplier brewed stinking domestic ink, and the smoke from the beehive ovens where Cassius our local breadman could char a loaf to the verge of destruction like no other baker in Rome.

These were dangerous byways: in a moment of lapsed concentration, I sank to the ankle in sticky brown dung. While I was muttering and cleaning my boot on a kerbstone, Lenia the laundress stuck her head round a line of tunics. Seeing me, she bustled out to deride me as usual. She was an ill-kempt bundle who approached with the gracelessness of a swan landing on water: wild writhings of luridly dyed red hair, watery eyes, and a voice that was hoarse from too many flagons of badly fermented wine.

'Falco! Where've you been all week?'

'Out of town.'

It was unclear whether she knew I meant in the Lautumiae. Not

13

that Lenia would care. She was too lazy to be curious, except in closely defined areas of business. Those included whether my filthy landlord Smaractus was being paid his dues – and she only became *really* curious about that after she decided to marry him. A decision made for purely financial reasons (because Smaractus was as rich as Crassus after decades of squeezing the Aventine poor) and now Lenia was preparing for her wedding with the clinical will of a surgeon. (Knowing that the patient would pay heavily for her services, after she had carved him up . . .)

'I gather I'm in credit,' I grinned.

'You finally found out how to pick a woman!'

'True; I rely on the Parian perfection of my face – '

Lenia, who was a harsh critic of the fine arts, cackled cynically. 'Falco, you're a cheap fake!'

'Not me – I come with a certificate of quality from a lady of good repute! She likes to pamper me. Well I deserve it, of course . . . How much has she contributed?'

I could see Lenia opening her mouth to lie about it; then she worked out that Helena Justina was bound to tell me, if ever I had the good manners to discuss my debt. 'Three months, Falco.'

'Jupiter!' That was a shock to my system. The most I ever reckoned to donate to my landlord's retirement fund was three weeks (in arrears). 'Smaractus must think he's been transported on a rainbow to Olympus!'

I deduced from a certain cloudiness in Lenia's expression that Smaractus had yet to discover his luck. She changed the subject rapidly: 'Someone keeps coming here asking for you.'

'Client?' Nervously I wondered if the Chief Spy had already discovered me missing. 'Take his details?'

'Oh I've better things to do, Falco! He turns up every day and every day I tell him you're not here – ' I relaxed. Anacrites would have had no reason to be looking for me until this afternoon.

'Well, I'm back now!' I felt too weary to be bothered with mysteries.

I set off up the stairs. I lived on the sixth floor, the cheapest of all. It gave me plenty of time to remember the familiar smell of urine and old cabbage ends; the stale pigeon droppings staining every step; the wall graffiti, not all of them at child height, of stickmen charioteers; the curses against betting agents and the pornographic advertisements. I knew hardly any of my fellow tenants, but I recognised their voices quarrelling as I passed. Some doors were permanently

14

closed with oppressive secrecy; other families opted for no more than curtained entrances which forced their neighbours to share their dismal lives. A naked toddler ran out of one, saw me, and rushed back inside screaming. A demented old lady on the third floor always sat in her doorway and gabbled after anyone who came by; I saluted her with a gracious gesture which set her off into torrents of venomous abuse.

I needed practice; I was stumbling when I finally reached the top of the building. For a moment I listened: professional habit. Then I operated my simple latch-lifter and pushed open the door.

Home. The sort of apartment where you go in; change your tunic; read your friends' messages; then find any excuse to rush straight back out again. But today I could not face the nightmares on the stairs a second time, so I stayed in.

Four strides permitted me to survey my premises: the office with a cheap bench and table, then the bedroom with a lopsided contraption that served as my bed. Both rooms had the worrying neatness that resulted when my mother had enjoyed three days of uninterrupted tidying. I looked around suspiciously but I reckoned no one else had been there. Then I set about making the place my own again. I soon managed to knock the sparse furniture askew, rumple the bedclothes, spill water everywhere as I revived my balcony foliage, and drop all the clothes I had been wearing onto the floor.

After that I felt better. Now it was *Home*.

Prominent on the table, where not even I could miss it, stood a ceramic Greek bowl which I had bought off an antiques stall for two coppers and a cheeky smile; it was half full of scratched bone counters, some with extremely odd streaks of colour. I chortled. The last time I saw these was at a ghastly family party where my little niece Marcia had seized them to play with and swallowed most of them: my betting tags.

When a child has eaten something you prefer not to lose, there is only one way – if you are fond of the child – to recover it. I knew the disgusting procedure from the time my brother Festus swallowed our mother's wedding ring and pressured me to help him find it. (Until he was killed in Judaea, which put an end to my fraternal duties, there was a tradition in our family that Festus was the one who was always in trouble, while I was the fool he always persuaded to dig him out of it.) Gulping down family valuables must be an inherited trait; I had just spent three days in prison wishing constipation on my feckless brother's sweet but feckless child . . .

No need to worry. Some hard-headed relation – my sister Maia probably, the only one who could organise – had gallantly retrieved these tags. To celebrate, I pulled up a floorboard where I had half a winejar hidden away from visitors and sat out on my balcony with my feet up on the parapet while I applied all my attention to a restorative drink.

As soon as I was comfortable, a visitor arrived.

I heard him come in, gasping for air after the long climb. I kept quiet, but he found me anyway. He pushed out through the folding door and accosted me chirpily. 'You Falco?'

'Could be.'

He had arms as thin as pea-sticks. A triangular face came down to a point at a dot of a chin. Above it ran a narrow black moustache, almost ear to ear. The moustache was what you noticed. It bisected a face that was too old for his adolescent body, as if he were a refugee from a province racked by twenty years of famine and tribal strife The true cause was nothing so dramatic. He was just a slave.

'Who's asking?' I prompted. By then I had warmed up enough in the late-afternoon sunshine not to care.

'A runabout from the house of Hortensius Novus.'

He had a faintly foreign accent, but it lay a long way back behind the common lilt all prisoners of war seem to contract in the slave market. I guessed he had picked up his Latin as a small child; probably by now he could hardly remember his native tongue. His eyes were blue; he looked like a Celt to me.

'You have a name?'

'Hyacinthus!'

He said it with a level stare that dared me to scoff. If he was a slave he had enough problems without enduring ribaldry from every new acquaintance just because some overseer with a filthy hangover had stuck him with the name of a Greek flower.

'Pleased to meet you, Hyacinthus.' I refused to present a target for the aggressive retort he held ready. 'I've never heard of your master Hortensius. What's his problem?'

'If you asked him, he'd say nothing.'

People often talk in riddles when they commission an informer. Very few clients seem capable of asking straight out, *What are your rates for proving that my wife sleeps with my driver?*

16

'So why has he sent you?' I asked the runabout patiently.

'His *relations* have sent me,' Hyacinthus corrected me. 'Hortensius Novus has no idea I'm here.'

That convinced me the case involved denarii, so I waved Hyacinthus to my bench: a hint of cash worth being secretive about always perks me up.

'Thanks, Falco; you're a regular general!' Hyacinthus assumed my invitation to sit included my winejar too; to my annoyance he dodged back indoors and found a beaker for himself. As he made himself at home under my rose pergola he demanded, 'This your idea of a gracious setting for interviewing clients?'

'My clients are easily impressed.'

'It stinks! Or is this just one of the drop-ins you keep around Rome?'

'Something like that.'

'It was the only address we had.' It was the only address *I* had. He tried the wine, then spluttered. '*Parnassus!*'

'Gift from a grateful client.' Not grateful enough.

I poured myself a refill, as an excuse to shift the winejar out of his reach. He was having a good squint at me. My informality made him doubtful. The world is full of straight-haired fools who think curly-tops who grin at them cannot possibly be good businessmen.

'This place has all I need,' I said, implying that to exist in such squalor I must be tougher than I looked. 'The people I want to meet know where to find me – while the ones I may be avoiding are put off by the stairs . . . All right Hyacinthus, I don't issue a prospectus of my services, but here's what I can offer: I do information-gathering of a mainly domestic type – '

'Divorce?' he translated, with a grin.

'Correct! Also investigating prospective sons-in-law on behalf of sensitive fathers, or advising recent legatees whether their bequests involve any hidden debt. I do legwork for lawyers who need more evidence – with a court appearance if required. I have contacts in auctioneering and I specialise in recovery of precious artworks after theft. I *don't* tackle draftdodgers or debt collection. And I *never* fix gladiatorial fights.'

'Squeamish?'

'Better sense.'

'We shall want to take up references.'

'So will I! All my business is legitimate.'

'How much do you charge, Falco?'

'Depends on the complexity of the case. A solving fee, plus a daily expense rate. And I give no guarantees, other than a promise to do my best.'

'What is it you do for the Palace?' Hyacinthus threw in suddenly.

'I don't work for the Palace now.' It sounded like official secrecy: a pleasing effect. 'Is that why you're here?'

'My people felt a Palace man came ready recommended.'

'Their mistake! If they hire me I'll do a decent job, and be discreet. So, Hyacinthus, are we in business?'

'I have to invite you to the house. You'll be told about the case there.'

I had intended to go anyway. I like to inspect the people who will be paying me. 'So where am I heading?'

'The Via Lata sector. On the Pincian.'

I whistled. 'Highly desirable! Are Hortensius and his relations people of rank?'

'Freedmen.'

Ex-slaves! That was new for me. But it made a change from vindictive officials and the hypocrisies I had run up against with some of the senatorial class.

'You object?' Hyacinthus enquired curiously.

'Why should I, if their money's good?'

'Oh . . . no reason,' said the slave.

He finished his drink and waited for another, but I had no intention of offering. 'We're on the Via Flaminia side, Falco. Anyone in the district will point out the house.'

'If Hortensius is to know nothing about this, when shall I come?'

'Daytime. He's a businessman. He leaves home after breakfast usually.'

'What's his business?' My question was a routine one, but the way Hyacinthus shrugged and ignored it seemed oddly evasive. 'So who do I ask for?'

'Sabina Pollia – or if she's unavailable, there's another called Hortensia Atilia – but it's Pollia who is taking the initiative.'

'Wife?'

He gave me a sly grin. 'Novus is unmarried.'

'Don't tell me any more! So the females of his household are hiring me to frighten off a gold-digger?' Hyacinthus looked impressed. 'When a bachelor has a houseful of formidable women – and don't tell me Hortensius Novus hasn't,' I growled, 'because you're here

18

behind his back on their behalf – why does he always decide that the solution to his troubles lies in marrying another one?'

'Now tell me you don't do gold-diggers!' the runabout retaliated.

'All the time!' I assured him glumly. 'Gold-diggers are wonderful women: the bedrock of my trade!'

As he left he said, 'If you ever do think of leasing a more respectable apartment – '

'I could be in the market.' I followed him as far as the balcony door.

'Try Cossus,' Hyacinthus offered helpfully. 'He's a letting agent in the Vicus Longus – a dozy pomegranate, but reliable. He has plenty of decent property for men of affairs. Mention my name and he'll be sure to look after you – '

'Thanks. I may do that.' I deduced that Hyacinthus thought his suggestion had earned him a tip. I keep a half-aureus sewn in the hem of my tunic, but there was no way I would part with that for a slave. All I could find was a thin copper *as* which no self-respecting latrinekeeper would accept as an entrance fee.

'Thanks, Falco. That should swell my freedom fund!'

'Sorry. I've been out of touch with my banker!'

I tried to make my spell in the Lautumiae sound like a secret mission in Lower Parthia, so he could go home with a good report for my prospective clients.

V

The freedman Hortensius Novus lived in the north of the city, on the scented slopes of the Pincian Hill. His house stood surrounded by a perfectly plain wall of sufficient height to prevent people peeping over the top, had any of his well-heeled neighbours lived near enough. None of them did. It was an area where the grounds of the private villas were even more spacious than the public gardens which were graciously allowed to fill the lesser spaces in between. If I say that one of *those* was the Garden of Lucullus, which the Empress Messalina had prized so highly she executed its owner when he declined to sell, this gives a fair idea of the scale of the private mansions on Pincian Hill.

I talked myself through the Hortensius gatehouse, then hiked along the hillside on their broad gravel drive. There was plenty of landscape to occupy me. Luckily I had stopped at a sweetmeat stall and made some enquiries, so I was to some extent prepared for the opulence of the freedman's estate. His box trees clipped like winged griffons, his pale statues of broad-browed goddesses, his intricate pergolas swagged with roses and vines, his massive alabaster urns with blush-pink veining, his dovecotes, his fishpools, his marble seats in intimate arbours with views across neatly scythed lawns, were a treat.

I was admitted past the bronze sphinxes guarding the white marble entrance steps into a formal entrance hall with heavy black pillars. There I tapped my boot gently on a white and grey geometric mosaic until a tired servant appeared. He took my name then led me through the delicate ferns and fountains to an elegant inner court where one of the three Hortensius freedmen had recently installed a new statue of himself, in his best toga, looking important and holding a scroll. This was, I decided, what my landing needed at the Falco residence: me in Carrara marble, like a plush prig with lots of money who felt satisfied with his world. I made a note to order one – some day.

I ended up in a reception room, alone. Throughout the house I had glimpsed burnt-out tapers and torches. A faint whiff of stale garlands hung round the corridors, and from time to time when a door opened I caught the sound of last night's dishes clattering. A message came from Sabina Pollia asking me to wait. I guessed that the lady was not yet up and dressed. I decided to reject the case if she turned out to be a rich party-giving slut.

After half an hour I grew bored and wandered off down a corridor, exploring. Everywhere was hung with lavishly dyed curtains, slightly crumpled; the furniture was exquisite, yet jumbled into the rooms quite haphazardly. The decor was a strange mixture too: white stuccoed ceilings, deliciously delicate, above wall paintings of grossly erotic scenes. It was as if they had bought whatever they were offered by every fast-talking salesman who came along, without reference to a design plan, let alone taste. The only thing the artwork had in common was that it must have cost thousands.

I was amusing myself putting an auction price to a Phidias 'Venus adjusting her Sandal' (which gave every appearance of being original, unlike almost every other Phidias you run across in Rome) when a door flew open behind me and a female voice cried, '*There* you are!'

I spun round guiltily. When I saw what she looked like, I did not apologise.

She was a peach. She had kissed farewell to forty, but if she ever went to the theatre she would attract more attention than the play. Her melting dark brown eyes were outlined with kohl, yet even left to nature those eyes would cause moral damage to any man with a nervous system as susceptible as mine. The eyes were set in a near-perfect face, and the face belonged to a body which made the Phidias Venus look like an out-of-condition eggseller who had been on her feet all day. She knew exactly the effect she had; I was swimming in perspiration where I stood.

Since I had asked for Sabina Pollia, I assumed this was she. From behind her two burly boys in vibrant blue livery surged towards me.

'Call off your dogs!' I commanded. 'I have an invitation from the lady of the house.'

'Are you the informer?' The direct way she spoke suggested that if it suited her she might not be a lady.

I nodded. She signalled the two flankers to back off. They stepped aside just enough for privacy though near enough to lather me soundly if I tried to cause offence. I had no intention of doing that – unless someone offended me first. 'If you ask me,' I said frankly, 'a lady should not need a bodyguard in her own home.'

21

I kept my face neutral while madam toyed with the suspicion that I had just accused her of being a common piece. 'I'm Didius Falco. Sabina Pollia, presumably?' I offered my paw for a handshake in a deliberately unconventional way. She looked unhappy, but accepted it. She had small hands with many jewelled finger-rings; short fingers with pale oval fingernails like a girl's.

Sabina Pollia made up her mind, and dismissed the two boys in the Adriatic uniforms. A lady ought to have sent for a chaperone; apparently she forgot. She threw herself onto a couch, rather untidily; the graceful Venus had the advantage of her now.

'Tell me about yourself, Falco!' A risk of my trade: she intended to enjoy herself, interrogating me. 'You're a private informer – how long have you been in that business?'

'Five years. Since I was invalided out of the legions.'

'Nothing serious?'

I gave her a dry, slow smile. 'Nothing that prevents me doing what I want to do!'

Our eyes met, lingeringly. Getting this beauty to discuss my commission was going to be hard work.

She was one of those classic kittens with a straight nose down the centre of a balanced face, clear skin, and extremely regular teeth – a perfect profile, though slightly lacking in expression since the owners of very beautiful faces never need to express character to get what they want; besides, too much expression might crease the paint they never need but always use. She was slight, and played on it – bold snake-headed bracelets to emphasise the delicacy of her arms, and a little, girlishly wounded pout. It was designed to melt a man. Never one to quibble when a woman makes an effort, I melted obediently.

'I hear you work for the Palace, Falco – though my servant tells me you are not allowed to say anything about that . . .'

'Correct.'

'Being a private informer must be fascinating?' She was evidently hoping for some scandalous revelations about past clients.

'Sometimes,' I answered unhelpfully. Most of my past clients were people I preferred to forget.

'You had a brother who was a military hero, I hear.'

'Didius Festus. He won the Palisaded Crown in Judaea.' My brother Festus would think it hilarious that I had gained status through being related to him. 'Did you know him?'

'No – should I?'

'A lot of women did.' I smiled. 'Sabina Pollia, I gather there is something I may be able to help you with?'

These doll-like creatures whip to the mark like artillery bolts. 'Why, Falco – what are you good at?'

I decided it was time to reassert my grip on the situation. 'Lady, what I'm good at is my job! Can we proceed?'

'Not before time!' Sabina Pollia retorted.

Why do I always get the blame?

'If I understood Hyacinthus, this is a family problem?' I asked somewhat dourly.

'Not quite!' Pollia laughed. She gave me the vulnerable pout again, but I had never been fooled by it; the lady was tough. 'We need you to keep the problem *out* of the family!'

'Then let's describe the "family" first. Hortensius Novus lives here; and who else?'

'We *all* live here. I am married to Hortensius Felix; Hortensia Atilia is the wife of Hortensius Crepito – ' Slaves intermarrying: a common development.

'Novus sits among this brotherly triumvirate, still a happy bachelor?'

'So far,' she replied, with tension in her voice. 'But they are not brothers, Falco! Who gave you that idea?'

I was thrown off balance slightly. 'The set-up; same names; you call yourselves a family – '

'We are none of us related. Though we *are* one family. Our patron's name was Hortensius Paulus.'

So to add to the normal inconvenience that every Roman is reverently named after his father, as are his brothers and sons, here I had a whole gang of ex-slaves, each bearing their old master's patronymic now they were free. Females too: 'Hortensia Atilia must be a freedwoman of the same household?'

'Yes.'

'But not you?'

'Oh yes.'

'Your name is different – ' Sabina Pollia raised the proud pared crescents of her eyebrows, amusing herself at my expense. 'I'm struggling here!' I admitted freely.

'I worked for the woman of the house,' she stated. The words 'belonged to' and 'was freed by' slipped by unsaid. 'I took her title . . . Falco, is this relevant?'

'It helps.' Mainly it helped me hold back accidental insults; I hate to offend my paying clients, in case they pay me less. 'To sum up: five of you were given your release for good service – ' Set free by the Paulus will, no doubt. 'You have lived together; married amongst yourselves; worked together, ever since.' As the minimum age for a slave's manumission is thirty, a shrewd glance at Pollia suggested she had been on the loose in society for at least ten years. More, I thought, forgetting to be tactful about the lady's age. 'You have a well-established household; visibly prosperous. I can work out the rest: enter an outsider – who may be a floosie but we'll come to that in a minute – and entraps your one loose end. You want me to fend her off?'

'You're sharp, Falco.'

'I like to eat . . . How far have things gone?'

'Hortensius Novus has had himself formally betrothed.'

'Rash man! Before I take the case,' I pondered thoughtfully, 'tell me why I should believe that you and Atilia are not simply annoyed at this clever operator for disrupting your routine?'

Pollia seemed to accept that it was a fair question. 'Naturally our concern is for our old friend's happiness.'

'Naturally!' I exclaimed. 'Though I gather there's an amount of cash at stake?'

'If Hortensius Novus brings home a bride who has the right motives we shall welcome her.' I found it a marvel that *two* women could share one household, let alone three. I said so. She explained the harmonious arrangements they had devised: 'Felix and I live in this wing; Crepito and Atilia have the far side. We meet for business and entertainment in the formal rooms at the centre of the house – '

'Where does Novus squeeze in?'

'He has a suite on an upper floor – more than ample, Falco.'

'We bachelors have restrained tastes. But if he weds, can you accommodate a third married couple?' I asked, wondering if all I had to sort out here was the normal sort of housing problem that blights family life in Rome.

'Easy enough.' Sabina Pollia shrugged. 'Our architect would build on a new wing.'

'We come to the crunch question then: if Novus taking a wife causes no problems domestically, what is so distressing to you and Atilia about his ladyfriend?'

'We believe she intends to kill him,' Sabina Pollia said.

VI

Informers are simple people. Given a dead body our response is to look for the killer – but we like the body first; it seems more logical.

'Lady, in good Roman society, mentioning a murder before it even happens is considered impolite.'

'You think I'm making this up!' Pollia rolled her magnificent eyes.

'It sounds so ridiculous, I'm taking you seriously! When people invent, they usually choose a story that's plausible.'

'This is true, Falco.'

'Convince me.'

'The woman has had husbands before – three of them!'

'Oh we live in slack times. Nowadays five weddings is the minimum to count as reprehensible . . .'

'None of her previous husbands survived long – ' Pollia insisted; I was still grinning evilly. 'And each time she walked away from the funeral far wealthier!'

I let the grin evaporate. 'Ah! Money lends this story of yours a genuine patina . . . Incidentally, what's her name?'

Pollia shrugged (negligently revealing her beautiful white shoulders between the sparkling dress pins on her sleeves). 'She calls herself Severina. I forget her other title.'

I made a note in my pocketbook with a stylus I kept handy. *'Forename, Severina; cognomen unknown* . . . Is she attractive?'

'Juno, how should I know? She must have something, to persuade four different men – men of substance – to marry her.'

I made another note, this time mentally: *bright personality*. (That could be difficult.) *And possibly intelligent*. (Even worse!)

'Does she make a secret of her past?'

'No.'

'Flaunts it?'

'No to that too. She just lets it be known as if having three short-lived husbands who happened to leave her everything were commonplace.'

25

'Clever.'

'Falco, I told you she was dangerous!' Things began to look intriguing (I was a man; I was normal: dangerous women always fascinated me).

'Pollia, let us be clear about what you want from me: I can investigate Severina, hoping to nail her with her past indiscretions – '

'You'll find no evidence. There was a praetor's enquiry after her third husband died,' Pollia complained. 'Nothing came of it.'

'Praetors miss things. It may help us. Even gold-diggers are human; so they make mistakes. After three successes, people like this start believing themselves demigods; that's when people like me can trap them. Tell me, is Hortensius Novus aware of her history?'

'We made him ask her about it. She had an answer for everything.'

'A professional bride would come prepared. I'll try to frighten her off anyway. Sometimes finding themselves under scrutiny is enough – they scuttle away to prey on an easier mark. Have you considered offering her money?'

'If it will help. We have plenty.'

I grinned, thinking ahead to my bill. I had known rich people who hid their wealth with decent secrecy, and I had known men who owned immense estates but treated it quite matter-of-factly. The open vulgarity of Sabina Pollia's boast made me realise that I had stepped into a brash new world. 'I'll find out her price then – '

'If she has one!'

'She will have! Bound to be less than Hortensius Novus imagines. Realising how small a value she sets on him has helped many an infatuated lover see his beloved with new eyes.'

'You are a cynic, Falco!'

'I've done a lot of work for men who thought they were in love.'

She was looking at me slyly through half-closed eyes. We were back on the suggestive tack again. 'Falco, don't you like women?'

'I love them!'

'Anyone in particular?'

'I'm *very* particular,' I retaliated rudely.

'Our information was different.' Their information was out of date. 'I ask,' Pollia justified the question with outrageous wide-eyed innocence, 'because I am wondering whether *you* will be safe from Severina's wiles . . .'

'Severina will grant me complete immunity – the minute she learns that the Falco bankbox contains only my birth certificate, my discharge from the legions, and a few suffocated moths!'

I screwed the subject back to business, obtained a few more facts I needed (an address, the name of a praetor, and most importantly, agreement on my fee), then I took my leave.

As I skipped down the broad white marble entrance steps, frowning because they were so slippery (like the householders), I noticed a sedan chair which had just arrived.

There were six carriers in cobalt livery, huge, broad-shouldered, glossy black Numidians who could push across the Forum of the Romans from the Tabularium to the Hall of the Vestals without once losing step despite the crowds. The chair had gleaming woodwork inlaid with tortoiseshell, crimson curtains, a lacquered Gorgon on the door and silver finials on the poles. I pretended I had twisted my ankle, so I could hang about to inspect whoever would descend.

I was glad I had waited.

I guessed it was Atilia.

She was a woman who wore a half-veil because it made her more attractive; above the veil's embroidered edge glowed dark, solemn eyes of oriental origin. She and Pollia had access to a great deal of money, and evidently spent as much as they could on themselves. She jingled with expensive filigree jewellery. She wore so much gold that such a weight on one woman was certainly illegal. Her dress was that shade of amethyst where the rich tint really looks as if ground-up gemstones created the dye. As she came up the steps I saluted her in a pleasant manner and stood aside.

She removed the veil.

'Good morning!' It was the best I could manage; I was struggling for breath.

This one was as cool as the icecap on Mount Ida. If Sabina Pollia was a peach, the new apparition was a fruit of rich, dark mystery from some exotic province where I had not yet been.

'You must be the investigator.' Her expression was earnest, and highly intelligent. I was under no illusions; in the old Hortensius household she was probably a kitchenmaid – yet she had the gaze of an articulate eastern princess. If Cleopatra could raise a look like this, it explained why respectable Roman generals had queued up to throw away their reputations on the mudbanks of the Nile.

'I'm Didius Falco . . . Hortensia Atilia?' She nodded assent. 'I'm glad of an opportunity to pay my respects – '

Her exquisite face grew sombre. A serious mood suited her; any mood would. 'Forgive me for not attending your interview; I was taking my young son to school.' A devoted mother: wonderful! 'Do you think you will be able to help us, Falco?'

'It's too early to say. I hope so.'

'Thank you,' she breathed. 'Don't let me take up your time now . . .' Hortensia Atilia gave me her hand, with a formality which made me feel gauche. 'Do come and see me, however, and let me know how your enquiries proceed.'

I smiled. A woman like that expects a man to smile; I imagine in most circumstances men try to avoid disappointing women like that. She smiled too, because she knew that sooner or later I would find an excuse to call. For women like that men always do.

Halfway down the hill I paused to survey their handsome views of Rome. Seen from the Pincian, the city lay bathed with a golden morning light. I loosened my belt, which was making my tunic feel damp against my waist, and cautiously steadied my racing breath while I took stock. Between them Pollia and Atilia had left me with a feeling, which I have to admit I was frankly enjoying, that I was lucky to get out of their house alive.

The omens were interesting: two glamorous clients whose vulgar lifestyle guaranteed to amuse me; a fortune-hunter whose past was so lively there must be a real chance to expose her where the official magistrate had failed (I love to prove a praetor wrong); plus a good fat fee – and all of this, with any luck, for doing nothing much . . .

A perfect case.

VII

Before I staked out the gold-digger, I wanted to explore the Hortensius ménage. People tell you more than they think by where they live and the questions they ask; their neighbours can be even franker. Now I had gained a general impression, the sweetmeat stall where I had been given directions earlier was ripe for a return visit.

When I got there a hen who liked the high life was pecking up crumbs. The place itself was just a shack opposite a stone pine. It had a fold-down counter and a fold-up awning in front, with a small oven tucked away behind. The accommodation in between was so scanty that the stallholder spent a lot of his time sitting on a stool in the shade of the pine tree on the other side of the road, playing Soldiers against himself. When a customer turned up he left you long enough to get excited over his produce, then sauntered across.

The freeholders of the Pincian discouraged shops; but they liked their little luxuries. I could see why they let this cakeman park on their hill. What his emporium lacked architecturally was made up by his bravura edibles.

The centrepiece was an immense platter where huge whole figs were sunk to the shoulder in a sticky bed of honey. Around this circular dish were tantalising dainties set out in whorls and spirals, with a few removed here and there (so no one need feel reluctant to disturb the display). There were dates stuffed with whole almonds the warm colour of ivory, and others filled with intriguing pastes in pastel shades; crisp pastries, bent into crescents or rectangles which were layered with oozing fruits and sifted with cinnamon dust; fresh damsons, quinces and peeled pears in a candied glaze; pale custards sprinkled with nutmeg, some plain and others cut to show how they were baked on a base of elderberries or rosehips. On a shelf at one side of the stall stood pots of honey, labelled from Hymettus and Hybla, or whole honeycombs if you wanted to take someone a more dramatic party gift. Opposite, dark slabs of African must cake drowsed beside other confections which the stallholder had made himself from wheat flour soaked in milk, piercing them with a skewer and drenching them with honey before adding decorative chopped filberts.

I was drooling over his specialities which were pastry doves filled with raisins and nuts before they were glazed and baked, when he popped up at my side.

'Back again! Find the house you wanted?'

'Yes thanks. Do you know the people at the Hortensius place?'

'I should think so!' The cakeman was a wizened stick with the careful movements of a man whose trade relies on delicate arts. The awning pole that was not labelled DOLCIA informed me he was called MINNIUS.

I risked a frank question. 'What are they like?'

'Not bad.'

'Been acquainted long?'

'Over twenty years! When I first knew that clutch of puffed-up bantams they were a kitchen-sweeper, a mule-driver, and a boy who trimmed the wicks of household lamps!'

'They have come on since then! I've landed an assignment for the women. Know Sabina Pollia too?'

Minnius laughed. 'I can remember *that* one when she was a hair-dresser called Iris!'

'Ho! What about Atilia?'

'The intellectual! I mean, she'll say she was a secretary, but don't suppose that implies a Greek bookish type. Atilia scribbled the laundry lists!' He chortled at his own anecdote. 'In those days I was hawking pistachios off a tray in the Emporium. Now I'm still vending confectionery – from a booth the Hortensius lamp-boy owns. If anything this is a step down for me; the customers are ruder, I pay that bastard too much rent, and I miss the exercise . . .'

He cut into a tipsy cake, oozing with honey, and gave me a taste. Plenty of people take one look at my friendly visage and find themselves afflicted by dislike. Luckily the other half of society appreciates an open smile.

'Ask me how they managed it!' I would have done, but my mouth was full of wondrous crumbs. 'Even when they belonged to old Paulus they were all entrepreneurs. Every one of them kept a jar under the bed filling up with coppers they earned privately. They all had the knack of running special errands for extra tips. If your Pollia – '

'Iris!' I grinned stickily.

'If Iris was given anything for herself – a hairpin or a length of fringe off a dress – she turned it into denarii straightaway.'

'Did old Paulus encourage this?'

'Dunno. But he let it go on. He was pleasant enough. A good master allows his servants to save up if they can.'

'Did they buy their own freedom?'

'Paulus saved them the trouble.'

'He died?'

Minnius nodded. 'By trade he polished marble. There was plenty of work, even if he never made much at it; the will was generous to his people when he went.' Paulus could manumit a percentage of his household by bequest; my clients had the bold look of slaves who would have ensured they were among the favourites he chose for the privilege.

'They soon made good with their savings,' Minnius mused. 'Is there some special scheme for cargo ships?'

I nodded. 'Incentives; for fitting out a grain transport.' By coincidence I had been looking into corn imports shortly before this and was well up on all the fiddles. 'The scheme was started by the Emperor Claudius to encourage winter sailings. He offered a bounty, dependent on tonnage, for anyone who built new vessels. Insurance, too; he underwrote any ships that sank. The legislation has never been repealed. Anyone who knows that can still reap benefits.'

'Pollia had a ship that sank,' Minnius told me rather dourly. 'She managed to acquire a new one quite rapidly too . . .'

He was obviously suggesting it was the original ship with its name changed – an intriguing hint of sharp practice among the Hortensius crowd. 'Had she fitted out the ship herself?' I asked. Under the Claudian scheme a woman who did so would acquire the honours of a mother of four children: what *my* mother called the right to tear her hair in public and be treated to constant harassment.

'Who knows? But she was soon wearing earfuls of rubies, and sandals with silver soles.'

'What did the men do to earn their fortune? What line are they in now?'

'This and that. In fact this, that, and pretty well everything else you could name . . .'

I sensed coyness creeping over my informant: time to back off. I purchased two of his stuffed pastry pigeons for Helena, plus some slices of must cake for my sister Maia – to reward her selfless gesture in recovering my swallowed bets.

The price was as exorbitant as I expected on Pincian Hill. But I did get a neat little basket containing a natty nest of vine leaves, to carry my confectionery home with clean hands. It made a change from the inky papers torn out of old scrolls of philosophy which were used to wrap up custards where I lived in the Aventine.

On the other hand, there is nothing to read on a vine leaf once you've licked it clean.

VIII

Next I risked raising my blood pressure with a visit to a praetor.

In the days of the Republic two magistrates were elected annually (*selected*, since it was an appointment from the ranks of the Senate so not exactly subject to a free vote), but by my time legal business had increased so much it kept eighteen of them busy, two solely on fraud. The one who had investigated the gold-digger was called Corvinus. The Forum *Gazette* had familiarised me with the ludicrous pronouncements of the current legal crop, so I knew Corvinus was a self-opinionated piece of pomposity. Praetors always are. In the scale of public appointments it is the last civil honour before a consulship, and if a man wants to parade his ignorance of modern morality then being praetor gives him dangerous scope. Corvinus predated the current Emperor's campaign to clean up the courts, and I reckoned the praetorship would be his last public position now Vespasian was in charge.

Unfortunately for my clients, before Corvinus was retired to his Latium farm, he had had time to make his pronouncement that poor little Severina had lost three wealthy husbands in rapid succession *purely through bad luck*. Well. That shows you why I think what I think about praetorian magistrates.

I had never met him, and in fact I didn't intend to, but after I came down from the Pincian I went straight to his house. It was a quiet mansion on the Esquiline. A faded trophy hung over the door, commemorating some ancient military show in which an ancestor had been honoured for not running away. Indoors were two statues of dour republican orators, an indifferent bronze of Augustus, and a huge chain for a watchdog (but no dog): the usual tired trappings of a family which had never been as important as it thought, and was now sinking into oblivion.

I hoped Corvinus would be in Cumae for the summer, but he was the sort of conscientious fool who probably sat in court on his own birthday; he grumbled about the pressure of business – yet fed his ego by bungling pleas all through the August heat. A bored porter let me in. Bundles of ceremonial rods and axes were lolling in the atrium, and I could hear a murmur from a side room where his honour's lictors were gnawing their midday snack. In a side passage a row of benches had been provided so clients and plaintiffs could hang about looking pathetic while the Praetor snored off his lunch. Sunlight slanted in from high square windows, but once my eyes grew accustomed to the harsh interplay of light and shade I discovered the familiar crowd of moaners who clog up the offices of famous men. All watching one another, while they pretended not to; all trying to dodge the mad-eyed know-all who wanted a conversation; all set for a long and probably disappointing afternoon.

I avoid sitting around catching other people's diseases, so I strolled briskly past. Some of the hangdog crowd sat up straighter, but most were prepared to let anyone who looked as if he knew what he was doing carry on doing it. I felt no qualms about queue-jumping. They had come to see the Praetor. The last thing *I* wanted was to endure a pointless interview with some tedious legal duffer. Praetors always have a clerk. And because litigants are so touchy to deal with, a praetor's clerk is usually alert. I had come to see the clerk.

I found him in the deep shade of an inner courtyard garden. It was a warm day, so he had moved a folding campstool out to the fresh air. He had a startling tan, as if it had been painted on – possibly the result of a week's concentrated vine pruning. He wore a large seal ring, pointed red shoes, and a glittering white tunic; he looked as sharp as a furnace-stoker on his festival day off.

As I expected, after a long morning up against senators' sons who had been caught peering into the changing rooms of women-only bathhouses and vague grannies who wanted to ramble through three generations of family history to explain why they stole four duck eggs, the clerk was glad to push aside his pyramid of petition rolls and enjoy a chat with me. I introduced myself straightaway, and he replied that his name was Lusius.

'Lusius, some clients of mine are worried about a professional bride. Name of Severina; I don't know her cognomen – '

'Zotica,' said Lusius abruptly. Perhaps he thought I was a time-waster.

'You remember her! Thank the gods for efficiency – '

'I remember,' growled the clerk, growing more expansive with this

34

chance to express his bitterness. 'There were three previous husbands, who had all lived in different sectors of the city, so I had to cope with a trio of disorganised aediles all sending me incomplete local details, four weeks after I required them – plus a letter from the Censor's office with all the names spelt wrong. I ended up co-ordinating the documents for Corvinus myself.'

'Routine procedure!' I commiserated. 'So what can you tell me?'

'What do you want to know?'

'Did she do it, basically.'

'Oh she did it!'

'That's not what your man decided.'

Lusius described his man in two brief words: the usual opinion of a praetor if you hear it from his clerk. 'The honourable Corvinus,' Lusius confided, 'would not recognise a boil on his own bum.' I was starting to have a lot of time for Lusius; he seemed a man of the world – the same shady world I inhabited myself.

'Routine again! So will you tell me the tale?'

'Why not?' he asked, stretching his legs in front of him, folding his arms, and speaking as if he thought anyone who worked as hard as he did deserved time off for anarchy. 'Why not, indeed? Severina Zotica . . .'

'What is she like?'

'Nothing special. But the madams who cause the most trouble never look much to outsiders who are not involved with them.' I nodded. 'And a redhead,' he added.

'I should have known!'

'Imported as a teenager from the big slave market at Delos, but she got there by a roundabout route. Born in Thrace – hence the hair – then passed about with different owners; Cyprus, Egypt, then before Delos Mauretania, I think.'

'How do you know all this?'

'I had to interview her at one point. Quite an experience!' he reminisced, though I noticed he did not dwell on it. In fact his expression became guarded, like a man keeping his own council talking about a girl he planned not to forget. 'Once she reached Italy she was bought by a bead-threader; he had a shop in the Subura; it's still there. His name was Severus Moscus. He seems to have been a decent enough old bastard, who eventually married her.'

'Husband number one. Short-lived?'

'No; the marriage had lasted a year or two.'

'Peacefully?'

'As far as I know.'

'What happened to him?'

'Died of heatstroke while he was watching a gladiatorial display. I *think* he had sat where there wasn't an awning, and his heart just gave out.' Lusius was evidently a fair man (or wanted to be, when he was assessing a redhead).

'Maybe he was too stupid or too stubborn to sit in the shade.' I could be fair myself. 'Did Severina buy his ticket?'

'No; one of his male slaves.'

'Did Severina weep and wail over losing him?'

'No . . .' Lusius pondered thoughtfully. 'Though that was in character; she's not the type to create.'

'Nice manners, eh? And Moscus liked her enough to leave her everything?'

'To an old man, a redhead – who was sixteen when he married her – is bound to be likeable.'

'All right: so far she looks genuine. But did her sudden inheritance supply her with an idea for getting on in life?'

'Could be. I could never ascertain whether she had married her master out of desperation or honest gratitude. She *may* have been fond of him – or she may have been a diplomat. The beadseller *may* have bullied her – or perhaps she coerced him. On the other hand,' said Lusius, balancing his arguments like a true clerk, 'when Severina realised how comfortable Severus Moscus had left her, she immediately set out to acquire greater comfort still.'

'Exactly how well off was Moscus?'

'He imported agates, polished them up and strung them. Nice stuff. Well, nice enough for senators' heirs to buy for prostitutes.'

'A flourishing market!'

'Especially when he branched out into cameos. You know – heads of the Imperial family under patriotic mottos. *Peace, Fortune,* and an overflowing cornucopia – '

'Everything one lacks at home!' I grinned. 'Imperial portraits are always popular with the creepers at court. His work was in fashion, so his ex-slavegirl inherited a thriving enterprise. What next?'

'An apothecary. Name of Eprius.'

'How did he die?'

'One of his own cough lozenges stuck in his throat.'

'How long had he lasted?'

'Well it took him nearly a year to get her to the priest; she put on a good show of dithering. Then he survived another ten months; perhaps she needed to steady her nerve.'

'The apothecary may have lingered because Severina wanted to acquire a knowledge of drugs . . . Was she there when he choked? Did she try to revive him?'

'Desperately!' We both laughed, certain we had the measure of that. 'She was rewarded for her devotion with three drugshops and his family farm.'

'Then what?'

'Grittius Fronto. He imported savage animals for Nero's arena shows. She was bolder that time. She must have been courting Fronto while the executors were still snipping the tape on the Eprius will. The circus manager only managed to survive four weeks – '

'Eaten by a lion?'

'Panther,' Lusius corrected without a pause. He was as cynical as me; I loved the man. 'Strolled out of an open cage below the stage at Nero's Circus and backed poor Grittius up against some lifting gear. They say the blood was horrible. The thing mauled a tightrope walker too, which seemed a bit superfluous but made the "accident" look more natural. Grittius had been making a lot of money – his empire included a sideline in unusual floor shows for sleazy dinner parties. You know – naked females doing peculiar things with pythons . . . Servicing orgies is like owning a Spanish gold mine. Severina danced away from the Fronto funeral pyre with what I estimated at half a million big gold ones. Oh, and a parrot whose conversation would make a galley overseer blush.'

'Was there a medical report on any of the bodies?'

'The old beadseller's heart failure looked too natural, and there was no point calling a doctor to examine the panther's handiwork – not enough left!' Lusius shuddered fastidiously. 'But a quack did see the apothecary.' I lifted an eyebrow and without needing to look it up he gave me a name and address. 'He saw nothing to take exception to.'

'So what put the law onto Severina?'

'Grittius had a great-nephew in Egypt who used to arrange shipping for the wild beasts; the shipper had expected to inherit the loot from the lions. He sailed home fast and tried to bring an action. We made the usual enquiries, but it never came to court. Corvinus threw it out after an initial examination.'

'On what grounds, Lusius?'

His eyes were darting angrily. 'Lack of evidence.'

'Was there any?'

'None at all.'

'So where is the argument?'

Lusius exploded with sardonic mirth. 'Whenever did lack of evidence stop a case?' I could tell what had happened. Lusius must have done the work for the aediles (young local officials, responsible for investigating the facts but keen only on pursuing their political careers). The case had gripped him, then when his efforts came to nothing due to the Praetor's stupidity he took it personally. 'She was clever,' he mused. 'She never overreached herself; the types she picked had plenty of cash, but were nothing in society – so seedy no one would really care if they had met a sticky end. Well, no one except the nephew who was a rival for one of the fortunes. Perhaps Grittius had forgotten to mention him; perhaps he forgot deliberately. Anyway, apart from that slip, she must have been extremely careful, Falco; there really was no evidence.'

'Just inference!' I grinned.

'Or as Corvinus so lucidly put it: *a tragic victim of a truly astonishing chain of coincidence* . . .'

What a master of jurisprudence.

A portentous belch from a room indoors warned us that the Praetor was about to emerge. A door pushed open. A sloe-eyed slaveboy, who must have been the tasty bite Corvinus used to sweeten his palate after lunch, sauntered out carrying a flagon as his excuse for being there. Lusius winked at me, gathering his scrolls up with the unhurried grace of a clerk who had learned long ago how to look busy.

I had no intention of watching the Praetor amuse himself rejecting pleas; I nodded politely to Lusius, and made myself scarce.

38

IX

I convinced myself it was now late enough to stop work for the day and attend to my personal life.

Helena, who took a stern view of my casual attitude to earning a living, seemed surprised to see me so early, but the Pincian confectionery persuaded her into a more lenient frame of mind. Enjoying my company may have helped too – but if so, she hid it well.

We sat in the garden at her parents' house, devouring the pastry doves, while I told her about my new case. She noted that it was an enquiry packed with feminine interest.

Since she could tell when I was evading an issue I described my day as it had occurred, glamour and all. When I got to the part about Hortensia Atilia being like some dark oriental fruit, Helena suggested grimly, 'A Bithynian prune!'

'Not so wrinkled!'

'Was she the one who did all the talking?'

'No; that was Pollia, the first tempting nibble.'

'How can you keep track of them?'

'Easy – for a connoisseur!' When she scowled I relented. 'You know you can trust me!' I promised, grinning insincerely. I liked to keep my women guessing, particularly when I had nothing to hide.

'I know I can trust you to run after anything in a pair of silly sandals and a string of tawdry beads!'

I touched her cheek with one finger. 'Eat your sticky cake, feather.'

Helena distrusted compliments; she looked at me as if some Forum layabout on the steps of the Temple of Castor had tried to lift up her skirt. I found myself mentioning a subject I had told myself I would let lie: 'Thought any more about what I suggested yesterday?'

'I've thought about it.'

'Think you'll ever come?'

'Probably.'

'That sounds like "*Probably not*".'

'I mean what I say!'

'So are you wondering whether *I* mean it?'

She smiled at me suddenly with vivid affection. 'No, Marcus!' I felt my expression alter. When Helena Justina smiled like that, I was in imminent danger of overreacting . . .

Luckily her father came out to join us just then. A diffident figure with a sprout of straight untameable hair; he had the vague air of an innocent abroad – but I knew from experience he was nothing of the kind; I found myself sitting up straighter. Camillus shed his toga with relief, and a slave took it away. It was the Nones of the month so the Senate had been in session. He touched on today's business, the usual wrangles over trifles; he was being polite, but eyeing our open cake basket. I broke up the must cake I had purchased as a present for my sister, and we handed it round. I had no objection to going back to Minnius' stall another day to buy something else for Maia.

Once the basket was empty, Helena tried to decide what she could do with it; she settled on making a gift for my mother, filling it with Campania violets.

'She ought to like that,' I said. 'Anything that sits in the house serving no useful purpose and gathering a layer of fluff reminds her of my father . . .'

'And someone else!'

I said to the Senator, 'I like a girl who speaks her mind. Was your daughter always so cantankerous?'

'We brought her up,' he answered between mouthfuls, 'to be a gentle, domestic treasure. As you see.' He was a likeable man, who could handle irony. He had two sons (both on foreign service), but if Helena had been less strong-minded she would probably have been his favourite. As it was, he viewed her warily but I reckoned their closeness was why Camillus Verus could never bring himself to send me packing; anyone who liked his daughter as much as I did was a liability he had to tolerate. 'What are you working on nowadays, Falco?'

I described my case and the Hortensius freedmen. 'It's the usual story of the wealthy and self-possessed, fighting off an adventurous newcomer. What makes it so piquant is that they are nouveaux riches themselves. I'll take the commission, sir, but I must say, I find their snobbery intolerable.'

'This is Rome, Marcus!' Camillus smiled. 'Don't forget, slaves from important households regard themselves as a superior species even to the freeborn poor.'

'Of which you're one!' Helena grinned. I knew she was implying Sabina Pollia and Hortensia Atilia would be too finicky to tangle with me. I gave her a level stare, through half-closed eyes, intending to worry her. It failed as usual.

'One of the things I find interesting,' I mentioned to the Senator, 'is that these people would probably admit they rose from next to nothing. The man who owned them polished marble. It's a skilled job – which means the piecework rates hardly pay enough to keep a snail alive. Yet now the ostentation of his freedmens' mansion suggests their fortunes must be greater than a consul's birthright. Still; that's Rome too!'

'How did they overcome their unpromising origins?'

'So far that's a mystery . . .'

While we talked I had been licking honey off the vine leaves from the cake basket; it suddenly struck me a senator's daughter might not wish to associate with an Aventine lout whose happy tongue cleaned up wrappings in public. Or at least, not associate with him in her father's townhouse garden, amongst the expensive bronze nymphs and graceful bulbs from the Caucasus, especially while her noble father was sitting there . . .

I need not have worried. Helena was making sure no currants from the must cake were left behind in the basket. She had even found a way of forcing the corners open so she could recapture any crumbs that had worked themselves among the woven strands of cane.

The Senator caught my eye. We knew Helena was still grieving for the baby she had lost, but we both thought she was starting to look healthier.

Helena glanced up abruptly. Her father looked away. I refused to be embarrassed, so I continued to gaze at her thoughtfully while Helena gazed back, in peaceful communion about who knows what.

Then Camillus Verus frowned at me, rather curiously I thought.

X

Although I had given up for the day, other folk were still labouring, so I popped along the Vicus Longus to see whether the letting agent Hyacinthus had mentioned was open for business. He was.

Cossus was a pale, long-nosed individual, who liked to lean back on his stool with his knees apart; luckily his green and brown striped tunic was sufficiently baggy to allow it without indecency. He clearly spent most of his day laughing loudly with his personal friends, two of whom were with him when I called. Since I wanted a favour, I stood by looking diffident while these orators dissected the various perverts who were standing in the next elections, discussed a horse, then hotly debated whether a girl they knew (another hot tip) was pregnant or pretending. When my hair had grown half a digit waiting, I coughed. With little attempt at apology the clique slowly broke up.

Alone with the agent, I found an excuse to drop the name of Hyacinthus as if I had known him since he cut his teeth on an old sandal strap, then I explained my yen for up-market real estate. Cossus sucked in his breath. 'August, Falco – not much shifting. Everyone's away . . .'

'Plenty of death, divorce and default!' Since my father was an auctioneer, I knew property moves at all seasons. In fact if I had wanted to buy something outright, my own papa could have put some ramshackle billet my way; but even he kept his hands clean of the rented sector. 'Still, if you can't help me, Cossus – '

The best way to screw activity from a land agent is to hint that you are taking your custom somewhere else. 'What area are you looking at?' he asked.

All I needed was lavish space at a small rent, anywhere central. The first thing Cossus offered was a boot cupboard beyond the city boundary stone, right along the Via Flaminia, an hour's walk out of town.

'Forget it! I must be near the Forum.'

42

'How about a well-established condominium, no snags, small out-goings, extremely appealing outlook, on the Janiculan Ridge?'

'Wrong side of the river.'

'It comes with shared use of a roof terrace.'

'Can't you understand Latin? Even if it comes with Julius Caesar's riverside gardens, Cossus, it's not my area! I'm not some damned itinerant matchseller. What else do you have?'

'Courtyard outlook, shaded by a pine tree, opposite the Praetorian Camp – '

'Rats! Find a tenant who's deaf!'

'Ground floor, by the Probus Bridge?'

'Find one who can swim in the spring floods . . .'

We worked through all the dreary dumps he must have had on the stocks for ages, but eventually Cossus acknowledged he would have to shift those onto some raw provincial visitor. 'Now this is just the thing for you – a short lease in the Piscina Publica. Someone else has expressed an interest, but seeing as it's you, Falco – '

'Don't make a drama. Tell me what it offers?'

'Four good rooms arranged conveniently on the third floor – '

'Over the courtyard?'

'The street – but it's a quiet street. The neighbourhood is most attractive, well away from the Aventine warehouses, and favoured by a genteel clientele.' What comedian writes their speeches? He meant that it was too far from the markets and peopled with snobbish hydraulic engineers. 'The premises are being offered on a six-monthly basis; the landlord is uncertain of his plans for the block.' That suited me, since I was uncertain of my plans for staying solvent enough to pay him.

'How much?'

'Five thousand.'

'Annually?'

'*A half-year!*' Cossus gave me a frosty stare. 'This is the market for men of means, Falco.'

'It's a market for fools, then.'

'Take it or leave it. That's the going rate.' I gave him a look to say in that case I was going. 'Well, I could probably come down to three thou for a friend.' Half the price was his commission, if I read him right – which made him no friend of mine. 'Because of the short lease,' he explained unconvincingly.

I sat frowning in silence, hoping this would beat him down: nothing doing. The Twelfth *is* a tolerable district. It lies east of the Aventine on the far side of the Via Ostiensis – nearly home to me. The public fishponds which supplied its name dried up years ago, so I knew the mosquitoes had decamped . . . I made an appointment to troop along with Cossus tomorrow and inspect the let.

By the time I approached Fountain Court that evening I was determined to take the Piscina Publica apartment whatever it was like. I felt tired of bursting blood vessels climbing up stairs. I was sick of dirt, and noise, and other people's sordid troubles intruding into my life. Tonight I came back into the tangled mass of those Aventine lanes which feed into each other like the underground filaments of some disgusting fungus, and I told myself that four rooms, conveniently arranged, anywhere else must be better than this.

Still dreaming, I turned the corner within sight of Lenia's laundry. Tomorrow I would sign the lease that enabled me to stop feeling ashamed whenever I had to tell a stranger my address . . .

A pair of feet stopped my happy plans.

The feet, which were enormous, were kicking at each other in the portico of the basketweaver's lock-up about ten strides away from me. Apart from their size, I noticed them because that was where I always parked myself if ever I had some reason to squint at my apartment discreetly before I showed myself.

Those feet were definitely loafing. The person they were attached to was taking no notice of the weaver's artefacts, even though he had lolled up against a gigantic pile of general purpose wicker carrying-hods which would be a boon to any household, while at his feet lay an excellent picnic basket which any genuine bargain-hunter would have snapped up fast . . . I squeezed behind a pilaster for a closer scrutiny. I knew he was not a burglar; burglars like to have something to steal. Even the incompetent ones steer clear of Fountain Court.

A client or a creditor would go in and chat to Lenia. These outsize platters must have been sent here by Anacrites, the Chief Spy.

I eased myself backwards, and nipped through a side alley to the back lane. The area behind the laundry appeared its normal self. On this muggy summer evening the open cess trench was polluting the nostrils vibrantly. Two starved black dogs lay asleep on their sides in the shade. From behind a cracked shutter above my head I could hear the spiteful daily conversation of a husband and wife. A pair of female chicken-pluckers were arguing, or just gossiping, by a pen of off-colour capons. And a man I had never seen before was sitting on a barrel, doing nothing much.

He had to be another spy. He was in full sun. It was the last place you would choose to sweat, if your only motive in planting your posterior on a barrel was to rest your legs. But it was the only place to sit if you wanted to survey comings and goings from Lenia's drying-yard. Unless he was in love with one of the teazle girls, he must be up to no good.

I opted for a strategic retreat.

A large family can be useful. I had numerous relations, all of whom assumed they owned me. Most would condescend to give me a bed in return for the chance to complain about my habits. My sisters would want to rant about our mother having to arrange my jailbreak, so I went to mother's instead. I knew that meant being obsequious about her standing sponsor but I thought I could put on a polite show. I did manage to play at being grateful for as long as it took to devour a bowl of her prawn dumplings, but when the strain of remembering to look humble became too oppressive I went home after all.

The watcher in the back lane must have been the well-organised one; he had fixed up a relief for himself. His replacement was now perched on the barrel trying to look inconspicuous; not a success, since he was a bald-headed, hook-nosed midget with a drooping left eye.

Around the front the monstrous feet were still outside the basket shop – all the more unconvincing since the weaver had taken in his produce, dragged across his sliding screen and bolted up. I slid into the local barber's, and paid one of his offspring to tell the feet that a homunculus wanted to speak to them in the lane. While footsie plodded round there for a fruitless chat with the midget, I planned to be pouring myself a goodnight drink six floors up on my balcony.

And so I was. Some days, some things actually go right.

XI

Next morning I was up early. Before Anacrites' scruffy assortment were back watching my warren, I had hopped out of my hole and off to an outdoor cookshop table two districts away. I was enjoying a slow breakfast (bread and dates, with honey and hot wine – nothing too lively for a man on surveillance), while *I* watched the home of the professional bride.

Severina Zotica lived in the Second Sector, the Caelimontium. Her street lay some way beyond the Porticus Claudia (at that time in ruins, but earmarked for restoration in Vespasian's public building programme); the gold-digger inhabited the sedate triangle which lies between the Aqueducts and the two major roads which come together at the Asinaria city gate. Cossus must have realised the Caelian Hill region was too select for me. For one thing, the streets had names. I expect he thought this might have worried me; I expect the beggar thought I couldn't read.

Severina had established herself in Abacus Street. It was a tasteful thoroughfare, a single cart's width. The junction at one end had a well-kept public fountain; the other had a small street market, mainly kitchen pottery and vegetable stalls. In between, the shopkeepers washed and swept their own frontages; they were doing this at the hour I arrived, in a way I found pleasantly businesslike. Both sides of the street were lined with artisans' booths: cutlers, cheese shops, picklesellers, cloth merchants, and locksmiths. Between each pair ran an entry with stairs to the apartments above, and a passage to the ground-floor accommodation which lay behind the shops. The buildings were about three storeys' high, brick-faced without balconies, though many had neat window boxes supported on brackets, while in other places rugs and counterpanes were already being given their daily airing over windowsills.

Residents came and went. A straight-backed old lady, quiet businessmen, a slave walking a lapdog, children with writing slates.

46

People rarely spoke, yet they exchanged nods. The atmosphere suggested most of them had lived there a long time. They were acquainted, though they kept to themselves.

There was a brothel four doors down from me. It was unmarked, but evident if you sat for any time. Patrons slipped in (looking strained) then strode out half an hour later (looking pleased with themselves).

I stuck with my breakfast. Though it made me remember mornings when I had woken warm from a night in companionable sleep, and enjoyed an extra hour in bed with some young lady I had lured home the evening before . . . Soon I was missing one in particular. I told myself there was no one in a brothel who could compensate for her.

Certainly, no one who would pay my rent.

It was still quite early when a slightly battered carrying chair emerged from the passage between the cheesemaker's booth and a tablecloth shop, which was where I had been told Severina Zotica lived. Curtains hid the occupant. The bearers were a couple of short sturdy slaves, chosen for the breadth of their shoulders rather than for cutting a dash on the Sacred Way; they had large hands and ugly chins, and looked as if they did everything from carrying water to mending boots.

I had paid for my food already. I stood up, brushing off crumbs. They marched past me and away towards the city. I followed, casually.

When we arrived at the first aqueduct they branched left, cut through some backstreets, came out on the Via Appia, then followed the road round the Circus Maximus towards the Aventine. I felt a shock: the gold-digger was apparently having herself ferried straight towards the Falco residence . . .

In fact she went somewhere more civilised. The chairmen dropped her at the Atrium of Liberty. A woman of medium height emerged, swathed so modestly in a russet-coloured stole it was impossible to see more of her than a slight figure, an upright carriage and a graceful walk. She entered the Library of Asinius Pollio, where she handed in some scrolls, exchanged pleasantries with the library clerk, then booked out another selection which he had already prepared. Whatever I had expected, it was not that the woman had set off from home purely to change her reading matter at the public library.

As she left, she passed quite close. I pretended to be browsing among the pigeonholes of philosophy, but managed to glimpse a white hand, clasping her new volumes, with a ring on her third finger with some red stone. Her gown was a subdued shade of umber, though its folds gleamed with an expensive lustre. The hem of the stole which still hid her face was embroidered and set with seed pearls.

Had I lingered to quizz the librarian, I should have lost the chair. Instead I tailed her to the Emporium where she purchased a Baetican ham and some Syrian pears. Next stop was the Theatre of Marcellus; she sent one of the chairmen to the ticket office for a single in the women's gallery that night.

After that the lady in brown had herself lugged back to the Caelimontium. She bought a cabbage (which I thought looked on the tough side), entered a female bathhouse for an hour, then minced out and went home. I had lunch at the cookshop (rissoles), then sat on there all afternoon. One of her slaves trotted out to get a knife sharpened, but Severina did not re-emerge. In the early evening she was taken straight back to the theatre. I excused myself from attending. It was a *pantomimus* performing a farce about adulterers pushing cuckolded husbands into conveniently open blanket chests; I had seen it; the dancing was terrible. In any case, observing a female subject at the theatre has its tricky side. If a good-looking specimen like me stares up at the women's seats too often, hussies from the cheap end of society start sending him shameless notes.

I went to see Helena. She had gone out with her mother to visit an aunt.

I met Cossus in a Piscina Publica wineshop, bought him a drink (a small one), then was taken to view the apartment. To my surprise it was not bad: up a rather narrow lane, but a plain tenement block where the stairs were dusty but free of other detritus. Metal lamps stood in one or two corners on the way upstairs, though they were dry of oil.

'You could fill them if you wanted to light the way up,' Cossus said.

'The lessor could light them.'

'True!' he grinned. 'I'll mention it . . .'

I suspected there had been a recent change of ownership: I glimpsed builders' props in a passageway, the shops at ground level were vacant, and although the principal tenant (who would be my landlord) reserved the large apartment behind them for his own use it was empty at present. Cossus told me I need not expect to see this main tenant; all the subletting was arranged through himself. I was used to spending so much time and trouble avoiding Smaractus, the new landlord's arrangements seemed sweet as a dream.

The apartment on offer was as good as any in the block, since they were all identical units piled on top of one another. In each the door opened into a corridor with two rooms on either hand. These were not much bigger than those I had at Fountain Court, but with four I could plan a more refined existence: a separate living room, bedroom, reading room and office . . . There were sound wooden floors and an encouraging smell of new plasterwork. If the roof leaked there were upper tenants whom the rain would soak before it dripped on me. I found no signs of pest infestation. The neighbours (if alive) sounded quiet.

Cossus and I smacked hands on the bargain.

'How many weeks' rent would you want at a time?'

'The full half-year!' he exclaimed, looking shocked.

'If the term starts in July, I've lost two months!'

'Oh well – the next four months' then.' I promised to cash in my betting tokens right away and bring him the money as soon as I could. 'And the deposit against lawsuits,' he added.

'Lawsuits?' He meant I might drop a flowerpot out of a window and brain some passer-by; the main leaseholder could be held liable, if I was just a subtenant. My current landlord Smaractus had never thought of demanding such indemnities – but most people on the Aventine find ways to right their grievances without becoming litigants. (They run up the stairs and punch your head.) 'Is this premium normal at your end of the market?'

'On new tenancies a deposit is traditional, Falco.' Since I wished to appear a man of the world, I gave way gracefully.

With Anacrites watching my old place, the sooner I moved into an address he didn't know, the easier life would be. In any case I could hardly wait for the pleasure of telling Smaractus he could hire a slow mule to Lusitania and take the lease for his filthy sixth-floor dosshouse with him when he went. Before I could move however, I would have to arrange some furniture.

At home the spies were still watching. I marched straight up to the one with the feet. 'Excuse me, is this where Didius Falco lives?' He nodded before he could help himself. 'Is he in at the moment?' The spy looked vague, now trying to disguise his interest.

Still playing the stranger, I went up to see whether Falco was in. Which he was, once I got there.

Anyone watching a building should record who goes in and make sure they come out again. I rigged up a trip rope attached to an iron griddle pan which would wake the whole tenement if it was kicked down the stairs in the dark, but no one followed me upstairs. Cheap expertise is all the Palace pays for. I knew that; I had once worked there myself.

XII

On the second day of my surveillance Severina Zotica must have stayed in to read her library scrolls. There were household deliveries – amphorae of olive oil and fish pickle – followed by a woman trundling a rackety handcart full of hanks of wool. It had badly set wheels, so I strolled over and lifted the base with the toe of my boot as she struggled to lever the thing up a kerb.

'Someone's going to be busy!' I commented nosily.

'She always buys a quantity.' The wool distributor backed her ample rear down the entry to Severina's house, huffing as she towed the load. 'She weaves it herself,' she told me, boasting on her customer's behalf. A likely tale.

It was a poor day if I was hoping to publish my diary to literary acclaim: breakfast; Lucanian sausage for lunch (with indigestion afterwards); hot weather; a dogfight in the afternoon (no interesting bites) . . .

The chair finally veered out of the passage in the early evening, followed by a thin maid with a cosmetics box in one hand and a strigil and oil flask dangling from her other wrist. Severina vanished into the same bathhouse as before, dragging the maid. An hour later she flounced back out down the steps. Her sandals were gilded, a lacing of gold threads embroidered every hem on her get-up, and what looked like a diadem came to a point beneath the inevitable stole. The maid who had tricked her out in this finery set off home on foot with her cast-offs and the cosmetics, while the chairmen hauled Severina north to the Pincian: a social call at the Hortensius house.

She stopped at Minnius' cake stall, where she acquired one of his leaf-lined baskets. I pursued her as far as the Hortensius gatehouse and winked at the porter, who confirmed for me that madam was dining with her fancy man. There seemed nothing to gain by waiting outside all evening while they gorged themselves and exchanged pretty nothings. I went back to see Minnius.

'Does Severina call here often?'

'Every time she goes to see Novus. He's a glutton for sweet stuff; they have a regular order up at the house, but she usually takes him a titbit.'

I bought another piece of must cake for my sister, but I ate it on my way to visit Helena.

'Marcus! How are you getting on with your enquiry?'

'All the evidence suggests the gold-digger is just a home-loving girl, improving her mind, who wants a classic tombstone. Apart from *She lived with one husband*, which we can assume she has abandoned, it's to be *Chaste, virtuous, and well-deserving . . . She spun and worked in wool –* '

'Perhaps she really *is* well-deserving!'

'And perhaps there will be a snowstorm in Tripolitania! It's time I took a closer look at her – '

'In her women-only bathhouse?' Helena pretended to be shocked.

'My darling, I'll consider most disguises – but I can't pass for a female once I'm in the nude . . .' Wondering whether I could somehow manage to infiltrate myself as a sweeper, I gave Helena a salacious grin.

'Don't flash your teeth at me, Didius Falco! And don't forget you're already on bail from the Lautumiae . . .' After a moment she added apropos of nothing, 'I missed seeing you yesterday.' Her voice was low; there was a true note of yearning in it for a man who wanted to be persuaded.

'Not my fault. You were out when I came.'

She stared at the toes of her shoes (which were leather in a discreet shade, but with dashing purple laces). I mentioned, also apropos of nothing, that I had taken a new lease. I was wondering how she would take it. She looked up. 'Can I come and see?'

'Once I've acquired some furniture.' No self-respecting bachelor invites a good-looking girl to his apartment until he can provide a mirror and anything else they might need. Such as a bed. 'Don't worry – as soon as word of my move gets round among my family, I expect to be showered with everything they've been longing to get rid of – especially my brothers-in-law's bodged efforts at carpentry . . .'

'My father has a battered reading couch he intended to offer you, but perhaps you won't want it now you're going up in the world?'

'I'll take it!' I assured her. Her gaze faltered. Helena Justina could always interpret my motives too easily.

Reading is not the only thing you can do on a couch.

I left early. We had run out of things to talk about.

One way and another I had hardly given my darling so much as a kiss. By the time we said goodbye she seemed rather standoffish, so I kept aloof too and strode away with just a nod.

Before I fetched up at the end of her father's street I felt a serious pang of misery, and wished I had been more affectionate. I nearly went back. But I had no intention of letting a senator's daughter see me behave like a dithering idiot.

XIII

I spent the rest of that evening turning my betting tags into cash. I found Cossus, clinched the deal, and received my key. I had a few drinks with the agent – business courtesy – then a few more later with my best friend Petronius Longus (in fact a few more than we meant to have, but we revelled in having something proper to celebrate). I ended up feeling far too happy to dupe the spies at Fountain Court so I stumbled to the new apartment, crashed inside, stretched out on the floor and sang myself to sleep.

Someone banged on the door and I heard a voice demanding whether everything was all right. Nice to know my new neighbours were such concerned types.

I woke early. The best-laid floorboards tend to have that effect.

Feeling pleased with life despite my headache, I went out to hunt for a snack. All-night cookshops in the Piscina Publica seemed a rarity, which could prove an inconvenience for my erratic way of life. But eventually I found a bar full of bad-tempered flies where a bleary-eyed waiter served me a slab of ancient bread with a pickled cucumber in it and told me I had to take it off the premises to eat.

It was too early for watching Severina's house. Even so, that rapacious little lady was firmly in mind. Clients have the unreasonable habit of expecting rapid progress, so I would soon need to report.

My feet took me east. They brought me up below the Esquiline, in the old part of town which people still call the Subura, though it had been variously retitled after Augustus enlarged the city and redrew the administrative sectors. Some folks grumble that was when Rome lost all its character; still, I dare say while Romulus was ploughing up the first boundary furrow there were hidebound old peasants standing about the Seven Hills and muttering into their frowsty beards that life would never be worth living in this wolf-man's newfangled settlement . . .

The Subura still kept its republican character. Much of it had been wiped out under Nero in the Great Fire. He had grabbed a large swathe of the blackened ground for his Golden House and its enormous parks and pleasure grounds. He then ordered Rome to be rebuilt on a classic grid pattern, with really strict fire regulations. (Even Nero had recognised that the Golden House was big enough for a petty prince, so there was no need to plan on any more Imperial land clearance.) In fact many streets had been rebuilt ignoring his proclamations, higgledy-piggledy on top of the old ones. I liked it. The Empire has far too many pious four-square towns all looking exactly the same.

This area had once been the most sordid in the city. There were plenty of rivals for that honour now. The Subura seemed like an elderly whore; it still had a tawdry reputation, though it was past living up to it. Yet you could still be robbed. Like everywhere else, the footpads in these tense one-man lanes were far from slack. They were set in their ways: an arm round the throat, a dagger in the ribs, lifting your purse and finger-rings, then kneeing you face-down in the mud while they hopped it.

I kept my wits about me. I knew the Subura, but not well enough to recognise the faces and not well enough for its villains to steer clear of me.

Coming this way was deliberate: to dig deeper into Severina's past. The Praetor's clerk Lusius had mentioned that her first husband, the bead-threader Moscus, used to own a shop which still existed somewhere here. I started looking for jewellers. They usually know where their rivals hang out. Sure enough, on the third try I was given directions and reached the right booth just as it was opening.

The new incumbent was probably another ex-slave from the Severus Moscus household, now free and self-employed. He sold every kind of gemstone work, from intaglios, where he cut into the jewel's surface, to cameos, where the design stood proud. He used all the semi-precious stones, but agates in particular – pale blues laced with milky striations; stone whites which blossomed with green or red ochre threads like lichen; translucent-streaked charcoals; handsome mixtures of matt buff and bronze. He was already at his bench, sorting tiny gold spacing beads. Apparently he did all the work himself.

'Hello!' I cried. 'Is this where Severus Moscus lives? I've been told to look him up; my mother knew his mother – '

He gave me a thoughtful glance. 'Would that have been in

Tusculum?' He had a curiously high-pitched voice for one whose manner was so completely confident.

Thinking it might be a trap I shrugged offhandedly. 'Could be. My ma has lived all over the place. She did tell me; I didn't bother to listen, I confess – '

'Moscus is dead.'

'No!' I whistled. 'I've had a wasted journey then. Look – my old biddy's bound to ask; can you tell me how it happened?' He leaned on the counter and told me the tale about the heart attack in the hot amphitheatre. 'That's bad luck. Was he very old?'

'Sixties.'

'No age!' No response. 'Did he have any family? Ma would want me to pay her condolences – '

I thought the man's face closed. 'No,' he said. That was odd; also inaccurate.

'What about you?' I pressed him cheerfully, like a crass stranger. 'You've got his business – were you involved with him?'

'I worked with him. He gave me a good apprenticeship; I ran the business when he started feeling his years, then I took over after he passed away.'

I admired his stuff. There was everything from strings of cheap coral to fabulous sardonyx pendants half the size of my fist. 'Beautiful! I know a lady who would happily accept anything I took her from your stock . . .' Not that I intended to, with a houseful of furniture to buy. Helena possessed enough jewellery. Most of it was better than I could afford; no point trying to compete. 'Look, don't get me wrong, but I'm sure my mother told me Moscus had a wife.'

'She remarried.' He sounded brief, though not particularly grim. 'I rent the shop from her. Anything else you want to know about Moscus, sonny? The position of his birthmarks, or the size of his feet?'

At his increasingly aggressive tone I backed off with a look of shamefaced innocence. 'Jupiter; I didn't mean to pry – my ma never has enough to do; she'll expect to hear a proper tale.'

'That's it. You've heard it,' stated the cameo-cutter tersely.

'Right! Thanks!' I risked a final impertinence: 'Don't you find it a bit galling to have kept the business afloat for old Moscus yet end up still a tenant, while his widow gaily flirts off with somebody new?'

'No.' The lapidary gave me a level stare. He was daring me to put it even more plainly – though giving notice that he would cut up rough if I did. 'Why should I?' he continued in his squeaky voice, apparently unperturbed by my badgering. 'She charges a fair rent; she has a decent business sense. Moscus is dead. It's up to the girl what she does with her life.'

If I wanted scandal, I stood no chance here. I grinned foolishly, and ambled off.

Back to watching the gold-digger's house in Abacus Street. The diary took its usual course. Breakfast. Hot weather. Wine delivery. Dog chasing a cat. Gold-digger to bathhouse . . .

This was reaching the point where I could describe Severina's day before she yawned and decided her plans. It was easy work, though so unproductive it made me depressed. Then, just when I was wondering how to initiate some action I acquired several new pieces of information in rapid succession.

The chair emerged just after lunch. I followed for five streets and watched it carried down an entry through a pottery shop. I stayed in the outer street. After over an hour, doubt set in. I walked through the shop, expecting to see Severina's chair waiting at the far end of the dark passageway.

The chair had vanished. While I was outside like a fool, being buffeted by piemen's trays and having mules stamp on my feet, the gold-digger had been carried indoors – then probably out afterwards through the garden gate. Clever work, Falco!

I walked up to the house. The ground-floor apartment was pretty unobtrusive. No windows; no potted creepers; no kittens on the step; just a dark painted door with a secretive grille. Beside it a small ceramic tile had been fixed to the wall. The plaque was midnight blue, with black lettering and a decorative border of tiny gold stars. It bore a single name in Greek script:

```
************
*          *
*  TUXH    *
*          *
************
```

I knew what sort of place this was. I knew just what sort of mad, withered hag this Tyche must be.

I braced myself. Then I raised my fist, and banged firmly on the door.

'Any chance of an appointment?'

'Do you want to see her now?'

'If there's nobody else with her – '

'It should be all right. Her last visitor left some time ago . . .'

I swallowed. Then in I went, for an immediate appointment with a female astrologer.

XIV

I dread these places.

I prepared myself for a filthy Babylonian, muttering gibberish. To my relief, the smoky caboose for predictions must be elsewhere in the house; the neat slaveboy led me instead to a disturbingly handsome reception room. It had a gleaming black and white mosaic floor. The walls were painted black above a simply patterned dado; their panels were divided by stylised candelabra and featured tiny gold medallions – scallop shells and flower sprays. There were two long-backed chairs such as women use, either side of a low white marble table that must have weighed half a ton. Positioned on the table (rather obviously, I thought) were an astrolabe at one end and at the other an open scroll of planetary records. Opposite the door stood a set of shelves holding a score of very old Greek vases which an auctioneer I knew would have drooled over – all perfect, all a substantial size, all in the ancient geometric style whose repetitive rows of whorls, circles and stylised antelopes must be the specialised choice of a collector with cool taste.

The antiques impressed me more than the atmosphere. Apart from a lingering scent of women's perfume, as though the room had been recently vacated, there were no wafts of incense or drugs to lull the unwary visitor. No tinkling bells. No subtle intoxicating music. No deformed dwarves leaping out of hidden cabinets . . .

'Welcome. How can I help you?' The woman who had slipped in through the door curtain was perfectly clean, calm, and possessed a pleasant, cultured voice. She spoke her Latin with a better accent than me.

She looked about sixty. Her straight dark gown hung from two small silver niello shoulder-brooches, so her arms were bare, though hidden in spare folds of the material. Her hair was rather thin, mostly black yet with broad silver streaks. Her face lacked professional mystique, except for severely hooded eyes. The eyes were no special colour. It was the face of any businesswoman in the male world of

Rome: accommodating, yet with an underlying stubborn strength and a trace, faint as snail tracks, of personal bitterness.

'You the astrologer?'

Her mouth was tight, as if she disapproved of me. 'I am Tyche.'

'Greek for *Fortune* – very nice!'

'That sounds insulting.'

'I have several less nice names for people who pointlessly raise the hopes of those in despair.'

'Then I must remember,' Tyche commented, 'not to raise yours!'

I was expecting to find myself the subject of some shrewd scrutiny. So I stared back openly. 'I can see you are not a customer,' she commented, though I had said nothing. Of course pretending to read minds would be part of her trade apparatus.

'The name's Falco – '

'I have no need to know your name.'

'Spare me the patter. Enigmatic piffle makes me grind my teeth.'

'Oh I see!' Her face relaxed into ruefulness. 'The régime here disappoints you. You wanted to be frightened to death. You expected a cackling harridan casting dried entrails backwards into a bright green fire? – I stopped doing spells. The smoke ruins the decor . . . You had better tell me when you were born.'

'Why?'

'Everyone who comes on other business expects a free prophecy.'

'I don't! March, if you must know.'

'Pisces or Aries?'

'Never quite sure. "On the cusp".'

'You would be!'

'I was right; you do disapprove of me,' I growled.

'Don't most people? Your eyes have witnessed too much you may not speak of among friends.'

'My feet have tramped too many uneven pavements on the trail of too many grasping girls who are conniving at death! *Her* name is Severina, by the way.'

'I know that,' said Tyche quietly.

'Oh?'

'Severina was a customer,' the astrologer explained, with mild reproof. 'I needed her name and address to send my bill.'

That did surprise me. 'What happened to crossing the palm with a silver denarius? I thought you people only did business on a strictly cash basis?'

'Certainly not! I never handle money. I have three perfectly adequate accountants who look after my financial affairs.' This must be one fortune-teller who had moved up a long way from telling half-truths to shepherds' girlfriends in hot little canvas booths. Tyche serviced the gilded-litter trade; I bet she charged for it too. 'What do you want, Falco?'

'A seer ought to know! What did Severina Zotica want?' The woman gave me a long stare that was meant to start a shiver between my shoulder blades. It did. But my work was as much based on bluff as her own. 'Was she buying horoscopes?' She assented in silence. 'I need to know what you told her?'

'Professional secret!'

'Naturally I'll pay the going rate for it – '

'The information is not for sale.'

'*Everything* is for sale! Tell me whose future she was putting a marker on.'

'I can't possibly do that.'

'All right; let me tell you! Her story goes, she is about to be married and wants to reassure herself about her prospects afterwards. One horoscope was her own; that was to make it look good. And the other subject was – '

'Her future husband.'

Tyche smiled wryly, as if she realised the news was bound to be misinterpreted: some people believe that to possess another person's horoscope gives you power over their soul.

XV

The first positive signal about Severina's motives: I felt my toes curling inside my boots, while my heels tried to press themselves through the unyielding tessellations of the mosaic floor. The coarse fibres of my worn woollen tunic prickled against my collarbones. Into this oddly civilised room with its austere occupant, horror had stalked.

Before I could comment, the astrologer took the initiative. 'I presume you are not a superstitious man?'

'The point,' I exclaimed, 'is whether *Severina* believes this gives her a hold over her fiancé!' Rome accepts anyone who takes a keen interest in their own destiny – but to peek at someone else's must be a sign of bad intentions. Indeed, in political life, to acquire an opponent's horoscope is a deeply hostile act. 'Future husband or not, Severina has broken a serious taboo of privacy. Tyche, you could be heading for indictment as an accessory to an unnatural death: if the freedman dies *I'd* be prepared to cite you for encouraging his murderer – unless you co-operate. What did you tell her?'

'I told her the truth, Falco.'

'Stop fencing! If Novus is supposed to die in the next few weeks, better warn me now – '

'If the man is *supposed* to die, then he will!'

'Next you'll tell me that we *all* die – '

'My gifts are passive; I can interpret fate. It is not my role to change it.'

'Ha! Don't you ever try?'

'Do you?' she chipped back.

'I was brought up by a good mother; compassion has a habit of intruding into my working life – '

'You must get very despondent!'

'I should be even more despondent if people with evil intentions were allowed to proceed unchecked – '

'Any force has its opposite,' Tyche assured me. 'Malign influences must be balanced by kindly ones.' Still standing quite motionless, she suddenly gave me a smile of such intensity it was impossible to meet head-on. 'Perhaps *you* are an agent of the stars?'

'Forget it!' I growled, fighting back a grin. 'No ethereal committee of management owns me; I am an independent spirit.'

'Not quite, I think!' For a moment she seemed to hesitate over whether to laugh. She let the desire pass and stood aside from the doorway.

I prognosticated (privately) that a handsome dark-haired man with intelligent eyes was about to make a brisk exit from her house. 'Tyche, if you refuse to tell me whether Novus is secure, at least say this: will Severina Zotica be executed for her crimes?'

'Oh no. She may never be happy, but she will live long and die in her bed.'

'You told her that?'

The wry look returned to the fortune-teller's face. 'We spoke only of her hopes for happiness.'

'Ah well, I imagine very few people ask you, *am I likely to be fed to the lions as a common criminal?*'

'True!'

'And what did you tell her about her marriage?'

'You will not believe it.'

'Try me.'

'Severina's next husband will outlive her in old age.'

I said that was good news for the husband!

Time to leave. I saluted the seer thoughtfully, with the respect I give anyone who can keep three accountants busy. They never let you get away that easily: 'Would you like a prediction, Falco?'

'Can I prevent it?'

'Someone who loves you may have a higher destiny.'

'Anyone who loves me could do better in life!' As we mentioned Helena I could not prevent the fortune-teller seeing the change in my face. 'The someone in question would not be in love with me now, if she had the sense to opt for a less cranky fate.'

'Your heart knows whether that is true.'

There was no damned reason why I should justify Helena to a postulating, nit-picking, Babylonian mountebank. 'My heart is at her feet,' I snapped. 'I shall not blame her if she gives it a nudge with her toe then kicks it around the floor a bit! But don't underestimate her loyalty! You have seen me, and made a few accurate deductions, but you cannot judge my lady – '

'I can judge anyone,' the woman answered flatly, 'by seeing the person they love.'

Which, like all astrological pronouncements, could mean anything you wanted – or nothing at all.

XVI

I retraced my steps to Abacus Street. Almost immediately Severina's chair appeared from the house. I had not even reached my usual place at the cookshop table, but was pausing at the opposite end of the street to buy an apple from an old man who kept a fruit stall there. He was telling me about his orchard, which was out on the Campagna and only a few miles from the market garden my mother's family ran. We were so deep in conversation about Campagna landmarks and characters that I could not easily disengage myself to pursue the sedan.

Then, while I was still trying to deflect the old chap's offers of complimentary fruit, who should slyly put her head out of the passage beside the cheese shop, but a heavily veiled woman who looked just Severina's shape and size? The maid at her elbow was definitely the gold-digger's . . .

My surveillance had been fairly casual. This gave every suggestion that my presence had been noted; that giving me the slip at Tyche's had been deliberate; and that sending out the chair was a decoy.

Both women were now looking towards the cookshop. I waited by the fruit stall until they seemed satisfied by my empty bench. Eventually they set off on foot, this time with me adopting my strictest procedures for tailing a suspect invisibly.

If the visit to the fortune-teller had been indicative, that was nothing to what happened next: Severina Zotica took herself to a marble yard.

She was ordering a tombstone.

I could guess who it was for.

After selecting her square of marble, I watched her depart. As soon as I felt sure she was heading homewards, I nipped back to see the stonemason myself.

His name was Scaurus. I found him deep in a narrow corridor amongst his stock. On one hand were room-high stacks of rough-cut travertine for general building purposes; on the other, pallets protecting smaller slabs of finer marble which would be made into self-congratulatory epitaphs for second-rate officials, monuments for old soldiers, and poignant plaques to commemorate sweet lost children.

Scaurus was a short, strong, dust-covered character with a bald dome, a broad face, and small ears which stuck out like wheel-bosses each side of his head. Naturally his dealings with clients were confidential. And naturally the size of bribe my clients could afford soon got us over that.

'I'm interested in Severina Zotica. She must be the kind of regular client you love – so much domestic tragedy!'

'I've done one or two jobs for her,' Scaurus admitted, not quarrelling with my jocular approach.

'Three husbands down – and the next looming! Am I right that she's just ordered a new memorial stone?' He nodded. 'Can I see the text of the inscription?'

'Severina only came in for an estimate, and to put down a deposit on the slab.'

'She give you the deceased's name?'

'No.'

'So what was the story?'

'Other people are involved – a subscription effort. She has to consult them about the words to use.'

'I bet! The fact is, this poor fellow's relations may have the good manners to want him dead first, before they commit themselves!' I was starting to feel angry. 'Does she normally have the tombstone cut in advance?'

Scaurus was becoming more cautious. A thriving trade was one thing, but he did not want to be identified as an accessory before the fact. I warned him I would be back for a sight of the finished carving, then I left it at that.

He had given me what I needed. The horoscope and the memorial stone spoke for themselves. If nobody weighed in to stop Severina, Hortensius Novus was a dead man.

XVII

Some informers with a telling piece of information rush straight off to report. I like to mull things over. Since I met Helena Justina most of my best mulling had been done in company; she had a sharp brain, with the advantage of a dispassionate view of my work. Her approval always reassured me – and sometimes she contributed a thought that I could hone up into a clever ploy for solving the case.

(Sometimes Helena told me I was a patronising ferret, which just proves my point about her perceptiveness.)

I arrived at the Senator's door at about nine, just before dinner. The porter on duty was an old antagonist. He eagerly told me Helena was out.

I asked where she had gone. The bathhouse. Which? He didn't know. I didn't believe him anyway. A senator's daughter rarely leaves home without mentioning where she is going. It need not be true. Just some tale to delude her noble father that his petal is respectable, and give her mother (who knows better) something new to worry about.

I shared a few choice witticisms with Janus, though frankly his intellect had never been up to my standard. I was turning away when their lost pigeon decided to wing in home.

'Where were you?' I demanded, more hotly than I meant.

She looked startled. 'Bathing . . .'

She was clean all right. She looked delicious. Her hair shone; her skin was soft, and perfumed all over with some distinctive flowery oil that made me want to move very much closer to investigate . . . I was working up a froth again. I knew she could tell, and I knew she would laugh, so I retreated into banter. 'I just encountered a fortune-teller who promised I was doomed in love. So naturally I dashed straight here – '

'For a dose of doom?'

'Works wonders on the bowels. *You're* due for "a higher destiny", by the way.'

'That sounds like hard work! Is it like a legacy? Can I pass it on hastily to somebody else?'

'No, madam, your stars are fixed – though luckily the prophetess has decided I am the constellations' agent. For a small backhander I can undertake to unfix fortune and unravel destiny . . .'

'Remind me never to let you near when I'm spinning wool . . . Are you coming in to make me laugh, or is this just a tantalising glimpse to make me pine for you?'

Since the porter had opened the door for her, I was already inside.

'Do you?' I asked nonchalantly.

'What?'

'Pine for me?'

Helena Justina gave me an unfathomable smile.

She whisked me further indoors and seated me under a pergola in a secluded colonnade. Helena slid onto a seat next to me and fastened a rose in my shoulder-brooch while she kept the houseslaves running about bringing me wine, warming it, fetching dishes of almonds, then cushions, then a new cup because mine had a minute chip in the glaze . . . I lay back in her own reclining chair and enjoyed the attention (gnawing my thumb). She seemed extraordinarily loving. Something was up. I decided some burnished bugger with a senatorial pedigree must have asked her home to see his collection of blackfigure jars.

'Marcus, tell me about your day.' I told her, gloomily. 'Cheer up. You need more excitement. Why not let some floosies flaunt themselves at you? Go and see your clients. The lapidary sounds a complete waste of time, but tell them about the astrologer and the mason, then see how they react.'

'You're sending me into a witches' lair!'

'Two overfed spenders, with no taste and even fewer scruples, both falling out of their frocks . . . I think you can handle them.'

'How do you know all this?'

'I've been to have a look at them.' Her face grew warmer, but she faced me out as I screwed round in the chair, full of alarm.

'Helena Justina! *How?*'

'I called on them this afternoon. I said I was trying to start a school for female foundlings, and – as women of feeling, and in one case a mother – could I persuade them to contribute?'

'Mars Ultor! Did they?'

'Only Atilia at first. That Pollia is an unyielding little bodkin – but I shamed her in the end. Then of course she gave me a *huge* donation, trying to impress on me what plutocrats they are.'

'I hope you never told them who you were?'

'I certainly did. There was no reason for them to connect me with you.' Cruel, but true. I was having a hard time connecting us myself. 'People who live on the Pincian are terrible snobs. They were delighted to have a senator's daughter sip mulled wine amid their outrageous artwork, while she entreated them to involve themselves in her modest civic works.'

'Did they get you drunk?'

'Not quite. Trust them to believe they were immaculate hostesses for giving a visitor monstrous goblets of boiling hot liquor, totally unsuited for the time of day; what I really needed was a nice finger-glass of herbal tea. Did they get *you* drunk?'

'No.'

'Bad luck! They wanted me to admire their solid silver goblets – too heavy to lift and too ornate to clean. Mine had the biggest topaz I have ever seen.' She looked thoughtful, then commented, 'They judge the world by what it costs. Unless the price is vulgar, nothing counts . . . Your rates are too reasonable; I'm surprised they employed you.'

'Thanks!' I barked, though I had the uneasy feeling my darling might be right. I buried my face in my hands for a moment then laughed. 'What will you do with the money?'

'Found a school. I'm not a hypocrite, Marcus.'

She was amazing. It seemed best to keep my admiration to myself. Helena needed no encouragement. I had witnessed her in public as endearingly shy – yet she forgot all about that whenever some daft idea like this invaded her head. 'I worry when you career off uncontrollably. Why ever did you go?' She would not answer me. 'Curiosity!' I slid my nearest arm round her and pulled her over against my chest, looking into her great dark eyes with their perplexing mixture of love and dismissiveness. 'So what did you think of my clients?'

'Rather too obvious – if I go again I must take them a present of some dress pins . . .' Her old sense of mischief was dancing there, I was glad to see. 'Sabina Pollia clawed her way up from nothing – and may still have dirt under her fingernails. The maternal one looks like the kind of tremulous sweetheart who begs for protection – while she savagely manipulates everyone around her . . . Did you meet her little boy, by the way? I suspect that tot has the full measure of his mama. Atilia has big plans for him. Her life's work will be putting him up for the Senate the minute he's old enough – '

I could think of bigger ambitions for a family who had the energy and funds to promote a child; tactless to say so to the daughter of a senator. 'But a wonderful mother!' I teased, without thinking: equally tactless, in fact.

'Lots of us might be wonderful mothers!'

Even before the violence flared I had enveloped her fiercely with both arms. 'You will!' We had never discussed this; no opportunity. I had assumed I was glad to avoid it; yet now I found myself launching into an urgent, prepared speech: 'My love, neither of us was ready; losing that baby may have been the best fate for the poor mite – ' Helena squirmed angrily. I glimpsed some dark mood I didn't care for, but I was not prepared to dump the girl and run just because she expected it. 'No, listen; I need to talk about this – Helena, I never rely on anything, but so far as I'm concerned we now have to find some way of being together; we'll enjoy that – and when it really seems a good idea we will start a new generation of quaint curiosities like us – '

'Perhaps I don't want to – '

'I'll win you round – '

'Marcus, I don't want to think about it; I need to live with what has happened first!'

'I know that – ' I suspected I would lose her altogether if she crashed the bolts home on me now. Besides, I was annoyed. 'Don't block me out of it – and don't suppose it had no effect on me!'

'Oh you and your old republican code!' Helena murmured with one of her sudden changes of mood, kissing my face. 'Stop being so reasonable – ' I said nothing. 'Didius Falco, somebody ought to explain to you, informers are tough; informers are hard men who lead mean lives, and whenever they have a lucky escape, informers speed off back to their own low world – '

'Wrong. Informers are soft slugs. Any woman in decent shoes can stamp on us.' That reminded me of something: 'Though I have no intention of letting the Hortensius females squash me on a garden path. There was no need for you to reconnoitre the terrain; my darling, I can look after myself . . .' I could certainly do that. My problem was looking after Helena. 'Don't get involved.'

'No Marcus,' she promised, with a meek air I knew was false.

'Well don't tell me afterwards!' She was still watching me. 'There's no need to worry about me. Those two women at the Hortensius house are trash. There's no one to compete with you. Besides, I have a rule: never sleep with a client.'

'Ever broken it.'

'Once.'

I gave her a sheepish grin. She gave me a twitchy smile. I tugged her head down onto my shoulder and held her close.

The colonnade where we were lurking was a completely private area. I stayed as I was, holding Helena. I felt relaxed, and more affectionate than I usually allowed myself to be. She still looked troubled; I stroked her hair, which soothed the look away. This encouraged me to range more widely, in case there were any other little tension spots that needed attention . . .

'Marcus!' I decided to carry on. Her sleek, soft skin seemed to have been oiled at the baths especially to attract an appreciative hand. 'Marcus, you're making things impossible for both of us . . .' I decided to prove I was as tough as she had said earlier; so I stopped.

Not long afterwards I chose to make my excuses; the various chinks of silverware which announced that her parents were at dinner were becoming an embarrassment. Helena invited me to dine, but I did not want Helena or her parents (especially her mother) to get the idea I was the sort of parasitic hanger-on who kept turning up at mealtimes in the hope of being fed.

On leaving the house I walked north, thoughtfully. Some informers give the impression that wherever they go ravishing women shed their scanty clothing without the slightest encouragement and want to fall into bed. I told myself it so rarely happened to me because I appealed to a more selective type of girl.

Well; I had appealed to her once.

71

XVIII

The ladies were at home. Their men were elsewhere. The ladies were bored. I turned up like a treat from the gods, to fill the vacant after-dinner entertainment spot. If I had brought along a flute and a couple of Phrygian sword dancers I might have been better use to them.

In all my visits to the Hortensius house, I would never be received for an interview in the same room twice. Tonight I was shown into a dramatic azure leisure suite, with heavy boudoir overtones. All the couches had expensive coverlets flung over them with suggestive abandon. Bulbous cushions with shiny covers were piled on top, with fringing and fat tassels much in evidence. The room was stuffed with furniture: bronze side tables held up by priapic satyrs; silver daybeds with lions' feet; tortoiseshell cabinets. The cabinets were displaying a job lot of spiralled Syrian glassware (including at least one vase which had been recycled in Campania recently), some ivory, a collection of quite pretty Etruscan hand mirrors, and an extremely large solid gold vessel of doubtful purpose which they probably called 'a votive bowl', though it looked to me like the personal chamberpot of a particularly gross Macedonian king.

With their burnished skin and antimonied eyes the women looked as plush as the drapery. Sabina Pollia occupied her couch with the thrusting sprawl of a sage bush taking possession of a herb garden. Hortensia Atilia lolled with a neater habit, though she held one foot up behind in a way which made it impossible not to notice the nakedness of her exposed leg. In fact, as they faced one another over a huge platter of grape bunches I could not forget Helena's disparaging comments (her intention, presumably). They both wore their gowns in luxuriant folds that were designed more for sliding off than draping the shapely forms beneath. I kept wondering whether Pollia's left or right shoulder-brooch would be the first to slither down a lovely arm further than decency permitted. Pollia was in emeralds; Atilia dripping with Indian pearls.

Atilia's son, an ordinary child, was with them, kneeling on the marble with a terracotta model donkey. He was about eight. I winked at him, and he stared back with the stark hostility of any little boy facing a strange beak in his nest.

'Well, Falco, what have you brought us?' Pollia demanded.

'Only news,' I apologised.

The left shoulder of Pollia's crimson dinner gown descended so far it was annoying her. So she twitched it up. This gave the right side more free play to droop appealingly over her breast.

'Do tell!' urged Hortensia Atilia, wriggling her raised toes. Atilia preferred to keep her brooches properly centred on her fine shoulders. This meant that as she lay on a couch the front of her gown (which was marine blue, verging on good taste but not quite making it) draped itself in a low parabola so anyone who was standing up at the time had a clear view straight down to the big brown mole two inches below her cleavage line: an abundant mother goddess, making good use of the area which mother goddesses love to display. (Naturally it left me unmoved; I was not the religious type.)

Without further preamble, I gave my two clients details of my findings so far. 'Regarding the astrologer, I don't want to dwell on the superstitious aspects, but better not to mention this if Hortensius Novus is likely to become anxious; nervous men tend to have accidents – '

'It proves nothing,' Pollia decided crushingly. She had wined well with her dinner. Now it was time to bring out the nutcrackers; I was the filbert she had her eye on, I could tell.

I kept cool. 'I'm the first to admit that. But ordering a memorial stone is rather a different matter! Severina Zotica is approaching her wedding with a practical grit which – if *I* was her intended – would send me scurrying for sanctuary.'

'Yes.'

The small boy crashed his toy donkey into the leg of a side table; his mother frowned, and signalled him to leave the room. 'To be fair to the girl,' suggested Atilia, 'perhaps we should not blame her if she wants to feel sure her previous ill luck will not recur. The horoscopes could be entirely innocent.' Of the two, Hortensia Atilia certainly had the most ample generosity. Like everything else which she possessed in abundance, the lady made it freely available to public view.

'What I want to do now,' I said, 'is tackle Severina at an interview – '

Atilia and Pollia glanced at one another. For some reason I recalled Helena's fear that something in this conundrum was not quite right.

'That sounds rather tricky.' Atilia's diffident expression implied she was a simple blossom looking for some manly type to fend off her troubles in the meadowland of life; I tried to strut like a city thug who liked to swipe the heads off marguerites for fun.

'Perhaps we should wait,' Pollia added, smiling at me brilliantly. 'You won't lose by it financially – '

My interest sharpened. 'Sabina Pollia, you and I agreed that I should discover the gold-digger's price.'

Pollia gave me a special pout which assured me there were other things we might agree. 'I was suggesting we try for more evidence first. But you are the expert, Falco. You must decide the moment; I'm sure your timing is immaculate . . .'

I eased the edge of my tunic where it sweltered against my neck. 'It's your choice; I can watch her some more. If you are willing to pay my expenses, I can watch her for as long as you like – ' I was never at my best while being treated as a plaything of the rich.

I normally prevent my clients running up unnecessary bills. With four empty rooms at home to furnish, and two females who could well afford to buy their puppet a new table, my upright morals were becoming more relaxed.

I left straightaway. The small boy was sitting on the steps of their mighty portico; his stare as he watched me skipping down the polished marble was full of dark scorn for the fact that I had obviously left too soon to have enjoyed myself.

I strode home, feeling aggressive. Everyone in Rome had just enjoyed their dinner; everyone except me. At this time of day cookshops in the Piscina Publica were more visible, though equally unpromising. I hoofed off to see my mother. I found several of my sisters there, so I ventured that if anyone had any unwanted furniture I could give it a home. Junia actually came up with a bed. Junia, who thought herself superior, had somehow entrapped a husband who was salaried, a customs clerk supervisor; they never kept anything longer than two years. Normally I avoided whatever they were turfing out since I hate feeling like some grovelling parasite, but for a decent bed I bent my pride. This bargain among the nearly-news had cost my sister's husband two hundred sesterces, I was pleased to hear. Might as well cadge quality.

It was after the wheeled-traffic curfew. My brother-in-law Mico could always lay his hands on a cart, so he and I whisked away the bed that night before Junia changed her mind, then we went round the rest of my family collecting their gifts of pans with crooked handles and stools with missing legs. As soon as I could get rid of Mico I enjoyed myself arranging and rearranging my apartment like a little girl playing with her dolls' furniture. It was late, but Ma had given me some lamps and Maia had thrown in half a jar of oil, spluttery but adequate. As I dragged stuff about, other people in the block banged on the walls from time to time. I banged back cheerfully, always glad to make new friends.

My new bed was fine, but the mattress had never seen much life at Junia's; it was like perching on a granite ledge halfway up a mountainside. Still, the nocturnal adventures I promised myself would soon create accommodating dents.

XIX

Since my clients had demanded more evidence, at first light I set off, armed with the name and address I had been given by Lusius at the Praetor's house: I was going to interview the doctor who had been called to Severina's second husband, the apothecary, after he had choked.

The quack was highly annoyed at being disturbed so early, though not so annoyed as I was when I discovered his uselessness. My frustration was nothing new to him; I gathered Lusius had been just as short with him at their previous interview.

'I told the clerk the facts, and facts don't change!' This presupposed that the self-opinionated duffer had the facts right in the first place – something I soon doubted. 'The apothecary went into convulsions – '

'Were you there then?'

'I was told! Then his servants ran away, while the wife did her best to revive him.'

'No luck?'

'She could hardly get near. The man was struggling violently – '

'You mean – '

'Don't you tell me my professional duty!' he interrupted angrily, though my unposed question had been perfectly subservient. 'I've already had all this from the Praetor's clerk! He wanted to convince me the wife may have suffocated her husband – ' So my friend Lusius had been diligent in his earlier investigation. 'It's nonsense. The poor woman was badly shaken and bruised, but she did her best. Eprius must have lashed out so hard he nearly knocked her senseless too – '

'Don't you find that suspicious, if she was helping him?'

'Certainly not. He had no idea what he was doing; he was having a fatal fit!'

'Try this scenario,' I insisted. 'Severina had tried to poison him; it was not working properly so she held him down; Eprius understood what was going on and fought with her – '

'Unnecessary speculation. I found the medicament that choked him.'

'Did you preserve it?'

'Of course,' he replied coldly. 'I gave the item to the Praetor's clerk.'

'I believe it was a cough lozenge. An apothecary ought to have known how to suck a jujube! Had you prescribed it for him?'

'I was not his doctor. I doubt if he had a doctor; he was qualified to make up medicines for himself. They called me to the accident because I lived nearby. Eprius was already dead when I got there; there was nothing anyone could do but comfort the widow. Luckily a freedman she knew happened to call at the house, so I was able to leave her being cared for by a friend – '

'She recovered!' I assured him. 'She remarried within the month.'

The arrogant noodle still refused to make an adverse report.

The story he told me was chilling, though it took me no further forwards. I left in disgust. Yet I was still determined to prove to Pollia and Atilia that my expenses were well earned. Since I had drawn a blank with the beadseller and the apothecary, my last resort was the importer of wild beasts.

I hired a mule, and rode out to the north-east part of the city. I knew that animals for the arena were housed beyond the city boundary, the other side of the main Praetorian Camp. Before I even reached the bestiary I could hear roaring and trumpeting, strangely incongruous in the environs of Rome. The Imperial menagerie had every strange creature I had ever heard of, and plenty besides. I made my initial enquiries with crocodiles snapping in cages behind me and ostriches looking over the shoulders of everyone I approached. All around were half-dead rhinos, sad apes, and lacklustre leopards, attended by long-haired men who looked as surly and unpredictable as the animals themselves. The smell was sour and disconcerting. Between all the cages there was a thin wash of sordid-looking mud underfoot.

I had asked for Grittius Fronto's nephew. I learned that the nephew was back in Egypt, but if I was trying to arrange party entertainment of a spectacular nature I ought to speak to Thalia. Since I never know when to cut and run, I followed directions to a striped tent where I boldly pulled back the entrance flap and even more recklessly went in.

77

'Ooh!' shrieked a voice that would sharpen ploughshares. 'My lucky day!'

She was a big girl. By which I mean . . . nothing. She was taller than me. She was big, all over; she was young enough to be described as a girl without too much irreverence; and I was able to see that her assets were entirely in proportion to the height of her. Her attire was what the well-dressed artiste was wearing that month: a few stars, a couple of ostrich feathers (which explained why some of the birds I had seen outside looked so miffed), a skimpy drape of transparent stuff – and a necklace.

The necklace might pass for coral – until you observed that its jewelled folds sometimes shuddered with a sluggish allure. From time to time an end of it slipped from her neck and she draped it back dismissively. It was a live snake.

'Unusual, eh?' She had a peaceful expression which told its own story; in any contest with a tricky reptile I would feel sorry for the snake.

'With a gem like that decorating your windpipe, I imagine you rarely encounter trouble from men!'

'Men are always trouble, darling!'

I smiled apologetically. 'All I want is a few kind words.'

She cackled with ribald laughter. 'That's what they all say!' Then she gazed at me as if she wanted to mother me. I was terrified. 'I'm Thalia.'

'One of the Graces!' This case was tilting into lunacy.

'Oh my word; you're a cheeky one – what's your name?' Against my better judgement I told her my name. 'Well, Falco? Have you run away from home to be a lion-tamer?'

'No; my mother wouldn't let me. Are you a contortionist?'

'Anyone would turn into a contortionist if they had a python looking up their – '

'Quite!' I interjected hastily.

'I am a professional snake dancer,' she informed me coolly.

'I see! Is this the snake you dance with?'

'What this? This is just for everyday wear! The one in my act is twenty times this size!'

'Sorry. I thought you might have been rehearsing.'

The snake dancer grimaced. 'What I do at a performance is dangerous enough if you're paid for it! Who needs to rehearse?'

I grinned. 'I'd like to see the act some time!'

Thalia gave me the shrewd, still stare of people who live with venomous animals. She was used to paying attention even when she seemed to be busy elsewhere. 'What do you want, Falco?'

I told her the truth. 'I'm an informer. I'm trying to finger a murderer. I've come to ask if you ever knew a man called Grittit Fronto?'

Thalia tidied her snake again. 'I knew Fronto.'

She patted the bench beside her. Since her manner seemed not unfriendly (and the snake appeared to be sleeping) I risked the close approach. 'I've been speaking to the clerk who helped the Praetor's investigation into Fronto's death; did Lusius ever talk to you?'

'Who trusts a female who does unusual things with snakes?'

'People should!' (It seemed a moment for gallantry.)

She nodded. I could see she was depressed. 'Some men are attracted to danger – at the time Fronto died my latest disaster was an unsteady tightrope walker so short-sighted he could never see his balls!'

I tried to look sympathetic. 'Wasn't a tightrope walker mauled in the same accident?'

'He would never have been the same again – but I nursed him through.'

'Still with him?'

'No! He caught a cold and died of that – men are such bastards!'

The snake suddenly unravelled and expressed a startling interest in my face. I tried to sit tight. Thalia tucked it back in place around her neck, two loops, then head and tail neatly below her ample chin. Since I was too faint to speak, she set off unaided: 'Fronto had an import business; had it for years. In some ways he was good at it, but his nephew did the hard work, finding the animals in Africa and India, then shipping them home. The best times for arena fighting were under Nero, but even during the troubles there were sidelines like mine – and plenty of private customers who wanted strange beasts to exhibit on their estates.'

I nodded. Rome had done its bit towards eliminating vicious species from the wilder provinces. Tigers stripped from India and the Caucasus. Whole herds of destructive elephants wiped out in Mauretania. Snakes too, presumably.

'What do you want to know?' Thalia enquired, suddenly more self-conscious.

'Anything that may have a bearing. As a matter of interest, did you know Fronto's wife?'

'Never met her. Never wanted to. She was obviously trouble; you could tell Fronto thought so too. He kept her out of things. He never let on to her he had that nephew, did you know?'

'I gathered as much. So what happened? I was told a panther ran Fronto and the tightrope walker up against some lifting gear?'

Thalia exclaimed mournfully, 'Well that's a lie for a start!'

'What do you mean?'

'It happened at Nero's Circus.'

Suddenly I caught on; unlike an ampitheatre, a racing circus is simply a level course. 'No substructures? Nothing underground at all – and so no requirement to lift the cages?' Thalia nodded. I wished she wouldn't; it disturbed the snake. Every time she moved, that creature perked up and started inspecting if I was properly shaved, and whether I had nits behind the ears. 'So did some cack-handed aedile write a report about the accident without even going to look?'

'Must have.'

That was good news; it left open the possibility of discovering new evidence. 'Were *you* there?' Thalia nodded; her curious pet unroped itself; she twined it back again. 'So what's the true story?'

'It happened inside the starting gates. Fronto had provided beasts for the morning interlude before the charioteers – a mock hunt. You know! Archers on horseback scampering about after anything spotted or striped that happened to be in the menagerie at the time. If you have a very tired old lion, with no teeth, you sometimes let a few sons of aristocrats in for a go . . .'

'Was the panther tired and toothless?'

'Oh no!' Thalia rebuked me. 'That panther was the real thing. He's beautiful. You can see him if you want. Fronto's nephew kept him afterwards – act of respect; just in case any of his uncle was still inside. The funeral, you know Falco, was very difficult – '

'I don't think I need to look at him; I don't suppose the animal would talk to me but even if he did, no court would accept his evidence! So what happened?'

'Someone let him out.'

'You mean, deliberately?'

'Look, Falco; for Nero's Circus they bring the cages all across the city. They do it at night but it would cause a commotion if even a very small lion got loose!' I had seen the special cages used for transportation of wild animals – just big enough to contain them and fit on ampitheatre lifts. The top section had the hinge. 'Fronto was very particular about the animals; they cost him enough! He checked the locks himself before a journey, and he checked them again while the cages were standing on site. There was no way that panther could have escaped by accident.'

'But the cages must have been unlocked at some time?'

'Just before the scene. Fronto would always be there to supervise. In an arena, he always waited to unlock them until the cages were on the lifting hoists; then there would be just a slip catch for the slaves at the top to undo – '

'But the procedure was different at the Circus?'

'Yes. The cages for the mock hunt were being kept in the chariot stalls; the plan was to release the animals through the starting gates. They would be lively after being cramped up overnight, so they would run well out into the Circus – which was set up with wooden trees like a forest – lovely it looked! Then the huntsmen would ride in after them . . .'

'Never mind the topiary. What happened by the gates?'

'Someone unlocked the panther early. Fronto and my tightrope walker were in one of the chariot lanes. They rushed to escape through the starting gates – but the gates were still roped up. They were trapped. I ran in the back with some of the men; we saw the panther just finishing his first course and going for dessert. The tightrope walker got in the open cage and pulled the lid down like a lover in a laundry box; that was how he escaped.'

'Oh Jupiter!'

'You can't blame the panther,' Thalia said kind-heartedly. 'He was hungry; and we reckoned that somebody had been annoying him!'

'Well this is the critical question,' I answered with more sobriety than I was feeling. 'Who upset him – and is that who let him out?'

Thalia sighed. From a girl of her size sighs tended to be considerable gusts. The snake shot out a portion of its neck and peered at her reproachfully. She tucked its head down her bosom; the ultimate sanction (or, possible, treat). 'We had a stockman,' said Thalia. 'A stockman I never liked.'

81

XX

I leaned forwards on my knees. Even Thalia's necklace was forgotten now. 'Will I have any chance of finding this stockman?'

'Do you think Fronto's nephew didn't try? Why do you reckon we said nothing to the lawmen? Why did Fronto's nephew drop his action?'

'You tell me.'

'The stockman's dead. An accident.'

'What was it?'

'He was walking past a derelict house. A wall fell on him.'

'Are you quite sure it was an accident?'

'Fronto's nephew was convinced. There was a local outcry about the way the building had been neglected, but since no one came forward to claim kinship with our stockman, there was no one able to prosecute the leaseholder. Fronto's nephew was hopping mad, because it ruined his case against the widow if somebody completely unconnected had caused Fronto's death. The vigilantes identified the stockman's body, you see, from a key in his purse which had Fronto's name on it – it was the missing key to the panther's cage.'

'So what had been his grudge against Fronto?'

'No one ever knew. He had only been with us a few weeks, and he had no traceable connections. We get a lot of temporary staff like that.'

'What did you call him?'

'Gaius.'

'That's a great help!' More than fifty per cent of the population answers to Gaius. Most of the rest are called Marcus or Lucius; it makes an informer's life very trying. 'Can't you do better?'

'He may have had another name. I racked my brains, but I simply can't remember it. Fronto was the only one who could have said.'

I asked the contortionist a few more questions, but she had nothing significant to add. She promised to go on trying to remember further details about the stockman. I left the menagerie, feeling dazed.

My early-morning's work had produced little concrete evidence, yet the pictures it had given me of Eprius and Fronto meeting their deaths were so vivid that when I made my way to the Caelimontium and took up my usual station I was abnormally subdued.

Abacus Street was baking; we were in for a scorcher. The pavements were drying almost as soon as buckets of water were sluiced over them, and the locksmith's singing finch already had a cloth tied round his cage to keep the sun off his little feathered head. When I arrived I raised my arm to the cookshop owner; he knew my order by this time so since I could see someone else at the counter I stayed outside, to bag the only table in the shade.

I was waiting for mine host to warm my wine. It was a pleasant morning (if you were the man with the shady table) and I knew Severina was unlikely to put in an appearance for a couple of hours. Happy with the prospect of being well paid for such easy labour, I linked my hands behind my head and had a good stretch.

Someone came out of the shop behind me. I thought it was the waiter but soon learned my mistake. As I dropped my arms, they were lassoed to my sides with a thick hemp rope. The rope jerked tight. And my cry of alarm was muffled by a large sack dragged swiftly over my head.

I flung myself upright, roaring. I felt the bench topple behind me but hardly knew where I was. Blinded, choked by a confusing smell within the sack, and utterly surprised, my instinctive attempts to free myself were thwarted; my attackers pushed me over violently, face down on the table. I twisted just in time – saved my nose from snapping, but took a hard knock that made one ear sing. I kicked out backwards, found a soft target, repeated the manoeuvre but kicked air. Still flattened on the table I jackknifed sideways. Hands grabbed at me; I thrashed in the other direction heavy as a shark – too far; I fell off the edge.

There was no time to reorientate my senses. Other people had their own ideas about where I was going: on my back, towed feetfirst at high speed. I knew better than to expect passers-by to assist. I was helpless. The villains had a leg of me each – dangerous if they ran two ways round a post. Most parts of me already hurt. Quarrelling with my abductors from this position could only make the pain worse. I went limp and let it happen.

The kerb down into the road posed no great problem; anticipating the next one up I arched my spine. The sack protected me to some extent, but the base of my neck took a scrape that made me feel like a chicken being boned. I grunted. Jolting over lava blocks was no tonic for my head either.

I knew we had turned, because my side wanged against the corner of a wall, grazing skin even through the sack. We passed into a cooler space: off the street.

A threshold bumped every knob of my spine, then finally my skull. More veering; more knocks. At last my heels crashed down; I had been dumped. I lay still and enjoyed the peace while I could.

The smell was lanolin, I decided. I was trussed in a sack that had been used for unspun wool: a clue so unwelcome I rapidly discarded it.

I listened. I was indoors, not alone. I heard movement; something unidentifiable, then clicks, like big pebbles knocking together.

'Right.' A female. Displeased, but not greatly disturbed. 'Get him out. Let's have a look at him.' I thrashed angrily. 'Careful! That's a good bag he's ruining – '

I recognised the sturdy slave with the big hands who unsheathed me from the hopsack. Then I identified the clicking sounds: big round terracotta loom weights, which swung against each other as someone tugged at the warp threads on the weights. She had just moved down the heddle bar to the next pegs on the frame, and was squaring up the cloth again. I had never seen her bareheaded, but I recognised her too.

So much for my professional expertise: I had been kidnapped in broad daylight by Severina Zotica.

XXI

The red hair was the crinkled gingery type. It was red enough to call for comment, though not too vivid. It would not distract nervous cattle, for instance – and it did not frighten me. With it came pale skin, invisible eyelashes, and sluice-water eyes. The hair was drawn back in a way that emphasised her brow; it should have given her face a childlike quality, but instead her expression suggested that Severina Zotica had passed through childhood too quickly for her own good. She looked the same age as Helena, though I knew she must be younger by several years. She had a witch's *old* eyes.

'You'll get the pip,' she said sourly, 'sitting out in the shade all day.'

I tested my limbs for broken bones. 'Next time, try sending me a simple invitation to come indoors.'

'Would you accept?'

'Always glad to meet a girl who has made a success of herself.'

The professional bride wore a sleeved overtunic in a shade of silver green which combined both simplicity and good taste. An eye for colour: the work on her loom was in happy shades of amber, oatmeal and rust. Her room had matt saffron walls, against which glowed the chair cushions and door curtains worked in brighter tones, while a great floor rug stretched in front of me, thickly tufted with flame, dark brown and black. I ached in so many places I gazed at it, thinking the floor would be a nice place to lie down.

I felt the back of my head, finding blood in my hair. Inside my tunic something trickled depressingly from my last mission's unhealed wound. 'Your musclemen have knocked me about. If this chat is going to be drawn out, could one of them bring me a seat?'

'Fetch it yourself!' She motioned her slaves to absent themselves. I folded my arms, braced my legs, and stayed on my feet. 'Tough, eh?' she mocked.

She started working at the loom. She was sitting sideways, pretending to give me little of her attention, but it was all there. The repetitive movements of the shuttle frayed my tender nerves. 'Lady, would you mind not doing that while you're talking to me?'

'You can do the talking.' Her mouth compressed angrily, though she kept her voice level. 'You have plenty to explain. You have been watching my house all week and following me around blatantly. One of my tenants tells me you were in the Subura asking crass questions about my private life – '

'You must be used to that!' I interrupted. 'Anyway, I don't follow you everywhere; I gave the pantomime a miss: seen it. The orchestra was flat, the plot was an insult, and the mime himself was a balding old paunch with goggle eyes, too arthritic to make a decent stab at it!'

'I enjoyed it.'

'An awkward type, eh?'

'I make my own judgements – do you have a name?'

'Didius Falco.'

'An informer?'

'Correct.'

'Yet *you* despise me!' I was not one of those pathetic worms who eavesdrop on senators in order to sell their sordid indiscretions to Anacrites at the Palace or to their own dissatisfied wives, but I let the insult pass. 'So, Falco, who is hiring you to spy on me?'

'Your fiancé's family. Don't blame them.'

'I don't!' Severina retorted crisply. 'They and I will reach an understanding in due course. They have his interests at heart. So do I, as it happens.'

'In love?' I demanded caustically.

'What do you think?'

'Not a chance! Is he?'

'I doubt it.'

'That's honest!'

'Novus and I are practical people. Romantic love can be very short-lived.'

I wondered if Hortensius Novus was more smitten than she was. A man who has survived so many years as a bachelor usually likes to persuade himself his reason for abandoning his freedom is a special one. The girl spoke to me with a cool competence she probably restrained in his company. Poor old Novus might be deluding himself that his beloved was demure.

Reaching into a basket for a new hank of wool, Severina lifted her head; she was watching me. I meanwhile was still trying to decide why she had taken the initiative today. It could be simple impatience at me following her about. Yet I sensed that she really loved playing with fire.

She sat up, and rested her pointed chin on tapering white fingers. 'You had better bring the family's anxieties into the open,' she offered. 'I have nothing to hide.'

'My clients' anxieties are those anyone would have, young lady – your sordid past, your present motives, and your future plans.'

'I am sure you know,' Severina interpolated, still composed but with a glint I welcomed, 'my past has been investigated thoroughly.'

'By an old praetorian bombast who had not enough sense to pay attention to his extremely able clerk.' The look she gave me might be renewed respect – or increasing dislike. 'I reckon the clerk took a shine to you – and not necessarily in secret,' I added, remembering Lusius as a straightforward type who might speak out. 'What did you think?'

Severina looked amused by the question but managed to make her answer sound genteel. 'I have no idea!'

'Lies, Zotica! Well, I'm the new boy here; strictly neutral so far. Suppose you whisper into my kindly ear what really happened. Let's start with your first manoeuvre. You had been dragged from the Delos slave market in your childhood, and ended up in Rome. You married your master; how did you wangle that?'

'Without trickery, I assure you. Moscus bought me because I looked quick; he wanted someone to train as a stock-keeper – '

'An aptitude for figures must stand you in good stead as a legatee!'

I saw her take a breath, but I failed to raise the flash fire I was hoping for. As redheads go she was pinched and secretive – the kind who broods on the ruin of empires. I could imagine her plotting revenge for imagined insults years after the event. 'Severus Moscus never touched me, but when I was sixteen he asked me to marry him. Perhaps *because* he had never abused me – unlike others – I agreed. Why not? His shop was the best place I had ever lived in, and I felt at home. I gained my freedom. But most marriages are based on bargains; no one can sneer at me for taking my chance.' She had an interesting way of anticipating both sides of a conversation. In private she probably talked out loud to herself.

'What did he get?'

'Youth. Company.'

'*Innocence?*' I chided.

That did make her burn more fiercely. 'A faithful woman and a quiet house where he could bring his friends! How many men can boast so much? Do *you* have that – or a cheap scut who shrieks at you?' I made no reply. Severina went on in a low, angry voice, 'He was an elderly man. His strength was fading. I was a good wife while I could be, but we both knew it would probably not last long.'

'Looked after him, did you?'

Her straight look rejected my sly tone. 'None of my husbands, Didius Falco, had cause for regret.'

'Truly professional!' She took the sneer on the chin. I stared at her. With that pallid skin, an almost brittle frame and her self-contained manner it was impossible to imagine what she must be like in bed. But men in search of security might easily convince themselves she was biddable. 'Did you send Moscus to the amphitheatre that day?'

'I knew he had gone.'

'Did you realise how hot it was? Had you ever suspected that he had a weak heart? Try to stop him?'

'I am not a nag.'

'So Moscus boiled over; you just wiped the froth off the cooking bench and moved up a clean pot! Where did you find Eprius, the apothecary?'

'He found me.' She was forcing too much patience into her tone; an innocent party would have sworn at me by now. 'After Moscus collapsed at the theatre someone ran to his shop for a draught that might revive the invalid – no use. Moscus had already gone to the gods. Life can be brutal; while I was mourning my husband, Eprius called to request payment for the cordial.'

'You soon won round your creditor!' Severina had the grace to let her small mouth slide into a smile, and I was aware that she noticed my answering twitch. 'Then what – he choked, didn't he?' She nodded. Those busy hands worked at their loom while I lost any temptation to sympathise: I was imagining those same little hands struggling to hold down the apothecary during his fatal convulsion. 'Were you in the house?'

'Another room.' I watched her mentally adjust to the new line of interrogation. She had practised this story far too many times for me to unnerve her. 'He was unconscious when they called me. I did what I could to make him breathe again; most people would have panicked. The lozenge was wedged a long way back. A doctor discovered it afterwards but at the time, distraught and fairly frightened, I admit

I failed. I blamed myself – but you can only call what happened an accident.'

'Had a cough, did he?' I demanded with a sneer.

'Yes.'

'Had it long?'

'We lived on the Esquiline.' Well known as an unhealthy area; she made her murder methods fit convincingly.

'Who gave him the menthol jujube?'

'I presume he had prescribed it for himself! He always kept a little soapstone box of them. I never saw him take them, but he told me they were for his cough.'

'Was it your habit to involve yourself in his business? A bright and helpful partner like you – I bet the first thing you did when he brought you home in your bridal wreath was to offer to catalogue his recipes and cross-reference his poison lists . . . What happened to Grittius Fronto?'

This time she shuddered. 'You must know that! An animal ate him. And before you ask, I had nothing to do with his business. I never went to the arena where it happened, nor was I there – or anywhere nearby – when Fronto died!'

I shook my head. 'I hear the scene was very bloody!'

Severina said nothing. Her face was so white normally it was impossible to decide whether she was truly upset now. But I knew what I thought.

She had too many well-prepared answers. I tried tossing in a silly question: 'Did you know the panther, by the way?'

Our eyes met. It felt an interesting clash.

I must have shaken her confidence. Severina was looking at me much more speculatively. 'You must be very brave,' I said, 'to contemplate making your flame-coloured veil stretch to yet another wedding.'

'It's good cloth; I wove it myself!' The redhead had rallied. Self-mockery stirred quite attractively behind those cold blue eyes. 'Single women without guardians,' she commented more sombrely, 'have a limited social life.'

'True – and it's miserable being a homemaker, with nobody left to welcome home . . .'

By this time, if I had not heard so many sordid details of what happened to her husbands I might well have let her win me over. I had expected some sort of dinner-party vamp. I hated the thought that Severina's quiet domestic habits were a front for calculated violence. Girls who weave and go to the library are supposed to be safe. 'You must be delighted to discover an astrologer who prophesies your next husband will outlive you?'

'Tyche told you that?'

'You knew she would. Did you warn her I would follow you in? She seemed extremely well prepared.'

'We professional women stick together,' replied Severina in a dry tone that reminded me of Tyche herself. 'Have you finished, Falco? I have things I want to do today.' I felt disappointed as she chopped off the discussion. Then I saw her stop herself. A mistake, trying to be rid of me; my grilling must have been making an impression. Rather feebly, she added: 'Unless you have anything more to ask?'

I smiled slightly, letting her know she was looking vulnerable. 'Nothing else.'

My bruises had stiffened up. The pain had become more nagging; it would take days to shift. 'Thanks for your time. If there is anything else I need to know, I'll come here and ask you directly.'

'How thoughtful!' Her eyes were back on the coloured hanks of wool she kept in a tall basket at her feet.

'Admit it,' I wheedled. 'A maid does the hard work for you after the visitors have gone!'

Severina looked up. 'Wrong, Falco.' She let a trace of sadness filter across her normally guarded face. A touching effect. 'Wrong about everything, actually.'

'Ah well; I loved your tale. I enjoy a well-turned comedy.'

Unperturbed, the gold-digger instructed me, 'Get out of my house.'

She was tough, and up to a point honest; I liked that. 'I'm going. One last question: the Hortensius mob seem a tight little clique. Don't you feel out of place?'

'I am prepared to make the effort.'

'Clever girl!'

'It is the least I can do for Novus!'

She was clever; but when I left, her eyes followed me more keenly than they should have done.

I limped into the first open bathhouse, pushed straight through the steam rooms, and eased my aches and grazes into a hot basin to soak. The sword-cut I had been nursing while I was imprisoned in the Lautumiae had cracked open partially when the gold-digger's house-slaves were slinging me about. I lay in the hot basin, letting myself sink into the next best mood to oblivion while I pulled at the loose scar the way you never should but always do.

Eventually I realised I had forgotten about trying to buy off Severina. Never mind. I could still make an offer. Have to go back to negotiate a price – another day. Another day, when I was mentally prepared for the encounter and my limbs could move freely again.

She was certainly a challenge. And the idea that *I* might pose a challenge for *her* didn't bother me at all.

XXII

I had had enough excitement. I could never have found the energy to struggle to the Pincian and report to my clients, even if I had wanted a further brush with feminine iniquity. I also decided not to irritate Helena by sporting around the Capena Gate the bruises another woman had given me. That left one attractive prospect: home to my new bed.

As I carefully scaled the three flights to my apartment, more grateful than ever that it was not the six gruelling sets of climbers at Fountain Court, I ran into Cossus.

'Falco! You look worse for wear – '

'Overenergetic girlfriend. What brings you here; collecting back rent?'

'Oh no; our clients all pay up prompt.' I schooled my face not to reveal he might be in for a shock later. 'The widow on the fourth floor has made a complaint; some idiot keeps disturbing the peace at midnight – singing raucous songs and crashing about. Know anything about it?'

'I've heard nothing.' I lowered my voice. 'Sometimes these old biddies who live alone imagine things.' Naturally Cossus was more prepared to believe the widow might be batty than that some other tenant – one who might thump him if criticised – had antisocial tendencies. 'I have heard the widow banging walls,' I grumbled. 'I would have mentioned it but I'm a tolerant type . . . By the way,' I said, changing the subject smoothly, 'doesn't the rent in a place like this normally include a porter to carry up water and keep the steps swept?'

I expected him to quibble. 'Of course,' agreed the agent, however. 'A lot of the apartments are empty, as you know. But organising a porter is the next thing on my list . . .'

He sounded so obliging I even tipped him for his trouble as he left.

My front door was open. No need to rush in with cries of outrage; familiar noises informed me of the cause. Mico, my unreliable brother-in-law, must have given away my address.

I leaned round the doorframe. A broomful of grit shot over my feet and stuck under my bootstraps. 'Good morning, madam; is this where the distinguished Marcus Didius Falco lives?'

'Judging by the dust!' She whisked the besom twigs across my toes, making me hop.

'Hello Ma. You found me then?'

'I suppose you intended to tell me where you were?'

'What do you think of my billet?'

'None of our family ever lived in Piscina Publica.'

'Time we moved up, Ma!' My mother sniffed.

I tried to walk as if I had just sprained myself slightly during a pleasant morning's exercise at the gym. It failed; Ma leaned on her broom. 'What happened to you this time?'

The enthusiastic girlfriend joke seemed a bad idea. 'Some people with rough manners caught me by surprise. It won't happen again.'

'Oh won't it?' This was not the first time she had seen me sooner than I wanted after a beating I preferred to hide. 'At least in prison you were in one piece!'

'Being gnawed by a big rat, Ma! I was lucky to be fetched out of it – ' She gave me a whack with the besom that told me she saw through that as easily as all my other lies.

Once I was home my mother decamped. Having me there grinning on a stool stopped her looking for evidence of my immoral life; she preferred to upset herself in solitude so she could make more of the occasion. Before she flounced off, she made me some hot wine from ingredients she had brought to stock my larder in case anyone respectable came to call. Consoled, I went to bed.

About halfway through the afternoon I woke, thoroughly chilled, since I had never acquired a bedcover for Junia's bed. After three days I was needing clean clothes too, and missing various treasures I normally kept around me wherever I called home. So, as if today had not been lively enough already, I decided to exert myself with an expedition to Fountain Court.

The shops were still shuttered as I hopped over the Aventine. In my old street everything looked quiet. My landlord's plug-uglies Rodan and Asiacus were treating the neighbourhood to a day of peace. There

93

was no sign of the Chief Spy's dog-eared minions. It was siesta at the laundry. I reckoned it was safe to go in.

I crept upstairs slowly, and slipped into my apartment. There I equipped myself with my favourite tunics, a useful hat, my festival toga, a pillow, two cooking pots which were more or less sound despite five years of wear, the waxed tablet where I wrote sentimental poetry, spare boots, and my favourite possessions: ten bronze spoons, a gift from Helena. I corded all these in a blanket I had brought home from the army, then set off back to ground level humping my bundle like any burglar leaving with his swag.

A burglar would have got away with it. Real thieves can strip a mansion of ten cartloads of antique marble, a score of bronze statues, all the vintage Falernian and the beautiful teenage daughter of the house – while nobody in the neighbourhood notices a thing. I emerged legitimately – only to have some gross female sausageseller whom I had never even seen before spot me and assume the worst. Even then, most robbers would have strolled on their way safely while the witness winked her eye. *I* met the only interfering citizen this side of the Aventine. The minute she spied me sauntering off, she hoiked up her coarse woollen skirts, let out a shriek they must have heard on Tiber Island, and scuttled after me.

Panic – and annoyance – lubricated my stiffened limbs. I hared off up the lane . . . just as Anacrites' two spies popped out from the barber's where they were having the top half-inch scraped off their beards. Next thing I was brought up short howling, with my left boot trapped inextricably under one of the monstrous feet.

I swung my bundle at the other spy. From inside it my biggest iron skillet must have caught the brute right across the throat; he flew backwards with a croak it hurt to hear. The owner of the feet was too close for me to swipe him, but his idea of overpowering a helpless victim was simply to yell for assistance from passers-by. Most of those knew me, so when they stopped guffawing at my plight they jeered at him. They were also bemused by the sight of the sausage-seller – who was all of three feet high – laying into us ferociously with her salami tray. I managed to angle myself so that coracle-feet caught the worst of it, including a violent thwack with a giant smoked phallus which must have put him off peppered pork for life.

But he still had his massive flipper planted on my toes. I was hampered by the need to cling onto my bundle, for I knew if I once let go some Thirteenth Sector layabout would run off with my chattels and have them auctioned on a street corner before I could blink. So

Footsie and I leaned against one another madly, like partners in some tribal wrestling match, while I tried to dance myself free.

I could see his fellow spy reviving. Just then Lenia rushed out of the laundry to investigate the racket, carrying a vast metal basin on her hip. She recognised me with a scornful look, then upended her cauldron over the man I had hit with my skillet: not his day with ironmongery. As his skull took the weight and his legs buckled, I managed to get enough purchase with my trapped foot to slew my other knee inwards; I aimed it angrily at a section of the spy which was much less well developed than his feet. His girlfriend would curse me. His toes curled in agony; I hopped free. Lenia was treating the sausageseller to some irreligious language. I finished off Footsie with a wack from my luggage, and did not stay to apologise.

Home again.

After the havoc in the Aventine it seemed ridiculously quiet. I livened things up by whistling a rude Gallic ditty, until the queer widow on the floor above began banging again. She had no idea of keeping time, so I drew my recitation to a close.

Exhausted, I hid Helena's spoons in my mattress, then rolled myself up in my moth-eaten blanket and collapsed on the bed.

Snoring away whole afternoons is an enjoyable pastime; one which private informers carry out with practised ease.

XXIII

Next day I woke refreshed, though aching. I decided to go and give Severina Zotica a piece of my mind while suitable phraseology was suggesting itself fluently.

Before I left I had breakfast. My ma, who believes home cooking keeps a boy out of moral danger (especially when he is the one stuck at home stirring the cooking pot), has organised a brazier, which would heat the occasional pannikin until I constructed a home griddle. That might have to wait. In August there was not much incentive to lug home stolen builders' bricks, only to fill my elegant new quarters with smoke, unwanted heat, and the smell of fried sardines. On the other hand, it might be easier to start at once than to keep defending myself to my mother for not getting round to it . . . Ma had never yet grasped that private informers might have more enterprising things to do than household jobs.

I drank my home-brewed honey drink, pondering the proposition that having fierce mothers may explain why most informers are furtive loners who look as if they have run away from home.

By the time I strolled into Abacus Street other people had forgotten their early-morning snacks and were musing on the possibility of lunch. I recalled my own recent breakfast with a refined belch – then joined the trend and considered acquiring further refreshments myself. (Anything I ate here could be charged up to the Hortensius mob as 'surveillance costs'.)

I was diverted from the cookshop by spotting the gold-digger. From the scrolls under her arm, this dedicated scholar had been to the library yet again. The cheese shop which fronted her apartment was having supplies delivered, forcing her to dismount from her chair in the street because her entry was blocked by handcarts carrying pails of goat's milk and made-up cheeses wrapped in cloth. As I approached, she was flaying the delivery men with sarcasm. They had made the mistake of complaining that they were only doing their job; this gave Severina Zotica a fine opportunity to describe how their job should be done properly if they had any consideration for fire regulations, local street bye-laws, the peace of the neighbourhood, other occupants of the building, or passers-by.

For Rome it was a normal scene. I stood back while she enjoyed herself. The men with the handcarts had heard it all before; eventually they edged aside a cream-encrusted bucket so if she gathered in her skirts she would be able to squeeze past.

'You again,' she threw back over her shoulder at me, in a tone some of my relations tend to use. Once again, I felt she was enjoying the sense of danger.

'Yes – excuse me . . .' Something had distracted me.

While I was waiting for Severina a lout on a donkey had ridden up to speak to the fruitseller, the one with the Campagna orchard to whom I had spoken yesterday. The old chap had come out from behind his counter and appeared to be pleading. Then, just as the lout appeared to be riding away from the lock-up, he backed his donkey savagely against the counter. Destructiveness was the creature's party trick; it swung its rump as accurately as if it were trained to entertain arena crowds between gladiatorial fights. All the careful rows of early grapes, apricots and berries spilled into the road. The rider snatched up an untouched nectarine, took one huge bite, laughed, then tossed the fruit contemptuously into the gutter.

I was already sprinting across the road. The lout prepared to back his mount a second time; I wrenched the bridle from his grasp and dug my heels in. 'Careful, friend!'

He was a seedy slab of insolence in a knitted brown cap, most of whose bulk was arranged horizontally. His calves were as broad as Baetican hams and his shoulders would have blocked the light through a triumphal arch. Despite the muscle he oozed unhealthiness; his eyes were gummy and his fingers sore with whitlows. Even in a city full of pimply necks, his was a marvel of exploding pustulence.

While the donkey bared its teeth against my grip on its bridle, the enforcer leaned forward and glared at me between its pointed ears. 'You'll know me again,' I said quietly. 'And I'll know you! The name's Falco; anyone in the Aventine will tell you I can't bear to see a bully damage an old man's livelihood.'

His rheumy eyes darted to the fruitseller, who had been standing cowed among his massacred pears. 'Accidents happen . . .' the old man muttered, not looking at me. Interference was probably unwelcome, but blatant intimidation makes me furious.

97

'Accidents can be prevented!' I snarled, addressing the bully. I hauled on the bridle to pull the donkey further from the stall. It looked as mean as a wild colt that had just been caught in a thicket in Thrace – but if it bit me I was angry enough to bite the brute straight back. 'Take off your four-hoofed wrecker to some other morning market – and don't come here again!'

Then I gave the beast a whack on the rump that set him wheezing in protest and cantering off. The rider looked back from the end of the street; I let him see me planted in the middle of the road, still watching him.

A small crowd had been standing by in silence. Most of them now remembered appointments and dispersed hurriedly. One or two helped me pick up the old man's fruit. He shoved the produce back anyhow, bundling the broken pieces into a bucket at the back of his lock-up, and trying to make the rest look as if nothing had happened.

Once the stall was more tidy he seemed to relax. 'You knew that oaf,' I said. 'What's his hold on you?'

'Landlord's runner.' I might have guessed. 'They want to increase the rent for all the frontage tenancies. Some of us with seasonal trade can't afford any more. I paid at the old rate in July but asked for time . . . That was my answer.'

'Anything I can do to help?'

He shook his head, looking frightened. We both knew I had caused him more trouble with the enforcer by defending him today.

Severina was still standing outside the entry to her house. She made no comment, though her expression was strangely still.

'Sorry for dashing off – ' As we turned down the entry I was still boiling with indignation. 'Do you have the same landlord as the people with the lock-ups?' She shook her head. 'Who owns the title to the shops?'

'It's a consortium. There has been a lot of trouble recently.'

'Violence?'

'I believe so . . .'

I had done the fruitseller no favour. It was preying on my mind. At least if I was hanging about this area while I tracked Severina I would be able to keep an eye on him.

XXIV

After her morning ride out of doors Severina had called for a recuperative beverage; I was invited to join her. While it was served she sat frowning; like me, preoccupied with the attack on the fruitseller.

'Falco, did you know that old man was in trouble with his landlord?'

'Once I saw him being bullied it was the obvious thing to suspect.'

She was wearing blue today, a deep sulphur-glass shade with a duller girdle into which she had woven strands of the vivid orange she favoured to add flecks of contrast. The blue brought unexpected colour to her eyes. Even that wiry red hair seemed a more luxuriant shade.

'So your better nature triumphed!' She seemed to admire me for doing my bit. I stirred the spoon round my drink. 'How long have you hated landlords, Falco?'

'Ever since the first one started dunning me.' Severina watched me over the rim of her cup, which was a ceramic redware beaker, inexpensive yet comfortable in the hand. 'Leaseholding is a foul infection. A great-uncle of mind – ' I stopped. She knew how to listen; I had already let myself be drawn in. 'My uncle, who was a market gardener, used to let his neighbour keep a pig in a shack on his land. For twenty years they shared it harmoniously, until the neighbour prospered and offered an annual fee. My great-uncle accepted – then found his immediate thought was whether he could insist that his old friend ought to pay for reroofing the shack! He was so horrified he returned the rent money. Great-uncle Scaro told me this when I was about seven, as if it was just a story; but he was warning me.'

'Against becoming a man of property?' Severina flicked a glance over me. I wore my normal patched tunic, workaday belt and uncombed hair. 'Not much danger of that, is there?'

'Fortune-hunters don't hold a monopoly in ambition!'

99

She took it with good temper. 'I had better confess, the reason I do not share a landlord with the shops – '

I had guessed. 'Your apartment is freehold?'

'I happen to control all the domestic leases in the block; but the shops are separate – nothing to do with me.' She spoke meekly, since this admission took us straight back to the issue of her swiftly acquired legacies. I had learned from the Subura lapidary that at least some of Severina's tenants were content. But I was more interested in the way she first acquired her loot than how she had invested it.

I stood up. We were in a bright, yellow-ochre room which had folding doors. I pushed them back further, hoping for greenery, but only found a paved and treeless yard.

'You have a garden here?' Severina shook her head. I tutted, turning back from the sad little patch of outdoor shade. 'Of course you always move on too quickly; planting is for people who stay put! . . . Never mind; with Novus you are acquiring half the Pincian – '

'Yes; plenty of scope to amuse myself with topiary . . . What sort of home do you have?'

'Just four rooms – one an office. It's a new lease I've taken out.'

'Pleased?'

'Not sure; the neighbours are behaving snootily and I miss having a balcony. But I like the space.'

'Are you married?'

'No.'

'Girlfriends?' She spotted me hesitating. 'Oh let me guess – just one? Is she giving you trouble?'

'Why should you think that?'

'You seem like a man who might overreach himself!' I scoffed but with five sisters, I had learned to ignore nosiness. Severina, who was brighter than my sisters, changed the subject. 'When you are being an informer do you have an accomplice?'

'No. I work alone.' At that she laughed; for some reason I still felt as if she was baiting me. A long time afterwards I discovered why.

'You look uneasy, Falco. Do you object to discussing your private life?'

'I'm human.'

'Oh yes. Under the firm-jawed cliché lurks a fascinating man.'

It was a line: straight professional flattery. I felt my spine stiffen.

'Cut it, Zotica! If you're practising winsome dialogue, I shall have to excuse myself.'

'Relax, Falco!'

I was still fighting back: 'Flattery's not what I go for. *That's* big brown eyes and smart repartee – '

'Sophisticated!'

'Besides, I hate redheads.'

She flashed me a sharp look. 'What have redheads done to you?'

I smiled faintly. A redhead ran off with my father once. But I could hardly blame the whole flame-haired tribe for that; I knew my father, and I knew it was his fault. My opinion was purely a matter of taste: redheads never appealed to me.

'Perhaps we should talk about business,' I suggested, without letting her question get to me.

Severina leaned across to a side table and refilled her beaker, then took mine and topped that up. Since I believed she was responsible for killing her three husbands and that one of them, the apothecary, might well have been poisoned, I experienced a qualm. Knowing Severina's history, a sensible man ought to have turned down hospitality from those graceful white hands. Yet in her comfortable house, lulled by the skilful turn of her conversation, when offered polite refreshments it seemed bad manners to refuse. Was I being disarmed by the same trickery with which new victims were lined up to be despatched?

'So what can I do for you, Falco?'

I put down my cup, then linked my hands, with my chin touching my thumbs. 'I'll pay you the compliment of being perfectly straight.' We were speaking in a soft, open tone, though the thrum of serious business heightened the tension. Her eyes were on mine, their calculation softened by the pleasure she obviously took in bargaining. 'My clients, the Hortensius women, have asked me to find out how much it will take to persuade you to leave Novus alone.'

Severina was silent for so long I began to run over the words in my head, in case I had made some mistake in phrasing them. But it must have been what she expected. 'That's certainly straight, Falco. You're well practised in offering women sums of cash!'

'My elder brother was a man of the world. He made sure I knew how to tuck half a denarius down a whore's bodice.'

'That's harsh!'

'This is not so different.'

I settled the Falco features into what she had called the firm-jawed cliché, while Severina drew herself up slightly. 'Well, this *is* flattering! How much are the dreadful Pollia and Atilia offering me?'

'Tell them what you want. If your claim is too exorbitant I'll advise them to reject it. On the other hand, we *are* talking about the price of a life – '

'I wonder what that is!' Severina muttered angrily, almost under her breath. She sat up even straighter. 'Falco, querying the offer was simple curiosity. I have no intention of breaking my engagement to Novus. Any attempt at bribery is insulting and a complete waste of time. I promise you, it is not his money that interests me!'

The last part of the speech was so passionate I felt obliged to clap. Severina Zotica breathed hard, but she suppressed her irritation because a visitor interrupted us. There was a scratching sound. The door curtain trembled. For a moment I felt puzzled, then beneath the hem of the curtain appeared a bad-tempered beak and a sinister yellow-rimmed eye, followed by a white face and twelve inches or so of grey bird, shading from moonshine to charcoal.

I saw Severina's mood change. 'I don't suppose you want a parrot, Falco?' she sighed.

To my mind birds belong in trees. Exotic birds – with their repulsive diseases – are best left in exotic trees. I shook my head.

'*All men are bastards!*' the parrot shrieked.

XXV

I was so astonished I laughed. The parrot mimicked my laughter, tone for tone. I felt myself colouring. *'Bastards!'* the parrot repeated obsessively.

'He's very unfair! Who taught him the social commentary?' I asked Severina.

'He's a she.'

'Oh foolish me!'

The bird, which looked as nasty a clump of feathers as you could find biting a perch, eyed me suspiciously. It shrugged itself free of the door curtain in a stubby flash of scarlet tail, then stalked into the room, dragging its rump over the floor with the air of a louche peacock. It stopped, just beyond reach of my boot.

Severina surveyed her pet. 'She's called Chloe. She was like this when I got her. A love token from Fronto.' Fronto was the wild-beast importer.

'Yes; well! Anyone who gets through men as fast as you do must accumulate more than her share of misjudged presents!'

The parrot fluffed its feathers at me; stray bits of down drifted loose unhealthily. I tried not to sneeze.

At that moment the curtain was pulled aside again, this time by one of Severina's two stocky slaves. He nodded to her. She got to her feet. 'Novus is here. He normally comes for lunch.' I was ready to vanish discreetly, but she signalled me to stay put. 'I'll just go and speak to him. Then would you like to join us?' I was too startled to answer. Severina smiled. 'I have told him all about you,' she murmured, revelling in my discomfiture. 'Do stay, Falco. My fiancé is extremely keen to meet you!'

XXVI

She left the room.

The parrot made chobbling noises; I had no doubt it was sneering at me. 'One word out of place,' I growled menacingly, 'and I'll glue your beak together with pine resin!'

The parrot Chloe heaved a histrionic sigh. *'Oh Cerinthus!'*

I had no time to ask the bird who Cerinthus was, because Severina came back with her husband-to-be.

Hortensius Novus was corpulent and self-absorbed. He wore a tunic so glistening he must change five times a day, together with double fistfuls of heavy rings. All the weight in his face was concentrated low in a swarthy chin; his fleshy mouth turned down with broodiness. He was about fifty, not too old for Severina in a society where heiresses were betrothed from the cradle and gross senators in mid-career married patrician snippets of fifteen. The parrot chuckled at him derisively; he ignored the thing.

'Hortensius Novus . . . Didius Falco . . .' A terse nod on his side; a quiet salute on mine. Severina, who had become the professional at work now, smiled at us without her usual sharpness – all milky skin and creamy good manners. 'Let's go to the dining room . . .'

Her triclinium was the first room I had seen here with wall paintings – unobtrusive trails of vine tendril and delicate urns sprouting blossom, on a formal garnet-coloured background. When Novus took his couch Severina herself removed his outdoor shoes, though I noticed the loving attention stopped there; she let one of her slaves wash his large, horny feet.

Novus swilled his hands and face too, while the slave held a bowl for him. The bowl was silver and of a good capacity; the towel from the slave's arm had a fine nap; the slave himself had been trained to high standards of competence. It all gave an impression that Severina Zotica could, with minimal fuss and extravagance, run a good home.

Even the meal was an affair whose subtleties disturbed me: the

104

most simple kind of Roman lunch – bread, cheese, salad, diluted wine and fruit. Yet there were flattering touches of luxury: even for three people a complete range of cheeses made from goat's, sheep's, cow's and buffalo's milk; tiny quails' eggs; refined white rolls. Even the humble radishes were cut into sprays and fantails, decorating a fabulous composition salad moulded in aspic – evidently made at home for it was turned out in front of us (with deliberate panache). Then to finish, a whole orchard of fruits.

This was plain fare all right: plain fare as afforded by the very rich.

Novus and Zotica seemed completely at ease together. They had a short conversation about arrangements for their wedding, the sort of short-tempered debate over avoiding unlucky dates which preoccupies most engaged couples for weeks (until they opt for some gouty aunt's birthday – only to find the old groucher is off on a cruise with a handsome young masseur to whom, without question, she will leave all her loot).

With so much to eat there were plenty of silences. Novus in any case was a full-blooded businessman fired only by finance and totally preoccupied with work. He made no reference to being the subject of my investigation; that suited me, yet left me awkwardly deprived of a social reason for my presence. In fact Novus contributed little; mainly a few remarks from which I gathered Severina had his full confidence.

'That shipment of mine from Sidon has arrived at last.'

'That will be a relief to you. What held it up?'

'Bad winds off Cyprus . . .'

She passed him the potted salad. He was the sort of lump who sweated freely and frowned a lot as he ate fast and greedily. He might be thought coarse – but a woman who yearned for comforts would overlook that if his presents were generous. Severina treated him with a kind of formal respect; if she married him, her attitude would certainly work – provided she could keep up the deference (and he could keep alive).

He *was* generous. He had brought his betrothed a necklace of twenty violet amethysts. He handed it over almost as a routine exercise; she received the gift with quiet pleasure; I kept my cynical thoughts to myself.

'Falco here had a run-in this morning with a representative of Priscillus,' Severina remarked eventually.

Novus showed his first signs of interest in me. While I chewed on an olive modestly, she described me rescuing the old fruitseller from his landlord's enforcing agent. Novus barked with laughter. 'You want to watch that! Offending Priscillus can be hazardous to health!'

'What is he? Property tycoon?'

'Businessman.'

'Dirty business?'

'Normal business.' Novus was not interested in my views on men who peddle real estate.

Severina tackled her fiancé in a thoughtful voice: 'Is Appius Priscillus getting above himself?'

'He's collecting his rents.'

'It seemed – '

Novus brushed her murmur aside: 'The tenant must have been owing – you cannot be sentimental about debt.' He behaved like a man who was used to being stubborn, though he did give her an indulgent look on the word 'sentimental'. I knew this type: hard as a Noricum knife – yet pleased to own a fluffy kitten who would act as a conscience for him. Fair enough – provided he listened when his conscience spoke.

Severina looked unconvinced, yet she fell silent without quarrelling. Just the sort of women to have at the lunch table: intelligent in conversation – but intelligent enough to show restraint . . . I began thinking about Helena Justina. When Helena had something on her mind she reckoned to make her point.

I found Severina quietly watching me; for some reason I revived the conversation Novus had crushed. 'Is this character Priscillus making you nervous, harrying the neighbourhood?'

The reassuring smile of a tactful hostess lit Severina's pale face. 'I take my advice from Hortensius Novus on business affairs!'

I should have known not to waste my breath.

As a final gesture to the Novus appetite we had cakes: just three (for it *was* lunch, not a banquet), but perfect gems of the pastry cook's art and elegantly displayed on a costly silver platter which Severina then presented to Novus. A gift from her to him looked as regular as her acquisition of the amethysts. It also gave him the indisputable right to lick the plate; his fat, sloppy tongue flickered over it, while I watched jealously.

He left shortly afterwards, with his platter under his elbow but still without any acknowledgement of why I was there. Severina went out with him, which gave an impression they were exchanging kisses in private. I heard a squawk of mockery from the parrot, anyway.

When the hostess came back I had swung myself upright on the dining couch and was giving the amethyst necklace a frank valuation, comparing its cost with her silver plate. 'I reckon Novus came out ahead financially today. That looks good, Zotica – nicely done!'

'You're so cynical it's pitiful.'

I stood up, and dangled the jewels from the fingers of one hand. 'Pretty – but one or two flaws which you'll soon spot. If it wasn't my job to drive a wedge between the two of you, I might warn the good Novus not to give gemstones to a girlie who has been through a lapidary's training . . .' She tried to take the necklace from me; I insisted on fastening it round her slender neck. 'Not quite right with blue.'

'No; amethysts are always difficult.' She remained impervious to my attempts to rile her.

'Time I was going.' I took both her hands in my own and bent over them gallantly. They were scented with a flowery fragrance which reminded me of the oil from the baths which Helena had taken to frequenting recently. Camomile must be the universal fragrance this month.

On her left hand Severina wore a massive gold betrothal ring with a red jasper stone. The false symbol of fidelity: one of those travesties where two hands, very badly drawn, are clasping each other. Novus had worn an identical ring. On the matching finger of her other hand was an elderly band of copper, its front flattened into a coin-shaped boss which was scratched with a simple picture of Venus. A cheap trinket. A memento, I guessed. Not many girls wear copper rings, because of the verdigris.

'That's pretty. From one of your husbands?'

'No; just a friend.'

'A man?'

'A man,' she agreed, as I pulled down my mouth to show what I thought of women who lived without a male protector yet had followers they called 'just friends'.

She took back her hands. 'What did you think of Novus?'

'He's too set in his ways, and you are far too bright for him – '

'Normal criteria for marriage!' she quipped defensively.

'Cobnuts! How long do you intend to waste your life coddling mediocre businessmen?'

'Better to do it while I have all my energy than later, when I may need coddling myself!'

'Ah, but meanwhile are you really the deferential type? . . .' She gave me an evasive smile. 'You implied Novus wanted to discuss something. He never told me.'

'He wanted to see if he liked you.'

'So did I impress the man?'

'I can tell you what he wanted, anyway. If you are going to be hanging round on hire to Pollia, there is something you could do for Novus too.'

'Sorry,' I replied at once, suspecting some plot of her own. 'I can only work for one client at a time. But I'd be interested in hearing what he wants.'

'Protection.'

'Ouch! I've still got bruises; don't make me laugh, Zotica!'

For once she lost patience. 'Must you always wield my slave-name like a Herculean club?'

'People should acknowledge their origins – '

'Hypocrisy!' she chipped back. 'You are a free citizen; you always were, you cannot know.'

'Wrong, Zotica. I know poverty, hard work, and hunger. I live with disillusionment. I face sneers from both the rich and rich men's slaves. My ambitions are as far beyond my reach as they would be for any chained wretch in a filthy hutch who builds the fires in bathhouses – '

'What ambitions?' she demanded, but things were already far too friendly for me.

We were still positioned in the dining room with me about to leave, but Severina seemed to want to delay me.

'I find I enjoy talking to you,' she grumbled. 'Is this your method of wearing people down?'

'Letting suspects enjoy themselves never achieves much.'

'It worries me when you're frank!'

'Lady, it worries me!'

Suddenly she smiled. It was a smile I had seen before in my life: the dangerous weapon of a woman who had decided we two were special friends. 'Now I shall tell you,' Severina promised, 'the real reason why I went to the astrologer. I hope it will show you why I worry about Novus.' I tipped my head on one side, preserving my neutrality. 'He has enemies, Falco. Novus has been the victim of threats – threats followed by inexplicable accidents. It started before he and I were introduced, and it has happened again recently. I consulted Tyche about the risk, with his full knowledge – in fact, on his behalf.'

I hid a grin. She did not know I had also watched her ordering a tombstone for the hapless man. 'Who are these enemies? And what exactly have they done to him?'

'Will you help us?'

'I told you; I cannot divide my interests in a case.'

'Then Novus would not want me to say any more.'

'Your choice.'

'What can he do?' she cried, putting on a good show of anxiety.

'The best way to treat enemies is to make friends with them.' Severina's eyes met mine, mocking my pious advice. For an instant we shared a dangerous sense of affinity. 'All right; I admit it: The best way is to nobble them.'

'Falco, if you won't help us, at least don't joke!'

If she was lying she was an impressive actress.

But I did not rule out the possibility that Severina was a liar.

XXVII

I spent the afternoon at the Forum, listening to the tired old rumours which the Rostrum lags were handing round as news; then I went on to my gymnasium for exercise, a bath, a shave, and to hear some *real* gossip. Next I devoted some attention to my private affairs: my mother and my banker. Both were trying events for the usual reasons, and also because I discovered that both people had been plagued with visits from Anacrites, the Chief Spy. His attentions were becoming a serious problem. Anacrites had made it official that Didius Falco was a jail-breaker. And when my mother had protested that she paid my surety, Anacrites snapped back that that made me a bail-jumper too.

Ma was very upset. What annoyed me was being portrayed as unreliable to my banker. Limiting my future credit was a really dirty trick.

By the time I had calmed my mother I felt in need of comfort myself, so I trailed along to the Capena Gate. Bad luck again: Helena was at home, but so were half her well-heeled Camillus relations; the Senator was giving an entertainment to mark the birthday of some aged aunt. The porter, who could tell from my informal get-up that I had not been favoured with an invitation, let me in solely for the pleasure of seeing me kicked out again by the people of the house.

Helena emerged from a reception room; sedate flute music trilled behind her before she closed the door.

'Sorry if this is an awkward time – '

'It's something of an event,' remarked Helena coolly, 'to see you at all!'

Things were not going well. A morning at Severina's had spoiled me for banter. I was tired; I wanted to be soothed and fussed over. Instead Helena reproached me that I might have been invited to the party if I had been on hand the night before, when her father had been arranging it. Apart from a nice impression that Camillus Verus must have forgotten his auntie's birthday until the last minute, I also glimpsed how Helena had been embarrassed by not knowing when (*if ever*) she might see her vague hanger-on again . . .

'Helena, my heart,' I apologised obsequiously, 'wherever I am, you are there – '

'Cheap philosophy!'

'Cheap, therefore simple; simple therefore true!'

Cheap meant simply unconvincing. She folded her arms. 'Falco, I am a woman, so I expect my loyalty to be taken for granted. I know my place is to wait until you roll home drunk or hurt or both – '

I folded my own arms the way one does, unconsciously imitating her. A lurid bruise just below one elbow must have become visible. 'Helena, I am not drunk.'

'You've taken some knocks!'

'I'm all right. Look, don't fight. I'm deeply involved in my case now; I have all the trouble I can handle – '

'Oh I forgot – ' she scoffed. '*You* are a *man*! The mildest criticism brings out the worst in you – '

Sometimes I did wonder what I thought I had been doing letting myself be smitten by an outspoken termagant with no sense of timing. Since I was off duty, and probably off guard, I allowed myself to mention this, then added a highly rhetorical description of her ladyship's hasty tongue, hot temper – and complete lack of faith in me.

There was a small silence. 'Marcus, tell me where you have been.'

'Nose to nose with the Hortensius gold-digger.'

'Yes,' Helena answered sadly. 'I thought that must be it.'

Her tone implied she had been moping. I took a critical look at her: Helena's idea of moping was to throw on a vivid carmine dress, adorn her hair with a rope of glass beads like a crown of hyacinths, then courageously enjoy herself in company. I was about to respond with some crabby badinage, when a young man stepped out from the party room.

In honour of the Senator's aunt's birthday he wore a toga whose luxurious nap rebuked the worn shine of my own workaday tunic. His haircut was crisp; a shiny wreath was parked on it. He had the sort of clean-cut aristocratic looks most women call attractive, even though the effect was simply due to phenomenal arrogance.

He expected Helena to introduce us. I knew better; she was too annoyed at his interruption. I beamed at him tolerantly. 'Evening. One of the family?'

'A friend of my brothers,' Helena interposed, recovering rapidly.

The aristo looked quizzical at my plebian presence, but she gave him his orders with her usual forcefulness. 'Falco and I were discussing business, if you don't mind.'

Quelled, he returned to the reception room.

I winked at Helena. 'Friend of your brothers, eh?'

'It's an elderly gathering; my parents provided him to talk to me. *You* were inaccessible.

'Just as well, sweetheart. They would not have wanted me.'

'Falco, *I* might have wanted you.'

'You seem to be making do.'

'I have to!' she accused me hotly. 'Anyway, father would have asked you, but who knows where you are living now?'

I told her my new address. She returned graciously that now her father would be able to send the cast-off couch they had promised me. 'Father was trying to contact you urgently yesterday. He had been approached by Anacrites.'

I swore. 'The man's a complete pest!'

'You will have to do something about it, Marcus. With him hounding you, how can you do your work?'

'I'll deal with it.'

'Promise?'

'Yes. Life's becoming impossible.'

I returned to the issue of my new address: 'I'm living in two rooms and another will be the office; that leaves one which could quite easily become yours. You know what I want – '

'A tolerant housekeeper, a free bedmate – and someone brave to catch the crawlies who scuttle out of the floorboards! – No; that's wrong,' Helena corrected herself. 'Someone timid who will let *you* batter the insects and look tough!'

'Well the offer stays open, but I don't intend to remind you again.' She knew it; pleading for her attention was not my style. 'Your noble pa will want you at his party; I'd better go.'

Helena reacted with her customary snootiness: 'So you had.' She relented: 'Are you coming again?'

'When I can,' I answered, accepting the weaker note in her voice as the nearest I would get to an apology. 'I just have a lot to think about. But now I've met the woman, it ought not to be beyond me to sort it all out pretty smartly.'

'Do you mean you won't come until the case is over?'

'That sounds like a brush-off.'

Helena stuck out her chin. '*I'm* getting the brush-off. It was a sensible suggestion.'

My teeth set. 'Gods, I hate sensible women! You decide. I'll come if you ask me. Whenever you want me you know where to find me.'

I waited for her to dissuade me, but Helena Justina was as obstinate as me. It was not the first time we had driven ourselves into some pointless deadlock.

I was leaving. She was letting me. '*Io*, my darling! What I *really* need is a girl to stay at home and take messages!'

'You can't afford to pay her,' Helena said.

XXVIII

Boasting that I would settle the case quickly had been rash. The case was nowhere near its end yet. In fact it was only just beginning, as I would soon find out.

As I sloped off home I was thinking less about work than about women. A normal preoccupation – though weighing on me more heavily tonight. My clients, Severina, my ladylove, my mother, all had designs on my peace of mind. Even my sister Maia, whom I had still not seen since Ma sprung me out of prison, loomed as a subject of guilt because I had not yet made any attempt to thank her for rescuing the betting tags which financed my new apartment . . . It was all getting beyond me. I needed to take action; the best kind of action, which is nothing at all: I had to stand back, give myself a breather, and let the ladies gently mull.

I planned to spend the next three days devoting myself to my own pleasure and profit. I even managed it for two of the days: not a bad success rate for a plan of mine.

First I spent a morning in bed, thinking.

Then, as I still officially worked for the Emperor (since I had never bothered to inform him otherwise) I went to the Palatine and applied to see Vespasian. I hung around the labyrinth of Palace offices for a whole afternoon before a flunkey deigned to tell me that Vespasian was away, enjoying a summer holiday in the Sabine hills. Now that he wore the purple, the old man liked to remind himself of his humble roots by kicking off the Imperial sandals and wriggling his toes in the dust of his old family estates.

Afraid I might run into Anacrites if I stayed too long, I left the Palace and put the Falco personality at the disposal of my private friends. That night I dined with Petronius Longus at his house. He had a wife and three young children, so it was a quiet occasion which ended early (and, by our standards, fairly soberly).

In the morning I redirected my request for an audience to Vespasian's elder son, Titus Caesar. Titus was governing the Empire in virtual partnership with Vespasian so he held ample authority to overrule Anacrites in my little bit of bother. He was also known as a soft touch. This meant my appeal had to take its place in a mountain of other scrolls full of hard-luck stories from ambiguous characters. Titus worked hard, but in August lavishing clemency on down-and-outs was bound to proceed at a slower pace than normal.

While I was waiting for my own screed to grab his Caesarship's jaded attention I went to a horse sale with my brother-in-law Famia. I hated to part with Little Sweetheart, but the chariot stables where Famia worked as a vet for the Greens could not be expected to house a horse of mine for ever – well, not for nothing, which was the present arrangement (unbeknown to the Greens). So Famia and I auctioned poor old Little Sweetheart, before the cost of keeping him in hay outstripped his winnings. With money in my pocket I made a trek to the Saepta Julia where I let myself be tempted by a dirty candelabrum which looked as if it might clean up (wrong, as usual) and an Egyptian cartouche ring (which fitted when I tried it on but felt too big when I got it home). Then I browsed in a couple of literary dealers and came away with an armful of Greek plays (don't ask me why; I hate Greek plays). I took some cash to my mother for her day-to-day expenses, and finally stowed what was left of the proceeds in my bankbox in the Forum.

Next day there was still no invitation to climb up to the Palace and make Titus laugh with my tale of woe, so I did go to see my sister Maia. She let me hang around her house for most of the morning, which led to lunch, followed by an afternoon asleep on her sun terrace. I promised her some of the Pincian cakes but Maia knew how to handle me; she managed to upgrade this to the offer of a house-warming in my spacious new abode. Like a speculator promising to square things with his banker I made a rapid escape: forgetting to agree a date.

Petronius and I spent that evening touring various wineshops to see if they were as good as we remembered from our youth. What with the free cups we were offered to encourage us to come more often, the flagons I bought him, and the drinks Petronius (who was a fair man) stood me in return, *this* occasion ended neither early nor soberly. I saw him home, since a watch captain risks all sorts of vindictiveness if villains he may have arrested in the past spot him stumbling about the city.

His wife Silvia had locked us out. Still, law officers know how to pick most locks and informers can force the ones that defeat them, so we got ourselves indoors without too many of his neighbours flinging open their shutters to bawl at our noise. We broke a bolt, but the door itself remained in one piece. Petro offered me a bed, but Silvia had come downstairs cursing us; she was trying to repair the door lock with a pair of eyebrow tweezers while Petro manhandled her affectionately with a view to a peace treaty (unlikely, I thought). Then their children woke up frightened, and Petro's youngest daughter started crying that her kitten had been sick in a sandal – so I left.

Like most decisions made after trying five or six amphorae of mediocre vintages in cheap commercial drinking rooms, this was not a good idea.

An important occasion: the first time I tried to find my new apartment when crazily drunk. I got lost. A big dog with a pointed snout nearly bit me and several prostitutes shouted uncalled-for abuse. Then, when I finally located the Piscina Publica, and found my own street, I failed to notice that a low-rank five-days-in-uniform Praetorian Guardlet was waiting to greet me – with a warrant from Anacrites, a painful set of leg irons, and three other baby-faced recruits in shiny breastplates who were all as keen as Baetican mustard to carry out their first official mission by arresting a dangerous renegade who apparently shared my name.

After they fastened the irons on me, I just lay down in the road and told them I would go wherever they wanted – but they would have to carry me.

XXIX

I spent the next two days recovering from my hangover, back in the Lautumiae jail.

XXX

By the second evening I was reacquainted with my old cellmate the rat. I tried keeping to one corner so as not to inconvenience him, but he was starting to look at me hungrily. I had to disappoint him. I was called away; someone very influential made enquiries about my case.

Two of the schoolboy Praetorians turned up to fetch me. At first I resisted. My hangover had been replaced by light-headedness. I was in no state to endure a confrontation with Anacrites and the bullies he used to encourage frank confessions. No fear of that! Anacrites had planned to imprison me until I was incontinent and toothless. With a kick to my kneecap the jailor let slip that a High-Up wanted a look at me. My petition to Titus must have surfaced on the pile . . .

The young troopers were bursting with excitement at the prospect of a royal audience. In the past the Imperial bodyguard had shown itself prone to replacing the Caesar who was entrusted to their care with anyone who caught their eye after a good night's carousing (Claudius, for heaven's sake, and that primped liability Otho). Not any longer. On his father's accession Titus had shrewdly taken direct charge of the Praetorians; so long as he gave them a good bounty on his birthday, they would stick by their own commander like burs on a shepherdess's skirt. Now Proculus and Justus (if you happen to get arrested, always find out the names of your guards) were about to come face to face with their famous new Prefect in their first week, thanks to me.

They were so wrapped up in their own glory they tactlessly escorted me across the open Forum, still in chains. But they were too new in uniform to have lost all their charity; they let me scoop up a drink from a public fountain to cure my dehydration before dragging me into the cool of the Cryptoporticus, that long galleried entrance which leads up to the various palaces that hog the crest of the Palatine. Outside the guardroom their centurion, a hardened regular, made them take the leg irons off me. He knew what was proper. We exchanged the imperceptible scowl of old soldiers as he inspected his inexperienced rankers for sloppy belts and smears on their armour. He came with us to the throne room, fretting in case his babes put a step wrong.

At the first waiting room an usher who claimed to know nothing about me shoved us into a side cubicle on our own. Proculus and Justus were starting to look rosy; the centurion and I had been through this stupid quarantine on other occasions so we saved our sweat.

Half an hour later we were moved to a corridor, which was full of tired people in limp togas hanging about. Proculus and Justus exchanged glances, thinking they would be stuck in this endless trail of ceremonial long after their watch was supposed to end. But immediately my name was called; minor flunkeys bustled us past the crowd; then we reached a cavernous antechamber where an elegantly spoken secretary inspected us like vermin while he crossed us off a list.

'This man was summonsed an hour ago! What kept you so long?'

A major-domo produced Anacrites, looking sleek in a grey tunic; like a conjuror's tame dove – but not so cute. In contrast to me he was well bathed and barbered, with his straight hair slicked back in a way I disliked intensely. It made him look like the trickster he was. At the sight of him I felt crumpled and crusty-tempered, with a mouth like the bottom of a cementmaker's hod. He narrowed his pale, suspicious eyes at me, but at this stage I forwent the chance of insulting him. Next minute Proculus and Justus had been ordered to march me in.

When we first entered through the grand travertine entrance pillars, Anacrites was the trusted official and I the seedy hangdog, under guard and in disgrace. But no protocol that I knew said I had to go along with it. Two days in bruising leg irons made it easy to adopt a brave expression and a limp. Which meant the first thing Titus Caesar asked me was, 'Something wrong with your leg, Falco?'

'Just an old fracture, sir. I broke a leg last winter, on that job for your father in Britain; it bothers me when I'm cramped up without exercise . . .'

'Cut the pathos, Falco!' Anacrites growled.

Titus shot a sharp glance at the spy. 'Britain; I remember!' His tone was clipped. The work I did for his father in Britain was too confidential to be mentioned in detail, but Anacrites would know of it. I heard him mutter with annoyance. I also noticed the secretary, whose job was to take shorthand notes, hold his stylus discreetly at rest as confidential subject matter came up. His exotic oriental eye caught mine momentarily; finely tuned to atmosphere, he anticipated fun.

Then Titus gestured to a slaveboy. 'Didius Falco needs looking after. Will you bring him a seat?'

Even at that stage Anacrites had no real need to worry. I had never made any secret of my rampant republican views. Dealing with the Imperial family always caused me difficulty. The Chief Spy knew as well as I did what to expect: M Didius Falco was about to be rude, ungracious, and a fool to himself as usual.

XXXI

So there we were. Titus relaxed on a throne, with one ankle crossed on the opposite knee, crushing the braid-encrusted pleats of his purple overtunic. To the slaveboy it seemed natural to place my cushioned footstool near the only other person who was seated, so he carried it right up onto the plinth at the base of His Caesarship's throne. He helped me hitch myself up. Anacrites took a step forward, then suppressed the protest as he was forced to accept his Imperial master's courtesy to me. I refrained from smirking; Anacrites was far too dangerous. I perched on my footstool, occasionally rubbing my leg unconsciously, as if it was a habit when my poor cracked bones were distressing me . . .

Titus was thirty. Too happy to be called handsome and too approachable for his rank, though a grave sense of public duty had recently sobered him. Even those forced to endure existence in the provinces knew from the coinage that he had a less craggy version of his father's bourgeois face, and curly hair. While he was a boy that mop probably caused his mother to pass the same remarks as mine did, but had Flavia Domitilla still been alive she could have relaxed now: a circus of hairdressers kept her eldest trim, so he would not let the Empire down in front of foreign ambassadors.

Titus and I made a nice friendly group, up on his plinth. My letter was in his hand; he tossed the roll back at me. There was a glint in his eye. Titus was always so gracious I suspected a joke – yet the charm was genuine. 'This is a moving narrative!'

'Sorry, Caesar. I'm a spare-time poet; my style tends to lyrical excess.' Titus grinned. He was a patron of the arts. I was on safe ground.

It was the wrong moment to force the Chief Spy to watch us enjoying ourselves. Infected by my own wariness, Titus gave Anacrites the nod to approach and state his case.

Anacrites took the floor without bluster. I had seen him in action

121

on other occasions so was prepared for the worst. He possessed the true bureaucrat's knack of sounding reasonable whatever lies he told.

In some ways I felt sorry for the unprincipled carbuncle. His was a classic case of career blight. He must have studied his craft under Nero, those crazy years of suspicion and terror, when prospects for intelligence agents had never looked more golden. Then as he reached his prime he found himself stuck with the new Emperor Vespasian, a man so irredeemably provincial that he did not really believe in palace spies. So instead of enjoying himself at the centre of some crawling network of undercover termites, Anacrites now had to devote every day to proving that his place on the payroll was justified.

No joke. Vespasian was tight with the salaries bill. One slip, one mistake in diplomacy, one door opening too suddenly to reveal him napping in his office when he had said he would be out on surveillance, and the Chief Spy would find himself selling catfish on some Tiber wharf. He knew it. I knew it. He realised I knew. Perhaps that explained some things.

I made no attempt to interrupt his speech. I wanted him to shoot all the dice from his cup. Out it poured, a subtle slime of misinterpreted facts, at the end of which *he* sounded like the honest professional whose superiors had lumbered him with a bungling outsider to work with. *I* emerged as a straightforward thief.

The facts were straightforward too: some ingots of lead from the Imperial mines had been stored in a warehouse. I knew they were there, forgotten by the Treasury. When I was sent to Campania I took the ingots with me, and sold the lead for waterpipes. I had never paid back the proceeds.

Titus listened with his hands linked behind his head. He himself was not a great speechmaker but he had served his time as a barrister before he came into higher things. Despite his impatient energy he knew how to listen. Only when he was sure Anacrites had finished complaining did he turn to me.

'The case against you was well put. The lead ingots belonged to the State; you took them without leave.'

'Anacrites is a good speaker; it was a good exercise in rhetoric. But Caesar, there's no case.' Titus shifted position. I had his full attention; he was leaning forwards now with both elbows on his knees. 'Caesar, I had a particular reason to respect those bars of lead; I probably hacked some of the ore from the seam myself!' I paused, to give those present time to absorb another reference to my mission in Britain,

122

where I had been forced to disguise myself as a lead-mine slave. 'Harsh, Caesar – but necessary, for your father's sake. And when I used up the ingots, I was in disguise again. We were seeking a fugitive. Anacrites can confirm it was a frustrating task, one on which he himself had spent several fruitless weeks – ' His jaw stiffened pleasingly. 'I was asked to try my own ingenuity. Unorthodox methods were, after all, why your father was augmenting his regular staff with me – '

'True,' said Titus to Anacrites pointedly.

'– acting as a black-market plumber helped me find the missing man. So the disguise worked, Caesar, as you know.'

In a silky voice Anacrites reminded Titus that the ingots I borrowed might have been needed as evidence in a conspiracy case.

'What prosecutor was going to produce multiple tonnage of metal in open court?' I asked. 'We all knew the ingots existed. There were documents to prove it: the Praetorian Guards had stacked them, and the victor of Jerusalem won't need me to tell him that the first thing military conscripts are taught is to *count* everything they handle . . .'

Titus smiled tolerantly. He was willing me to explain the charge away. I was not naïve. I knew why it probably suited the Empire to set me loose: Titus and his father must have some real pig of a problem they wanted me to solve for them.

'I suppose,' Anacrites suggested heavily, 'you intended to repay the money from selling the ingots? Or have you blown away your profits on women and drink?'

I looked shocked. Just *one* woman (Helena Justina); though on holiday in Campania she and I, and a nephew of mine, and Petronius Longus, and Petro's wife and family, had freely eaten and drunk the Treasury's cash, using my imperial mission as our excuse. 'Don't blame me for the delay, Anacrites! Being thrust into the Lautumiae hampered me unfairly – though I did make use of my few days of freedom to see my banker on the very subject of transfering funds to the Privy purse . . .'

'Good news!' Titus sounded relieved. Having to write off the money was his main stumbling block to releasing me.

'I must warn you though, Caesar,' I apologised swiftly, 'since I was selling the metal on back-door terms, the sum involved is not as great as it would have been using official franchises . . .'

'He's lying!' snarled Anacrites. 'I have a complete list of his assets – ' A short list! 'This windbag hasn't a bean!'

So much for my banker keeping his client's confidence . . . Yet I knew that Anacrites had pried open my private money chest the day before I sold my racehorse; I now possessed funds he must have overlooked. Now there was no escape. Even if it ruined me I was not prepared to let a pernicious undercover agent do me down. Sighing, I kissed goodbye to Little Sweetheart (or what was left of the poor nag after my Saepta Julia spending spree).

'There is a liar in this throne room, but it's not me!' I pulled off my signet ring. 'Caesar, if you will send someone to my banker we can settle this tonight – ' Suddenly suspicious, Anacrites chewed his lip.

'Spoken like an upright citizen!' Titus, embarrassed, aimed a frown at the spy while a minion took my ring away as sanction to my financier to bankrupt me. 'That does seem to cover your charges, Anacrites!'

'True, Caesar – if the cash comes!'

'You can trust me! Mind you,' I grumbled touchily, 'I don't want to be cleared on false pretences. If this is just a gag in order to make me available for some filthy undercover mission which none of your regular Palace employees will handle, frankly I prefer jail – '

Titus soothed me, too eagerly for honesty: 'Didius Falco, there are no complications; I pronounce you a free man!'

'And a free agent?' I haggled.

'As usual!' he chipped – but then, overcome by his keenness he jumped straight in: 'So, are you free to do something for my father?'

Excellent: one bound from prison, straight back in favour. Anacrites glowered. He need not have worried. 'Love to, sir – but prison didn't suit me; I need to recuperate.' Back in favour – then straight back out in one more bound.

Titus Caesar had known me for the past four months; long enough. He became his most agreeable, always a civilised sight. 'What can I do to persuade you back, Falco?'

'Well,' I mused. 'First you could try paying me for the *last* mission I carried out for Vespasian . . .'

'And then?'

'It might help, sir, to pay me for the mission before that!'

He drew a sharp breath. '*Britain?* Have you never been paid for Britain?' I looked humble. Titus barked something at a secretary standing in the shadow of his throne, then assured me that immediate arrangements would be made.

'Thank you, Caesar,' I said, letting him know I thought 'immediate' was a Palace codeword for 'indefinitely deferred'.

'Once you receive the money perhaps you will feel able to resume your official career?'

'Once I receive it!' I challenged him. 'By the way – ' I leaned sideways to include Anacrites in this comment ' – if today's verdict is that I should not have been in prison in the first place, can I assume you will be repaying to my elderly mother the money which she lodged with the jailor as my bail?'

The bastard was stuck; do it, or expose the fact that the jailor had accepted Mama's savings as a bribe. At present the Lautumiae staff were in the Spy's pocket and gave Anacrites the run of the cells. Naturally Anacrites wanted to preserve the status quo . . .

Titus told him to see to it. (Titus came from an odd family: the women respected their menfolk and the men respected their mothers.) Anacrites cast one furious glance at me, promising revenge later, and slunk off. *His* mother probably took one look at him when he was born, then let out a screech and abandoned him over a drain in an alleyway.

After him Proculus and Justus, with their centurion, were also dismissed. I sensed the attendants relaxing as Titus yawned and stretched; he must have saved interviewing me, like the olive in the middle of an omelette, as his last treat of the day. Then, since I was a free man and a free agent, Titus asked if I was also free to stay on at the Palatine and dine with him.

'Thanks, Caesar. This reminds me that there are *some* pleasant reasons why I let myself be coerced into political work!'

The chief jewel of the Empire gave me a sweet grin. 'Maybe I am keeping you on hand – in case your banker fails to send a certain sum . . .'

I had been right in the first place. Getting involved with politicians is complete stupidity.

XXXII

Like everyone else, I had heard that the parties Titus gave tended to be riotous, late-night affairs. People like to believe in scandal; I like to believe in scandal myself. After my second stint in prison I was ready to handle a riot at the Empire's expense, but that night on the Palatine we only enjoyed a pleasant meal with unobtrusive music and easy talk. Perhaps Titus was just a good-looking, unmarried lad who had seen in the dawn with his cronies (once or twice, when he was younger), and now he had a reputation for loose living which would be held over him whatever else he did. I sympathised. I was a good-looking, unmarried lad myself. My own wicked reputation was so hard to shift, I didn't even try.

Before we ate I had made myself respectable in the Imperial baths, so once I was fed and comfortably wined my energy renewed and I excused myself, with a plea of work. Might as well air my new haircut around the city while the Palace barber's lotions were still exuding interesting whiffs. When he saw a slave strapping my sandals back, Titus called out, 'Falco – I have not forgotten your present, you know!'

'What present was that, Caesar?' I asked cautiously, thinking he meant the promise of work.

'To thank you for my luck at the races!' Thundering Jupiter; something else I really did not want.

That horse, Little Sweetheart, had been a mixed blessing. Titus had backed him, and I knew he was eager to demonstrate his pleasure at winning. I remembered now what my reward was to be – and I would need my most devious resources to deal with it.

'An honour and a treat, Caesar – ' I lied diplomatically, adding (with less good sense) that Titus might like to drop into the Falco residence to sample a sliver . . . He promised he would remember (while I prayed he would forget).

My present, in case you wondered, was a fabulous fish.

126

I left the Palatine feeling thoughtful. Titus intended to send me a turbot.

Turbot was strange meat to me – me and most of Rome. I had seen one once in a fishing boat; it was half a yard across. That one fish would have cost five or six times my annual income – though in fact they rarely hit the markets since most fishermen who catch a turbot present it smartly to the Emperor.

Now I was in a dilemma. I could cook. I quite enjoyed it. After five years of living solo in squalor I was the king of one-man cuisine; I could grill or poach or fry most edibles, in cramped spaces, with no decent utensils and only a basic range of condiments. My best efforts were delectable, and my worst blunders had gone into the scrap bucket before they made me ill. But it was obvious not even I could barbecue a *turbot* in a dribble of olive oil on a household skewer over a few burning twigs. The marvel Titus promised me would call for a monumental fishpan and a massive serving platter, the high arts of a first-rate sauce chef who had access to a sophisticated cooking range, a train of uniformed bearers to present the royal creature handsomely to my slavering guests, an orchestra, and an announcement in the *Daily Gazette*.

My only real alternative was to give the fish away.

I knew that. And I knew what I would probably do instead.

Wandering into the Forum, I paused by the Temple of Vesta. To my left, at the Rostrum end, some magnate was being taken home from a banquet in a canopied litter flanked by eight marching body-guards whose torches bobbed like well-drilled fireflies as they nego-tiated the steep curve of the Vicus Argentarii.

At the Palace I had lost all track of time. It was a hot August night, with serene violet light tinting open skies. Cookshops were still doing heavy business, and although some booths were shuttered and bolted I passed a cabinetmaker, a mirror-seller and a goldsmith who had all kept their folding doors open and lights burning in the interior; dogs and toddlers and companionable women could be glimpsed inside. Folk still hogged pavement tables, reluctant to abandon their wine beakers and gaming-boards. The dangerous men who took control of Rome during darkness were probably about by now, but the citizenry had not yet surrendered the streets to them.

There was plenty of action. I stopped to gape at a house fire. It was a four-storey block, smouldering from the ground up. The lesser tenants had come rushing out with their possessions in bundles; the main householder was struggling to drag his tortoiseshell bedstead out of the doorway, hampering the municipal firefighters as they and their buckets waited to go in. Eventually he and they were all driven away as the whole building flared ablaze. The man sat on the pavement with his head in his hands sobbing, until some passing tycoon jumped out of a greasy brown sedan chair and offered to buy up the ground lease. I could hardly believe it. The oldest fiddle in the world – but the fool with the burning bed just clutched a pillow to his heart and accepted on the spot.

I thought everyone had heard how Crassus came by his legendary millions – touring Rome looking for fires then preying on people while they were still in shock. And I thought everybody nowadays knew to reject any helpful shark who popped up offering a pittance for a smoking building site – aiming to redevelop at a profit as soon as the ashes cooled. Evidently there were still idiots who would succumb to the lure of cash in hand . . . For a second I considered intervening, but the acceptance of terms was too far advanced; thwarted property developers are notoriously vindictive and I could not risk involving myself in a breach of contract case.

Halfway along the next dark alley I kicked something which turned out to be a tinderbox; it was lying near a tangle of rags which someone in a hurry had dropped in the street.

Apparently speculators no longer relied on luck when looking for their next site. It would be hard to prove now the building was burnt to a cinder, but that fire had been arson without any doubt.

Stars winked above the Capitol. Small slaveboys slept on their lanterns as they waited in doorways for masters who were still being entertained. The air was full of rumbling wheels as the carters plied their evening trade; then above the chinks of cheap metal on harnesswork came the sweet shiver of silver bells on the slim ankles of the dancing girls in some overpriced saloon. Passing along the gloomy lanes I knocked into empty amphorae which careless tavernkeepers had put out in piles; among the dried mud and mule droppings on broader streets I trod upon loose flower petals which had flittered from dinner garlands as their wearers came and went. It was a vibrant night. I was a free man in my own city – and not yet ready for bed.

It was too late to call at a senator's house. I also failed to drum up any desire to visit my own relations. Instead my feet took me northwards. The Hortensius crowd always gave the impression theirs was a home which kept long social hours. I would be fully justified if I apologised to Sabina Pollia and Hortensia Atilia for having been out of action for the past few days. Besides, I did need to ask the ladies if they had noticed any developments after my meeting with Hortensius Novus at Severina's lunch party.

The whole Pincian area was lively at this hour. By day these private palaces seemed sedate enough. By night houses and grounds throbbed with activity. Contracts for business and pleasure of every kind (legitimate or otherwise) were being worked out on this elegant mount. Some were already sealed and concluded. One of those affected me.

From the Forum to the Pincian, avoiding dossers, drabs and happy drunks, takes half an hour. By the time I turned off the Via Flaminia a subtle change had transformed Rome. The violet had drained from the skies, leaving greyness and a more wary atmosphere. Now the good would go home while the bad came out to play. Even my own mood was different. I slipped along, keeping to the centre of each street. My concentration stayed on the alert. I wished I had a knife.

There was no one at the Hortensius gatehouse. I walked through the gardens, staring twice at every darkened bush. Near the house torches lined the driveway, some still lit, a few atilt and smoking, but most burned out.

Clearly the family had been entertaining. The main door still stood open, with lamps aglow throughout the reception halls. I could smell the kind of perfume which is used to drench dinner guests – that light but cloying odour of rose petals, which to me always seems too close to the tang of decay. But there was no music, and nobody about. Then a gaggle of servants emerged through a curtain, with a relaxed air that betrayed the fact they were unsupervised.

One of them was fooling about with a tambourine; another was swigging wine, spilling it down his tunic as he took it straight from the lip of a golden ewer. They noticed me just as I recognised the runabout Hyacinthus, the thin slave who had first commissioned me. Like the others he was wearing a tunic with more ornament than cloth, a bawdy concoction of glittering guilloche which must be the Hortensius party livery – on a night like this, unbearably heavy and hot. 'Looks like you've been having fun here tonight!' I said.

'Welcome, stranger! Rumour had it you were in prison.'

'Malicious gossip! What was the party – special occasion?'

'Just dinner with an old acquaintance.'

'Business or pleasure?'

'Business.' I should have known. Everything was business in this

129

house. 'Did you have an appointment? Pollia and Atilia have both gone up to bed – '

I grinned. 'I'm not brave enough to disturb either of them in the bedroom!' One of the slaves giggled.

'The men should still be available,' Hyacinthus added.

I had had no dealings with Crepito or Felix. It might be useful to speak to Novus, but if I wanted to improve on our minimal chat over lunch I would need to see him on his own. 'Is Severina here tonight Hyacinthus?'

'She's been here since the afternoon but I haven't seen her lately.'

Someone else said, 'Her chairmen have gone; she must have left.'

'Can I see Novus then?' A young lad volunteered to ask.

The slaves were still joshing among themselves, and they wanted to be rid of me. Luckily the delay was short; the lad returned to say Novus was not in his own bedroom, nor with Crepito and Felix though they were expecting him to join them for a late-night glass of wine.

The houseslaves lost interest but after I had walked so far, heading back with nothing to show for my blisters was too dispiriting. 'Novus must be up and around somewhere!'

The man with the golden wine flagon laughed. 'Last I saw he was up all right – doubled up and running!'

'Something he ate disagreed with him?' It was a sultry night. My tunic stuck to my neck and chest unpleasantly as I asked.

'Probably the amount!' sneered the drinker. I remembered the ill-mannered gusto with which Novus licked his plate.

'How long ago did you see him on the trot?'

'About an hour.'

I glanced at Hyacinthus. 'Any chance he's stuck in a lavatory – flaked out, or still chucking up?' The slaves exchanged bored glances. 'Would he call for an attendant if he had a bad attack of the gyp?'

'Only to bawl at us to leave him on his own – he likes privacy when his gorging upsets him. Anyway – ' the man with the flagon was a caustic social satirist ' – there's not much help you can offer; shitting is one thing the rich have to do for themselves . . .'

Hyacinthus, who had been standing silent, finally returned my thoughtful stare. 'No harm in looking,' he said. The others refused to make the effort, so the search was left to Hyacinthus and me.

As in most houses which possess their own facilities, the Hortensius lavatories were situated alongside the kitchen so any water which was sluiced out of pots and sinks could be utilised to swill the channels clean. The freedmen's house boasted a triple-seater, but we only found one occupant.

Hortensius Novus must have burst in and let the heavy door swing behind him; the clatter from the kitchen where the remains of the dinner party were being cleared would have suddenly stilled; after that he was alone, in this dark, quiet place. If he was sober enough to understand what was happening, he must have been terrified. If he had called out, before the ghastly purge became paralysis, no one would have heard.

It would have been painful and degrading. But the speed of it had some mercy. And it was a private death.

XXXIII

'*I-o!*' exclaimed Hyacinthus. He instinctively turned away towards the kitchen, but I clapped my hand over his mouth and held him still.

'Don't raise the alarm yet!'

Hortensius Novus was lying on the floor. He had been felled in mid-stride; halfway between the door and the latrine seats. Cut down by death, the last embarrassment of all. If he was lucky, he was gone before he crashed face first onto the slabs.

Stepping carefully I bent to feel his neck, though I knew it was a formality. Then I saw his wild grimace. Something far worse than the violent purge had overwhelmed him. Perhaps the horrific certainty of approaching death.

He was warm, though not warm enough to be revived. I was no doctor; but I knew it was more than the strain of digesting too much dinner which had stopped the freedman's heart.

'Somebody got to him after all, Falco!'

The slave became hysterical; I felt a rush of panic myself, but I had been in this situation often enough to control it. 'Steady. Don't let's overreact.'

'He's been murdered!'

'Could be. But people often pass away during a fit of diarrhoea . . . and gluttons do die from overeating occasionally Hyacinthus – '

The speech, too, was a formality. I was filling in time while I looked around.

Novus had clutched his light banqueting gown up around his waist. I steeled myself then tugged away his left hand, with its jasper betrothal ring, and dragged the garment down. The dead deserve some decency.

I stood up quickly. Then I gripped Hyacinthus by one elbow and wheeled him outside the door. There might still be time to find some evidence before it was destroyed – either accidentally or by someone with a vested interest. 'Hyacinthus, stand there and don't let anyone go in.'

One glance in the kitchen confirmed my fears. The house was slackly run. Flies circled over the work surfaces with a languidly possessive air. But the used utensils from the banquet, which might have furnished clues, were already lost to me. The tousled skivvy who washed the platters knew she would have to do it some time so she had already made a start at scraping away, before the food on the dishes and serving tureens had caked too hard. When I strode round the door she was on her knees beside a cauldron of greasy water, surrounded by finished piles of gold plate. I saw her squint at a huge silver dish, which I recognised as the one Severina gave Novus the day we had lunch; the tired drudge tried to persuade herself the comport was clean, but found a sticky smear and listlessly dunked it into her tub.

Only the skivvy was working. (Any skivvy will tell you that is a perfectly normal event.)

Some of the cooks and carvers were lolling around now the toffs had dispersed. They were picking at the leftovers with the sluggish air of kitchen workers who knew some of the meat had looked slimy when it came from the butchers, which of the sauces had not wanted to thicken, and how many times the vegetables had fallen on the floor among the mice droppings in the course of being prepared.

'Who's in charge here?' I demanded. I guessed it was the kind of slapdash servery where no one would be in charge. I guessed right. I warned them that one of the guests had been taken ill, and none of the underlings looked surprised. I then said that the illness was fatal, at which they did suddenly lose their appetites. 'If you can find a dog that no one likes, start feeding him these leftover titbits one at a time . . .'

I strode back to Hyacinthus. 'We'll put a bar across this door – ' That would serve my purpose; people would think the lavatory had flooded: common enough. 'Now before some busybody tidies it up, I want you to show me the dining room – '

A house where nobody empties the rubbish pails and the kitchen boards are never scrubbed may nonetheless feed its visitors amid breathtaking opulence.

The blazing candelabra were beginning to die down now, but not enough to dim entirely the gilding on the pedestals and finely fluted pillarwork, or the shimmer from the brocaded swags of curtaining, cushioning and valencing which made the room and its three gigantic couches suitably luxurious for a set of jumped-up lamp-boys and the female trash who married them. I could not be bothered to take in all the details, but I remember there were huge paintings of battle scenes and highly polished onyx urns. Grilles overhead in the vaulted ceiling remained open after raining down a sickly perfume which made my throat clench.

A pageboy was curled up with his thumb in his mouth and a peach in his hand. He was so fast asleep he looked as if all breath had left him. Hyacinthus kicked at him anxiously, but the child started awake and stumbled away.

I gazed around, searching for clues. Here the worst signs of domestic upset were the wine-stained napery which would pose problems for the Hortensius linenkeeper, and a sea of spilt lamp oil on one of the couch coverlets. I kicked a hardened bread roll out of my path. 'Who was here tonight, Hyacinthus? How many of the family?'

'All three, with both women.'

'The guests?'

'Just one. A business associate.'

'And Severina.' Seven. Plenty of elbow room on the couches. 'What was the table plan?'

'Mealtimes are not my province, Falco. You want the chamberlain.' The chamberlain would be full of himself, a wearying talker (I had met them before). He could wait.

I walked all round the triclinium, but nothing caught my eye. Wine flagons and water jugs had been left on several side tables after the meal, with a litter of spice bowls and straining equipment. The only relic of the food was a complicated structure on a low central table. It was a tree, sculpted from golden wire, which must have arrived festooned with the fruit for dessert. Bunches of grapes and apricots still hung from its twisting arms and loaded its plinth.

I was still lost in thought, and Hyacinthus was hunched miserably on a dining couch, when the stillness was interrupted by a man arriving explosively.

'Someone has died – yes?'

'Someone may have done,' I answered sombrely, giving this wild apparition a once-over. He had a bald forehead, a wide mouth, a nose two sizes bigger than his other features and darting mid-brown eyes. His stature was unexceptional but he filled extra space by exuding the operational energy of a well-oiled Cretan windmill left with its brake off in a steady gale. 'Who gave you the information?'

'A skivvy ran and told me!'

'Why? What is it to do with you?'

Hyacinthus looked up. 'If you are blaming the food for poisoning Novus,' he told me, with a faint trace of amusement, 'he thinks you're after him – he's the chef, Falco!'

XXXIV

'*Novus!*' The wild-eyed chef grew still. He was visibly upset.

'Steady! What's your name?'

'People here call me Viridovix,' he informed me stiffly. 'And if my master has been poisoned – then you want to talk to me!'

'If you're the chef,' I commented, 'most of the people who ate here tonight will want to do that!'

If I needed confirmation that the Hortensius crowd were a clutch of social amateurs, I would have found it in the fact that they had a Gallic cook.

It was a hundred years since Rome decided to civilise the Gauls; since then we had moved on from genocide at Julius Caesar's hand to taming the tribes with commodities which came cheaper for the Treasury: ceramic bowls, Italian wine, and the finer points of democratic local government. Gaul's response was to fill Rome's artists' studios with life models who specialised in posing as Dying Barbarians, then later to inflict on us a rash of heavy-going middle-class bureaucrats in the mode of Agricola. Many prominent Gauls come from Forum Julii, which was graced by what passed for a university – plus a port, so they could easily ship themselves out to Rome.

I am prepared to concede that one day the three cold Gallic provinces will come up with a contribution to the civilised arts – but nobody is going to convince me that it will be mastery of cuisine. Even so, I never imagined that Hortensius Novus died because his cook came from Gaul. His dinner almost certainly killed him – but that was nothing to do with the cook.

Calming Viridovix was my first priority; he might become less agitated without an audience. I winked at Hyacinthus, who obligingly disappeared.

'I'm Didius Falco. I'm investigating this tragedy – and frankly, after finding your master's body I need a drink! Considering that he was poisoned, I imagine you'd like to join me – let's try and find something we can assume has not been tampered with . . .'

I sat him down to simmer off boiling point. I found one wine flask, an elegant sky-blue fluted glass affair with a silvery, lustrous finish, which stood with its bung out, breathing, like a special vintage set aside for the after-dinner toasts. The amber wine was brimming well up the neck of the vessel; the diners had plainly overlooked their treat. I took a risk that anything that was meant to be partaken of by the company in common was probably safe. It was a big risk; but Viridovix was obviously badly shaken, and I was desperate.

'This should do us –' The contents were thick as nectar and probably of great age. Although I took my own cup neat Viridovix asked for spices; I found a little bowl in matching blue glass standing handy beside the flask and, thinking a cook would appreciate flavour, I emptied the entire contents – myrrh and cassia, by the sniff of it – into his cup.

One gulp convinced me the person who should be enjoying this was my expert friend Petronius. It was fifteen-year-old Falernian, if I was any judge. I recognised the way it slid down my throat like molten glass, and the warm burn of the aftertaste. I knew it because Petro used to treat me on his birthday; he always said it was a waste pouring this noble grape juice into a cluck like me, but Falernian should not be drunk alone (a philosophy I encouraged).

We quaffed. The cook immediately looked less pale. 'Better? Viridovix, the fact is Novus has died, but no one is likely to blame you – unless you had a grudge against him.' I wanted to remind the cook that when a free citizen died by violent means the first suspects were his slaves, but to offer a hope of my protection if he was innocent. 'The best thing you can do to help clear yourself – '

'I have done nothing wrong.'

'I realise that.'

'Yet others may not agree with you?' I liked his wry attitude.

'They will if I identify the real killer.' Viridovix looked uncertain. 'I was hired to prevent this,' I grumbled. 'So yours is not the only reputation under threat, my friend.'

My glum mood had convinced him. We took another swig, then I persuaded him to go through the dinner menu. Obviously a worrier, he had been carrying it around, written on a scrap of parchment which was still in a pouch at his waist:

DINNER FOR SEVEN; HOSTED BY HORTENSIUS NOVUS

Appetisers:
Salad of Lettuce and Mallow Leaves
Peacocks' Eggs
Sausage in a Ring
Baian Oysters Hortensius
Artichoke Hearts
Olives

Main Dishes:
Hare in Rich Wine Sauce
Lobster in Saffron
Pot Roast Pork Crowned with Laurel
Wild Crane
Halibut Pancakes
Fennel; Potted Peas; Stewed Leeks and Onions; Mushrooms

Dessert:
White cheeses
Fruits Presented on a Hesperides Tree
Purchased Pastries

Wines:
With the Appetiser, Mulsum (first pressing), warmed
with Honey and malabathron flavouring
With the Main Dishes, a choice of Red or White Chian
Served to Individual Taste
For the Toasts after Dinner, Setinum

'And who devised this elegant collation?' I asked.

'I myself,' boasted Viridovix, then added, 'with some suggestions from Severina Zotica . . .'

I was not ready to think of Zotica. 'Was the evening a success, Viridovix?'

'Certainly.'

'Your creations were well received?'

'Good ingredients,' he shrugged. 'You cannot go wrong. I am free to buy the best.' He was evidently conscientious. I discarded my private joke earlier about shiny meat – and with it any lingering doubt that his master might have been poisoned by accident, simply through eating unsafe food.

Rereading the list, I put some further queries to the cook, not all of them for professional reasons. 'What are Oysters Hortensius?'

'Poached in a light bouillon of white wine, laurel leaves, juniper berries and lovage –'

'Invented by one of the family?'

'Invented by *me*!' I was corrected. Of course. No one as pretentious as these freedmen would allow visitors to be served up with a recipe named after a Celtic slave. Viridovix provided the creative skill; they took the credit.

'Mushrooms make people think twice nowadays . . .' I was referring to the infamous murder of the Emperor Claudius by his wife. Viridovix, who was well down his winecup, merely sniffed. 'Did the pastries come from Minnius along the road?'

'As usual. His work is not bad, and he gives us special rates.'

'Because one of the freedmen leases him the stall?'

'I don't know why. I am a cook.'

'How did that come about?'

'Prisoner of war. Novus acquired me,' Viridovix murmured rather sweetly, 'because the slavemaster declared I was a tribal leader.'

'Snobbery!'

'He likes having his porridge stirred by a ruined prince.' The cook was not a bitter man. I enjoyed the light way he mocked his master's vulgarity.

'Were you one?' He smiled in silence. 'Still, perhaps you were once something better than a cook . . . Was it hard, coming here?'

'This is how I have to live,' Viridovix said quietly.

'So you knuckle down?'

'This is my work – I choose to do it well,' he added, with the dignity of the mildly drunk.

'An individual's privilege!' I must have been drunk too. I noticed he wore the same overdone uniform as Hyacinthus, laden with gaudy braid. The cook also sported a twisted silver torque. 'Did that necklet come with you when you were a prisoner?'

'Hardly! I have been supplied with it.'

'Extra colour? Do I gather from the full fancy dress that you supervised the servers personally?'

'Bad carving can ruin my best work.'

'I intended to ask the chamberlain who ate what.'

'He will not know,' said Viridovix dismissively.

'But *you* noticed?' I hazarded. 'You know what they all took – and what they all left on their plates!'

He glanced at me, pleased by the compliment, then graciously answered my query. 'I should say everyone sampled almost everything. Pollia left every scrap which she could call gristle; Felix looked for fat to peel off; the guest pushed his food around all night –'

'Any reason?'

'A man who does not know how to eat.'

'Or how to live!' I cried, glancing enthusiastically at his menu.

Viridovix accepted the compliment. 'As you say! Novus as usual devoured a large plateful, then called for a further helping. But none of them really noticed what they ate.'

'Disappointing?'

'Normal, Falco. In this house.'

'Does that rankle with you?'

'Not enough,' responded Viridovix shrewdly, 'to make me want to murder them!'

'It's my theory cooks commit their murders when they overheat in the glare of the ovens – then their method is to run amuck with meat cleavers.'

'Poison would be highly unprofessional!' he smiled.

'Tell me – as an observant man – were any of those present nervous?' I carefully avoided naming Severina Zotica.

'All of them,' he replied at once.

'Even Novus?'

'Especially him.' Somehow that was a surprise.

'What accounted for this edginess?' He gave me a wide-mouthed Gallic smile again, full of intelligent charm. I laughed. 'Oh sorry; you will not know details; you are just the cook!'

'Ah, cooks are all ears while people eat their food!'

'Going to tell me?'

'It was because of the business they had gathered to discuss.' I waited. He timed it nicely for effect: 'I think, forming a new partnership.' This time he actually grinned at me.

'In what field?'

'City property.'

'Did you learn any details?'

'No, Falco. When they were ready to talk, all of us serving were dismissed. I expect you want to ask me,' Viridovix suggested quietly, 'if I saw Hortensius Novus eat or drink anything that nobody else touched?'

'I would probably have worked around to it!'

'Nothing,' the cook disappointed me. 'Most of them dipped into most of the dishes and all of the wines. If poison was in the food, they are all dead. The servers were being attentive – but it was also a party where people made much of passing delicacies to their neighbours –'

'Best behaviour night?'

'Much graciousness. *Too* much.'

'So the general mood was amicable?'

'It seemed so, but the tension was high. I was afraid it would infect the servers; something would be dropped. A harpist had been engaged, but he was paid off without playing. They finished fairly early –'

'Did you see what happened then?'

'Of course; we were waiting to clear . . . After they came out, Crepito and Felix stood in the portico for some time, with their guest –'

'Still discussing?'

'Low voices – something Novus had done seemed to be causing controversy. Then I overheard talk of them going on drinking, but nothing came of it; the guest said he had something else to do. When he left, Felix and Crepito disappeared, heads together.'

'Happy?'

'No; I would say.'

'Where was Novus?'

'Novus had stomped off somewhere.'

'With Severina Zotica?'

'No,' said the cook. 'I should have told you earlier – Severina Zotica was never there!'

At that point a shoe scratched on marble. Viridovix dropped a warning hand on my arm. I turned on my seat. Standing in the doorway in a waft of garlic and frankincense was a man who could only be another of the Hortensius triumvirate.

XXXV

He looked older than Novus, though similar: the same skin tones and well-fed solidity. A fleshy body with a heavy head, and a bushy black moustache which hid the movements of his mouth.

He exhibited a strange lack of curiosity about who I was or what I might be talking about here in their family dining room, with the family cook. Instead, he crossed in front of us and seized the fluted blue flagon from which Viridovix and I had helped ourselves. Luckily I had previously put down my cup on the floor where it was hidden behind my feet. Viridovix somehow let *his* winecup burrow invisibly into the folds of our couch's coverlet. The freedman glanced at the flask, spotting that some of the liquor was missing.

'Novus couldn't wait!' he grumbled.

I detached myself from Viridovix. 'Excuse me, sir. Are you Crepito?'

'Felix.' The one married to Pollia. He was still scowling at the flask as if accusing Hortensius Novus of starting it. Neither Viridovix nor I disillusioned him.

'I'm Marcus Didius Falco. Here on an assignment for your wife . . .' Impossible to tell if he knew anything about it. 'If Hortensius Crepito is anywhere around can I request an urgent interview?'

He lifted the flask. 'Special vintage! Crepito and Novus are both about to join me –'

'Not Novus, sir. Something has happened. May we talk – with Crepito as well, if possible?'

Still more concerned with the flask than this mystery, Hortensius Felix shrugged and led me out.

The three freedmen had meant to marshal and sample their Falernian in a small room on the other side of their main hall. Another which was new to me. It was exuberantly foreign – Nilotic paintings, fans, statuettes of ibis-headed gods, vibrantly striped cushions and ivory couches with sphinxes for arms.

'Our Egyptian salon.' Felix noticed me step back a pace. 'Like it?'

'Every home should have one!' Like a wasps' nest, or a door that will never stay closed.

Another gust of garlic billowed in after us: Crepito – who must have been searching for Novus. 'I can't find the fool; what's he playing at?'

Although Pollia had assured me these freedmen had no direct blood relationship, now that I had seen all three they definitely sprang from the same eastern tribe. Crepito had a smaller moustache than Felix, less flesh than Novus, and a louder, bluffer voice than either, yet the same jowls, swarthiness, and irritable temperament. Novus must have been the youngest of the three.

I introduced myself a second time. 'Hortensius Crepito? I'm Didius Falco, on hire to your wives.' Crepito grunted, so I proceeded on the assumption that I was a known quantity. 'I'm sorry to be the one who breaks this; Hortensius Novus has had a sudden accident – a fatal one.'

Both showed proper evidence of surprise. 'Impossible! We were with him no time ago –' That came from Crepito.

'I found him myself,' I declared quietly. 'He must have had some kind of seizure, immediately after your meal tonight.'

The two freedmen exchanged glances. 'You mean –'

'Yes; it looks like deliberate poisoning.'

'How?' demanded Felix, with the urgency of a man who realised all too keenly that he had just eaten the same meal as the murdered man.

I reassured them sympathetically. 'What happened to Hortensius Novus seems to have struck with great rapidity. If anyone else was affected, I'm sure they would know by now.'

Despite this, Felix put down the fluted blue flask on a side table, and stepped away hastily.

I was wishing I had met Crepito and Felix earlier. Breaking news to strangers is always unsatisfactory. It's harder to judge which of their reactions are due to shock – and how much of the shock is genuine.

Hortensius Felix had grown sombre and uncommunicative. Crepito requested details, so I described how I had found Novus dead on the floor of the lavatory, which was where he remained. 'You may feel,' I suggested, 'you ought to call in a magistrate before you have him moved.'

'Is that normal?' demanded Felix abruptly. 'Normal to call in the authorities?' Under stress he had revealed for the first time signs that the freedmen had come to Rome from some different culture.

'Best to act responsibly, sir. Most householders report a suspected murder to the Praetor of their own accord, rather than have him sending his aedile round after tip-offs from their neighbours.'

'People don't –'

'People do,' I said grimly. 'Don't expect solidarity from the folks you used to dine with, once the nasty rumours start to fly.' Once again the two of them exchanged glances. 'I know Hortensius Novus was like a brother to you both,' I said, more gently. They received this with a distinct air of reserve. My sense of dealing with foreigners increased. I thought I needed to reassure them again: 'I'm trying to advise you. If the murderer were fleeing from the scene, you should send for the vigilantes to dash in pursuit. But poisoners normally hope they will remain undetected; so they stay put, looking innocent. You can rely on the magistrate's office to investigate tomorrow. Then the matter will be handled with greater sensitivity –' I meant, polite incompetence.

'Where do you fit in?' Felix asked brusquely.

'I can continue to act for you privately. I'm so angry about this, I may beat the Praetor to the truth.' As businessmen I hoped Crepito and Felix might contribute the local Praetor's name; no luck. 'There was no way I could prevent this,' I told them levelly. 'But I shall not rest until I have exposed the poisoner. Severina has to be the prime suspect. My next move is to interrogate her. I'm intrigued to hear she was an absent guest tonight?'

'She gave some excuse to Novus,' Felix said.

'But she was here earlier?' Both Felix and Crepito shrugged. 'Well, if she thinks being off the scene is enough to clear her, I'll have news for that young lady!' Once again the two freedmen made eye contact.

A silence fell, which warned me to disappear. 'I'll be on my way . . . Ought I to see Sabina Pollia and Hortensia Atilia first?' I hoped to witness the ladies' first reactions to the tragedy.

'Not necessary,' Felix replied, with a curtness which just fell short of hostility. He rang a bell to reinforce the message.

'Fine! Well, I will call again tomorrow of course. I want to pay my condolences in person . . . By the way,' I asked in a neutral tone, just as I was leaving. 'Were relations between you and Novus fairly friendly this evening?'

For once, they avoided looking at each other; in fact the rigidity with which they kept their eyes fixed ahead was suspicious in itself.

Both solemnly assured me the party had been relaxed and harmonious.

Thanks to Viridovix I knew they were lying. Which raised an interesting question: why?

I guessed there would be some vivid debate later that night in the Hortensius house. I wished I could overhear it. I wondered what part the two women who employed me would play.

But in the meantime I was speculating on something else: how I would face Severina with news of this crime.

It was only then, as I walked south through the streets full of delivery wagons, trying to avoid having my toes crushed under a cartwheel, that a thought I had been too busy to frame consciously finally found space to present itself: *what was the point of it?*

Hortensius Novus had died too soon. Severina had no hope of inheriting his fortune, except as his wife. At this stage in their affairs she would be lucky to get a sack of apples and his kind regards. Whatever was the woman playing at?

XXXVI

Most of Abacus Street lay in darkness. A few dim lights showed, but the passage to Severina's accommodation was pitch-dark; I stubbed my toe on a bucket left outside the cheesemakers. Her house itself looked dead.

It took a quarter of an hour to rouse one of her slaves. I tried to attract attention discreetly, but I could only batter the metal knocker continually. The noise must have carried all over the Caelimontium, though no one threw open their shutters to investigate or protest. How unlike the intolerant types I knew on the Aventine!

The slave recognised me; he made no comment on the time. Perhaps Severina knew other men who called on her during the silent hours. As he admitted me I noticed the house seemed muffled, with few lamps lit, all apparently at rest.

I was left to wait in the room where the girl and I first met. The work on the loom had been changed to a new pattern. I glanced at a library scroll lying on a couch: something about Mauretania. I lost interest. I was listening for movements elsewhere in the house.

The slave put his head round the door curtain. 'She'll come down,' he muttered grudgingly.

'Thanks. Tell me,' I asked, 'have Novus and Severina fixed a date for their wedding yet?'

'Ten days' time.'

'When was that agreed?'

'Earlier this week.'

'So Novus may have announced it to the world at large tonight?'

'She'll be down!' the slave reiterated, giving me a caustic look. He could tell that I was just firing off ballista bolts in the dark.

I never heard her coming.

She was tricked out as if the slave really had roused her from her bed: unshod feet; bare-armed in a short white undershift; face slightly puffy; the drift of that coppery hair all spread loose down her back.

146

She probably *had* been in bed: lying awake, waiting for a messenger to bring the news.

'You've got some talking to do, Zotica!' She met my bald scrutiny and held my gaze. I expected that. There would be no faltering from this one. 'Novus is dead.'

'Novus?' She said it, quickly, then frowned as if confused.

'Did you know?'

'*Dead*?' she repeated.

'Keep it up, Zotica!' I teased insultingly.

Severina drew an indignant breath. 'Do you need to be so brutal?' She came into the room, putting both hands to her face. 'What has happened? Tell me properly.'

'I found your intended tonight, face down in a lavatory. Poisoned, Severina. Don't tell me this is unexpected news.'

She bit her lip when I mentioned the details, but she was angry now. Excellent. She walked over to a couch and sat, apparently shivering. 'What time is it, Falco?' I had no idea. 'The question people always ask,' she murmured abstractedly, 'when time no longer matters anyway . . .'

The stricken look failed to convince me. 'Cut the pathos! What kept you from the dinner party?'

Her face clouded. 'I was feeling unwell, Falco. Women's problems.' Her chin came up defiantly as she hugged her stomach. 'You know what I mean!'

'Or I'm supposed to be too embarrassed to ask? Forget it! I grew up with five sisters, Zotica. Victorina was the prize artist – she could make "a bad time of the month" last three weeks, especially if there was some boring religious festival she wanted to miss.'

'I did go up to the house this afternoon,' Severina said shortly. 'But in the end I could not face a long evening of strained formality among people who make no secret of their dislike for me –'

'Yes; you would need courage – to recline alongside your victim while he sampled the poisoned sauce!'

'That's slander, Falco!' she fought back. 'I went to reassure the cook. Novus has been fussing ever since he sent out the invitations –' I noticed she used the present tense, the way people continue to do after a genuine bereavement: a delicate touch! 'It was a big responsibility for Viridovix –'

'Whatever possessed Novus to buy himself a Gallic cook? If a man must have a chef from the ends of the Empire, surely he turns to Alexandria?'

147

'You know how they are in that house – their captive "prince" is a novelty.'

'He's certainly a rarity: he makes the best of things.' I could see this temporary diversion was making no impression, so I abandoned it. 'Tell me about tonight's party. Why the grand performance? Who were the guests?'

'Appius Priscillus.'

For a moment I was at a loss. 'Oh the property tycoon! The beater-up of fruitsellers. What is his link with the Hortensius crew?'

'Same interests. Leasing; property; land use. Relations between their two empires had deteriorated badly. They were all acting against their own interests by prolonging the rivalry, so the dinner party was suggested to resolve their differences.'

'*Who* suggested it?' I asked, frowning. I already knew.

'I did. But, Falco, bringing them together was your idea originally . . . Excuse me a moment.' Severina murmured abruptly. She looked as if she was going to be sick.

She slipped from the room. I gave her a few minutes, then set off to look for her.

Intuition led me into an anteroom alongside the gracious triclinium where Novus and I had been given lunch. Severina stood motionless in the darkness. I held up a lamp I had carried in with me. 'Are you all right?'

'So much to think about.'

I stepped closer carefully. 'Zotica?' Her intense quiet and fixed gaze were signs of true shock. For a moment she stood with one hand to her forehead. Then she started to cry.

Restraining my annoyance, I said, 'The first rule for an informer is: women who burst into tears are up to no good.'

'Keep out of their way then!' Severina snapped. I put two fingers under her elbow and moved her to a couch. She sat down, without arguing, then turned away and sobbed. I perched alongside and let her get on with it. 'Sorry about that,' she murmured finally, bending forwards to mop her face on the skirt of her shift. I had a glimpse of knee, which I found oddly distracting.

She breathed slowly, as if coming to terms with some unexpected trouble. She was obviously acting. She had to be. I remembered the Praetor's clerk Lusius saying that Severina was naturally undemonstrative under stress, and friend Lusius had seemed observant enough. Yet I still felt that the need to release all this emotion had been partly genuine.

'I hope you've got your story composed for the enquiring magistrate.' She stared ahead, still in a kind of trance. 'Better still,' I suggested, 'why not tell your nice Uncle Marcus exactly what happened, and let him take charge?'

Severina sighed, stretching her minute feet in front of her. Her feet, and what I could see of her legs (more than usual), were freckled; so were her bare arms. 'Oh leave it alone, Falco!'

'You are not going to talk to me?'

'If I did poison Novus, certainly not!'

'Did you?'

'No. Juno and Minerva – if all I wanted was his money, what would be the point?'

'I had thought of that.'

'Brilliant! So what twisted explanation have you come up with instead?'

'I feel certain that you killed him – but I have no idea why.'

She had jumped to her feet. 'Didius Falco, you have no reason to be here! Either arrest me, or go away –'

'What are you doing, Zotica?'

'I'm fetching a wine jug from the dining room – then I intend getting drunk!'

My heart was pounding out a warning – but I told myself this might be the only chance I ever had of persuading Severina to say something indiscreet. 'Oh sit down, woman! I'll get the jug. Take some advice from an expert: getting drunk is quicker, as well as much more cheerful, if you have a friend to help!'

XXXVII

Why do I do these things? (Why does anyone?)

I found cups on a sideboard, and a half-filled amphora of something which tasted brash enough for the kind of deliberate drinking which is bound to make you ill. Severina fetched a ewer of cold water. We did not bother with flavourings. Our mutual suspicion would provide a bitter spice if we needed it.

We ended up sitting on the floor, leaning our heads against a couch behind us. At first we drank in silence.

Even after five years as an informer, finding a corpse always unsettled me. I let the memory come surging in as it was trying to do: Novus, bare-buttocked in that undignified spasm. Novus, pressed face-down against the floor slabs, with that expression of stark terror . . .

'Are you all right, Falco?' Severina asked quietly.

'Murder offends me. Like me to describe the death scene?'

I noticed that her knuckles whitened as she gripped the stem of her ceramic cup. 'I can probably endure it!'

I had told her the worst of it. I spared myself dwelling on any more details.

Severina topped up her winecup. We had been serving ourselves – not letting formal manners interfere. It was like drinking with a man.

'Do you do this often?' I asked.

'No!' she conceded. 'What about you?'

'Only when the memory of the headache I had the last time has faded . . .'

'If we are going to do this, shall I call you by your first name?'

'No.'

She chewed the side of her thumb for a moment. 'I thought you were my nice Uncle Marcus?'

'I'm Falco – and I'm not nice.'

'I see! Drunk but distant!' She laughed. Whenever Severina

150

laughed she sounded arrogant – and that irritated me. 'I think you and I have more in common than you admit, Falco.'

'We have nothing in common!' I splashed more liquor into my cup. 'Novus is dead. What next, Zotica?'

'Nothing.'

'*What* was the wrong word. I should have asked, *Who?*'

'Don't be so offensive!' she told me – but she said it with a half-smile and a glint behind these pale eyelashes. She was daring me to ask fiercer questions. Interrogation was a thrill.

I knew better than to fight a suspect who so loved to be the centre of attention. Instead, I stretched lazily. 'Never again, eh? Sounds like what I always used to say, when some flighty piece took my cash and broke my heart.'

'Past tense?' Severina immediately wormed at me, unable to resist prying.

'Too old. Flighty bits want boys, who go like fire in bed and let themselves be bossed about – '

'You're romancing, Falco,' she scolded, as if something had suddenly made her more wary. 'Why can you never hold a straight-forward conversation?'

'I get bored,' I admitted. 'That straightforward enough?'

We both fizzled with tipsy laughter.

Severina was sitting cross-legged, with her back very straight. She was on my left. So I had lolled with my right knee bent, supporting my winecup hand. It enabled me to turn inwards, and watch her unobtrusively.

She filled her cup again. 'I'm drinking more than you!'

'I had noticed.'

'You intend to stay sober, so you can winkle out my secrets . . .'

'I like a woman with secrets – '

'You don't like me! Stop inventing . . . I should have asked,' she murmured, with what she probably thought was a sly approach, 'if anyone is waiting up for you at home?'

'No.' I drained my cup. The action was more drastic than I intended; I nearly choked.

'You surprise me!' she taunted in a soft voice.

When I stopped coughing I said, 'You were right the other day; I overreached myself.'

'Tell me!'

'Not much to tell. One of us is yearning to settle down and start

151

a family; the other wants to stay footloose.' Severina looked uncertain, as if she missed the joke. 'Women are so feckless!' I complained. 'They can't take the responsibility – '

'So how will you entrap her?' Severina now joined in the game, though with a scornful expression.

'I have my methods.'

'You men are so devious!'

'Once she discovers my wonderful cooking and my sweet devoted nature, I'll tie her down . . .'

'Does she help you in your work?'

'You asked me that before. I keep her out of my work.'

'I wondered if you sent her to spy on people in places you can't go?'

'I'd never let her go anywhere I couldn't go myself.'

'How considerate!' Severina said.

We had both stopped drinking and were staring ahead like crass philosophers. The effect of a harsh young grape-pressing on top of the subtle Falernian I had quaffed earlier, not to mention the smooth dinner wines Titus had served up at the Palace, was beginning to make me wonder if it would be possible to stand upright when I wanted to. Even Severina was now breathing drowsily.

'A night of revelations!'

I grunted, feeling bilious. 'Bit one-sided so far! The plan was that I would open up, then lure you into a confession . . .'

'Plan, Falco? You won't wheedle confessions out of *me* by such a transparent trick as getting me drunk!'

'You got yourself drunk.'

'I hate you when you're logical.'

'And I hate you – Oh forget it,' I sighed. 'I'm too tired to rise to the challenge of cheap dialogue.'

'You're falling asleep!' Severina chortled next. Perhaps I was. Perhaps I just wanted her to think so. (Perhaps I could no longer help myself.)

When I made no answer she tipped back her head, groaning. Then she pulled from her finger the red jasper ring with the two hands clasped; she tossed it wryly in the air, caught it, then set it down beside her on the floor. A spark seemed to leap from the gemstone to glint in her hair. Her action was not irreverent, yet obviously marked a formal end of her betrothal to the dead man. 'Nothing left to do . . . no one who needs me . . . no one to turn to . . . What is it all for, Falco?'

The jewel she had removed looked almost as heavy as the one Novus himself had worn: far too massive for Severina's fingers, which were tiny as a child's. 'For profit, lady! That ring at least was a decent piece of gold!'

Severina moved the jasper ring dismissively on the mosaic. 'Gold wears thin. Like the love it pretends to represent.'

'Some lasts.'

'Do you really believe that?' she demanded. 'Does your famous ladyfriend?'

I laughed. 'She's a realist. She keeps me on a short rope, just in case.'

After a moment Severina lifted her right hand, showing the cheap ring with a crudely etched Venus and a small blob that was meant to be the Cupid nestling her knee. 'Now copper – ' she declared obscurely, '*that's* for eternity!'

'Eternity comes cheap! Did you know, copper is named for the mountains of Cyprus, where the oxhide ingots come from?' I collect obscure facts. 'And Cyprus is the birthplace of Venus, so that's why copper is the metal of Love – '

'It gives you verdigris in the soul, Falco!' she murmured.

'You ought to see a doctor about that.' I refused to ask her what she meant. There is nothing you can do with a woman when she wants to be mysterious. 'So who gave you the copper ring?'

'Someone who was a slave with me.'

'He have a name?'

'Only among the Shades in the Underworld.'

I smiled wryly. 'Like so many of your friends!'

Severina leaned to collect the flagon. I raised my palm in protest but she shared the last of the wine between us.

She sat back, slightly closer. We drank, slowly, both deep in the glum privacy that passes for thought when drunk.

'I ought to be leaving.'

'We can give you a bed.'

What I desperately needed was untroubled sleep. In this house I would lie awake expecting a mechanical ceiling to lower itself and crush me . . . I shook my head.

'Thank you for staying anyway.' Severina compressed her lips, like a girl who was all alone but trying to be brave. 'I needed somebody tonight – '

I turned my head. She turned hers. I was two digits away from kissing her. She knew it, and made no attempt to move away. If I did, I knew what would happen: I would start to feel responsible.

Leaning on the couch behind me, I hoisted myself to my feet.

Severina scrambled upright too, holding out her hand for me to steady her. The wine, and the sudden motion, made us both sway. For a moment we lurched together, still clutching hands.

Had it been Helena, I would have found my arms were round her. Severina was smaller; I would have to stoop. She was not the birdlike bony type who gave me goosepimples; under her loose shift I could see inviting flesh on her. Her skin always looked clean and smooth; it was poignantly perfumed with some familiar oil. In the lamplight, and so close to me, the wintery grey of her eyes was suddenly a deeper, more interesting, blue. We both knew what I was thinking. I was relaxed, and susceptible. I was missing my lady; I too needed company.

She made no attempt to stand on tiptoe; she wanted the decision – and the blame – to be all mine.

Too tired out and tipsy to think fast, I searched for a way to escape with some tact. 'Bad idea, Zotica!'

'Not tempted?'

'Too far gone,' I pretended gallantly. At that moment I felt so overcome with weariness I could easily have agreed to any procedure which allowed me to lie down. 'Another time,' I promised.

'I doubt it!' she answered – pretty vindictively.

I managed to stagger home.

I had not been back to my Piscina Publica apartment since Anacrites arrested me. I would have been relieved to find a message from Helena Justina: some signal that she missed me, some reward for my own good faith. There was nothing.

Still, I could hardly blame a senator's daughter if she was too proud to make overtures. And, having said I would wait to hear from her, there was no way on earth that *I* was going to approach her first . . .

I went to bed, cursing women.

Severina didn't want me; she wanted me to want her; not the same thing.

Nor, I thought angrily (for the drink was now making me belligerent), was there any way that a pair of cool blue eyes would make me forget the girl who really made me furious; the girl I wanted to think about; the girl whose brown eyes once said so frankly that *she* wanted *me* . . .

Frustrated beyond endurance, I crashed my clenched fist as hard as I could against the bedroom wall. Somewhere close by, within the building fabric, a shower of falling material rattled disturbingly as if I had shifted a joist. The debris trickled for a long time.

In the darkness I moved my hand over the wall surface. Unable to find any damage to the plasterwork, I lay rigid with guilt and foreboding, listening for noises.

Pretty soon I forgot to listen and fell asleep.

XXXVIII

I woke earlier than I might have done, due to my dreams. Dreams which disturbed me so badly I won't bother you by revealing what they were.

To avoid further nightmares I sat up and dressed – a drawn-out procedure, given that it only consisted of pulling on a clean tunic over the crumpled one I had slept in, then finding my favourite boots where Ma had hidden them. During this struggle, I could hear some sort of racket going on. The old woman upstairs was bawling away at some poor soul as if he had thieved her only daughter's virginity.

'You can only regret it!' a man's voice raged. Pleased that for once *I* was an innocent party in her delusions, I stuck my head out just as Cossus the letting agent tumbled downstairs past my door. He looked flustered.

'Trouble?' I asked.

'She's a mad old bag – ' he mumbled, glancing back over one shoulder as if he feared the woman would call down a witch's curse on him. 'Some people never know what's good for them – '

He seemed disinclined to dispel my curiosity so I contented myself with chivvying, 'What's happening about that water-carrier you promised me?'

'Give us a chance . . .'

This time I let him depart without a tip.

I left home without any breakfast. Nursing a sore head, I set off to see the women on the Pincian. It took me some time to get there. My feet had apparently taken a vow against walking anywhere today. I fooled them by hiring a mule.

Novus was being honoured in a brave style on his departure across the Styx. Throughout the house there was a dark smell of embalming oils and incense. Instead of a few indicative cyprus boughs, each doorway was guarded by a pair of whole trees. They must have

156

uprooted a small forest. Trust this lot to create a spectacle even out of a funeral.

The slaves were in strict black. The cloth looked brand-new. The freedwomen must have had sempstresses working all night.

When I managed to get in to see them (for they were putting on a show of being too overwrought for visitors), Pollia and Atilia were veiled in elaborate swathes of exquisite white: the upper-class colour for mourning wear (more flattering).

I muttered condolences then squared up to the situation: 'You may ask me how I dare to show my face . . .'

Sabina Pollia cackled briefly. Grief can affect some people with irritability. As usual her face was beautifully presented, yet today it was apparent that her voice was ten years older than the face.

I braced myself. 'Look; I did my best – which is all I ever promised you.' Hortensia Atilia's huge dark eyes, which looked more frightened than sorrowful, fastened on me anxiously. Sabina Pollia glared. 'You were right about Severina – though her timing seems inexplicable . . . There was no way to prevent what happened. But she won't escape justice this time – '

'How can you be so confident?' Pollia asked me cuttingly.

'Experience.'

'You were confident before!'

'No; I was cautious before. Now I'm angry – '

'The matter has been reported to the Praetor,' Pollia broke in.

'Yes; I suggested that myself – ' I already guessed what was coming.

'Then *I* suggest we leave the Praetor to deal with it!'

After the whiplash of scorn from Pollia subsided, I started again cautiously: 'You commissioned me because I worked for the Palace, which happens to be where I was detained last evening – '

'Our husbands have instructed us to discontinue your services.' This was Atilia, who had always appeared the more timid of the pair. Neither of these women would care a bent hairpin for what their husbands said; Felix and Crepito were mere ciphers. But one excuse was as good as another when clients were set on dismissing me.

'Of course,' I said, 'you must respect your husbands' wishes!'

'You failed, Falco!' Pollia insisted.

'Apparently!'

Even with a raging hangover I knew how to be professional. They were both tense, expecting an angry outburst; I could relieve my feelings later so I disappointed them. 'Ladies, I never stick around if I have lost my clients' confidence.'

I saluted them politely (since I wanted them to pay me). Then I left.

The end of the case. Ah well; if I failed to recruit any other business I could always go back to working for the Palace.

Signed off.

Signed off *again*! It was always happening to me. Somehow the only clients who ever commissioned me were vacillating types. Hardly had I drummed up interest in their tawdry lives, than they changed their fretful little minds about needing me.

I could have solved this one. I would have enjoyed doing so. Never mind; for a few weeks' surveillance I could now charge the two women extortionate expenses, then nip off out of it before the messy part. It was the best way to do business, for a philosophical man. Let the local law and order people give themselves headaches puzzling how Severina managed it this time. Let the Pincian magistrate try to bring her to court where the Praetor Corvinus on the Esquiline had failed. I was laughing. I could send a bill for my expenses, spend some time at the baths, enjoy myself, then read about official bungling in the *Daily Gazette* . . .

But that was not the end of the case.

I was about to stride haughtily past the ornate lodge where the Hortensius porter lurked, when I spotted somebody waiting nearby in the shade: thin arms and a black wire moustache bisecting his face.

'Hyacinthus!'

He was waiting for me. 'Falco – can we talk?'

'Certainly – '

'I have to be quick. We have all been ordered not to speak to you.'

'Why's that?' He glanced nervously up towards the house. I drew him off the main path and we squatted on our haunches beneath an elderly pine tree. 'Never mind why then – what's up?'

'You were talking to Viridovix – '

'Yes; I intended to have another word today – '

Hyacinthus laughed briefly, then picked up a pine cone and hurled it among the trees. 'Did they pay you off?' he demanded.

'Well I'm sent off – it remains to be seen whether I get paid!'

'Just present your bill. They don't want trouble.'

'Trouble? What trouble?'

He was silent for a moment, then out it came: 'You won't be able to talk to the cook, again. Viridovix is dead!'

XXXIX

As soon as he said it I felt a cold sweat. 'What happened?'

'He died last night. In his sleep.'

'The same way as Novus?'

'Don't think so. He looked quite peaceful. It appeared to be natural – '

'Hah!'

'He was healthy,' frowned Hyacinthus.

'Cooks can always scavenge nourishment.' Viridovix was no age either; thirty, I reckoned. Like me; a boy. 'Is anyone looking into it?'

'No chance! Someone suggested foul play to Felix – but he retorted that maybe Viridovix was so ashamed Hortensius Novus died after one of his meals, he committed suicide – '

'Is that likely?'

'You met him!' Hyacinthus scoffed.

'Yes! Are the rest of you going to do anything about it?'

'If the freedmen say no, how can we? He was,' pointed out my companion dourly, 'just a slave!' So were his friends.

I chewed a fingernail. 'The Praetor who is investigating what happened to Novus ought to hear of this!'

Hyacinthus scuffled to his feet in the loose earth. 'Forget that, Falco! The Praetor has a large loan underwritten by Crepito; he is bound to co-operate. The family want Novus buried quietly – and no other distractions.'

'I thought they wanted to protect his interests? I thought that was why they hired me!'

Hyacinthus looked shamefaced. 'I could never understand why they chose you,' he let slip. 'You had a reputation for bungling . . .'

'Oh thanks!' I bit back an oath. Then I spat it out after all. It was one of my brother's: particularly colourful: the slave looked impressed. 'If they believed that, why commission me?'

'Perhaps they thought you would be cheap.'

160

'Then perhaps that was just one of their mistakes!'

I remembered Helena saying that what impressed these ghastly people was expense.

Even without seeing the body I shared the runabout's doubts about the cook's death. 'Viridovix was poisoned too,' I said. 'Though not with the same violent paralytic that dispatched Novus. 'You saw both corpses afterwards: do you agree?' The runabout nodded. I made up my mind. 'I needed to talk to Viridovix in more detail about yesterday afternoon. Now he's gone, can you possibly find me someone observant who would have been in the kitchens while the food for the dinner party was being prepared?'

He looked uncertain. I reminded him that no one else would lift a finger to avenge the cook's death. Fellow feelings made him promise to find someone who would help. I told him my new address. Then, since he was growing anxious about being seen here with me, I let him scamper back to the house.

I sat on under the tree, thinking about the man from Gaul. I had liked him. He accepted his fate but kept his own style. He had integrity. He was dignified.

I thought about him for a long time. I owed him that.

He had definitely been murdered. It must have been a slower poison than the one which struck down Novus, a less vicious kind. Presumably this too was intended for Novus – thought I could not rule out the possibility he was not the only victim hoped for.

Nor could I yet be certain that the same person had prepared both poisons. Or why at least two different attempts had been made; insurance, possibly. But I did know how the second drug was administered; that would haunt me for a long time. The poison must have been among the bitter-smelling spices which the cook took in his cup of Falernian.

I still remembered how I mixed the wine for him: I had killed Viridovix myself.

XL

As I rode the hired mule south again, part of me was now saying this case would not be over until I had solved it, even if I had to work without a fee. That was the brave and noble part. Another part (thinking of Viridovix) merely felt sordid and tired.

I went home. There was no point going anywhere else. In particular, there was no point tangling with Severina Zotica until I had some unbreakable hold over that freckled female snake.

Half an hour later she knocked on my door. I was thinking. To help, I was doing something practical.

'Holiday, Falco?'

'Mending a chair.' I was in a pedantic, bad-tempered mood.

She stared at the battered wicker article, which had a semicircular back curving into boudoir arms. 'That's a woman's chair.'

'Maybe when I've mended the chair I'll get a woman to go with it.'

The redhead smiled nervously.

She was wearing not black exactly, but some dark purple berry-juice shade; in her unconventional way this managed to imply greater respect for the dead than Pollia and Atilia had shown with all their yardage of dramatic white.

I continued my work. The job had turned into one of those treasures where you start off intending to wind back a few strands of loose material, but end up dismantling half the piece of furniture and rebuilding it from scratch. I had already spent two hours on it.

To fend off Severina's annoying curiosity I snapped, 'The chair comes from my sister Galla. My mother produced some new cane. It's a pig of a job. And all the time I'm doing it I know that once Galla sees the thing serviceable, she will coo "*Ooh, Marcus, you are clever!*" – and ask to have her chair back again.'

'You have the cane too dry,' Severina informed me. 'You ought to dampen it with a sponge – '

162

'I can manage without advice.' The cane I was weaving snapped, halfway along a row. I fetched a wet sponge.

Severina found herself a stool. 'You go to a lot of trouble.'

'Thoroughness pays.'

She sat quiet, waiting for me to calm down. I had no intention of obliging. 'An aedile came to see me today, on behalf of the Pincian Hill magistrate.'

I negotiated a tough end change, tugging at the cane to keep the work taut. 'No doubt you bamboozled him.' I repositioned the chair between my knees.

'I answered his questions.'

'And he blithely went away?'

Severina looked prim. 'Perhaps *some* people can see that without a motive, accusing me is illogical.'

'Perhaps the Praetor likes a holiday in August.' I soothed my aching fingers on the wet sponge. 'Anyway, here's another bonus: so long as you can fend off this aedile of his, no one else will bother you.'

'What?'

I got up from my knees, righted the chair, and sat in it. That put me higher than her slight, neat, shawl-wrapped figure as she still hugged her knees on my stool. 'I'm off the case, Zotica. Pollia and Atilia have dispensed with my services.'

'Stupid of them!' Severina said. 'Anyone who cared about Novus would have let you carry on.'

'They always did seem strangely half-hearted.'

'I'm not surprised.' I suppressed any reaction. Whatever was to follow could only mean trouble. Still, with Severina that was nothing new. 'The fact they have dismissed you,' she continued, 'proves everything I say.'

'How's that?'

'Pollia and Atilia hired you to throw suspicion on me.'

'Why?'

'To disguise their own ambitions.'

'What ambitions would those be?'

Severina took a deep breath. 'There was serious friction between the three freedmen. Crepito and Felix disagreed with the way Novus handled their business affairs. Novus hated trouble, and wanted to end the partnership.'

Much as I distrusted her, this reminded me what Viridovix had

163

said about sensing disagreement among the freedman following their dinner. 'The other two would lose badly if he broke with them?'

'Novus had always been the leader; he had all the initiative and ideas.'

'So he would take a large sector of their business away with him?'

'Exactly. Meeting me had not improved matters; if he married – especially if we had children – his present heirs would suffer.'

'Felix and Crepito?'

'Felix, and Crepito's son. Atilia is obsessive about the boy; she was relying on an inheritance to found the child's career.'

'What about Pollia?'

'Pollia wants to plunder her husband's share of the cash.'

What she said was making sense. I hated that: having established in my own mind that Severina was a villainess, I could not bring myself to readjust. 'Are you claiming that the freedmen, or their wives, would go so far as to kill Novus?'

'Maybe they were all in it together.'

'Don't judge other people by your own perverted standards! But I have to agree, the timing of the murder – when you and Novus had just announced the date of your wedding – does look significant.'

Severina clapped her small white hands triumphantly. 'But it's worse than that: I told you Novus had enemies.' She had told me a number of things that were probably lies. I laughed. 'Listen to me, Falco!' I made a small gesture of apology, yet she kept me in suspense for a moment, sulkily.

'What enemies?'

'Apart from Crepito and Felix, he had also antagonised Appius Priscillus.

'Do I gather *he* runs a rival organisation with overlapping interests? Tell me about that, Severina. What was the form at last night's dinner?'

'A reconciliation; I've already told you. It was Priscillus I tried to warn you about before.'

'He was threatening Novus?'

'Novus, and the other two as well. That was why Atilia hardly lets her son out of her sight – one of the threats was to abduct him.' I knew Atilia took the child to school herself, which was highly unusual.

'So which of these multiple suspects are you fingering?' I asked sarcastically.

'That's the problem – I just don't know. Falco, what would you say if I asked to hire you myself?'

I'd call for help, probably. 'Frankly the last thing I want is a commission from a professional bride – especially when she's midway between husbands, and tends to react unpredictably – '

'You mean what nearly happened last night?' Severina coloured.

'We can both forget last night.' My voice sounded lower than I had intended. I noticed that she started slightly, so her shawl slipped back, revealing her flame-coloured hair. 'We were drunk.' Severina gave me a straighter look than I liked.

'Will you work for me?' she insisted.

'I'll think about it.'

'That means no.'

'It means I'll think about it!'

At that moment I was ready to throw the gold-digger downstairs. (In fact I was in two minds whether to give up my career altogether, hire a booth and take up chair mending . . .)

There was a knock; Severina must have left my outer door ajar, and before I could answer it was pushed open. A man staggered in, gasping. His predicament was clear.

He had just struggled up two flights of stairs – to deliver the biggest fish I ever saw.

165

XLI

I stood up. Very slowly.

'Where do you want him, legate?' He was a small man. As he lurched in from the corridor he was holding my present up by its mouth because he could not get his arms round it: the fish looked almost as long as its deliverer was tall. It was wider than he was.

'Slap him down here . . .'

The man groaned, leaned back, then launched the fish sideways so it landed across the small table I used to lean my elbows on sometimes. Then, being a game trier, he jumped up and down, each time hauling my slippery present further on. Severina bobbed upright, daunted by a tailfin the size of an ostrich feather fan, which stuck over the edge of the table a foot from her nose.

There was no smell. He was in beautiful condition.

The delivery man seemed to take sufficient pleasure from the drama his arrival had caused – but I decided for once to squeeze out the half-aureus I kept in my tunic for really serious gratuities.

'Thanks, legate! Enjoy your party . . .' He left, with a much lighter step than when he came.

'Party?' hinted Severina, looking coy. 'Are you going to invite me?'

I felt so weak I might have let her persuade me. It would have created a Mount Olympus of complications for myself.

Then the door swung open a second time, to admit someone who never reckoned to knock if there was half a chance of interrupting something scandalous. 'Hello Mother!' I cried valiantly.

Ma raked Severina Zotica with the look she reserved for unpleasant squashy things found at the back of dark kitchen shelves. Then she glanced at my extravagant present. 'That fishmonger of yours needs a talking-to! When did you start buying by the yard?'

'Must be a mix-up: all I ordered was a cuttlefish.'

'That's you all over. Palace ideas on pigsty money . . . You'll want a big plate!'

I sighed. 'I can't keep this, Ma. I'd better send him as a gift to Camillus Verus; do myself some good that way – '

'It's one way to show your respect for the Senator . . . Pity. I could have made a good stock from the bones.' My mother was still blocking Severina out of the conversation, but letting her know that I had influential friends. Redheads always upset my mother. And she generally disapproved of my female clients.

Ma made herself scarce so I could rid us of this inconvenience. 'Severina, I'll have to think about your offer.'

'Will you have to ask your mother?' she sniped.

'No; I have to consult my barber, look up the "black days" on my calendar, sacrifice a beautiful virgin, and peruse the internal organs of a sheep with twisted horns . . . I know where I can get the sheep, but virgins are harder to come by and my barber's out of town. Give me twenty-four hours.' She wanted to argue, but I gestured at the turbot so she could see that I was serious about having things to organise.

My mother promptly reappeared, stepping out of Severina's way with insulting delicacy. Severina retaliated by giving me a much sweeter smile than usual before she closed the door behind her.

'Watch that one!' muttered Ma.

Ma and I gazed sadly at the giant fish.

'I'm bound to regret giving him away.'

'You'll never get another!'

'I'm itching to keep him – but how could I cook him?'

'Oh I dare say we can improvise . . .'

'Camillus Verus is never going to approve of me, anyway – '

'No,' agreed Ma, obliquely. 'You could invite him to eat some of it.'

'Not here!'

'Invite Helena then.'

'Helena won't come.'

'She never will if nobody asks her! Have you upset her?'

'Why do you assume it's my fault? We had a few words.'

'You never change! . . . So that's settled,' decided my mother. 'Just a family party. Mind you,' she added, in case this news had somehow cheered me up, 'I always reckon turbot is a tasteless fish.'

XLII

Sometimes I feared my mother must have led a double life. I resisted the thought, because that is not what a decent Roman boy wants to suspect about the woman who gave him birth.

'Where on earth have you eaten turbot?'

'Your Uncle Fabius caught one once.' That made sense. No one in our family had the nous to present a turbot to the Emperor; anything my relations got their hands on went straight in the pot. 'It was a baby. Nowhere near as big as this.'

'If Fabius caught it, that was predictable!' Everything about Uncle Fabius was small: a family joke.

'You don't want him bitter. I'll take out the gills for you,' volunteered mother.

I let her. She liked to delude herself I still needed looking after. Besides, I enjoyed the thought of my tiny, elderly mother laying into something quite that big.

Ideally I would bake him in an oven. That called for a clay pot (no time to have one made), then entrusting him to the dopey rakemen at some public bakery. I could have built my own oven, but apart from having to lug the bricks home I was frightened of the fire risk and strongly suspected that any structure big enough to contain this turbot might cause my floor to cave in.

I decided to poach him. Flatfish only need gentle simmering. I would have to find a huge pan, but for that I had had an idea. In the roof space at my mother's house, where members of the family stored unattractive New Year gifts, was a huge oval shield which my late brother Festus brought home. It was made of some bronzed alloy, and Festus maintained it was a pricey Peloponnesian antique. I upset him by swearing it had to be Celtic – which meant it was just another cheap souvenir my daft brother had won in a bet or picked up on the quay at Ostia. Festus would have been even more annoyed at me turning his dusty prize into a monstrous fishkettle.

I nipped off to mother's. When I clambered up to get the shield I found a nest of mice in one end, but I tipped them out and said nothing. The handle inside had already lost one securing bolt when Festus was larking about; the other was rusted fast with verdigris but I managed to shear it off (cutting open a few knuckles). The pointed boss on the front might cause problems. I reckoned I could suspend the shield on two or three steaming pans of water over braziers and just keep the fish going if I heated his liquor first. I spent an hour burnishing the metal, washed it at a public fountain, then carried it home. It was indeed big enough for the turbot – but too shallow. I put him in, filled up with water, and found it reached the rim of the shield before it fully covered the fish. The scalding stock would swoosh about. And turning the turbot over half-way through cooking time might be difficult . . .

As usual my mother let me devise my own solution, then sat at home brooding how my brilliant plan would fail. While I was still staring at the half-covered fish in the shield she rattled into my apartment, almost invisible under a huge copper washtub from Lenia's laundry yard. We tried not to think what might have been trampled clean in it. 'I gave it a good scrub . . .' The tub was shorter than the Celtic shield, but the turbot could be crammed in diagonally if I turned up his great triangular head and his tail. Ma had also brought some cabbage nets to lift him out after he turned gelatinous.

Now I was ready.

I invited my mother, my best friend Petronius and Petro's wife Silvia, with a couple of my relatives. At least my family was so large that nobody could expect me to entertain the entire tribe at once. I chose Maia, to thank her for the betting-token feat, and Junia, to repay her for the bed. I did not invite my brothers-in-law, but they came anyway.

I told the guests they could arrive early, since watching the fish cooked would be part of the fun. None of them needed encouragement. They all turned up before I had time to look out a clean tunic or go for a bathe. I let them wander about criticising my new quarters and rearranging my personal property, while I worried over the fish.

I was planning for us to eat in the room I had earmarked as my office, but they all brought their stools and crowded into the living room, where they could get in my way and clammer advice.

'What stock are you using, Marcus?'

'Just water with wine and bay leaves; I don't want to destroy the natural flavour; it's supposed to be delicate –'

169

'You ought to add a dash of fish pickle – Maia, shouldn't he add fish pickle?'

'I reckon he ought to cook it in the sauce –'

'No; the sauce will be handled separately –'

'You're going to regret that, Marcus! Is it Saffron or Onion?'

'Caraway.'

'Caraway? Ooh! Marcus is making a Caraway Sauce –'

In the midst of this babble, I was pestling the herbs for my sauce (should have been lovage but Maia had thought I asked her to bring parsley; should have included thyme but I had left my pot at Fountain Court). Someone knocked; Petronius answered the door for me. 'Camillus Verus has sent you a reading couch – where do you want it?' Petro bawled. I wanted the couch in my office, but that was where I had laid out everything for our meal (everything that had not yet been removed again by my visitors). 'Shall we stick it in your bedroom?'

'Not enough space; try the empty one opposite –' One of my braziers flared up dangerously, so I had to leave him to it.

My mother and Junia had chosen this moment to hang up door curtains for me, so I could not see out into the corridor for their arms waving amongst folds of striped material. Both my brothers-in-law had involved themselves in banging up nails to carry the lintel string; the simple task of putting up a straight line had developed into a major surveying project. Whatever was happening in the rest of the house I could hear distressing indications of damage to both my doorframes and Petronius' good temper, but the liquor for my fish was beginning to sizzle on the sides of the washtub so I had to ignore the raised voices outside. I was red-faced from stabilising a brazier beneath the weight of the hot washcopper; I had just heaved up the turbot into my arms to introduce him to the pan when I heard Maia shriek, 'Sorry; this is a private family party; Didius Falco is not on call to clients –'

There was an uneasy lull. I turned round, fish and all. For one horrid moment I expected Severina, but it was far worse. Petronius, with desperate eyes, was shepherding someone in the doorway, someone who was a stranger to most of my family, but certainly not to me . . . Helena Justina.

For a moment she failed to grasp the situation. 'Marcus! I thought you must have been developing other interests, but I never expected to find you with your arms locked round a *fish* –'

Then the lull sank to a silence. And all the sparkle died in her

170

eyes, as Helena absorbed the houseful of merrymaking visitors, the fabulous gift I was cooking – and the fact that I had not invited her.

XLIII

After five years in the Aventine watch Petronius had a keen eye for trouble. 'Someone take hold of the man's fish for him!'

My sister Maia leapt to her feet and grappled with me for the turbot, but with the stubbornness of someone in shock I refused to let it go. 'This is Helena,' Petronius announced to everybody helpfully. He had planted himself behind her to stop her backing out. She and I were both helpless. I did not want to talk to her in front of other people. With people watching, Helena would not speak to me.

I gripped the fish like a drowning sailor clutching a spar. It was all my fault as usual, but it was Helena who looked horrified. She struggled against the avuncular arm which Petronius had slung round her. 'Marcus, Helena came to supervise the delivery of your reading couch – Helena,' Petronius battled on, 'Marcus has been presented with a wonderful treat from Titus – are you going to stay and dine with us?'

'Not where I am not invited!'

'You are always invited,' I spoke up at last unconvincingly.

'It's considered convenient to tell people!'

'Then I'm telling you now –'

'That's gracious of you, Marcus!'

With the strength of the tipsy, Maia dragged the turbot away from me. Before I could stop her she placed him on the edge of the copper, over which he slipped as gracefully as a state barge on its maiden trip. A tide of scented water surged over the opposite edge making all the braziers crackle; members of my family cheered.

Maia sat down looking proud of her efforts. My brothers-in-law started passing round the wine I intended for later. The turbot was safe temporarily but he had started to cook, before I had time to count the spoons, thicken the sauce, change my tunic – or reconcile the girl I had insulted so appallingly. Petronius Longus was fussing over her, trying to apologise for me, but with a final effort Helena forced herself free. 'Marcus will see you out –' he got in hopefully.

'Marcus has to cook his fish!'

Helena disappeared.

The water in the fish copper boiled.

'*Leave it!*' squealed Maia, fighting me over the braziers.

My mother, who had been sitting in silence, pushed us both aside with a mutinous growl. 'We can look after it – *go on!*'

I rushed out into the corridor: empty.

I threw open the outer door: no one on the stairs.

With my heart bumping angrily I ran back inside, and glanced in the other rooms. Alongside the Senator's reading couch in the cubicle I never used stood a trunk I had seen Helena travel with . . . *Oh Jupiter.* I guessed what *that* meant.

Petronius had cornered her in my bedroom. Helena was normally so resilient he seemed more upset than she was. I strode in, to his immense relief. 'Would you like us all to leave?' I shook my head vigorously (thinking of the fish). Petronius slunk away.

I placed myself between Helena and the door. She stood shaking with anger, or possibly distress. 'Why didn't you invite me?'

'I thought you wouldn't come!' Her face was white, and tense, and miserable. I hated myself for making her hate me. 'I was still waiting for you to contact me. You obviously didn't want to. Helena, I could not face staring at the door all evening, waiting for you –'

'Well, I came anyway!' she retorted crisply. 'And now I suppose I'm expected to say "Oh that's just Marcus!" the way your family do!' I let her rant. It did her good, and gave me time. I could see that she had completely despaired. That trunk of hers had told me why. Not only had I slapped her in the face; I did it on the very day she had decided to come and live with me . . . 'Don't try anything!' she warned me, as I started walking towards her. 'I cannot deal with this any longer, Marcus –'

I put both hands on her shoulders; she braced herself against the weight. 'My darling, I do know –' I pulled her towards me. She resisted, but not hard enough.

'Marcus, I cannot bear seeing you go away and never knowing if I shall ever see you come back –'

I gathered her closer. 'I'm here –'

'Let me go, Marcus.' Helena was leaning away from me; I must have stunk of uncooked fish.

'No; let me make things right –'

'I don't want you to!' she answered, in that same thin, despondent voice. 'Marcus, I don't want to be bamboozled by some clever piece of oratory. I don't want to co-operate in cheating myself. I don't want to hear you squirming, "*Helena Justina, I didn't invite you because I knew you were coming anyway; Helena, I'm letting you blame me because I deserve it*"–'

'I am sorry. Don't tell me I'm a bastard; I'll say it myself –' Helena nodded rapidly. 'I won't insult you by saying I love you, but I do, and you know it –'

'Oh stop pretending to be so strong and comforting!'

Grateful for the hint, I wrapped myself around her. 'Forget I've been cuddling a turbot; come here . . .'

Her face crumpled as she leaned against my fishy chest.

Maia poked her head in through the new door curtain, saw us and blushed. 'Shall we lay another bowl?'

'Yes,' I said without consulting Helena. Maia disappeared.

'No Marcus,' said Helena. 'I'll be friends; I cannot help it – but you will never make me stay!'

She had no time to finish. Before she could demolish me utterly, someone else started banging at my door. Petro would go. I could imagine his dread in case he found another girlfriend smirking on the threshold . . . I grimaced at Helena and started off to assist. Before I reached the doorway he burst in.

'There's a panic on, Marcus; can you come?' My quiet friend looked highly excited. 'It's a posse of damned Praetorians! Only Mars knows what they are after – but apparently you asked Titus to bring his dinner napkin, to sample your fish . . .'

This had all the makings of a social disaster.

I winked at Helena. 'Well! Are you just going to stand there looking beautiful – or are you going to rally round?'

XLIV

She saved me. She had to. She was a girl with a conscience. She would not risk exposing Titus Caesar to embarrassment from a clutch of raucous plebians. Helena ground her teeth, I grinned at her – and for one night at least I had a senator's daughter to act as my social hostess. I did not expect her to be able to cook, but she knew how to supervise.

The members of my family saw no reason to alter the habits of a lifetime just because I had produced an Imperial guest. Titus had already edged in, looking startled, before Helena and I could emerge with the kind of refined welcome he had learned to expect. My relations immediately grabbed him and sat him on a stool with a bowl of olives on one knee, to watch his turbot cooking. Next thing I knew, everyone seemed to have introduced themselves without waiting for me, Helena was testing the fish with a knife-point, Petronius shoved a full winecup under my elbow, and the chaos redoubled while I stood there like a drowned vole in a thunderstorm.

After five minutes and a cup of inferior Campanian wine, Titus had grasped the house rules and joined in with the rabble shouting advice. None of my family was snobbish; they accepted him as one of us. Most of them were much more curious about the superior young lady whose sweet-scented head was bent close to mine over my makeshift cooking pot.

The Praetorians had to wait outside. Luckily, when the Didius women bring bread rolls for a party they supply enough to send out several basketfuls if any high-ranking visitor happens to bring his bodyguard.

'What kind of sauce?' Helena murmured, dipping in her finger.

'Caraway.'

'It hardly tastes.' I was looking up the recipe – one I once stole from Helena herself. She peered over my shoulder and spotted her own handwriting. 'You ruffian! . . . It says a scruple; I'll put more – did you squash them?'

175

'Have you tried grinding caraway seeds? They sit there and laugh at you.'

She tipped in more from the bag. 'Don't crowd me; I'm doing this!'

'You're the staff; I'm the chef – I'll get the blame.' I sampled it myself. 'Rasps a bit!'

'That's the mustardseed and peppercorns.'

'Stir in a spoonful of honey while I make the thickening –'

'This man is good!' cried Titus; the kind of guest I like.

'My younger brother is extremely self-sufficient,' Junia boasted complacently. (Junia had always cursed me as an incompetent clown.) I caught Helena's eye. My sister Junia took great pride in her civilised behaviour and good taste; somehow at any family gathering she seemed stiff and out of place. I was pleased to detect it was Maia the madcap whom Helena already liked best.

It took four of us to transfer the fish from his bath. I hooked up the cabbage nets on the end of a spoon; the cooked turbot proved firm enough for us to ease him out whole, then swing the cradle onto my brother's Celtic shield which Petronius was holding. As we fiddled about removing the nets, the heat of the fish, conducted through the metal shield with amazing rapidity, was burning his arms. When he complained we told him it was a test of character.

'Be careful of the prong on the underside!'

'Gods, Marcus; have I got to hold up the fish tray all evening? How can I put this thing down with a spike underneath?'

My brother-in-law Gaius Baebius, the customs clerk, stepped forward. Gaius Baebius (who would not dream of being mentioned in somebody's memoirs by less than two of his names) silently swung an iron cauldron onto the table top. Petro dropped the boss into the pot, which supported the shield quite steadily; Gaius Baebius had created a two-piece comport of some style.

My brother-in-law must have been secretly planning this coup since he got here. What a creep.

The turbot looked wonderful.

'Oh Marcus, well done!' Helena cried – almost letting some affection show.

Now the company had expanded, there were the usual party problems: not enough dishes and not enough seats. Titus pretended he did not mind squatting on the floor with his dinner served up on a lettuce leaf, but with my mother present better standards were required. While Mama took a carving knife to the turbot I sent Maia, who had no inhibitions after wine on an empty stomach, rushing off to knock up my neighbours and demand a loan of extra stools and bowls. 'Most of the other apartments are empty, Marcus; your block is a sanctuary for ghosts! I cadged these for you off an old lady upstairs – do you know who I mean?' I knew.

Remembering what the pretentious Hortensius family served up to Priscillus at *their* dinner party, you may like to know the menu I produced at *mine:*

FISH SUPPER AT THE HOUSE OF M. DIDIUS FALCO

Salad

The Turbot
More Salad

Fruit

Plain – but none of it was poisoned, I could guarantee.

We did have an exquisite wine which Petronius had brought (he told me what it was, but I forgot). And perhaps I exaggerate. My mother's brothers were all market gardeners so our family's idea of a salad had never been just a sliced hard-boiled egg on a bunch of endive leaves. Even my three uninvited sisters sent contributions to make me feel guilty; we had a large tray of white cheeses, plus cold sausage and a bucket of oysters to gobble with the basic greenery. There was food flowing out of the doors – literally, since Junia enjoyed herself more than once taking dishes down to our guest of honour's loitering Praetorians.

Everyone told me the turbot was delicious. As the cook, I was too busy worrying to taste it myself. The Caraway Sauce must have been an effective side dish, since when I looked round for it the serving jug had been scraped bare. By the time I sat down to eat, the only space was in the corridor. There was so much noise my head ached. Nobody bothered to talk to me since I was merely a tired scullion. I could see my mother squashed in a corner with Petro and his wife, discussing their offspring, probably. My brothers-in-law just ate and drank, or farted surreptitiously. Maia had the hiccups, which was hardly surprising. Junia was taking pains to look after His Caesarship, which he tolerated pleasantly – though he appeared much more taken with Helena Justina.

Helena's dark eyes constantly watched over my guests; she and Maia were doing good work for me, nudging along the conversation and passing round the food. Helena was beyond my reach. If I called out she would never hear me. I wanted to thank her. I wanted to go across and fetch her, then take her to one of my empty rooms and make passionate love until neither of us could move . . .

'Where did you find *her*?' squealed Maia's voice behind my right ear, as she lurched up to spoon more of the glutinous turbot onto my plate.

'She found me, I think . . .'

'Poor girl, she adores you!'

I felt like a man stumbling out of the desert. 'Why's that?'

'The way she looks at you!' giggled Maia, the only one of my sisters who was actually fond of me.

I toyed with my second helping. Then across the hubbub of eight people talking at once Helena raised her head, and noticed me watching her. Her face had always contained a mixture of intelligence and character which jolted me. She smiled slightly. A private signal between us, to tell me everybody was enjoying my party; then a shared moment of stillness after that.

Titus Caesar bent sideways to say something to Helena; she was answering him in the quiet way she conversed with people publicly – nothing like the tyrant who trampled over me. Titus seemed to admire her as much as I did. Somebody should tell him that when an Emperor's son indulges himself with a visitation to a poor man's house, he could eat the fish and swig the wine and leave his guards outside to amaze the neighbours – but he should draw the line at flirting with the poor man's girl . . . He had effortlessly impressed all my relations. I hated him for his happy Flavian skill at mucking in.

'Cheer up!' someone chaffed me, the way people do.

Helena Justina appeared to be lecturing Titus; she glanced at me, so I realised I was the subject. Helena must be attacking him over the way the Palace treated me. I winked at him; he smiled back sheepishly.

My sister Junia squeezed past me on her way somewhere. She tossed a glance at Helena. 'Idiot! You must be heading for a tumble there!' she chortled, not bothering to wait and see if I was upset.

Once again I was the typical host: tired and left out. My fish had gone cold while I brooded. I noticed glumly that where my landlord had had a wall replastered it must have dried out and now there was a crack the whole length of the corridor, wide enough to insert my thumb. So here I was, presiding over an ideal Roman evening: a tasteful dinner for my family, friends, and a patron I respected. Here I was feeling depressed and with a dry mouth; insulted by my sister; watching a handsome Caesar attempt to capture my girlfriend; and knowing that when everyone else reeled off cheerfully, the debris they left behind would take me hours to tidy up.

One good feature of my family was that once they had eaten and drunk everything they could get their hands on, they vanished speedily. My mother, with the excuse of her age, was leaving first, though not before Petro's wife Silvia had shrieked to prevent Titus from helpfully throwing away the turbot remains. Of course Ma had fixed on carrying off the skeleton and the jelly from the serving tray for stock. Petronius and Silvia were taking my mother home (with her bucket of bones). Titus remembered to say something complimentary to her about Festus (who had served under Titus in Judaea). Still reeling from his near disaster with the fish tray his honour decided it would be tactful if he left too. He had already thanked me and was taking Helena lightly by the hand.

'Camillus Verus' daughter has been defending your interests, Falco!' I wondered if he had heard that my relationship with Helena was more than professional; and if he knew how intensely I was trying to keep her here. He appeared unaware of it. A smooth operator, this one.

I shook my head at her gently. 'I thought we agreed: your role here tonight was to pass round the olives nicely and to count up the winecups before anybody left!'

Titus was offering Helena transport home.

'Thank you, sir,' she responded in her firm style. 'Didius Falco has a commission to look after me –' (I used to be her bodyguard.) Titus tried to insist. 'He needs the money!' she hissed, quite openly.

Titus laughed. 'Oh I'll give him the money –'

'No use, sir,' Helena quipped. 'Without the work he won't take any payment – you know how touchy Falco is!'

But she was a senator's daughter. I had no public claim on her. It was impossible to cause the Emperor's son offence by quarrelling on the doorstep over a matter of simple etiquette, so finally I lost Helena among the noisy throng which was escorting Titus downstairs to the street.

It was rude of me, but I felt so depressed I stayed upstairs. Once my relatives had trampled down three flights to the thoroughfare and waved my Imperial visitor back to the Palatine, they saw no reason to march back up again, merely to say goodbye to me. They went home. The respectable citizens of the Piscina Publica must have winced at the racket as they left.

The apartment was dismally quiet. I braced myself for a long night clearing up. I flipped some strands of watercress into a rubbish pail, straightened a couple of cups lethargically, then collapsed on a bench in the traditional manner of a weary host, as I stared at the mess.

A door closed behind me. Someone with gentle fingers and a delicate sense of timing tickled my neck. I bent forwards to give her more scope. 'Is that you?'

'It's me.' A girl with a conscience. Naturally she had stayed behind me to help me wash the plates.

XLV

I should have expected it. The real question was, whether I could persuade her to stay with me afterwards.

I decided to do the housework first, and the hard stuff when I was too tired to feel any pain.

Helena and I made a useful team. I could square up to hard work. She was fastidious, but shrank from nothing that needed to be done. 'Which end of the street is the midden?' Grasping two disagreeable slop buckets she paused in the outer doorway.

'Stand them out on the landing tonight. The neighbourhood seems peaceful, but never take the risk in the dark.' Helena was sensible, but there were a lot of things I needed to teach her about plebian domestic life.

Still from the corridor she called, 'Marcus, have you seen this crack in your wall? Is it structural?'

'Probably!'

We finished in the end. The smell of fish still pervaded the house but everything was clean except the floor, which I could wash down tomorrow. 'Thanks; you're a gem.'

'I quite enjoyed it.'

'I enjoy knowing it's finished! There's a difference, my love, between doing the work of twenty servants once for fun – and doing it every day.' I sat for some minutes, polishing my good bronze spoons; taking my time. 'Something you're not telling me?' Helena said nothing. 'You might as well spill it: you've run away from home.' Even when we were on the best of terms she grew restless if I seemed to understand her private motives too well. In fact with Helena, nudging her into opening up had always been part of the challenge. She scowled. I scowled back at her. 'I am a professional informer, Helena – I can decipher clues! As well as your father's reading couch, there's a box here with your second-best dress and your life savings –'

'I'm wearing my second-best dress,' she contradicted me. 'The box is for the title deeds from my Aunt Valeria's legacy –'

When I fall in love as heavily as I had done with Helena Justina, I soon enquire what I have let myself in for. I knew her aunt's Sabine farm was a fraction of Helena's portfolio. I knew Helena too; it sounded as if she was deliberately turning her back on any income which her father had allowed her.

'Fallen out with your family?'

'If I'm disgracing myself I cannot take family property.'

'That bad, is it?' I frowned. Helena was not the usual spoiled society kitten, stamping her foot and demanding the freedom to be scandalous. She loved her family. She would hate upsetting them. I was none too keen on having persuaded her to do it – then letting her down.

She surprised me by trying to explain: 'I'm twenty-three; I have been married and divorced; but it *is* a disgrace to leave my parents' house – I simply cannot settle down at home any more.' There was a difference between running away from the conventional life of a dutiful daughter and running to me. Which was this?

'They trying to make you marry again? Some stiff-backed senatorial stripe?'

'Now you live here,' she suggested (ignoring the question), '*I* could take over your old apartment –'

'Not on your own.'

'I'm not afraid!'

'Then you ought to be. Fountain Court frightened me.'

'I'm sorry,' Helena said glumly. 'I should have let Titus take me home –'

'To Hades with Titus.' We had an unfinished quarrel, which was impeding a sensible decision here. If we started fighting at this time of night, the results might be disastrous. 'If you want to go, *I'll* take you home. But tell me first what you were coming here to say.' She closed her eyes wearily, blocking me out. 'Helena, you owe me that!'

'I wanted to ask if there was still a vacancy for a girl to take messages.'

'For the right applicant.' She said nothing, but she looked at me again. 'Stay here tonight and think about it,' I said quietly. 'I'll give you a good home. I'd hate to find you sleeping rough in temple doorways and begging coppers from passers-by at the Probus Bridge!' Helena was still uncertain. 'We have a bed and a couch; you can choose; I'm not asking you to share with me.'

'You have the bed,' Helena said.

'All right. Don't worry; I can keep my hands off you.' Luckily I was exhausted, or that might not have been true. I heaved myself upright. 'In my bedroom there's a wicker chair begging for an owner. Here's a lamp; here's some warm water you can take to wash. Is that enough?'

She nodded and left me.

We had achieved something. I was not certain what. But Helena Justina had taken a huge step – and I would have to see it through with her.

Restless, I tried to scrub the fishiness off myself, then pottered about like a regular householder: fixing shutters; dousing braziers; feeling big. Now that I had Helena to look after, I locked the outer door. I was not sure whether this was to keep out cat burglars, or keep Helena in.

I whistled as a warning, then went in, carrying two beakers of warm honey drink. Lamplight flickered in the draught I caused. Helena was curled up on her father's couch, plaiting her hair. With Galla's chair and Helena's box and other things, the little room looked cosy; it felt right. 'I brought you a drink. Anything else you need?' *Me, for instance?* She shook her head apprehensively.

I put her beaker where she could reach it, then shuffled towards the door. 'I usually add cloves, but tell me if you don't like it and I'll leave them out next time.'

'Marcus, you look unhappy. Is it my fault?'

'I think it's the case.'

'What's wrong?'

'That freedman was murdered despite my pitiful efforts. His cook is dead too – and it's partly my fault. I have to decide tomorrow what I want to do.'

'Will you tell me about it?'

'Tonight?'

Helena Justina smiled at me. Taking an interest would be part of her new role. She intended to ask constant questions, vet my clients, interfere . . . I could handle that. Fighting over my work with Helena would be glorious. Her smile grew; she had seen my grin. I sat in Galla's chair, balanced my hot drink on my knee, and finally told Helena everything that had happened since we last had a chance to talk.

Almost everything. Being nearly seduced by Severina seemed not worth mentioning. 'Is that all?' Helena asked.

'First the Hortensius women hired me to entrap Severina. Now they've dumped me, and *she* wants me to indict *them* . . .'

Helena considered my options while I gazed fondly at her. 'Pollia and Atilia have excluded you from the Hortensius house, which is a blow. I think you should accept Severina as a client. If she is innocent, what's to lose? And if she's guilty it gives you more chance to prove it and do right by your late friend the cook. Besides,' Helena concluded, 'Severina has to pay you if you work for her.'

'Can't object to that!' I did not mention my fear that the gold-digger might be expecting to pay me in kind.

'Feel better?'

'Mmm. Thanks. I'll go and see Severina tomorrow.' Time for bed. 'Also, daughter of Camillus Verus, I must call on your noble papa to explain how I have dishonoured you –'

'No case to answer! I dishonoured myself.'

'Your father may quibble. A scruff who lures off a senator's daughter is held to have injured her father's good name.'

Helena dismissed it: 'Any father should be proud to discover his daughter dines on turbot with the elder son of the Emperor as her fellow guest.'

'Sweetheart, sometimes in the Falco house, we do not dine at all!' She was looking tired. I picked up the lamp. Our eyes met. I walked to the doorway. 'I won't kiss you goodnight. But that's only because if I did, I could not trust myself to stop.'

'Marcus, at the moment I cannot tell what I want –'

'No. But it's plain what you *don't* want –' She started to speak but I hushed her. 'The first rule of this household is, don't argue with the master; however, I expect you to break that.' I quenched the lamp. Under cover of darkness I added, 'The second rule is, be kind to him because he loves you.'

'I can do that. What else?'

'Nothing. That's all. Except, Helena Justina – welcome to my house!'

XLVI

Severina spotted the change in me immediately. 'What happened to you?'

'A good dinner last night.' Since relations with Helena were on such a tentative basis, I had decided to keep news of my lodger to myself. Anyway, vetting clients might be Helena's business but Helena Justina's position was no concern of my clients.

'Is that all?' Severina demanded jealously. The words sounded familiar.

I told her I was accepting her commission. I would investigate two avenues: relations between the Hortensius and Priscillus empires, and the exact details of the dinner the night Novus died. She asked if she could assist, and looked surprised when I said no. 'You were a suspect, Zotica. Best stand back.'

'Well, if I think of anything helpful I can call in at your apartment –'

'No, don't do that. I let one of my rooms to a subtenant, whom I don't trust alone with female visitors. I'll come to you.'

'I want to know what you are doing though –'

'You will!' I already had to explain my every move to Helena. One overseer was enough.

Severina's light eyes flickered. 'What made up your mind to help me?'

'I hate unfinished business.'

I was on my way out. 'Going so soon?' She followed me. 'You are my only hope now, Falco,' she said clingingly. 'Everyone distrusts me –'

I fixed her with a playful finger, squashing the tip of her small freckled nose. 'Not when I've proved your innocence.' Now she was paying for the privilege, I let myself sound protective. In fact the pose was so convincing I startled myself. Even half a commitment from Helena had made me feel light-hearted. 'By the way; are you still trying to find your parrot a new home? I know someone who might like a pet for company.'

185

'Who's that?'

'Distant relative of mine.' Well, someone who might *become* a relative in some distant aeon. But actually I had reasons of my own for wanting the bird. 'I can't promise to make it permanent, but if you like I'll take Chloe on a month's trial . . .'

After I left I made a long detour riverwards, to drop in on Petronius Longus at the booth which the Aventine watch used as its lock-up and chophouse. It was full of his men, dicing and complaining about the government, so we sat outside watching the bumboats scull up the Tiber.

Petronius was my best friend, so telling *him* about Helena was obligatory. To forestall awkward jokes, I also had to mention that arrangements were slightly precarious. He shook his head, smiling into his hands. 'You two! You never do anything the easy way . . .'

'*Is* there an easy way for a plebian to entice away the daughter of a senator?'

'No one but you would try!'

He started to thank me for last evening but I cut him short. 'My pleasure; I owed you and Silvia hospitality – Petro, tell me, what's the word these days about the world of high-finance property?'

'Nothing unusual – all swindles, scams and harassment. You working on something?'

'Could be. Ever come across a shoal of real-estate predators by the name of Hortensius?' Petro shook his head. 'What about Appius Priscillus?'

'Oh I've heard of him! If you intend to go and see Priscillus, wear a peg on your nose.' I lifted an eyebrow quizzically. 'Everything he does stinks!'

'Any stink in particular?'

'I've never run across him myself, but I do know half the shop-keepers on the Via Ostiensis hide their heads in a cauldron at the mention of his name. Do you want some background? I can ask around.'

'Appreciated . . .'

'You're trying to net a big one, Falco!' Petro told me in a warning voice. Size as such – or even size as a measure of social status – never worried Petronius; he meant the man was dangerous.

Back home I found an immaculate factotum, with her nose in a scroll of poetry. She had been to the baths; the disturbing undernotes of some perfume I half disliked were filling the house. She gave me a swift sneer as if I had six legs and mandibles, then carried on brazenly skiving in office time.

I adopted a furtive whine. 'Falco live here?'

'On and off.' She refused to raise her well-groomed head from the scroll.

'Can you give him a message?'

'If I feel like it.'

'It's just that I might have a job for him – if he's not too particular.'

'Falco's not fussy.' She laughed bitterly.

'So what are his prices?' She looked up from her reading at last. 'No; don't tell them, fruit. The answer is *more than you can afford by the look of you!*'

'Why? I can tell them. I know what you charged me –'

'You were a beautiful woman and I wanted to impress you. I gave you special rates.'

'Specially dear, you mean!' Beneath the surface of this bonhomie I had been throwing out hard messages of domineering lust. Helena was starting to flounder. 'Am I doing this right?' she asked.

'Cut down on the friendliness! Clients only mean trouble. Why encourage them?'

'What's that fighting in the bag?'

I untied the string and Chloe hopped out angrily. *'Don't just stand there, woman,'* she cackled, *'give me a drink!'*

Helena was furious. 'Didius Falco, if you want to bring home presents, I draw the line at pets who answer back!'

'I wouldn't insult you! Job for you, my darling. I reckon this flying ferdango may give us a clue. It's female; name of Chloe; eats seeds, I'm told. As witnesses go she's the tricky kind, and thoroughly unreliable. Better keep her in a room with the shutter closed in case she tries to do a flit before she's squawked. I'll find you a slate – just write down anything she says.'

'What sort of clue am I listening for?' The parrot obliged with three words which are mostly seen on the walls of tavern latrines. 'It will be a pleasure!' Helena muttered rebelliously.

'Thanks, beloved! If you see the letting agent – name of Cossus – will you ask him to look at that crack for me?'

'I can tell him it's interfering with your plans for a thousand sesterces' wall painting of *Bellerophon and Pegasus*.'

'That should do the trick. Any questions, fruit?'

'Staying in for lunch?'

'Sorry; no time.'

'Where are you going?'

'Knocking on doors.'

'Who does the dinner?' She was a single-minded girl.

I dropped some money in a bowl. 'You buy it; I cook it; we eat it together while we talk about my day.'

I gave her a swift, chaste, parting kiss which left her unmoved but had a troublesome effect on me.

XLVII

The address I had for Appius Priscillus turned out to be a gloomy fortress on the Esquiline. This made him a close neighbour of the Praetor Corvinus, inhabiting the area which had once been notorious for fevers but was now host to pestilence of a different kind: the rich.

The house reeked of money, though the owner displayed his wealth in a different way from the Hortensii with their flash parade of interior design and art treasures. Priscillus emphasised how much *he* possessed by the pains he took protecting it. His property had been stripped of any balconies or pergolas which could offer cover to a thief's approach; its few upstairs windows were permanently barred. Private guards playing board games sat in a pillbox on one corner of the street, all of which was taken up with the sombre mansion where this grandmaster of real estate was supposed to live. His outer walls were painted black: a subtle hint of character.

Two white eyeballs, belonging to a big black African, squinted at me through a grille in a particularly solid black front door. The eyes let me in, but raced through the formalities with a speed designed to prevent anyone becoming too familiar with the layout. The entrance hall contained a brace of British hunting dogs (on chains), who were just fractionally friendlier than the leather-clad bodyguards; I counted at least five of those, patrolling the precincts with glittery daggers prominent in their handspan belts.

I was shunted into a side room where, before I could get bored and start writing my name on the wallplaster, a secretary stepped in with the clear intention of despatching me whence I came.

'May I see Appius Priscillus?'

'No. Priscillus greets his followers in the morning, but we keep a list. If you're not on the list, there is no chance of dole. If you are a tenant, see the rent clerk. If you are seeking a loan see the loans clerk –'

'Where do I find the personal information clerk?'

He paused. His eyes said information was at a premium. 'That's possibly me.'

'The information I'm after is extremely sensitive. Priscillus may prefer to give it to me himself.'

'He's not the sensitive type,' said his man.

Clearly Priscillus had not lashed out much on his secretarial services; this was no high-flown Greek who could speak and write five languages. He had an uninspiring north European face. The only indication that he acted as a scribe was the fact he had a split-nibbed reed pen stuck in the swag of brown cloth that he used as a belt, and ink all over him.

'My name is Didius Falco,' I said. He hadn't thought it polite to ask me, but I thought it polite to say. 'I would like you to inform Appius Priscillus that I have certain questions regarding events at the Hortensius house two nights ago. Clearing up these questions will be in his interests as much as mine.'

'What questions?'

'Confidential.'

'You can tell me.'

'Maybe – but I'm not going to!'

The secretary disappeared grumpily, without telling me I could sit down. In fact there were no stools or benches. The room contained only heavy coffers which were probably stuffed with money. Anyone who sat on the strongboxes would imprint himself with a vicious pattern of studs, bands, and bolts. I decided to keep my delicate posterior unmarked.

If I had been a barrister the court usher would barely have had time to set the waterclock to time my speech before my messenger returned. 'He will not see you!' he informed me triumphantly.

I sighed. 'So what's to be done?'

'Nothing. You're not wanted. Now you leave.'

'Let's go through this again,' I said patiently. 'My name is Marcus Didius Falco. I am investigating the poisoning of the freedman Hortensius Novus; also, incidentally, the murder of his cook –'

'So what?' jeered the secretary.

'So somebody has suggested to me that Appius Priscillus may be implicated in these deaths.' This accusation raised not a flicker. 'It did seem to me,' I suggested, 'in view of the serious charges, Priscillus might like a chance to vindicate himself –'

'If he did anything, you'd never prove it! If you could prove something, you would not be here!'

'That sounds persuasive – but it's the rhetoric of a thug. Now tell Priscillus this: if he did it I will prove it. When I prove it I'll be back.'

'I doubt it, Falco. Now I suggest you leave quickly of your own accord because if I ask the Phrygians to convey you outside, you may land rather heavily.'

'Give Priscillus the message,' I repeated, making my own way to the door. As I reached the smirking stylus-pusher I did a quick twirl and yanked his arm up his back at the very moment his vigilance relaxed. 'Let's give the message to him now, shall we? We can deliver the second part together – and try him out with the first, because I think he may not have heard it yet . . .' The fool started to bluster. 'Stop fidgeting, or taking shorthand notes will be painful for a week or two –' I gave his arm a jerk to emphasise the point. 'Don't take me for an idiot – you never saw Priscillus. You were only gone long enough to scratch your lice.'

'He's not here!' gasped the inkblot.

'Where is he then?'

'This is his business address. He has a house on the Quirinal and two others opposite the Salarian Gate; or he may be over the river at his new place on the Janiculan. But he only sees his private friends in his private homes.'

'So when do you expect him here again?'

'No way of telling –' Suddenly he squirmed free and let out a shout which attracted the attention of one of the bodyguards.

'Keep cool. I'm going – but give your master my message just as soon as he turns up!'

'Don't worry! And when I do, Falco, you can expect to be hearing from him!'

I smiled. Some threats do lead to inconvenience. But mainly they evaporate.

As I crossed the hall, keeping half an eye on the Phrygian muscle, I noticed a sedan chair. Whatever Priscillus spent his takings on, it was not this conveyance: this was a stained brown leather veteran, so crumpled and grimy it was conspicuous. I had seen it before: at that housefire, the night Hortensius Novus died. Which meant that I had seen Priscillus too: leaping out of it.

Tough life, being a businessman. Hardly time to take a well-earned break after murdering your rival, before you had to be back out on the streets, greeting sobbing arson victims with a contract in your hand . . .

191

The presence of the chair probably meant Priscillus *was* here. But I left without further argument. I had hurt the scribe's arm enough to ensure he would rush to his master to complain. My message would get there now.

I recognised something else unpleasant outside the street door: descending from his mule was the pustulent piece of aggravation I last saw attacking the old fruitseller in Abacus Street. I braced myself for a fight, but the bleary bug failed to remember me.

I amused myself that afternoon at the Temple of Saturn, going through the Censor's register of citizens and their property, which was kept for safety at the Treasury. Appius Priscillus was a freedman of long-standing, attached to the Galerian voting tribe. We were long overdue for a full Roman census, but he should have featured somewhere in official documents. He had managed to hide his existence. I was not surprised.

I found myself more eager than usual to wander off home. This had less to do with the sour taste left by Priscillus than a certain smile I might encounter in my own den.

She was out. That was just about acceptable. I would have to let her stroll around loose occasionally. Sceptical types might think that I was holding her to ransom otherwise.

At home there was evidence that the morning had been lively. Severina had assured me her parrot was house-trained, but apparently this only meant Chloe was trained to eat household effects. There were beakmarks scarring several doorframes, and a broken dish in the rubbish pail. Something, presumably not Helena, had attacked my office stool ferociously and bitten halfway through its leg. Now the parrot was missing too.

Helena had left me a list of the bird's sayings, brightly annotated by herself:

> *Chloe's a clever girl.   (Doubtful. H.)*
> *Manicure set.*
> *Where's my dinner?*
> *Let's go out to a party!*
> *Eggs in a basket.   (Is this rude? H.)*
> *Three obscenities.   (I refuse to write them. H.)*
> *Chloe, Chloe, Chloe.   Chloe's a good girl.*
> *Gone to Maia's; taking your stupid bird.*

192

The last line confused me until I realised it was a joke addressed to me in my sister's strange spiked handwriting.

I dashed off to Maia's in a state of annoyance; I had intended to censor news of Helena's arrival. I should have known that after the fish supper my family would come poking round, on the lookout for scandal and leftovers.

Helena and my sister had settled themselves on Maia's sun terrace. A wide variety of empty plates, bowls and mint-tea glasses littered the edge of the stone parapet and the rims of Maia's great flowerpots. Neither Maia nor Helena roused themselves to suggest feeding me. They must have been nibbling most of the afternoon and were too well stuffed to budge.

Helena put up her cheek which I brushed with a kiss. Maia looked away. Our formality seemed to embarrass her more than a passionate clinch.

'Where's the parrot?'

'Hiding,' said Maia. 'It thought it was going to terrorise my children but they fought back. We had to cover it with a stewpot for its own protection.'

'I saw what that pest did at home,' I complained, still pecking round for crumbs like a forlorn sparrow. 'I'll get a cage.'

I managed to find a few lacklustre almonds at the bottom of a bowl. They tasted off. I should have known no titbit which had already been rejected by my lass and my youngest sister would provide much sustenance.

'I believe "two eggs in a basket" is a reference to testicles,' I informed them, using clinical neutrality to indicate I saw them both as women of the world. 'Though if "manicure set" is a soldiering term its translation escapes me.' Maia pretended she knew, and she would tell Helena afterwards.

They let me sit down, threw me a few cushions, then condescended to hear about my day. I soon deduced Helena had told Maia all about my case. 'I never managed to see Priscillus. But he seems what I thought – high rents and low motives. It's beginning to look as if Severina may have a point.'

'Don't you dare start feeling sorry for her!' my sister instructed. It seemed to me she and Helena had exchanged a knowing glance.

Their set reaction immediately made my own attitude to the fortune-hunter more sympathetic. 'Why not? What if everyone has misjudged her? What if she really is just a home-loving girl, acting from the best of motives with regard to Hortensius Novus, and has simply had bad luck with everything she touches?' This fair-minded attitude surprised even me. I must be going soft.

My sister and my lady bestirred themselves to jangle their bracelets at me, then I was ordered to report on Severina Zotica in detail so they could systematically destroy her character. Maia, who had been a professional weaver, was particularly interested in her domestic handicrafts. 'Does she really do it herself? How fast can she work? Was she using a pattern? When she changed colours did she have to think, or could she choose the next hank of wool automatically?'

'Oh I can't remember.'

'Marcus, you're useless!'

'I reckon she's genuine. Isn't this dutiful Penelope act more likely to mean she's innocent? Sitting at a loom seems a nice quiet occupation – '

'Sitting at a loom quietly,' Maia rebuked me, 'gives her plenty of time to scheme and plot!'

'Traditional life of a decent Roman matron. Augustus always insisted that the women of his household wove all his clothes at home.'

Helena laughed. 'And his female relations all ended up a byword for debauchery!' She gazed at me, considering. 'Are scratchy homespun tunics what *you* want?'

'Wouldn't dream of it.' I wouldn't dare!

'Good! Tell us about all these trips to the library. What is she studying?'

'Geography.'

'That's harmless – apparently,' Helena agreed, though she and Maia exchanged another silly glance. 'Perhaps she is searching for a pleasant province where she can go into voluntary exile with her ill-gotten loot!'

'Doubt it. The only scroll I noticed had some reference to Mauretania. Who wants to retire to a desert, overrun by plagues of elephants?'

'If she had taken out three volumes on taming parrots,' Maia giggled, 'there might be some point. Are you attracted to this female?'

Helena was scrutinising me out of the corner of one eye, so to cause trouble I said, 'She's not bad, if you like redheads!'

Maia told me I was disgusting; then she instructed Helena Justina to take me (and my parrot) home.

Not long after we reached the apartment I discovered that my sister had taught the parrot to squawk, '*Ooh! Marcus has been a naughty boy!*'

XLVIII

Next morning, while I was making fruitless attempts to track down Appius Priscillus at one or other of his fancy bivouacs, Helena Justina bought a parrot cage and later took two messages.

'You had a visit from a slave, who refused to leave his name – though he must be the runabout from the Hortensius house.'

'They owe me a packet.'

'He brought that. I counted and wrote a receipt for it. Am I going to keep your accounts for you?'

A cold sweat struck me, faced by aspects of togetherness I had never allowed for. 'Certainly not! My brains and my body are at your disposal, but a man needs some privacy . . .'

'We'll see!' Helena looked unimpressed. 'The runabout has found someone who can help you; he will bring her tomorrow morning. Can you be here? She works in the kitchen so it has to be early. Also, the cook's funeral will be on Thursday, if you want to go.'

'Yes; I owe Viridovix a respectful gesture.'

'I said I thought you would. The other message was from Petronius Longus; he wants to see you urgently.'

Petronius was working, so I found him on the Aventine. He took time out from policing the Emporium to snatch a glass of wine with me. I told him about my morning chasing around the Priscillus properties and being shown the door at all of them. 'Apparently he was out shopping for Alban holiday retreats. If he can't decide which location he wants, he'll just buy them all . . .'

'Priscillus was why I wanted to see you.' Petro gave me one of his sombre looks. He swilled the wine round his gums, as a sign that it tasted like toothpowder. 'Falco, what muleshit are you stepping in? Everyone I asked about this mogul reckons he's about as safe to deal with as a bucket of snakes. And come to that,' added Petro, with relish, 'your Hortensius brothers – or whatever they are – have little more to recommend them!'

'What's the dirt?'

'Start with Priscillus. The story is pretty sordid. He first surfaced on a big scale during the clearances after the Great Fire. He was "doing the public a service" preying on the dispossessed tenants Nero had kicked out to make space for the Golden House. Priscillus moved in on them, with his greedy eyes fixed on compensation claims – '

'I thought "compensation" was a bad joke?'

'Is this Rome? What actually happened was that Nero removed the corpses and the rubble free of charge – though that was a ploy so he could pick over the debris and grab anything left to loot. The Fire Relief Fund, to which we citizens all contributed so graciously – ' Petro meant, it was screwed out of us by the taxfarmers, ' – went no further than the Emperor's own coffers. Thousands were left homeless and absolutely desperate. So firstly there were good pickings for contractors providing temporary shelters outside the city. Then racketeers were able to make their piles building cheap slums for the refugees who had salvaged anything, and even cheaper billets for the ones who had nothing left. They cleaned up: as soon as the refugees were settled in, the rents soared. Once the costs bit, cynical Priscillus moved in again – this time as a loan shark.'

Most of Rome lives on credit. Everyone from temple-cleaner to consul tends to be in debt for most of their lives. People at the upper end of society can juggle their mortgages; the less fortunate spiral down under the burden of five per cent interest into selling their sons as gladiators and their daughters as cheap brothel fare.

'What about the Hortensius triumvirate, Petro? Is their operation similar?'

'Yes, though slightly cleaner. Their interests appear more diversified – '

I mentioned what the cakeman had told me about Pollia's venture into fitting out corn ships. 'Looks as if Novus believed in a well-balanced portfolio: mercantile fiddles nicely balanced against land-lease fraud!'

'Their business style is less brutal than the one Priscillus adopts. As landlords they seem to be merely bad managers. Why should they care if their tenants can see daylight through the walls?'

'Almost as friendly as Smaractus!' I joked.

'Not funny. Three children died recently at an apartment in the Third Sector when a floor fell in. The Hortensii average a lawsuit a month from pedestrians who have narrowly escaped falling roof tiles or pieces breaking off balcony balustrades. A whole wall gave way and killed a man not long ago, somewhere on the Esquiline. Neglecting a dangerous structure is second nature; their collateral stays solid, even though their property is always collapsing – '

'And rebuilt at a profit?'

'Oh yes!' Petro confirmed with a delicate lift of both wrists. 'But their main method of raising finance is the multiple-pledge fiddle.'

'What's that?'

'You still in the cradle, Falco?' Petronius seemed unable to believe I was serious. He was more alert to fraud than me; as a salaried officer he sometimes had cash to invest. Sometimes he lost it – but not as often as most people; he had a canny business sense. 'The legal term is a "hypothec". Are you with me?'

'I'm not stupid . . . So what does it mean?'

'It means a fiddle, Falco!'

'I have heard the word, or read it somewhere; isn't it just the term lawyers use for a pledge, when the pledge is on property? How can a fiddle operate?'

'What happens is: the Hortensii own a piece of property, and raise a loan secured on it. Then they repeat the process – same property but a new lender; and again, as many times as possible. They pick simple-minded investors who don't know – or don't enquire – that there are previous secured debts.'

'So they mortgage the building, to its full value, as often as they can?'

'Insight is penetrating that drunken little brain! Next, as you'll guess, the Hortensii default. Of course they lose the original property, but they don't mind that! They have raised its value several times over in loans.'

'But what about their creditors, Petro? Can't they sue?'

'Paid off in strict order of precedence; earliest contract date first. One or two will recoup when the building is sold; but once its selling price is covered, the rest have no claim.'

'What? No protection at all?'

'They should protect themselves by checking first! If not; hard luck. It's a fraud which relies on punters' laziness.' Petro sounded unsympathetic. Like me, he was a man who took trouble over things. 'I had all this from a Syrian financier. Normally he just shakes his greasy ringlets and I can't get a word out of him, but this Priscillus is so notorious everyone in the Forum would like to see his operations limited. My contact told me about the Hortensii out of sheer spite at their success with the duplicate loans charade. None of the professional moneylenders touch it – but there are always fools in the private market who can be intrigued by clever talk of quick percentages. The regular dealers are grousing that the Hortensii are pinching all the spare collateral, while Priscillus, with his brutal methods, is making everybody nervous on the fringe.'

'What,' I suggested, 'if the two groups joined forces?'

Petro winced. 'That's the big fear.'

I sat and thought. Now that I had an inkling how the Hortensius and Priscillus empires worked there seemed plenty of scope for them all to make a profit – but that also encouraged endless jealousy about making even more. The poor get used to making do; people with real money never feel it is enough.

'Thanks, Petro. Anything else I ought to be aware of?'

'Only that my informant says if you're going to upset Appius Priscillus I ought to ask where you deposited your will.'

'Ma knows,' I said tersely.

His quiet brown eyes surveyed me. 'Wear a body belt under your tunic and keep a dagger in your boot! If you get in trouble, let me know.'

I nodded. He went back to work; I lingered over my drink.

I won't say I felt apprehensive – but the little hairs were standing to attention all over my skin.

To give myself something else alarming to think about, I went to see Severina.

'As promised: come to report.'

'How is my parrot?'

'I hear she's been making herself at home . . .' I described Chloe's trail of destruction, being careful to omit the fact that the aviary she was destroying was my own.

'What do you expect?' rebuked the gold-digger crossly. 'She's a sensitive female. You have to introduce her to a new habitat gradually!' I smiled, thinking not of Chloe, but Helena Justina so warily agreeing to unfurl her tent at my water hole. 'Falco, what are you grinning at?'

'I may have to chain the birdie to a perch.'

'No; don't do that. If she tries to fly she may fall and just dangle there!'

'Thought you were anxious to get rid of her?'

'I am. Chloe,' declared Severina, 'was a gift from Grittius Fronto, whose unpleasantness I want to forget as soon as possible.'

'Relax! I gave your feather duster to a person of humane tendencies; a proper cage has been purchased . . . I want to talk to you about more rapacious birds. Sit down, keep a clear head, and don't give me the "I'm just an ignorant little woman" tale again.' Before she could argue I told her what I had found out so far about Priscillus. 'It does fit with your story – but *proves* none of it. Tell me what you know about relationships between Priscillus and your group on the Pincian. You mentioned a quarrel, which the dinner was supposed to reconcile. What caused the initial rift? Would I be correct if I guessed that the Hortensii had somehow double-crossed the other organisation with their duplicate hypothecs scam?'

'That's sharp of you!' Severina admitted. 'Hortensius Novus always claimed it had happened accidentally, but he *had* tricked Appius Priscillus into underwriting one of those dubious schemes of his. That was why Priscillus started threatening the family, and why Felix and Crepito, who had less nerve than Novus, wanted to end the feud by accepting an offer from him to co-operate in future.'

'I get the impression they were shaking hands on more than just compensation for rooking him! *I* think Felix and Crepito desired a full business merger – Mars Ultor, they could still do it, and stitch up the whole of residential Rome! Was your Novus resisting it?'

'You could be right,' she suggested doubtfully. I recognised the simple woman act again, so left the conversation there. The trick with Severina, I had discovered, was to move one line ahead in the board game, then force her to follow your move.

'Will you stay to lunch with me, Falco? I need some decent conversation; my girlfriend at the baths was too busy to stop, and I'm missing my fiancé – '

For a moment I forgot Severina was my client now. 'Don't worry,' I smiled sweetly. 'You'll soon find another to fill the void.'

Her parrot's wilful damage in my apartment must have eroded my natural tolerance.

I wanted to see Helena; I was anxious to mend relations by helping her cope with the truculent bird.

Walking home, I did feel I was advancing on the case. Not that it cleared any undergrowth: I still had three sets of suspects and there were more motives than fleas on a cat. The only thing they had in common was that none could yet be proved.

I was enjoying myself though. This was much more satisfying than some dead-end mission for Vespasian. It offered a livelier challenge, and if I managed to solve it I should not just be removing some tired political grub whose disappearance would hardly be noticed by the man in the street; here there were real social undesirables to unearth and convict.

I had flushed one of them out already, apparently. Waiting on the bottom step to my apartment was a messenger. A pasty youth with a stye and a stammer told me Appius Priscillus had received my messages. If I wanted to meet him I was to be in the Forum of Julius in half an hour.

There was no time even to pop up and mention it to Helena. I thanked the youth (who looked surprised anyone should be grateful for an introduction to Priscillus) then I set off hot-foot.

I knew Petronius would have warned me against going solo, but I had my knife and my self-reliance, which had seen me through plenty. Besides, the Forum of Julius Caesar is an open public place.

I approached by what I thought was the subtle way, walking through the Curia and letting myself out of the great double doors at the back. It *would* have been a discreet approach – but Priscillus was not yet there so I had been wasting my time.

Everywhere seemed quiet. I had the big public lavatory on one hand and the shops on the other: ready for anything! Caesar had built his overspill Forum with a gracious surrounding colonnade; I moved out into the open, just in case.

The brown sedan turned up five minutes later. It entered from the eastern end and parked there, just inside the arch.

I had a good look round for ambushers: none in sight. In the end I ambled over. The carriers were standing motionless, staring ahead, ignoring me. They could be mute or stupid or foreign – or all three. I glanced back over both shoulders, then approached. When I whipped aside the lank leather curtain I had already convinced myself that Appius Priscillus would not be there. But I was wrong.

'*Get in!*' he said.

XLIX

It was like coming face to face with another rat: he was all teeth and piercing eyes. I got in, but I would rather have been tangling knees with my cellmate in the Lautumiae.

No one could accuse Priscillus of indulging in luxury. He had the skinny frame of a man who was too preoccupied to enjoy eating. He wore a dull old tunic, which had nothing actually wrong with it but was so depressing even I would have tossed it out for a tramp (though most tramps I knew had more sartorial style). A barber had made a few practice feints over his narrow chin fairly recently, but that was probably only because businessmen believe the barber's chair is a place to pick up tips. (I don't know why; all *I* ever pick up is a rash.) Attending to the Priscillus toilette had stopped short of the expensive frills. His thin hair was too long; his talons needed cleaning and clipping. And I could not imagine his razorman ever bothered offering any little flasks of cedar gum for contraceptive purposes . . .

Priscillus was unmarried; now I knew why. Not because a woman would be too fastidious to have him (most would tolerate grimy fingernails in return for all those strongboxes), but this mean runt who barely kept himself alive would begrudge paying board and lodging for anything so inessential as a wife.

Even with two passengers the chairmen set off at a cracking pace. 'Where are we going?' I demanded in some alarm, before I even introduced myself.

'Business on the Campus Martius.' Well, I realised it had to be business; he would never spare time to visit a temple or indulge in exercise! 'So, you're Falco. What do you want with me?' His voice had a wheeze in it, as if he hugged in his breath as grudgingly as everything else he did.

'A few answers, please. I'm working on the Novus case – '
'Who are you working for?'
'I'm being *paid* by Severina Zotica,' I answered pedantically.
'More fool you! You want to look at your own client, Falco!'

'Oh I treat her very warily – but I'm looking at you first!' It was difficult to concentrate, for the bearers were still running and the chair jogged every syllable we tried to speak. 'Severina's a professional bride; she had no motive to kill Novus before she was in line to inherit his loot. You and the Hortensii must be much more viable suspects – ' The rat's eyes flashed a threat which made me shiver. 'Sorry, but I'm judging by the facts: it looks black for you if you are planning to merge operations with Felix and Crepito – when all Rome knows their dead partner was so strongly set against it. Why was that, by the way?' Priscillus only glared at me; I answered it myself. 'He saw it not as a merger but a takeover – by you. He was used to being top cockerel on his own dungheap; he refused to take second place to anyone . . . different for the other two, since they had always been subordinate to Novus anyway – '

The chair had stopped.

'You annoy me, Falco.' Priscillus spoke with the tired slur thugs always use for threats. He could have been any overstuffed off-duty guardsman who had crossed the street for the simple pleasure of shoving me aside.

'Then help me.'

'Help yourself!' he snarled insultingly. 'This is where we get out.'

I could tell we were well out on the Campus, on open ground. I experienced a sudden yearning to stay safe inside this chair of his, even joggling along and trying to keep from being bruised by his bony knees. He pulled back the curtain and climbed out himself. This almost had the foolish effect of reassuring me.

I got out. My foreboding had been correct. If I had clung on, the waiting Phrygians would simply have rolled the sedan chair onto its side and tackled the problem like poking a limpet to death inside its shell. Being out of it was no better. We had stopped in the middle of an exercise ground, and they all held javelins. The heads of the javelins were not weighted with practice dummies, but sharp Noricum steel – *really* sharp. When I climbed out and straightened up I was pinned between them so that a move in any direction would slit my hide.

I said nothing. One spearhead was nuzzling my windpipe. Speech would have cut my own throat.

Nowadays the Plain of Mars is well built up with monuments but some parts are still desolate. We were in one of those. A dry wind off the river lifted my curls but barely brushed my sweating arms. A few cantering horseriders were visible, too far away to notice what was happening even if they were willing to interfere.

None of the Phrygians spoke to me. There were eight of them: taking no chances. They were slight, but all sinew. They had high-cheekboned features, distinguished one from another only by old scars. Aliens, from the mountainous interior of Asia; probably straight descendants of the Hittites – whose fame was based on cruelty.

They tired me out first. Playing, they nudged me this way and that. Some lifted away their spearheads; others shoved me towards them; I would lurch on my toes as the first javelins engaged again, then be pushed off another way. Too little interest on my part was corrected by a warning nick. Too much effort would spit me. All the time we all knew I was looking for a chance to break away and make a run for it – but it would be a long sprint. Even if I could ever put distance between us, the javelins would come winging after me . . .

The signal to act must have come from the man behind me. He grabbed me. The Phrygians all flung down their weapons. Then they played a new game – throwing me from one to another while they battered any parts of me they could reach. Not too hard: they wanted the fun to last.

I did manage to jackknife and land vindictive punches of my own, but that only made the jeers louder and the returns harder while my own anger burned more vilely in my mouth.

I knew by then Priscillus did not want me dead. He would have had them slash my throat at once and leave my corpse for the early-morning riders to stumble across next day, damp and stiff in the river mist. He wanted me to be able to warn anyone else who looked at him too closely what crossing the mighty Appius Priscillus would entail.

At the end of all this I would still be alive.

Just so long as the Phrygians knew how to follow orders and were sufficiently well trained. Otherwise, there seemed a fair chance they might finish me off by accident.

L

For thugs, they were neat. They put me back where they first found me – in the Forum of Julius. When sensation returned, I could recognise the dictator's equestrian statue as his honour stared loftily at the world he had conquered (though he omitted to notice me).

I started to crawl. I had no idea where, since my eyes blurred. When I found the steps, I told myself carefully it must be the Temple of Venus Genetrix.

I passed out on them.

Next time I came round, I looked up and confirmed my impressive knowledge of topography. Here was the high platform, with me sprawled upon it, and up there were the gorgeous Corinthian columns. If any foreign visitors had stooped to ask me about the temple I could have informed them that inside they would find fine statues of Venus, Caesar, the youthful Cleopatra, and two ravishing pictures (by Timomachus) of Ajax and Medea. Meanwhile, they could make a note in their tour diary that *outside* they had seen the slightly less glorious informer M. Didius Falco, calling for help so croakily no passers-by thought it safe to hear.

Nice work, Falco. If you have to be immobilised it may as well be on the steps of a world-famous temple in the most beautiful forum in Rome.

A priest came out. He gave me a kick and passed on quickly, thinking I was one of the usual beggars who loiter on temple steps.

Hours later he came back from his errand. I was ready for him now. 'Aid me, sir, in the name of the Divine Julius!'

I was right: most priests can be swayed by a plea in the name of the patron who provided their livelihood. Perhaps they are afraid you maybe one of the cult's auditors, testing them in disguise.

Once I managed to stop him, the priest condescended to clear my leaking carcass off his previously pristine marble steps, and load me into a litter which would be paid for by Petronius.

I missed the sensation my bloody arrival must have caused, by dint of being unconscious. A good trick if you can do it. Avoids fuss.

It was not the first time I had had myself delivered to Petronius like a package of overripe provisions which had been left steaming too long in the midday heat. But I had never before been tortured to a jelly quite so efficiently.

He was at home, luckily. I became aware I was in Petro and Silvia's house. Silvia was braising meat. Her small daughters were thundering about like a legion on rapid drill somewhere directly above us in the upstairs rooms. One of the children had a squeaky flute, adding to the agony.

I felt Petro cutting away my tunic; I heard him curse; I heard my boots thud into a bucket; I smelt the familiar potpourri of Petro's unlocked medicine chest. I let him force cold water into me to counter the shock. I swallowed some of a burning draught, though most seemed to trickle down my chest on the outside. After that it did not really matter if I passed out while he worked on me; so on the whole I did.

He had the sense to soak off the dirt and the loose blood, before he allowed his wife to leave the house to run for Helena.

LI

It was impossible to speak to her.

She said nothing either. Only the light pressure of her hand on mine altered fractionally. My swollen eyes could hardly open, but she must have detected the moment when I woke. I could see her against the dazzle: the familiar outline of her body; the shape of her hair, turned up the way she sometimes wore it, with boxwood combs above her ears. Her hair was too soft; the left-hand comb always ended up lower than the right.

Her thumb was moving faintly, caressing the back of my hand; she was probably unaware of doing it. By aiming through the left side of my mouth I managed to make some unintelligible sound. She bent forwards. Somehow she found the only square inch of my face which did not hurt for her gentle kiss.

She went away. Unreasonable panic swept over me, until I heard her voice. 'He's awake. Thank you for looking after him; I can manage now. Could you possibly find someone with a litter to carry him?' Petro's bulk filled the doorway, protesting that it was best to keep me here. (He thought Helena was too refined to deal with the nursing I would need.) I closed my eyes, waiting for it; the convincing voice of ownership: 'Petronius Longus, I am perfectly capable! I am not a schoolgirl, *playing* at house with pots and pans in miniature!'

'You're in serious trouble, Falco!' Petro said laconically. He meant, all this pain from Priscillus, and now another tyrant taking me over and shouting at my friends.

I could only lie there and let Helena fight it out. She certainly intended to get her own way. Could she cope? Petro thought not. What did I think? Helena Justina knew that too. 'Lucius Petronius – *Marcus wants me to take him home!*'

Petro muttered some swearwords; then he did as he was told.

The journey passed quickly but the men with the litter refused to attempt the stairs. I walked it. The whole three flights. There was no alternative.

When I swam fully back to consciousness I was propped upright against my own bedroom wall. Helena glanced across at me, then continued preparing my bed; Silvia had provided her with an old sheet in case I bled on my own decent one. Women are so practical.

I watched Helena's figure as she worked, with rapid movements and an economy of effort that would soon have things ready. Not soon enough.

'I'm going to fall over – '

'I'll catch you . . .'

I could trust Helena's promises. She reached me in one stride. Thank heavens for small rooms.

Without knowing how I got there, I found myself on the bed. I could smell that floral perfume all the women's bathhouses seemed to be using nowadays. What had brought me round was the sensation of being unwrapped from the cloak Petro rolled me in for travelling. Underneath all I had on were bandages.

Helena caught her breath. 'Well! This is going to take more than a bowl of hot soup inside you and a bean-meal mash outside . . . I've seen your manly attributes before, but I can throw a cover over you if you're shy.'

'Not with you.' In my own home I had recovered enough to slur a few words. 'You know everything about me; I know everything about you – '

'That's what you think!' she muttered, but delirium was taking hold and I was laughing too much to be sensible.

When she leaned over to square me up neatly on the pillow, I got my arms round her. Helena snorted. She struggled, on principle, but she was trying too hard not to hurt me as she landed; she missed her chance to escape. There was nothing else I could manage, but I held on tight. She gave in; after some mild squirming of a different kind I heard her sandals drop on the floor, then she unhooked her earrings and laid them aside. I kept my arms locked round her as I drifted off into oblivion. She was lying quiet; she would still be there waiting when I awoke. If I had known this was all it would take to get her back in bed with me, I would have run out and had myself beaten up by some bully long before.

LII

She was there. Sitting at my bedside in a clean grey gown with newly pinned hair. Sipping something from a beaker, thoughtfully.

The changed light told me it was the next morning. Every part of me that had been swollen yesterday had now become stiff as well. Helena did not ask if I felt better; she could see I was worse.

She looked after me, in her sensible way. Petronius had supplied her with painkilling cordial, ointments and wads of lambswool; she had already mastered the medical régime. Anyone who had ever had charge of a baby understood my other needs.

When I was lying still, recovering from being cleansed and dosed, she sat on the bed and held my hand again. Our eyes met. I felt very close to her.

'What have you got to smile at?'

'Oh, any man feels a special attachment for the girl who washes his ears and empties his chamber pot.'

'I see this hasn't stopped you talking nonsense,' Helena said.

I was woken next by the parrot having one of its shrieking fits. A good scream several times a day seemed its way of taking exercise. Chloe's throat must have had the best toned-up set of muscles in Rome.

When the antisocial mobster finally shut up, Helena came in to see me.

'I'll suffocate that voice box!' I had never had to endure the full performance before. I was horrified. 'The old lady upstairs will be complaining – '

'She already has!' Helena informed me. 'I met her when I took back the bowls your sister borrowed for the fish supper. I was getting on with her quite nicely, but the bird stopped that. I feel sorry for the pathetic old thing; she has a running feud with the landlord; he keeps trying to winkle her out. Ranting at you is her only joy in life – I suppose I'll be like that one day . . .'

It must have been a couple of hours since I was last awake. Helena now had a different beaker; hot honey, which she shared with me. While I was still recovering from the effort of sitting up to drink it, someone knocked.

It was Hyacinthus. He had brought with him the scullion I remembered from the Hortensius kitchen. I glanced at Helena in desperation; I could never cope with this.

Nothing disturbed Helena Justina, once she deemed herself in charge. She patted my bandages. 'Didius Falco has had a slight upset as you can see.' The gods only know what I looked like. The visitors were crowding against the doorframe, completely quelled. 'There's no need for you to have a wasted journey; we'll fetch some stools into the bedroom and you can talk to me instead. Marcus will just lie still and listen in.'

'What happened to him?' Hyacinthus whispered.

Helena replied briskly, 'He tripped over a step!'

The washtub princess was called Anthea. She was three-foot high, and looked about twelve, though Helena and I agreed afterwards that we reckoned her secondary function had been warming the chef's bed. Her miserable life had given her a bad complexion, a sad face underneath it, a depressed outlook, chapped hands, and probably sore feet. Her threadbare scrap of a tunic barely reached down to her reddened knees.

I lay there and listened dreamily while Helena Justina tried to tease information out of this poor little mite: 'I want you to tell me everything about the day of the dinner party. Were you in the kitchen all the time? I expect there were plenty of pans and ladles to wash, even while Viridovix was just preparing the food?' Anthea nodded, proud to have her importance recognised. 'Did anything happen that *you* thought seemed peculiar?' This time the girl shook her head. Her dry, colourless hair had an annoying way of constantly falling over her eyes.

Helena had apparently remembered the entire party menu, because she mentioned most of the dishes. She wanted to know who stirred the saffron sauce for the lobsters, who jointed the hare, who folded over the halibut pancakes, even who tied the damned dessert fruit onto the golden tree. Hearing it made me so queasy I only just held out. 'And was the lady they call Severina in the kitchen at any time?'

'From about halfway through.'

'Talking to Viridovix?'

'Yes.'

210

'Did she help him at all?'

'Mostly she sat up on the edge of a table. Viridovix used to get very excited when he was working and hot; she was keeping him calm. I think she tasted some gravies.'

'Was it a busy period? So you could not pay much attention?'

'Yes, but I did see her whisking the egg whites.'

The pot-scourer had a sniff sometimes, caused by neither grief nor a nasal infection; wrinkling her snitch merely added variety to her empty life. 'Sometimes eggs take ages don't they?' Helena chirped; she was more patient than I would have been. 'It's a good idea to pass the bowl around – what were they being used for?'

'A glaze.'

'A glaze?'

'It was her idea.'

'Severina's?'

'Yes. He was too polite to argue, but Viridovix thought it wouldn't work.'

'Why? Was the glaze spread on something the people were going to eat?' Helena asked, her dark eyes narrowing.

'No; just a plate.'

'A plate?'

'No one ate it. It was to decorate a plate.'

Under pressure the scullion was starting to look angry and confused. I was about to issue a signal, but Helena moved on anyway. 'Anthea, can you tell me how long Severina stayed with you, and what happened when she left?'

'She stayed all the time.'

'What – during the dinner?'

'Oh no; not that long. Until the party had started. Just started,' she repeated, shoving that hair out of her eyes again while I gripped my bedcover.

'Then what?' Helena queried pleasantly. I think she knew I was getting annoyed.

'Severina sighed a bit and said she was feeling poorly so she would go home.'

'By then all she had done was taste some things, talk to Viridovix, and decorate a plate?'

'She inspected the dishes before she went.'

'What happened about that?'

'Nothing. She said it all looked lovely, and Viridovix should be proud of himself.'

If Helena was feeling the strain of this interview, no one would have known. 'So Severina left, then Viridovix went up to the triclinium to oversee the carvers. Did anyone except your own household servants come into the kitchen after that?'

'No.'

'Did you ever see any of the dinner guests?'

'They might have gone past to the lavatory. But I was busy by then.'

'None of them came in, for instance to say thank you for the splendid food?' I choked with mirth, echoed by Hyacinthus. Helena ignored us. 'Anthea, in your house where are the prepared dishes kept while they wait for the bearers to take them upstairs?'

'On a table by the kitchen door.'

'Inside the room?'

'Yes.'

'Could anyone have tampered with them without being seen?'

'No. A boy has to stand by the table to keep off the flies.'

'Ah! I expect there are quite a lot of flies in your house,' Helena allowed herself to jibe sarcastically. She had run out of questions for a moment.

'There was one thing,' Anthea broke in, almost accusingly. 'Severina and Viridovix were giggling about the cakes.'

Helena stayed calm. 'These were the bought pastries which had come up to the house from the cakeseller Minnius?'

'One was a very big one.'

'A special one!' Helena exclaimed.

'Yes, but it can't have been the one that poisoned the master –' For the first time Anthea was carried away by what she had to impart. 'I know about that cake; no one else does! Severina said it was going to cause a quarrel, because everyone would fight to snatch it off the plate. She *said* she would take it away, and keep it for Hortensius Novus to have afterwards in his own room by himself –'

Helena's head spun in my direction. We were both holding our breath, and even the runabout tensed, realising what this tale implied. But the scullion, having built up her big moment, deflated us. 'He never ate it though.'

She sat, enjoying the anticlimax she had caused. Helena murmured, 'How do you know that?'

'I found it! After the dinner was over, when I was scraping off scraps from the big gold plates so I could wash them. I saw that cake in one of the slop buckets. I remember, because at first I was going to pick it out again and eat it, only it was all covered with wet onion peel. I don't like onions,' Anthea added, as if she would have eaten the cake regardless, but for that.

'I wonder,' pondered Helena, 'who can have thrown the cake away?'

'Nobody knew. I was mad; I called out, what miserable rat dumped this good cake in here? I would have belted them – but no one knew.'

I roused myself. 'Anthea, had all the other cakes been eaten when the serving dish came back?'

'I'll say. We never see pastries sent back to the kitchen in our house!'

'How were they served – on the vine leaves Minnius sends them wrapped in?'

'No; just on a platter. I washed it,' she added bitterly. 'Not a crumb left; not a crumb! I nearly didn't bother to wash it at all.'

I fell back on my pillow. The cakes had to be a false lead. Most people present must have eaten one, and none of the other diners had suffered ill effects.

Helena said quietly, 'Falco's tired. I think you must leave now – but you have been of immense help. Viridovix will be avenged, I promise you.'

She was shepherding them out, but that brain of hers was still reasoning rapidly for as they went I heard her ask Anthea whether the platter the cakes had been served on was the one with the egg white glaze.

Hyacinthus called out that he would see me on Thursday if I was able to attend the funeral, then he led off the little washer-upper. (Another thing Helena and I agreed afterwards, was that if we were right about Anthea's relationship with Viridovix, Hyacinthus had probably taken her over now.)

At the outside door I heard the runabout mention to Helena that downstairs in the street there were two men prominently watching our block. Rough types, he said.

Helena went into the living room alone. She would be thinking about what Hyacinthus had just said, not wanting to worry me. I heard her battering something in a bowl to take her mind off it.

Eventually she reappeared. 'Omelette for dinner.'

'What's that?' She was holding a dish covered in a thin layer of wet white froth.

'Egg white. I think if it's left it will set on the dish. It doesn't look

213

much. But I suppose if it was Severina's own idea she could have convinced herself it resembled a decorative bed of snow.'

'Especially on silver.'

Helena was surprised. 'The dishes were gold!'

'Not all. Anthea said she nearly didn't wash up the cake plate; I saw that. It was a giant silver comport Severina had given to Novus.'

'I still think she was wasting eggs,' Helena muttered, inspecting our own crock doubtfully.

'All right. Tell me instead what the runabout said about men watching the house.' She concentrated on the egg white; Helena did not believe in sharing her troubles with an invalid. 'I think we're safe,' I told her, because I knew who the watchers would be.

'Marcus –' she began indignantly.

'When you go out, march straight up and ask who sent them here.'

'You know?'

'Petronius. He has equipped us with a highly visible vigilante guard.'

'If Petronius thinks that necessary, it frightens me even more!' We stared at each other. Helena must have decided there was no point creating a fuss. 'Did I ask the right questions?'

'You always ask the right questions!'

'The cakes are important, Marcus; I *know* they are. You could poison cakes individually. But ensuring the right victim took the right cake . . . I thought it must be the extra large one.'

'I know you did,' I smiled at her.

'That would have been perfect, Marcus! Hortensius Novus was the host. In such a vulgar house I bet they offer platters to the host first; Novus could be guaranteed to grab the best!'

I smiled again. 'Yet Severina took it off the plate!'

'This is a complete puzzle.'

'Perhaps not. It could be that Severina is innocent. Maybe she went to the house, even though she was feeling off colour, because she had realised the banquet could be dangerous for her beloved. Maybe she really wanted to check for anything suspicious in the food.'

'Is that what she says?' Actually, that was one line she had not inflicted on me yet. 'It could be,' Helena retorted bleakly, 'this is just what Severina *wants* you to think. Do you believe Viridovix knew she was checking for people trying to get at his food?'

'Viridovix was no fool.'

Helena growled. 'Perhaps you were meant to discover the business with the giant pastry; it could be a clever double bluff, while the poison was really somewhere else –'

'Oh it was somewhere else!' We both fell silent. 'If he was poisoned at the dinner,' I said, 'it may rule out any connection with Priscillus. His business rival could not easily snuff him out in his own house.'

'Could not Priscillus have bribed one of the Hortensius slaves?'

'Risky. Slaves fall under suspicion so easily. It would take a large bribe – and then there is a risk that a slave with too much money becomes conspicuous.'

'Not if the slave was Viridovix; and if Viridovix is now dead!'

'I won't believe it was the cook.'

'All right. You met him!' She noticed I was really too tired to go on. 'Are we any further forwards?' she asked, smoothing my bedcover.

I lifted a scratched finger tenderly to her cheek. 'Oh I think so!' I leered at her cheekily.

Helena put my arm back under the cover. 'It's time I fed the parrot; go to sleep!'

'The parrot is old enough to feed itself.'

She was still sitting quietly with me. 'You sound better; it's a good sign when you can talk.'

'I can talk; I just can't move.' Something was on her mind. 'What is it, fruit?'

'Nothing.'

'I know my girl!'

'Marcus, how do you bear the pain?'

'At the time you're being beaten up, you tend to be too busy to notice it. Afterwards, you just have to be brave . . .' I was watching her. Sometimes Helena's dogged way of tackling life made her close in on herself. It was hard for anyone to reach her then, though sometimes she would turn to me. 'Sweetheart . . . when you lost the baby did it hurt?'

'Mmm.' Despite the brief answer, she was prepared to communicate. There might never be another opportunity like this.

'Is that why having another frightens you?'

'I'm frightened of everything, Marcus. Not knowing what will happen. Not being able to do anything about it. The *helplessness* . . . Incompetent midwives, crass physicians with terrifying instruments – I'm frightened I'll die. I'm terrified that after all that effort the *baby* will die, and how will I bear it? . . . I love you very much!' she said suddenly. It did not seem irrelevant.

215

'I would be there,' I promised her.

She smiled sadly. 'You would find some urgent job to do!'

'No,' I said.

Helena wiped away her tears while I lay trying to look reliable. 'Now I'll go and feed the parrot,' she said.

She made the mistake of looking back from the door.

I grumbled plaintively, 'You're only using that parrot as a handy alibi!'

'Look at the state of you!' Helena scoffed. 'Who needs an alibi?'

Then before I could reach out and grab her she had to run, because a grinding noise announced that the damned parrot was learning to bend open the bars of its cage.

'Oh stop being so wicked and tell me who did it!' Helena roared.

But Chloe only shrieked back, *'Marcus has been a naughty boy!'*

Untrue, unfortunately.

LIII

Helena decided *she* would visit her parents before the Senator (with a large cudgel) came to visit *me*.

I was half dozing when I thought I heard her returning; I lay low until someone came into the bedroom, when I shouted out, 'Is that you?'

'*Oh Juno!*' Wrong voice! 'Yes; it's me – you frightened me!'

Severina Zotica.

I sat up abruptly. She had the parrot on her forearm, so she must have been into the office where we kept its cage. I wondered if the prying cat's little feet had also invaded Helena's room. Her nose would have brought her tripping in here, for Helena was a determined believer in fenugreek poultices, continually applied (unlike Petronius, who cleaned wounds once with his balsam resins, then tended to lose interest).

My mashed features stopped the gold-digger short. 'Oh no! Oh, Falco, whatever happened to you?'

'Appius Priscillus.'

She was at the bedside, fluttering with concern. 'But you need looking after –'

'Someone takes care of me.'

Her eyes darted round quickly. She had already absorbed the fact that despite half a week's dissolute growth of beard, I was well sponged down, combed, and fitted out like an eastern potentate with cushions and bowls of figs. My abrasions and swellings had finished growing worse, though they had not yet begun to improve; the bandages were off to air them, but I had been covered up with a clean tunic – not for modesty, but to stop me prodding the bumps and scabs to check progress every five minutes.

'Your mother?' Severina queried sharply.

'Girlfriend,' I stated, for some reason not wanting her to know.

Severina's white face seemed to become taut. At that moment the parrot crooned softly in its throat, so she stroked the feathers on its

217

grey neck. 'You lied to me, Falco – about this bird – and about your woman friend too.'

'Not at all.'

'You said –'

'I know what I said. It was true at the time. It's my girlfriend who needs Chloe for company. They both have tricky tempers; I think they're taming one another . . .' These jolly jests were making little headway. 'I'm sorry I couldn't keep in touch; I've not left the house since this. What can I do for you?'

'One of my slaves heard a rumour Priscillus had had you worked over, so I rushed round here of course – I never imagined it would be so bad!'

'It's getting better. No need to get fluffed up.'

Helena's wicker chair was by my bed, so I motioned Severina to sit down. 'Nice to have a visitor.' The atmosphere seemed tense and I wanted to loosen the screw.

She scowled. 'So where is your attendant?'

'Helena?' The girl's insistency was irritating me, but stretched out on my own bed in comfort, I could not be bothered to fight. The redhead seemed to have an envious urge for possession, like a child snatching at other infants' toys before it has been taught self-control. 'Helena Justina has gone to explain to her father, who happens to be a senator, why *I* have yet to put in an appearance to apologise for pinching his noble child. If a man rushes in with red crescents on his boots –' (the traditional patrician uniform) '– bearing a sharp sword and a furious expression, just step aside and let him get to me!'

'You unspeakable hypocrite – you're after her money!'

'Oh she's after mine. I have great difficulty keeping her away from my accounts!'

People never believe the truth.

There was a silence. I was still too sick to concern myself with other people's touchiness.

'What's this, Falco?'

I had a slate on the bed. 'Today's diagnosis was boredom; I was left here with orders to write a poem. Thought I might scribble a satire on why I hate parrots.'

'What a rude man!' crooned Severina to the parrot.

'*What a rude man!*' Chloe instantly answered her.

'Quick learner!' I observed.

Unabashed Severina turned back to me. 'Does this mean the investigation has ground to a halt?'

'Ah! The investigation . . .' I joked, teasing her with flippancy. There were several queries I could have put to her: concerning egg-white glazes for instance, or thrownaway patisserie. But I had decided to complete my enquiries before I let Severina Zotica confuse the issue with more easy answers. I adopted my brave professional voice: 'I need a week at home in bed – but I shall have to make do with three days. Tomorrow morning is the funeral of the Hortensius chef, which I want to attend.'

Severina looked troubled. 'What happened to Viridovix, Falco? I heard he had died, very suddenly. Is it something to do with what happened to Novus?'

I smiled reassuringly. 'Viridovix died peacefully in his sleep.'

'Then why are you going to his funeral?'

'Firstly, I liked him. Also, it gets me near the house.'

'Looking for clues?'

'Could be.'

'Falco, I don't understand you sometimes! I am your client, Falco. Why is it necessary to be so secretive?'

'No complicated motive. All right: I think it might be useful to show the Hortensius family – and probably through them to warn that bastard Priscillus – that contrary to rumour I am still able to get about.' She looked down at me, as if she was afraid I might not manage it. 'Tell me, have you ever encountered this Priscillus?'

She frowned suspiciously, though in fact the question was mere curiosity. 'When I was married to the apothecary, we lived near that house of his up on the Esquiline. Then when things between him and Novus were at their worst recently, I went to see Priscillus myself. I acted as go-between and took his invitation to the dinner –'

'Novus agreed to that?'

'Of course! I would never have gone otherwise.' I nodded gravely, amused by this shocked protest; of course no respectable female visits men. But then who is respectable? 'If it was Priscillus who killed my fiancé, I helped bring it about!' She had a quaint way of overlooking ironies.

'Calm down,' I clucked. 'A property war was about to erupt well before you took a hand in it. And now I've been on the receiving end of Priscillus when he felt disgruntled, I reckon Hortensius Novus was destined for Hades whatever you did.'

'Do you think it *was* Priscillus? Did he attack you because you had some evidence?'

'Priscillus would probably have killed Novus if he could get away with it. I am not sure yet. My money is on Pollia and Atilia at the moment –' She looked satisfied with that alternative, as any woman would.

I was starting to worry why Helena had been gone so long; I missed her if she left the house. I suggested Severina could stay and meet her. 'No; I was on my way to the baths –' So much for making a special journey to see me! She persuaded the parrot to hop on to the post at the end of my bed. 'Now: you are going to the cook's funeral; I still don't really know why –' She paused, as if she did not entirely trust me. I scowled, which may not have given the reassurance she required. 'Will you come and see me afterwards?'

'If madam requires.'

Before she left she told me to take care of myself (though I thought we had established someone else was doing that), then at the last moment she leaned over and kissed my cheek.

I swear she expected me to grapple her onto the bed. Some people show no respect for an invalid.

'Alone at last!' I sighed at the parrot.

'More front than the beach at Baiae!' the parrot returned colloquially.

I started my poem.

Afterwards I did some thinking.

Anyone else who had been battered to cow-heel glue by Appius Priscillus might decide that alone convicted him of any unsolved deaths that month. I was not so sure. The sequence of events seemed illogical. Hortensius Novus had invited Priscillus to dinner, promising a pact; there was no way Priscillus could have known until the night was over that Novus would reject a merger after all. When things were looking hopeful, why come armed to murder him?

The over-ostentatious cake rang with the women's resonance. Obvious and vulgar. Too obvious, it seemed to me – but crimes are often committed with ludicrously poor judgement. Criminals are supposed to be cunning and clever. Sometimes fools get away with a crackpot scheme because no one can believe they would have behaved so stupidly. Not me though. After five years as an informer, I was prepared to believe anything.

I had been thoughtful too long.

'*So tell me who did it!*' Chloe screamed.

I threw my boot at her, just as Helena came in. She rushed out again, giggling helplessly.

'How was your father?' I shouted after her.

'He wants to talk to you.'

'I thought he might!'

She poked her head back round the door curtain and gave me a smile which ought to have warned me there was worse to come. 'Actually, my mother does as well . . .'

Helena Justina reckoned Falco's *Satire* I.1 ('*Let me tell you, Lucius, a hundred reasons why I hate this parrot* . . .') was the best work I had ever done.

Just my luck.

LIV

I make it a rule never to go to the funerals of people I have killed myself. But it seemed fair to make an exception for someone I had killed by accident.

Helena was still sleeping on the reading couch in the other room, on the poor excuse that she would not disturb my convalescing frame. Something would have to be done about that. I was already enjoying myself, planning schemes for changing things.

I got up quietly on my own. The day before I had dressed and mooched about the house to test my strength, but there was a subtle difference now I knew I was going outside. For the first time since I was hurt I made my own morning drink; watered the sleepy parrot; and looked about like a proprietor again (noticed that the crack in the wall seemed to be growing steadily). I took a beaker in to Helena. Hiding her anxiety, she pretended to be half asleep though an inch of warm cheek emerged from the coverlet to be kissed goodbye.

'Take care . . .'

'And you.'

On legs which felt like cotton floss I walked downstairs, then I noticed a carrier staring at my bruises so I walked all the way back to find a hat. In case Helena had heard me and was frightened, I popped in to reassure her it was me.

She had gone.

Puzzled, I turned back into the corridor. The apartment was silent; even the parrot had hunched up and gone back to sleep.

I pushed aside the curtain to my bedroom. Her beaker of hot honey now stood among my own pillowside litter of pens, coins and combs; Helena was in my bed. As soon as I left she must have scampered out and curled up here, where I had been.

Her brown eyes stared at me like some defiant dog, left alone, which had jumped up on its master's couch the moment he left the house.

She did not move. I waved the hat in explanation, hesitated, then

crossed the room to kiss her goodbye again. I found the same cheek
– then as I moved away she followed; her arms came round my neck,
and our lips met. My stomach tensed. Then a brief moment of
questioning dissolved into certainty: this was the old, sure welcome
only Helena could give – the girl I so badly wanted, saying that she
wanted me . . .

I made myself stop. '*Work!*' I groaned. No one would hold up the
cook's funeral if I stayed to play.

Helena smiled, still hanging round my neck as I feebly tried to
free myself while my hands began to travel over and round her more
deliberately. Those eyes of hers were so full of love and promise I
was ready to forget everything. 'Work, Marcus . . .' she echoed. I
kissed her again.

'I think it's time,' I murmured, against Helena's mouth, 'I started
coming home for lunch like a good Roman householder . . .'

Helena kissed me.

'Stay there!' I said. 'Don't stir – stay there and wait for me!'

LV

This time as I reached ground level some contractor's men were unloading their tools from a hand-drawn cart. A helpful sign. If the landlord was bringing in the finishing trades at last, maybe we should soon have new tenants too. Make the place less like living in a mausoleum. And some time – though probably not today! – I might persuade those fellows to stuff some hair and plaster in our crack.

I felt good. Even though I was going to someone else's funeral, *my* life was cheering up.

It was the Kalends of September. In Rome, still hot well into the evening, though in the northern parts of the Empire – Britain, for instance, where I had served in the army and later met Helena – there would be a damp chill now in the mornings and the long winter dark would already be making its approach felt on the late afternoons. Even here, time had taken a new turn round the spindle. I felt like a stranger. I had that uneasy mood which besets the emerging invalid, as if the city had lived through centuries in the few days I was confined to my sickroom.

I had come out too soon. The air felt troublesome on my fragile skin. The bustle disconcerted me. Noise and colour shouted alarm signals to my brain. But the first real shock of my working day was that when my hired donkey blundered up the slope of the Pincian, the stall where Minnius used to sell his cakes had gone.

There was nothing left. The stall, the awning, the delectable produce had all vanished. Even the oven had been dismantled. Someone had completely levelled the cakeman's pitch.

Within the extensive Hortensius grounds, smoke from a portable altar led me to the scene of the funeral. Members of the household were still winding out in convoy from the mansion; I stood back while they assembled in a space among the pine trees. Viridovix would be in famous company. Pincian Hill boasts the Emperor Nero's surprisingly tasteful monument.

There were no shocks at the funeral. Revelations at the bierside are a cheap device employed by epic poets. I was a satirist now, so I knew better than to expect surprises; we satirists are realists.

In my Greek brimmed hat, and the black cloak I wear on these occasions, I tiptoed discreetly among the mourners. I may not have passed entirely unnoticed, since the normal rule at funerals is that half the people present spend most of their time peering about for family celebrities; the keen-eyed, looking for long-lost half-brothers to complain about, would have worked out that I was an unknown quantity who might be good for a few hours of speculative gossip later on.

Crepito, Felix, and their two wives made a cursory appearance as their loyal servant was bundled into the Underworld with the minimum of fuss. The sweet oils were pleasant though not overpowering. A plaque had been commissioned; it would be set in the high boundary wall. I noticed it had been purchased and dedicated not by the masters of the house, but by his fellow slaves.

Once the Hortensii had paid their brief respects while the fire was lit, they went about their business; probably racing off to the slave market to acquire a new cook.

I pushed back the hat and made myself known to Hyacinthus, who was standing with the household chamberlain. As the flames burned up, we talked.

'Falco! You still look ready to step up on the pyre there with him!'

'After four days on nothing but grape jelly in milk, don't sneeze, or you'll blow me over. I was hoping to cheer myself up with some tipsy cake – what happened to Minnius?'

'Some trouble about his lease for the stall. Felix cancelled it and kicked him out.'

'So where has Minnius gone?'

'Who knows?'

Now the owners had departed I could sense undercurrents of bad feeling here among the slaves. The cook's death had caused rumours, however much the Hortensii convinced themselves it had been hushed up.

'It hasn't helped,' grumbled Hyacinthus, 'that they buried Novus in high old style – whereas poor old Viridovix had to wait around at the embalmers for the best part of a week, and now his send-off is as brisk as possible. He was a slave – but so were they once!'

'So much,' I said, 'for the concept of family!'

Hyacinthus introduced the chamberlain, an uneasy type with pointed ears who had been glancing at me curiously. 'Hello! I'm Falco. Viridovix and I shared a drink and some good conversation the night he died, that's why I'm here. Do you mind if I ask you something?' He looked shy, but let me proceed. 'I was talking to Viridovix about that dinner party; he told me how smoothly it passed off –' Without a remit from the family I had to be quick and careful. 'Do you know what happened after the diners settled down in private?'

The chamberlain had remained within call after the servants were shooed out. He was classy enough to know he ought to keep things confidential, and human enough to want to spill his tale. 'There was a bust-up,' he let out.

'What was the problem?'

He laughed. 'The problem was Novus!'

'What – he let the rest of the party know there would be no joint stock confederation as they hoped?'

'That's right. He refused to play; they could all put their knuckle-bones back in the drawstring bag . . .'

So that was it; I sucked air through my teeth. 'When Novus stomped off afterwards, leaving Felix and Crepito with Priscillus, did those three get their heads together? Wasn't it hugs all round on the doorstep when Priscillus left?'

'If you ask me –' he lowered his voice '– Crepito and Felix have been hooked up with Priscillus for a long time.'

'Unknown to Novus,' I commented. Then I realised. 'No . . . no, that's wrong – of course! *Novus* had found out!'

That explained everything – his partners and Priscillus believed he had invited them to dinner to reconcile their differences – but in fact, Novus was planning a spiteful scene: once the doors were closed and the conversation became sub rosa, he confronted them with his knowledge of their previous canoodling – to which his solution was: marry Severina Zotica, abnegate the time-honoured partnership, probably move house when he got married, set up solo – and take the business off with him. That would horrify Felix and Crepito – because not only would they lose their share of the Hortensius business empire, they would also forfeit any passing interest they had held for Appius Priscillus. He was no man to take on dud partners. They were dumped off both sides of the boat!

'Felix and Crepito must have been shitting Nile delta mud – how did Priscillus take it?'

'Surprisingly well,' said the chamberlain.

Up until then I had been surviving, but I suddenly felt too much aware that it was my first day out of doors. Excitement and the heat from the pyre were threatening to keel me over. I stopped talking. I had to concentrate on fighting this sudden sweat.

The chamberlain had done enough that day for truth and justice; I could feel him closing up.

A small group of us watched the last spurt of the sweet-scented flames as Viridovix went in the Roman fashion to his own remote gods.

'He was a prince!' I murmured. 'Though a dedicated cook. A classic. He and I saw out his last night in the way any cook would have wanted – with a good drink, pilfered from the higher-ups . . . in fact,' I sighed, 'I wouldn't mind knowing what the vintage was, so I can buy myself an amphora and drink it in his memory –'

'Here's your man then –' The chamberlain stopped a youngster, with the swollen eyelids of a late-riser up before his natural time, who was on his way forward to pour a libation on the pyre. 'Galenus keeps our cellar –'

'Thanks! Galenus, can you tell me what variety of Falernian Crepito and Felix drink – would it be Faustianum?'

'Falernian?' He pulled up. 'Not here! You must mean the Setinum – they reckon it's superior – one of their fads.'

Setinum was what Viridovix had listed on his menu, certainly.

'Are you sure you hadn't made an exception for a special occasion? There was a nice wine here the night your master died. It was in a blue glass flask with silver lustre on the shoulders . . .'

The lad became even more definite. 'Not one I ever put out that night.'

'We were on orders to impress,' confirmed the chamberlain. 'Nothing less than the gold jugs and anything set with gemstones.'

'Your flask isn't one of mine,' Galenus assured me. 'I don't recall even seeing one like that.'

'It never came back to you in the buttery?'

'No; I'm sure. I keep my eye open for fancy glass, for when the ladies want a tipple served up daintily in the afternoons.'

'That's very interesting!' I said. 'I wonder if it could have been a present someone brought?'

227

'Priscillus,' inserted another lad, a round and red-faced little apple who had been listening to us avidly. 'I was on shoe duty,' he explained. In the thick of it, removing people's sandals as they arrived. 'Priscillus brought the sparkling blue flask.'

I smiled at the russet. 'And was there a little bowl in matching glass?'

He did not hesitate. 'Oh Priscillus had that in a satchel put aside with his cloak. When he was leaving he suddenly remembered, and rushed to put the bowl on the sideboard with the flask. He had even brought some myrrh in a little bag, which he tipped in to make the present all complete . . .'

What a touching thought. I could hardly contain my admiration: a model guest!

LVI

I looked around for the skivvy Anthea, but the burning pyre seemed to have brought the cook's death fully home to her; the wheyfaced scullion was sobbing in the arms of two weepy cronies the way teenage girls do. I had a couple of questions ready, but I abandoned them.

Not long before the smoke died down, I recognised a figure approaching from the gatehouse. It was one of Severina's slaves.

'She wants you to come for lunch.' It was typical of this solid doorstopper that he grunted it without preliminaries.

'Thanks, but I won't be able to manage it.'

'She won't like that!' he said.

I was tired of his mistress trying to make demands on me when I had busy plans of my own, but to get rid of him I said I would break my previous appointment if I could (not meaning to try). Then I slung one end of my black cloak over my shoulder and studied the pyre like a mourner who was lost in melancholy thought: the transience of life, inevitable death, how to avoid the Furies, how to placate the Fates (and how soon can one politely make an escape from this funeral . . .).

When the slave had gone I cast my garland and poured my oil, said a few words in private to the cook's soul, then collected my hired donkey and left the scene.

At the site where the cake stall once stood I reined in thoughtfully.

I had to be clear what I intended doing now. I had been working for Severina simply to stay close enough to study her as a suspect. It must be nearly time to choose where I really stood.

Yet it was beginning to look as if Severina's theories about who killed Hortensius Novus might be accurate. Priscillus for one had attempted it, after Novus took his stubborn business stand. And apparently either Pollia or Atilia was responsible for another try, with a poisoned cake.

I considered the one line of events which I could now trace

229

satisfactorily: Priscillus planting the poisoned spices which killed Viridovix. A murder which did remove a key witness to what had happened that day in the kitchen – yet a murder brought about by chance. If I had not gone into the dining room for professional reasons that evening, Viridovix would never have rushed in there too. No one could have planned that. Poor Viridovix was an accident.

For obvious and very strong reasons I wanted to avenge the cook. For equally strong social reasons, there was no future in doing it.

True, I had enough evidence to ask a magistrate to indict Appius Priscillus. But face facts: Viridovix was a slave. If I showed that Priscillus had killed him – especially without intending to – what would probably happen if it ever reached a court would be not a murder trial, but a civil suit by the Hortensii for the loss of their slave. The worst charge levelled against Appius Priscillus would be a compensation claim for lost property. No court would put much value on a Gallic prisoner of war; a cook, and not even Alexandrian! Two hundred sestercii, at the outside.

That left my only hope of exacting retribution for Viridovix in the indirect approach: through proving what had happened to his dead master and bringing *that* culprit to book. All I knew was what had *not* happened. I could name suspects with motives, but possessing a motive to kill someone was not, in these enlightened days, enough to have them denounced publically. They had made attempts; yet as far as I knew the attempts had failed. Again, probably no charge.

Lastly, there was Severina Zotica. Severina, who had established a wonderful motive for herself when Novus agreed to marry her – and lost it, the moment he died before their wedding contracts were exchanged.

Perhaps she had *another* motive. But if so, I could not fathom what it was.

Why do funerals always arouse such a tearing appetite? I had to stop thinking about life, death, and retribution. All I could apply my mind to was the now futile memory of delectable cakes.

What ineptitude makes a landlord destroy such a boon to the community? Minnius would have been an asset to the neighbourhood whatever rent he paid. By clearing him out, Hortensius Felix must have made his name a byword for pointless destructiveness all over the Pincian. Well, landlords are used to that. Who knows what labyrinthine form of reasoning churns in a lessor's perverted mind?

Though in this case the answer was unfortunately obvious: Minnius knew too much.

What could he have known? Simple: Minnius knew who bought the dinner-party cakes.

It was dangerous knowledge. For a moment I even wondered if the cakeman might be dead. Perhaps one dark night after Hortensius Novus was poisoned, sinister shapes had come flitting down the hill from the freedmens' mansion, battered the unlucky pastry king while he was sleeping, and buried the corpse in a shallow grave on the site of his flattened oven and stall . . . No. I was still sick and rambling. One glance round the area convinced me that no soil had been disturbed. (I was a market gardener's grandson – but more than that, I had been in the army; the army teaches you all there is to know about digging hostile ground.) After a long hot Roman August it would be obvious if anyone had attempted to scrape at this hard-baked hillside. Only the sun had forced open these giant cracks where furiously aimless ants ferried themselves to and fro with specks of chaff while the more sensible lizards basked. Only wheels and hooves had ever packed down the surface of this road.

Minnius might be dead, but if so he wasn't here. And if he wasn't here, in the absence of other evidence I might as well hope he was alive.

So where would he go? Thinking back to my previous conversations with him, it was possible he had told me the answer himself: '. . . *in those days I was still selling pistachio nuts off a tray in the Emporium . . .*'

I turned the donkey down the hill, and set off across Rome.

It took me an hour to find him, but I managed eventually. So it was an hour well spent.

The Emporium sits on the city side of the Tiber bank, under the shadow of the Aventine. It is the main exchange in Italy for produce imported by sea, quite simply the greatest, most fascinating commodity market in the Empire – the hub of world trade. You can buy anything there, from Phoenician glass to Gallic venison; Indian rubies; British leather; Arabian peppercorns; Chinese silk; papyrus, fish pickle, porphyry, olives, amber, ingots of tin and copper or bales of honey-coloured wool; and from Italy itself all the building bricks, roof tiles, ceramic dinner services, oil, fruit and wine you could ever want – provided you are prepared to buy it in wholesale quantities. No point asking the man politely if he will pick you out just one nice nutmeg; it must be twenty caskfulls, or you'd better be on your way

231

before he reinforces his raucous sarcasm with the sole of his boot. There are stalls outside for timewasters who only want something tasty for the family lunch.

I had known the cavernous interior of the Emporium building, the wharves where the Tiber wherries jostled in queues before they landed, and the unloading bays for the creaking wagons that rumbled overland from Ostia, since I was knee-high to a Macedonian. I knew more people in the Emporium than my brother-in-law Gaius Baebius did, and he worked there (mind you, unless he landed you with the calamity of his marrying your sister, who would want to know Gaius Baebius?) I even knew that although the place appeared to be stuffed with produce, there were good days at the Emporium; but when the right ships had just landed there could be even better ones. Mind you, the normal rules of human life applied here as well: if you dropped in for that special rose-tinted marble your architect had recommended to face your reconditioned atrium, the odds were that the very last sheets in stock would have gone out yesterday to some baker who was building himself an atrocious mausoleum, and as to when another consignment could be expected, legate – it would depend on the quarry, and the shipper, and the winds, and frankly, *who could say?* Odds on, you would buy yourself a Syrian perfume jar to save being altogether disappointed by the trip – then drop it on the doorstep when you reached home.

Leave that aside. *My* trip was a success.

The main building was the usual throng of porters and patter. Pushing my way round this noisy bazaar was not the wisest occupation for a recent invalid. But I did find him. He had gone down from a stall but was still one up from his old tray; he was now selling from a stone-faced counter, though he told me he had to take his wares to be cooked first at a public bakery.

'So why did Felix chuck you out?'

'Novus was the sweet tooth in that house,' Minnius mentioned warily.

'Oh I know that! I'm working on a theory that his sweet tooth was what finished Novus –' I stopped short. Best to avoid too much stress on the possibility that Minnius sold cakes that caused poisonings – even if it was somebody else who put the poison into them. 'So how are you managing?'

'Oh it's home from home. I should have come back years ago. I kept telling myself I ought not to leave there because I had built up a good passing trade, but you just as soon create your regulars in a place like this.'

'You like the bustle. On Pincian Hill even the fleas are snobs.' Minnius served a porter with a giant-sized slab of tipsy cake. 'So – three questions, my friend, and then I'll leave you to get on!' He nodded. People like to know there will be set limits to the invasion of their time. 'One: tell me about the batch of confectionery you sent up the hill the night Hortensius Novus died. Were there any special instructions, or was the choice left to you?'

His face set slightly. My guess was, somebody had warned him to keep his mouth shut, but he decided to tell me anyway. 'The original request was for seven luxury pastries. The runabout ambled down the day before and placed the order – a mixture, my choice; but on the afternoon somebody came by and picked another out.'

'Much bigger than the ones you sent,' I said quietly. 'It was to go in the centre of the platter for effect. It would have caused an effect all right!' I commented, leaving Minnius to work out why. 'Question number two, therefore: who picked the extra cake, Minnius?'

I had money on two of them, mentally. I would have lost. Minnius, with his eyes steady, answered, 'Hortensia Atilia.'

The meek one! *That* was an unexpected treat. I thought about it. 'Thanks.'

'And your third question?' he nagged. Behind me a queue was waiting to be served.

I grinned at him. 'The third is; how much to buy two of your raisin-stuffed pastry doves, for me and my special lady?'

'How special?'

'Very.'

'Better do you a special price.' He wrapped two of the biggest in vine leaves, and gave them to me for nothing.

I put the cakes in my hat, which I carried. Then I set off for home and the special lady who was waiting for me there.

I left the donkey in the hiring stables since I expected to be indoors some while; there was no need to deprive him of shade, hay and companionship. Besides, I hate paying standing time.

The stables were just around the corner from where we lived. From this corner, you could see the entire block. I was like a lad with his first sweetheart, staring round in wonder at everything. I looked up, which you normally never do at your own house since you are thinking about wherever you have just come from, and trying to find your latch-lifter.

The sun was above me, hitting my left eye. I started to squint, looking away from the apartment. Then I had to look back.

Something produced an odd effect. I shaded my eyes. The building seemed to shimmer for a second, though not with light. I was about fifty yards away. The street was busy; no one else noticed anything at first.

The entire frontage of my apartment block crumpled, quite quickly, like a human face dissolving into tears. The building swayed, then visibly hung in the air. All the natural forces which keep a structure upright had lost their effect; for an instant every component was suspended in space individually. Something maintained the shape of the building – then nothing did. The block neatly folded, with a strangely compact motion, falling in upon itself.

Then the noise overwhelmed the street.

Immediately afterwards we were swamped by a great cloud of masonry dust which enveloped everyone in its stinging, suffocating filth.

LVII

First the incredible silence. Then people start to scream.

You have to clear the dust from your eyes first. Shaking yourself makes it worse. You cannot move until you can see. Your senses are fighting to catch up with what is happening.

The first screams are the people in the street, startled and shocked, but grateful that they at least still have breath to scream. After that there may be others, from underneath the rubble, but it is difficult to tell until the panic quietens down and someone starts to organise. Someone always will.

There is a procedure to follow. In Rome, buildings often come falling down.

Word goes round the neighbourhood quickly; the noise assures that. In no time men run up with shovels and props. Others will follow with carts, grapplers, barrows from building sites, makeshift stretchers and perhaps even a hoist. But not soon enough. If the building was known to be occupied, those of you on the spot don't wait. Before the men come with shovels you start in with bare hands. It achieves little. But how can you just stand?

All I had in the world to worry about was two pastries in a hatful of dust. I put the hat down on a doorstep and laid my cloak over it. A gesture really; while I tried to cope.

Stay there . . . Don't stir – stay there and wait for me!

The walk to what had been our apartment seemed to take a year. Others were moving forwards with me. Even if you are a stranger you do what you can.

I wanted to shout; I wanted to roar. I could not bear to speak her name. Someone did shout: a cry, just a noise to say we were there. So next we stood, listening to the debris settling. That is the procedure; you shout or you knock on something; then listen; then dig. With luck, you are digging for someone. But you dig anyway. You wrench away whole beams as if they were cordwood, turn over doors which are still attached to frames, bend jagged spars, and scrabble among tons of anonymous rubble which somehow no longer bears any resemblance to the materials which originally went into the block. All around the air is cloudy. Shapes move. The mass beneath your boot sinks suddenly, with a lurch that makes your heart race, amid more sick clouds of filth. A four-inch nail, still as bright as the day it was first hammered home, gouges your bare knee. The backs of your hands are in shreds from scraping against bricks and concrete. Your sweat can hardly manage to trickle through the thick coating of pale dust that dries your skin. Your clothes are stiff with it. Your boots will never be worth pulling on again. Through their thongs your toes and ankles bleed. That dust clogs your lungs.

Every now and then people stop again and call for silence; then somebody who has the heart for it shouts. And you listen to the slow trickle of loose mortar among the broken bricks and tiles and papery lathes that were once your home.

If it was a large building, you know before you listen that there is very little chance of anybody ever answering.

While we were working I hardly spoke to anyone. Even strangers must have realised the place was known to me. When the first spades came I snatched one at once; I had proprietary rights. At one point there was a sudden rattle of subsidence so we all jumped back. I took the lead then, to supervise the forcing of props into place. I had been in the army. I was trained to take command of civilians when they were running round like chickens. Even in a catastrophe, you have to be businesslike. Even if I had lost her, she would expect that. The girl would expect me to do what I could, in case I could save someone else. If she was here, at least I was close to her. I would stay here, day and night if necessary, until I knew for certain where she was.

What I felt would have to come later. The later the better. I was not sure I could ever endure what my brain already said I felt.

When they found the woman's body, everything went quiet.

I never knew who said my name. A space cleared. I forced myself to stumble over there and look; they all waited and watched. Hands touched my back.

She was grey. Grey dress, grey skin, grey matted hair full of plaster dust and fragments of building material. A complete corpse, made of dust. So covered with filth that it could be anyone.

236

No ear-rings. The wrong curve to the lobe, and no gold there – in fact no tiny hole to take the hook.

I shook my head. 'Mine was tall.'

Besides, once I was certain it was safe to look properly, I could tell that under the grey dust this woman's hair would still be grey. The hair was thin – just a sad trail in a braid no broader than my little finger, which petered out to a few strands after a foot or so. Mine had a thick plait, hardly varying in width, down to her waist.

Someone dropped a neck scarf over the face. A voice said, 'Must be the old woman on the upper floor.' The mad old bag who had so often cursed me.

I went back to work.

It had upset me. I was beginning to imagine now what I was going to find.

I paused, wiping the sweat from my filthy brow. Someone who knew he had more will than me at that moment took the shovel from my hand. I moved aside, as he attacked the swamp of masonry where I stood. Standing idle for a moment, something caught my eye.

It was the handle of a basket. I recognised the shiny black raffia wound round it by my mother when the original canework started to unwind. I dragged it to the surface. Something of mine. It used to hang beside the doorway in our living room.

I walked aside. Bystanders were quietly handing drinks to slake the rescuers' throats. I found a beaker shoved into my hand. There was nowhere to sit. I squatted down on my heels, swallowed the liquid, put down the cup, shook the dirt off the basket and looked inside. Not much. All I had left. The pride of our household: ten bronze spoons Helena once gave me; she had refused to let me hide them in my mattress now they were needed for daily use. A dish that belonged to my mother, put aside for her. My best boots; hidden from the parrot . . . And a cheese grater.

I had no idea why the grater had been singled out. I would never be able to ask. So much unfinished business: the worst result of sudden death.

I replaced everything in the basket, shoving my arm through the handles right up to the shoulder. Then my bravery ended; no longer any point to it. I buried my head in my arm and tried to shut out everything.

Somebody was shaking my shoulder. Someone who must have

known me, or known her, or both of us. I looked up, full of rage. Then I saw him point.

A woman had turned round a corner, just as I did half an hour ago. She had a big circular loaf in her arms. She must have been out to buy something for lunch; now she was coming home.

Home was no longer there. She had stopped, as if she thought she had turned into the wrong street in a daydream. Then the truth of the collapsed building struck.

She was going to run. I spotted her before she started moving, but her intention was clear. She thought I might have been in the apartment; now she thought I was dead underneath. There was only one way to let her know.

I whistled. *My* whistle. She stopped.

I was on my feet. She had heard me. At first I could see she could not find me. Then she did. There was no need any longer, but I was already shouting. At last I could say it. *'Helena!'*

'My lass, my love – I'm here!' The loaf crushed to a thousand fragments between us. Then she was in my arms. Soft – warm – living – Helena. I gripped her skull between my two open palms as if I was holding treasure. 'Helena, Helena, Helena . . .' Her hair caught on my roughened fingers where I had been dragging beams aside in search of her. She was clean, and untouched, and crying her heart out helplessly because for one fraction of a second she had believed she had lost me. 'Helena, Helena! When I saw the house fall down, I thought –'

'I know what you thought.'

'I said you were to wait for me –'

'Oh Didius Falco,' Helena sobbed, *'I never take any notice of what you say!'*

LVIII

People were slapping us on the back; women kissed Helena. I would have returned to the digging, but the crowd voted otherwise. We were jostled into a tavern where a flask, which I needed, appeared in front of us followed by hot pies, which I could have done without. My hat and cloak were brought in to me. Then, with that gentle tact which strangers discover for one another at the scene of a catastrophe, we were left alone.

Helena and I sat close, heads together. We hardly spoke. There was nothing to say. Just one of those times of deeply shared emotion when you know that nothing can ever be the same again.

A voice I knew cut through my concentration when almost nothing else would have broken it. I turned. A sleepy-eyed gawper in a brown and green striped tunic was buying himself a drink while he stood unobtrusively in the shade of the awning and peered outside. He was surveying the extent of the damage. It was the letting agent: Cossus.

I got to him before he received his order. I must have sprung out, still covered all over with dust, like a spirit from the Underworld. He was so amazed he had no time to dodge away.

'Just the man I want to see!' I gave him the elbow treatment, and fetched him indoors. 'If you want a drink, Cossus, come and have one with us –'

Helena was sitting on the nearest bench so I made Cossus take the other. There was a table in the way of it, but I lifted him, slewed him sideways, and threw him across there anyway. I leapt the table myself with a one-handed vault, landing astride his bench. Cossus gasped. 'Helena, this is Cossus; Cossus is the wonderful chap who controlled our lease! Sit down, Cossus –' He had been trying to struggle upright but sank down immediately. 'Have a drink, Cossus –' I gripped him by the hair, screwed his head against my side, seized the flagon and poured all that was left of it over his head.

Helena did not move. She must have realised it was a pretty awful draught of wine.

'That's your drink. Next,' I said, still in the same convivial tone, 'I'm going to kill you, Cossus!'

Helena reached across the table. 'Marcus –' Cossus looked up at her sideways with what must have been (for a letting agent) gratitude. 'If this is the man who controlled our apartment,' said Helena Justina at her most refined, 'I should like to be the person who kills him myself!'

Cossus squeaked. Her measured, aristocratic tones were more chilling than any grit of mine. I let him go. He straightened up, rubbing his neck. He flashed a glance round the tavern in search of support. All he saw were turned backs. They knew his pedigree. If I killed him no one would help him; people were hoping that I would. Helena had made herself popular in the neighbourhood. If *she* killed him, people would probably help.

I walked back round the table and sat with my lass.

'You chose the wrong day, Cossus,' I said grimly. 'The Kalends of September is a white day in the calendar; it's tomorrow people mark with the sign of bad luck. No style, Cossus! How can your tenants plan ahead?' He started to mutter. I cut him short. I turned to Helena and asked her quietly, 'I noticed this morning the landlord's contractors had turned up to do some work on the ground floor. Were they still there when you went out?'

'They were just finishing,' Helena returned. 'They were taking away all that scaffolding that used to be in the entrance.'

'Bit of a mix-up,' Cossus mumbled, still too crass to know when to stop the bluff. 'Must have disturbed something –'

'Me, for instance!'

'Sorry, Falco,' Cossus reluctantly answered, knowing his skull was in danger of being shattered by my fist.

'So am I, Cossus.'

'The landlord will offer compensation –'

'He will, Cossus! That would be very sensible!'

'How,' Helena enquired levelly, 'can he compensate the old lady from the fourth floor, who is dead?'

'Unforeseeable miscalculation by our civil engineer,' he hedged, trying out the excuse they must keep rehearsed for appearances in court.

'Rather drastic solution to your problems with her lease!' I weighed in. Cossus sighed. At last he appreciated that my grasp of the situation

240

made resistance irrelevant. He was lazy; he hated trouble. My inter-ference made him too depressed to answer, so I elaborated myself: 'The landlord was trying to terminate the old woman's tenancy so he could pull down the building and replace it with a more prestigious block. When she refused to leave, this charitable man saved her lawyers the trouble of fleecing her by demolishing the building anyway!'

'But why not simply give her notice?' demanded Helena.

'We did. Well,' the agent admitted, 'we should have done. The old biddy had been living up there for so long, I forgot she was there. We have a huge number of clients. I can't remember everyone. In June she tripped into the office and paid up, grumbling into her chin like they all do, so I just got rid of her as quickly as possible and only noticed her address after she had scuttled off cursing me. The owner had never really given me firm instructions about the place so I just let it lie. Come July, he suddenly made up his mind to rede-velop, but we were stuck with the old mother for another year.'

'Why exactly,' Helena enquired, 'did you then grant a new tenancy to us?'

He forced his aggravating features to appear ashamed. I would not trust him as far as I could see up a camel's backside at midnight; Helena might have put it more elegantly, but she felt the same.

'Make it look good,' I stated. 'When the place crashes down, it is easier to justify if the landlord pretends he was filling the empty apartments; then it's not deliberate demolition, but an accident during refurbishment. Tough luck, tenants (if you happen to have survived the shock): here's some of your rent back, so make sure you look grateful; now go away!'

'I told you the lease was temporary,' Cossus grumbled self-righte-ously.

'Excuse me! I must have misread my contract. I never realised it ran *"for six months – or until your house falls down."* '

'We can give you a pro rata rebate –' Cossus began. His mouth was like the doors on the Temple of Janus: never shut.

'Wrong!' snapped Helena. 'You will give Didius Falco a *full* refund, plus compensation for the loss of his effects and furniture!'

'Yes, madam.'

The concept of men making eager promises then changing their minds later was familiar to my love. 'You will write out a banker's draft for us here and now,' Helena decreed decisively.

'Yes, madam. If you want to put a new roof over your heads

urgently, I may be able to find something –' He was a true landlord's agent; a complete fool.

'Another of your temporary specials?' I sneered. Helena took my hand. We stared at him.

Helena Justina stormed off up the road to the local stationer's while Cossus and I agreed a price for my lost furniture. I enjoyed myself, and the agreed price was better than the furniture.

When she came back, Helena dictated the draft. 'Make it out to the lady,' I instructed. 'Her name is Helena Justina; she keeps all my accounts.' Cossus looked surprised. I cannot say how Helena looked, since I avoided her eyes.

We had reached the point where we either had to let the agent leave or have him arrested. It was Helena who said quietly, 'I should like to know our careless landlord's name.'

Cossus looked uneasy; I confirmed his fears: 'Getting our money back is just the start.'

'He has to be brought to justice,' Helena said.

Cossus started to bluster but I cut him short. 'Your principals have made a slight error. This lady who was nearly killed today by your so-called accident is the daughter of a senator. When her father hears what happened to his treasure he is bound to raise the issue of landlords' derelictions in the Curia – and that won't be the end of it!' The last thing Helena wanted was to let her father know how dangerous life with me could be. But he was bound to find out, and Camillus Verus was one of the few in the Senate who would be prepared to tackle the issue. 'I want to know anyway,' I continued. 'Just tell me, Cossus. So I can sleep tonight with a clear conscience – tell me I did not entrust myself and this precious lady to that calamity Priscillus!'

He looked relieved. 'Oh no, Falco!'

'Well then?'

Edging away, his voice withered to a croak as he tried to confess: 'I work for the Hortensii. Novus controlled your lease.'

LIX

I gripped the front of his baggy tunic in my two blackened claws and gave him a shake that would loosen his teeth.

'Don't blame me,' pleaded Cossus. 'I would have thought it was obvious!' He was waiting for me to let go of him, but I kept hold.

'Novus is dead! Novus died last week!'

'So what's the panic?'

'On whose instruction did the demolition go ahead?'

'Novus told me to put in the order weeks ago –'

'And when Novus died, did you never think of checking with his heirs?'

'I did check.' Something in the bluff way he said it rang untrue.

'With Felix or with Crepito?' I stopped shaking him, but screwed the tunic tighter round my fists. I felt certain he had been too idle to go up to the house and ask.

'She was in the office,' he muttered. 'She often gave me messages from Novus before, so I asked her. She said not to bother the others during the period of mourning, but to proceed as Novus planned . . .'

'Who, Cossus?'

'Severina Zotica.'

'The woman had no jurisdiction,' I replied immediately. I said it without passion, though I meant the words to go home. 'Cossus, she's made you an accessory to murder –' I lost interest in the agent, as the full meaning of what he had told me sank in: Severina, ordering the destruction of my apartment; trying to lure me away this morning; making no attempt to warn me that Helena was in danger . . .

Disgusted, I gave Cossus a shove. People who were standing at the bar helped push him along. As he reached the street he stumbled. Someone outside must have recognised him. I heard a shout and he started off running. By the time I reached the door he was past saving even if I had wanted to help.

Angered by unearthing bodies, the crowd cornered the agent, and battered him with the tools they had been using to dig. Then they strung together a cross, using beams from the rubble, and hoisted him up on that. But I reckon he was gone before they lashed him to the spar.

I sat down again, and put my arm round Helena. She put both hers around me.

I spent some time talking very quietly, not to Helena in particular but to the world at large. I was raging against landlords – the whole disgusting class of them. The mean; the shoddy; the grasping; those who acted with violent malice like Priscillus; and those like Novus who relied on slack, incompetent agents so they could distance themselves from the filthy conduct of their crimes.

Helena let me finish, then quietly kissed my grimy face. The pain eased slightly.

I leaned back far enough to look at her. 'I love you.'

'I love you too.'

'Should we get married?'

'Now? With no money?' I nodded. 'Why?' she asked. 'I'm happy as we are. Who needs ceremonies, and contracts, and idiots throwing nuts? If we live together in trust and love –'

'Is that enough for you?'

'Yes,' she replied simply. My strong, sarcastic lady had a strangely romantic streak. Besides, she had experienced the ceremony once and knew it guaranteed nothing. 'Is it not enough for you?'

'No,' I said. I wanted to make the full public statement.

Helena Justina laughed softly, as if she thought *I* was the romantic one.

We left the tavern. I had things to do. Bad things. I was not sure how I could tell Helena I would have to leave her now.

We walked slowly to the ruin of the building that had so briefly been our home. Now I understood why the crowd who caught Cossus had felt so violent: there were other bodies laid in a sorry line – a whole family, including three children and a baby. More 'temporary' occupants; we had never even known this sad group shared the tenement with us.

The diggers were still working. Only a few bystanders remained. Overnight the looters would descend. Tomorrow morning the Hortensii, looking diligent, would send the carts which they must already have on order to clear the site.

'At least we are together,' Helena whispered.

'We will be. Helena, I have to –'

'I know.'

She was wonderful. I held her tight and told her so. 'Do you still want to live with me?'

'We belong.'

'Oh my darling, we belong somewhere better than this!' As usual she calmed me down. 'We can find somewhere else, but I shall look into it more carefully than this place! Helena, I may not be able to rehouse us today – better go to your father's, and I'll meet you there later –'

'Slinking home with my tail between my legs?' Helena sniffed. 'I don't care for that!'

'I want you to be comfortable –'

'I want to be with you.'

'And I want you! Believe me, I don't want to leave you alone now; all I do want is to lock us away and hold you tight until *you* feel safe, and *I* feel better –'

'Oh Marcus, look!' Helena interrupted. 'There's the parrot!'

It was perching on a pile of rubble. Totally bedraggled, but not in the least cowed. Helena called, 'Chloe! Chloe, come here –'

Perhaps the cage had saved it. Somehow the creature had emerged alive and was now staring around at the wreckage with its normal air of dissolute superiority.

Small boys (whose mother would not thank them) were approaching with the aim of catching it. Chloe never liked men. She let them come within arm's reach, then fluffed up her feathers, hopped a yard in the other direction, and took off. Her tail flashed scarlet as she lifted. I joked, 'Better warn the local starlings they are likely to be mobbed!'

Helena was straining up to watch the parrot's flight. Chloe swooped in a defiant circle near her head.

'Marcus, can she live, if she's loose?'

'Oh that bird leads a charmed life.'

Chloe landed briefly. 'Chloe! Chloe!' Helena cried.

More desperate to catch her now someone else was interested too, the small boys lunged. Chloe slipped away from them, and fluttered to a rooftree far out of reach.

'Come down here and tell me who did it!' Helena screamed with frustration.

'*Oh Cerinthus! Cerinthus! Cerinthus!*' squawked Chloe obligingly.

245

Then we watched the parrot soar in ever-diminishing parabolas away into the hot blue Roman sky.

LX

There was nothing to gain by delaying any longer.

'Sweetheart! This job I do is stupid. You get knocked about; your house falls down; the most gorgeous woman you ever went to bed with is telling you she needs you; and yet off you go to round up villains – when you've just found out that the man the villains murdered is someone you would only have kept alive so you could murder him yourself!'

Shivering, I flung my black cloak round me. That reminded me; in my hat there were still my two cakes from Minnius, wrapped in his vine leaves so more or less free from dust. 'Take these; we'll eat them together at your father's house tonight,' I said, trying not to acknowledge Helena's painful need to stay close. 'Promise!'

She sighed. 'Father wants to see you anyway, now you're up and about.'

'It should cheer him up if I have to give you back to him!'

'We can talk about that,' Helena said; implying that there was nothing to discuss.

I banged my hat to shift some of the mortar dust, and rammed it on.

'You look like a messenger of vengeance! Anyone who sees you outlined in an archway will want to turn and run . . .'

'Good!' I said.

The dirt on my skin and in my hair was obsessing me; I sluiced off quickly at a bathhouse while I laid my plans.

It was midafternoon. Enough of this mosaic now existed for me to feel confident that once I started to manipulate the tesserae, I could fill in the gaps by guesswork and good luck. I had to see Priscillus, the Hortensius women, and Severina Zotica. Cerinthus could be a false lead. But if I could discover where this Cerinthus hung out, I had to see him too.

I chose Appius Priscillus first, and at his house on the Janiculan. Fired by my new incentive, I chose well.

Tension cramped my guts at the thought of meeting the Phrygian bodyguards, but the Priscillus organisation had been stood down – off watch during the siesta. I knew from the disgusting brown sedan in the hall that Priscillus himself was there.

The first mistake his porter made was letting me in. The second was going off to tell his master a visitor had called, without noticing that the visitor was padding behind.

'Thanks!' I smiled at the porter, steering him out of the way as I went in. 'No need to introduce us – Appius Priscillus and I are old friends.'

I had a grudge against Priscillus, which was embellished with bitter envy once I entered the room.

It was a spacious study, with large pannelled doors folded back to give an amazing view across the Tiber towards Rome. In the hands of any competent designer, the effect would have been spectacular. Priscillus probably bought the house for its position, but then he completely wasted it. It was full of natural light – and nothing else but heavily sealed strongboxes. Priscillus begrudged the most basic sticks of furniture. He had confined himself to such dingy paint and fixtures that he managed to ruin everything; there should be a law against spoiling the potential of such a perfect spot.

I felt my nose wrinkling. Its glorious position made the house much more palatable than his business address on the Esquiline; but there was a sordid smell of neglect.

'The game's up, Priscillus. Time for you to leave Rome!'

Priscillus, the same rat-faced runt in what looked like exactly the same frowsty tunic, found his voice with a venomous wheeze. 'Don't waste my time, Falco!'

'Or you mine! I'm calling you to account for the murder of Novus.'

'You've nothing on me, Falco!'

'Oh no? What about your party gift – the excellent Falernian!'

'There was nothing wrong with the Falernian,' Priscillus assured me a little too smugly.

'I'll go along with that!' I grinned. 'I tried a drop. A connoisseur might have said it overheated while it was standing in the dining room – but it was as smooth as I have ever drunk. On the whole best taken neat, however! The spices that came with it were a rather queer selection . . .' He shot me a glance. 'Myself,' I said, 'I never take myrrh and cassia in a wine of real character. Too bitter. Though it's true that in an inferior vintage, myrrh will disguise a multitude of sins . . .'

Enough said. I walked further into the room.

Priscillus started to run round under his fingernails with the pointed end of a stylus. 'What do you want, Falco?'

'Revenge, actually.'

'You'll be disappointed!'

'I don't think so.' My confidence was baffling him. He was too amazed even to send for reinforcements. I liked that. He was afraid I might have something on him so all I had to do was let him know I had. 'Priscillus, I know how Hortensius Novus was murdered. If it ever comes to court I'll be subpoenaed as a witness –'

'It won't.' He carried on digging out grime. Some of that silt probably found its way under his talons when he still had his milk teeth.

'Wrong. What I know is far too incriminating for Crepito and Felix to buy off the investigating praetor, however deeply he's in hock to Crepito.'

'How come you know so much?' Priscillus sneered.

'I found out while I was being hired to fend off the little gold-digger –'

'The girl did it!' he tried; a half-hearted attempt. 'She sat in this room, when she brought the invitation, and actually admitted that if she ever felt like disposing of an unwanted husband, she would poison him!'

'Novus was never her husband,' I responded logically. 'Useful though! Severina's presence must have seemed an ideal cover for the rest of you who wanted Novus dead. Don't think she didn't realise! I reckon her involvement was to come here and give you the idea. She set you up! You were supposed to do it after they were married – but unluckily for her you couldn't wait.'

'What's your evidence?' Priscillus mooned morosely.

'I went up to the house on business that evening. I witnessed your spice being stirred into the winecup; I saw the poison drunk. Well!' I exclaimed, as if I were still startled by the memory, 'I don't know what you were expecting, but poor old Novus certainly doubled up with surprise! Next minute he was stretched out on the latrine floor!'

This quaint mixture of detail and informed bluff started to have the desired effect. 'How much?' asked Priscillus wearily.

'Oh I'm not looking for a bribe!'

'*How much?*' he repeated. Evidently he had dealt with coy extortionists before.

I shook my head. 'You can't buy me. Things have gone too far. For one thing, I was pretty upset when you had me knocked about the other day – so anything I said to the Hortensius mob while under the stress of injury is your own fault!'

'Cut the pretty talk, Falco,' Priscillus growled, but I could see him wondering what I had said.

I straightened up. 'Here's my theory: Crepito and Felix had discussed with you the possibility of getting rid of Novus if he kicked up rough. He did, so you left him the extra present. When he died, those two went along with it at first.' Priscillus agreed none of this; though he failed to deny it either. 'It came as rather a shock when I pointed out to them that by poisoning the Falernian – which you rushed off without sharing – you must have been hoping to polish off not just Novus, but the entire Hortensius clan.'

He was good. He was so good it was dangerous. 'Why,' Appius Priscillus asked me serenely, 'would Felix and Crepito imagine I wanted to do that?'

I smiled. 'Did you warn them not to take any spice?' He said nothing. That was a mistake; it dropped him into my hands. 'Felix and Crepito are not the brightest boys on the Via Flaminia, but even they finally realised: you wanted a clear field. They only escaped by accident. Novus could never wait; it was just like him to start into the wine on his own. Before he knew Novus was dead, Felix had carried the flask to another room – their Egyptian salon –' I added, for extra conviction. 'He left the spice bowl behind. At first Felix and Crepito thought you had accomplished the Novus killing by some brilliant and undetectable method –'

'But you told them otherwise!' Priscillus threatened coldly.

'That's right,' I said. 'And now Pollia and Atilia also know you tried to poison their husbands. They have sent Felix and Crepito running to the law.'

Priscillus scowled. His narrow, secretive mentality would fight me all the way. 'You're stupid coming here today – I'm going to wipe you out, Falco!'

'No point. This is out of my hands. You'll be convicted by the Hortensii. Their servants saw you hand over the flask. They saw you run back with the spice bowl after quarrelling with Novus. Felix and Crepito may even corroborate that there was a prior conspiracy.'

'They're stupid enough to do that! What are you up to?' Priscillus demanded with contempt in the wheeze.

I let my hands drop. 'I hate the lot of you. I hated Novus; I was a tenant of his. The apartment he leased me was overpriced and undermanned, and today it fell down. Nearly killed my girlfriend; nearly killed me –'

Priscillus had such a spiteful spirit he could understand this kind of anger. 'You're fingering them for it?'

'What else?' I snarled. 'If I could implicate those bastards in the poisoning too I would! And now while they are spilling the dirt to their own pocket magistrate, denouncing you and preening themselves, I've run up here. I wanted to see your face when I told you I've already watched the law officers making enquiries at your house on the Esquiline, and their next stop must be here –' I could tell from his rat's face that Priscillus was already working out that this place was outside the city boundary, so the vigilantes might not arrive immediately.

'Time to move if you want to pack a sponge and a few moneybags!' I insisted. 'Rome's too small to hide in now, Priscillus. Your only hope of survival is to nip off and see the high spots of the Empire for a few years –'

'Get out!' he said. He was too preoccupied with his urgent need for escape even to shout for the Phrygian bodyguards to make their mark on me.

I scowled, as if I didn't like the order. Then I tipped my hat back on its string, flung my cloak around me bitterly, and left.

The grimy brown sedan chair scurried off a few minutes later.

Lying among the garden bushes, I watched some ponderously heavy trunks departing with him, supported on their shoulders by the sweating Phrygians. I could hear Priscillus bawling at them to hurry, as he was carried down the Janiculan towards the Via Aurelia and the Sublician Bridge.

There were more than thirty mileposts between here and the port at Ostia. I hoped he would make those Phrygians run all the way.

LXI

Easy really.

Just a handful of pathetic suggestions and a few lies. Bullies are so sensitive. You can bamboozle them with any soft tale which threatens their way of life.

What next?

Before I could tackle his rivals, those sly females on the Pincian, frankly I needed a rest. I found it – and possibly more than I bargained for – by taking a quiet stroll along the Transtiberina bank.

I walked north. I had to go north anyway. There was nothing to lose by trekking up past the farthermost spur of the Janiculan, and looking in at the scene of an old crime.

The Circus of Caligula and Nero – as lurid a pair of characters as you could meet at the back of a bathhouse – lies opposite the great right-hand bend of the river which encloses the Plain of Mars. As luck would have it, there were no races that week but there *was* a small exhibition of caged wild animals, surrounded by the usual nervous schoolboys wondering if they dared throw things, a little girl who wanted to pat a tiger, and a desultory trainer who rushed out from time to time to warn people away from the bars. On show were a hippopotamus, the inevitable elephant, two ostriches, and a Gallic lynx. There were a few bales of wet, dirty straw and a sad smell.

The showfolk owned some canvas booths in the shadow of the starting gates; as I went past to enter the Circus, I overheard a familiar female voice relating some tawdry tale. '. . . I thought he had just gone for a tinkle with his winkle, but he was *hours*; anyway I forgot all about him – why bother? – but when I went to feed the python, there he was; he must have stripped for action before he saw the snake – I found him cowering up against the awning, too scared to shout – all knobby knees and his poor little set of equipment dangling there like a three-piece manicure set . . .'

I pulled back a battered curtain and beamed. 'I shall never be able to look at an earscoop again! Thalia! How's the performing snake business?'

'Falco! You still trying to run away from home to do something adventurous? How did you know it was me?'

'Oh – I think I've met a parrot you must have known at one time . . .'

'That terrible bird!' she said.

Her companion – a thin specimen who must be the woman who fed the man who watered the hippopotamus – gave me a prim smile, and slipped out of the booth.

Thalia became more serious. 'You're dressed up like a messenger with bad news for somebody.'

'For villains, I hope. That talk we had the other day helped me a lot. Have you got a moment?'

'Let's get some air,' she suggested, perhaps afraid of being overheard.

She led me outside, and into the Circus. We paused slightly at the starting gates, where once the panther must have made its meal of Severina's husband Fronto. In silence Thalia and I climbed up a few rows and sat on the marble seats.

'I'm developing a theory about Fronto's death. Thalia, you said you never met his wife. So I suppose you wouldn't know whether Severina had a fancy man?'

'Couldn't say. But Fronto thought she did.'

'Did he suspect who?'

'I never heard a name. But Fronto seemed to believe there was someone she had known for a long time who could be hovering offstage.'

'That fits,' I said. 'She's mentioned a fellow slave from her original master's; she wears a ring he gave her. And a doctor who attended another of her husbands told me a "friend" came to comfort her afterwards. But there's no sign of this fellow anywhere now.' In fact when we were getting drunk together she had said he was in the Underworld. 'Tell me, Fronto and Severina were only together a few weeks. She seems to think badly of him. Did he knock her about?'

'Probably.'

'A rough type? All sweetness until they were married, then he cut up sour?'

'You know men!' she grinned. But then she added, 'Fronto didn't like to be made a fool of.'

'And he reckoned Severina had pulled a fast one on him?'

'Didn't she?' We sat brooding for a moment. 'Have I got to go to court, Falco?'

'Not sure.'

'Who would take care of my snake?'

'I'll try to keep you out of it . . . But I know a girl who's kind to animals, if it comes to anything.'

'I've been thinking about that stockman,' Thalia said, explaining why she was so worried about matters going further. 'I'm sure he came to work for us about the time Fronto got married – I can't be sure, but I had an idea that *she* persuaded Fronto to take him on.'

I smiled. 'That's the theory I've devised.'

'The thing is,' she told me slowly. 'I reckon I can remember the stockman's name now –'

'The mysterious Gaius?' I sat up straight. 'The one who let the panther out, who was then crushed by a falling wall?' Something else had clicked into place while we sat here quietly; details I had heard from Petronius: "Three children died when a floor fell in . . . The Hortensii average a lawsuit a month . . . *A wall gave way and killed a man, somewhere on the Esquiline* . . ." 'The name wouldn't be Cerinthus, I suppose?'

'You rotten bug –' Thalia accused me laughingly. 'You knew all along!'

I knew something else too. I now understood the real reason why Hortensius Novus died.

LXII

Time had gone by. It was dusk when I reached the Hortensius mansion, but its owners were so fond of displaying their lucre that they had already set up rows of resin torches and dozens of flickering lamps. As usual I ended up in a reception room which was completely new to me, alone.

The freedmen had bravely set aside their grief for Novus and were entertaining friends. There was a faint lick of perfumed garlands, and from time to time when a door opened I caught a distant swell of laughing voices with the shiver of a tambourine. The message which I sent in was framed to intrigue, with a warning beneath. A slave came back from Sabina Pollia asking me to wait. To while away the time while the company gorged she had me provided with a few titbits of my own: a feast, nicely presented on three silver trays, accompanied by a flagon of their well-aged Setinum wine. I discovered it was good quality because I was in no mood for tasting titbits so imbibing at least their Setinum seemed only polite.

On the wine tray were a matched pair of jugs with hot water and cold, a small charcoal burner, bowls of herbs, a pointed strainer, and fine twisted winecups of green Syrian glass: I amused myself for half an hour with these, then sat back on a couch decorated with silver lions and gazed thoughtfully about the vividly furnished room. It was too splendid to be comfortable but I had reached the stage where reclining amid tastelessness, despising it, suited my bitter mood.

Before long Sabina Pollia did appear. She was swaying slightly, and offering to serve me more wine with her own fair hands. I told her mine was a large one, leaving out the herbs and the water. She laughed, poured two, sat beside me, and then we both dashed off daring quaffs of Setinum, neat.

After days on an invalid diet, it tasted richer than I could handle. But I polished it off, swung to my feet and poured myself some more. I came back to sit beside Pollia. She laid one elbow on the back of the couch just behind my head, leaning on her hand as I gazed into her exquisite face. She smelt of some drowsy perfume squeezed from the glands of animals. She was slightly flushed and she watched me through experienced half-closed eyes.

'Have you something to tell me, Falco?'

I smiled lazily, admiring her at close quarters while her hand idly tickled my ear. The excellence of the wine burned comfortably into my windpipe. 'There are many things I could tell you, Sabina Pollia – most of them not relevant to the reason why I've come!' I drew my finger along the perfect line of her cheek. She gave no sign of awareness; I asked quietly, 'Do you and Atilia realise there are witnesses to what you tried to do with the poisoned cake?'

She grew very still. 'Perhaps Atilia should be here?' She spoke with neither embarrassment nor any other kind of feeling that I could recognise.

'As you wish.' She made no move to send for her crony, so I went on, 'Hortensia Atilia at least had the excuse that she thought she was providing for her young child. What about you?' Pollia merely shrugged. 'No children yourself?'

'No.' I wondered if that was a conscious choice to preserve her figure. Then she asked, 'Falco, have you come to threaten us?'

'In theory I am on my way to see the Praetor and report what I know. I realise,' I broke in as she tried to interrupt, 'the Pincian Praetor is heavily in debt to your family. But I shall remind him that under Vespasian's new administration, if he wants to win a consulship it will be in his interest to demonstrate how impartial he can be. I'm sorry; impartiality tends to be tough on a Praetor's private friends!'

'Why should he listen to you?'

'I have influence at the Palace, as you know.'

Pollia moved. 'Atilia will want to hear this. Atilia is involved in this, Falco; Atilia bought the cake –' She tailed off. I guessed she had been drinking steadily all night.

I had kept them separate long enough to disturb their composure; I nodded. She clapped her hands for a slave and not long afterwards Hortensia Atilia hurried in. Pollia spoke to her in a low tone on the far side of the room, while I played with the stuff on the wine tray.

'So what have you come to tell us?' Atilia asked, advancing towards me and taking the brisk role.

'Actually, I thought you would like to know that Appius Priscillus has just left town.' Atilia frowned immediately; Pollia, who was the more drunk, followed her lead. 'It was my suggestion. I informed

256

him,' I said, sounding helpful, 'that Crepito and Felix had found out how Novus was poisoned by the flask of wine Priscillus left here, and that they had realised he also meant to kill them. Priscillus saw that this news might rouse them to some heat! He thinks they are denouncing him.' I sat down on the couch with the lions, threw my head back, and smiled at them. 'May I ask you, ladies, what you did with the flask?'

Pollia giggled. 'We poured the wine as a libation on the pyre –' At the funeral of Novus, this must be; not when we buried the cook. 'And then,' she explained with a mild explosion of silliness, 'we added the flask to the fire too!'

'Destroying the evidence? Never mind; it wasn't relevant.'

'Not relevant?' Atilia queried. For the mother of a future senator, she was unfashionably sharp.

'The Falernian was harmless. Priscillus had poisoned the spices which he left to be mixed with it. It was Viridovix who took the spices, poor fellow. So you see, Priscillus only killed your cook.'

'Then what happened to Novus?' Atilia demanded.

'Hortensius Novus was poisoned by something he ate.' They were at full attention. 'I expect you noticed,' I told them, 'that when the cake platter came to the table, your special item had been removed?' Atilia went rigid; Pollia would have done, but she was too drunk. They must have geared themselves up to do the poisoning, then relaxed when they thought someone had thwarted their efforts. Now I was telling them they were murderers, when they were no longer prepared to deal with it. 'Unfortunately, the cake had been removed by Severina Zotica, who thought Novus would enjoy it as a treat after dinner on his own . . . I presume you realise,' I said gravely, 'that if this comes to court, the penalty for murder is to be fed to the arena lions?'

Guilt blinded my listeners to any holes in this tale. They came to sit either side of me. 'What are you saying?' Pollia murmured. '*If* it comes to court?'

'Well; I've had to deposit details in a place where I keep my records – in case anything ever happens to me, you know . . . But at present, apart from Zotica, I'm the only one who knows.'

'Are you and she intending to do anything about it?' Atilia asked.

I scratched my chin. 'I've been thinking about that on my way up here.' They were cheering up. 'The redhead won't bother you. Zotica will have to cut her losses; I hold evidence about her past husbands' deaths which she can't risk having exposed.'

'And what about you?' Atilia cooed sweetly.

'This could bring me a good bonus.'

'Who from?' snapped Atilia, changing tone.

'Any prosecuting barrister who wants a juicy case; several of them buy my information to provide lustre for their careers. Your story is guaranteed to pack the courts and make lawyers' names overnight. I could earn a lot of money if I turned you in.'

Pollia said bluntly, 'Then you can earn a lot of money if you don't!'

She deserved the Novus empire: a really snappy businesswoman, full of practical ideas! I gazed at each of them in turn. With the evil reputation some informers have, I knew I could convince them of anything. The blacker the better. 'I'm open to offers. There is a scheme which I run with my girlfriend for simplifying movements of large sums of cash.' Deplorable suggestions were what they understood. 'You've met her actually; I sent her up here to get a second opinion when you were hiring me – Helena Justina.'

'The senator's daughter?'

I laughed. 'Is that what she told you? She's with me! That school she pretended to be founding – well, that's how we operate. If you want to, you can donate an endowment for Helena's school.'

'How much?' rapped Atilia. I plucked a huge figure from the air. 'Falco, that's enough for a Greek university!'

'Got to make it right,' I assured her. 'We shall need to build a real school or the cover's no good. Luckily I know where there's a piece of land you can give us – one of your own apartments fell down this lunchtime in the Piscina Publica – *My* apartment!' I growled, as Pollia started to protest.

There was a small silence. I turned genuinely serious. 'People were killed. Too many people. Questions will be asked in the Senate. Better warn Felix and Crepito that that lackadaisical agent of theirs has already been strung up on a street crucifix, and they are facing intense public interest in their affairs. Face facts, ladies; you need to clean up the business methods Novus used – and you need to do it fast. I suggest a rapid programme of civic works: start paying for public fountains. Erect a few statues. Get yourselves a better name, because at present your standing couldn't be worse. For instance,' I suggested, 'we might name the new school after the Hortensius

258

family. That's a decent and respectable project, to impress the community!'

No one laughed, though one of us was trying to.

Pollia swayed to her feet. She was feeling ill. I raised my winecup as she fled the room. Silence fell, as I drained the cup and made ready to leave.

Atilia had turned her head; she came so close her breath tickled my cheek. I began to sweat. Then there was nothing to do but wait while Hortensia Atilia lifted her beautiful face into position for my kiss.

'Sorry,' I said gruffly. 'The night is too young, I have too much to do – and besides, I'm a good boy!'

LXIII

On Pincian Hill the scent of the stone pines wafted cleanly to my jaded brain. Rome lay clothed in blackness ahead, its geography distinguished only by faint lights on the Seven Hills; I could make out the Capitol and the twin peaks of the Aventine; in the other direction what must be the Caelimontium. A cake would have been nice, to speed my steps. But I had to do without, as I turned down through the lively early-evening streets, to face my last ordeal.

On the way to tackle Severina, I completed one further piece of outstanding business; I called at the marble yard. It was open, but lit with only a taper or two. The mason approached through the eery lines of rough-cut stone; his unforgettable ears stuck out like roundels either side of his bald dome. He peered at me anxiously as I stood waiting at the end of an alley among the travertine, still shrouded in my shapeless black cloak and shadowed by the wide brim of my hat.

'Scaurus! Has Severina been in about her commission? You told me she had to consult other people.'

'Her other friends backed out. Severina paid for the monument.'

'She can afford the occasional tribute to the dead! Scaurus, I never forget a promise; I told you I would be back when she'd made up her mind . . .'

Scaurus grunted. 'The stone's already gone.'

'Where to?'

'Tomb on the Via Appia.'

'Not in the family name of Hortensius?'

'Name of Moscus, I believe.'

The mason was mistaken if he thought that would be good enough; I was in a mood for perfecting things. 'I'm not traipsing out there among the ghosts at this time of night.' I smiled at him. 'Don't try it on, Scaurus. I can always go another day, but I know that I won't need to . . . All I want is the wording. Just show me your pocket scribble-board . . .'

He knew I could see the waxed tablets which he used to take notes, hanging from his belt. So he turned back a couple containing more recent orders, and there it was.

Not what I had assumed the first time I made enquiries. But exactly what I was expecting now:

```
        D + M
     C+CERINTHO
    LIB+C+SEVER+
    MOSC+VIXIT+
   XXVI+ANN+SEV
   ERINA+ZOTICA
   +LIB+SEVERI+
        FECIT
```

I read it aloud, slowly deciphering the monumental shorthand: ' "*To the spirit of the departed, Gaius Cerinthus, freedman of Gaius Severus Moscus, lived twenty-six years: Severina Zotica, freedwoman of Severus set up this*" . . . Very subdued. There's spare space on your diagram. What have you deleted at the end?'

'Oh . . . she couldn't make up her mind whether to add, "well deserving of him". In the end she left it out for some reason.'

An innocent enough phrase – much used on tombstones set up by wives, or their informal equivalent. Sometimes, no doubt, the tribute was ironical. But anybody reading it would infer a close relationship.

So I could tell the mason the reason why Severina made herself omit those words: however much she wanted to speak well of her fellow freedman, the girl was too professional to leave the slightest clue.

LXIV

It seemed an age since I had visited the house in Abacus Street. It was night now, but the house was flooded with light; she had three hefty legacies to pay for oil in her candelabra. In most homes work would have stopped. But Severina was doing the only thing left to a home-loving girl who had no prospective husband this week; sitting at her loom, planning how to catch another one.

I watched her, remembering what my sister Maia had told me about noticing whether the weaving was genuine. I reckoned it was. Even if nothing else about her could be trusted, she worked with a sure touch. When I came in she was able to keep the shuttle moving even though she glanced up angrily.

'Lunch has been cleared, Falco!'

'And dinner too! Sorry.' I walked to the couch, so she had to skew round from her work. I buried my face in my hands wearily. 'Oh Zotica! Today's been one trial after another; gods, I'm tired . . .'

'Anything we can get you?' she felt compelled to ask.

'No. All I want is honest company and conversation with a friend!' I breathed in heavily, then expelled the air hard to clear my lungs. When I looked up, she had dropped her wool altogether and was watching me nervously. 'I just left the Hortensius place. Before that, Priscillus.'

'What happened?' By now she was prickling with delight at facing a grand occasion. She knew I had come to finish things. Excitement was her medium; I would have to tip her over unexpectedly, or I would never succeed.

'Bad acting and lies mostly! Anyway, I've wrapped it all up for you . . . afraid the women filled me up with wine; I'm not myself –' I forced a grin, then flung up my hands. 'I feel soiled, Zotica! I resent being toyed with. I particularly resent the none-too-subtle implication that I am just another attractive artwork any freedwoman with more cash than discrimination can buy!' I had set off rambling pleasantly. 'I like to be a genuine find. The years have given me one or two knocks that will never be hammered out again, but my personality has been burnished into a choice investment for a connoisseur . . .'

'What's the matter, Falco?' Severina giggled.

'Nothing. Actually, I think it's all right. I think that without a shred of proper evidence I put the frighteners on all of them!'

'Tell me then!'

I ticked them off on my fingers. '*Crepito and Felix* know Priscillus would happily have poisoned them – so the dangerous idea of a joint partnership is scuppered. Now Novus is gone, their grip on the Hortensius empire has slipped a bit – especially since I've said that they are liable to a senatorial enquiry. They should be hastily cleaning up their business habits and devoting their lives to public works . . . *Priscillus* believes the other two are turning him in to the law. He's rushed off on a long sea cruise. That should be good news for his tenants. With any luck, he'll drown before he dares return to Rome.'

'How did you achieve all this?'

'It was nothing! Persuasiveness and charm. Meanwhile *Pollia and Atilia* are terrified that if they put a foot wrong I'll send them to the arena for their attempts to poison Novus. In return for my silence they are taking up noble deeds – in their own lavish style of course. I persuaded them to apply their energy to an establishment for orphaned girls. You're an orphan, aren't you; I could get you a place if you want –'

'How much liquor have they given you?'

'Not enough; it was a highly acceptable vintage!'

Severina laughed at me. I beamed at her. Suddenly she realised the merriment was a ploy and I was sober after all.

'My house fell down today,' I said. I let the smile go out of my eyes. 'But of course, you know all about that.'

LXV

I watched Severina's uncertainty gnawing.

'How ironic it would be, Zotica, if I brought you to court not for any of your husbands – or even for killing Novus – but charged with murdering the people who died today! An old lady I only heard banging on walls, and a family I had never even realised were living there.'

We both sat motionless.

'Why don't you ask?' I sneered.

She forced out the words: 'Is your friend all right?'

'What is it to you?' The danger of her situation had long informed those still blue eyes, but whatever she thought lay too deep to penetrate. 'You knew her didn't you?' I asked. There was enough steel in my voice for her to think Helena *might* be dead. 'She used the same baths as you.'

'I thought you sent her –'

'Yes, I realise that. You were wrong. It was her own idea. She must have wanted to know what I was dealing with. She never told me, or I would have forbidden it – tried to, anyway. Helena's resistance to domineering was one of the things I first fell for.'

'What happened to her?' Severina managed to ask.

'The apartment collapsed. Everyone who was inside was killed.' I paused. 'Oh there's no need to sit there wondering whether you should confess, Zotica! I know who to blame. Cossus told me. You knew. You gave the order, in effect. Then the nearest you came to warning me was a pathetic attempt to lure me here today – never mind anyone else who might be there!'

There was a change in Severina's face, but so imperceptible I could not define it. Not that I wanted to. Even if she felt regret I was hardened against her.

'I hold out no hopes of indicting you. I've lost my witness; Cossus is dead. He let himself be recognised, and the locals dealt with him.

In any case, the Hortensii were the landlords. Their agent should never have taken instructions from you. Why did you do it? To dispose of me, because I became a threat to you? What made you change your mind? A hope of using me after all?'

She spoke at last. 'You should be grateful I tried to keep you away!'

'While you eliminated Helena?' She was sharp; she realised I would not have been able to discuss it at all if that were true. 'Helena was out of the building, or you'd be dead. You had a reason for what you did today. Don't pretend you wanted me. Even if you did, do you really believe I would have turned to you – or any woman – if I lost her in that way? But your motive was much more complicated. I knew you were jealous – yet you were jealous of us both. You hated the thought of other people possessing what you had lost . . .' I leaned forwards so I came closer, down to her level as she crouched on her stool. 'Tell me about Gaius Cerinthus, Zotica.'

It was the first time I was ever certain I surprised her. Even now she refused to give anything away: 'You obviously know!'

'I know you and he both came from the Moscus household. I know Cerinthus killed Grittius Fronto. I could prove it; there was a witness. But the Fates decided for me that Cerinthus would not come to trial. I know Cerinthus was then crushed by a falling wall. I know Hortensius Novus owned the wall.'

She closed her eyes, a bare acknowledgement.

I could guess the rest: 'Cerinthus was a slave with you. What happened – you grew fond of him? After you were married to Severus Moscus, or before?'

'Afterwards,' she said calmly.

'Once Moscus died, you were a free woman with a handy legacy. You and Cerinthus could have been married and led pleasant lives. Why so much greed? Was amassing a huge dowry his idea or yours?'

'Both.'

'Very businesslike! How long were you intending to carry on?'

'Not after Fronto.'

'So first there was Moscus – was it Cerinthus who chose his master's seat in the hot amphitheatre?'

'Cerinthus bought the ticket; you cannot blame him for the sun!'

'I can blame him for not keeping old man Moscus out of it! Then the apothecary, Eprius; you managed that yourself somehow. And finally the wild-beast man. Two mistakes there – Fronto never told you he had a nephew who was expecting to inherit, and he also battered you. Cerinthus must have been able to cope with you going to bed with other men, but he took against brutality. His solution was as vicious as he could make it. But Cerinthus soon walked under some typically unstable Novus masonry. You ended up with a sticky reputation, a dead lover, money you had probably lost the taste for – and nothing to occupy you but revenge.'

Her skin had a yellowy papyrus look, yet her spirit was unchanged. 'You can say what you like, Falco.'

'And you won't budge? I'm not so sure. You must have worked your way close to Novus with real passion in your heart, but the night I told you he was dead it shook you, Zotica. Don't pretend otherwise! I think you realised the truth: hate was an empty motive. Novus was dead, but so was your lover. Cerinthus would never know you had avenged him. This time there was no one to share your triumph. This time you were alone. What, as you said to me, was the purpose of it all? Killing Novus was nothing like the joy of planning a future with someone you loved, was it, Zotica?' Severina was shaking her head, refusing to accept my arguments. 'I know, Zotica! I know just how you felt when you lost him, and I know how you still feel now. Once you have shared yourself like that, the other person becomes part of you for ever.' This time she let out a small exclamation of protest. It was too late; forcing her to admit the kind of emotion I felt for Helena only sickened me. 'What I cannot understand is how a person who had experienced real loss herself could deliberately inflict the same on anybody else! At least, dear gods, when Cerinthus died you did not have to stand in the street and watch the falling wall!' There was a tremor in her face; I no longer wanted to see it. 'I know you killed Novus.'

'You don't know how.'

'I have some pointers.'

'Not enough, Falco.'

'I know you nudged Priscillus into thinking of poison, and probably the Hortensius women too –'

'They never needed pushing!'

'I know you prevented the women's feeble effort, and would probably have stopped Priscillus, but you had left the house before the meal. Nerve failed, did it – without Cerinthus to support you? But why set the others up as suspects, then keep them all out of it? Why risk destroying your alibis by hiring me? Oh you do love flirting with danger, but you did chance it, Zotica. I'm not completely useless;

I've cleared them, even if I can't convict you. And why not let them take things to their conclusion, and carry out the deed for you?' She said nothing. I realised the answer; it lay in her obsessiveness. 'You hated Novus so deeply, you had to finish him yourself!'

'No proof, Falco!'

'No proof,' I agreed gently. No point pretending otherwise. 'Not yet. But evidence is bound to exist, and I'll find it. You condemned yourself by what you tried to do to Helena today. She's safe – but I'll never forgive you. I can be just as patient as you were with Novus, and equally devious. You may never rest now, Zotica. One false move, and I'll be on to you –'

She stood up. She was fighting back. 'Helena will never stay with you, Falco! She was brought up in too much comfort and she knows she can do better. Besides, she's too intelligent!'

I gazed up at her benignly. 'Oh she'll stay.'

'Stick with your own kind, Falco.'

'I'm doing that!' I swung myself upright. 'I'm leaving now.'

'I'll thank you and pay you then.'

'I want neither from you.'

Severina laughed ruefully. 'You're a fool then! If you want to live with a senator's daughter, you need money even more than Cerinthus and I did.'

Her jibe failed to rouse me. 'I need money all right. I need four hundred thousand sesterces; let's be precise.'

'To qualify as a middle ranker? You'll never manage it!'

'I will. And I'll keep my integrity.'

My ludicrous social position seemed to fire her with a desperate hope of suborning me after all. 'You should stay with me, Falco. You and I could do good work in this city. We think alike; we both have ambitions; we never give up. You and I could make a useful partnership in any area we chose –'

'We have nothing in common; I told you before.'

She gave me her hand, with a strange, grave formality. I knew I must have nearly broken her. I knew I never would achieve it now.

I pressed my thumb against the copper ring, her love token from Cerinthus. 'So all this was a clever vengeance campaign, eh? All for Venus? All for love?'

Sudden laughter lit her face. 'You never stop trying, do you?'

'No.'

'Or failing, Falco!'

It was her familiar vindictive farewell.

As I left the house, someone else was just arriving. A figure as smart as a bookmaker's uncle: bright tunic, bronzed skin, buffed boots, plenty of hair tonic – but not all swank. He was as sharp as pepper. Although it was a long time since I had seen him, I recognised him immediately: 'Lusius!'

It was the Esquiline Praetor's clerk.

LXVI

As soon as I realised who it was, my heart bumped: I guessed that there had been a new development.

We danced round one another on the doorstep. 'I'm just leaving,' I smiled.

'Corvinus heard there was another case to answer –' We carried on dodging, and squinting like rivals. 'How have you got on?' Lusius asked.

'She's clear again. I did manage to work out who arranged to do in the animal importer – but the perpetrator's dead. He was her lover, but without him there's not enough to take her to court alone. I made her admit she had a partner until recently, but that's all.'

'No other evidence?' asked Lusius.

'Zilch.' I gained the impression he was holding something back. I gripped his elbow and drew him into the pool of light from a bronze lantern which hung on Severina's porch. He made no resistance. 'What's the idea, Lusius? You look pretty pleased with yourself!'

The clerk grinned. 'This is mine, Falco!'

I raised both hands, backing off. 'If you found something . . . It's a bargain, Lusius.'

He told me in a quiet voice, 'I've got her on the apothecary.'

I had thought we had both run the apothecary angle into the ground. 'How? Will that doctor who examined him make a report at last?'

'No. But did he tell you that he never attended Eprius normally?'

I nodded. 'Apparently he was called in after the choking because he lived across the street.'

'And probably because Severina knew he was a fool . . . What I've found out,' Lusius continued, 'is that Eprius *did* have a physician of his own.'

'For the famous cough that killed him?'

'Eprius never had a cough.'

'I gather you spoke to his regular quack?'

'I did. And I discovered that for years his own doctor had been treating him for piles. The medicine man reckoned Eprius was very vain – and so embarrassed about his problem that Severina may not have known.'

'Does this have a bearing on our enquiry?'

'Ah well!' Lusius was really enjoying himself. 'I showed the normal doctor the remnants of the cough lozenge that allegedly choked Eprius – though I didn't tell him what it was supposed to be. It was rather mutilated, and partly dissolved, but he was fairly sure the thing was his own handiwork.'

'Then what?'

'When I did tell him which end of his patient the lozenge had been recovered from, he was extremely surprised!' I was beginning to guess. 'That's right,' said Lusius cheerfully. 'She must have known Eprius possessed a little box of magic gumdrops – but he lied to her about their purpose. The "cough lozenge" which Severina says choked him was actually one of his suppositories for piles!'

I said, trying not to laugh too hard, 'This will make a sensation in court!'

A narrow expression crossed the clerk's face. 'I told you this was mine, Falco.'

'So what?' He said nothing. I remembered he liked redheads. 'You're mad, Lusius!'

'I haven't made up my mind yet.'

'If you go in there to see her, she will make your mind up for you . . . Whatever do you see in her?'

'Apart from quiet habits, interesting looks – and the fact I would be living on the verge of danger every minute I was with her?' the clerk asked, with a rueful lack of delusion.

'Well you know exactly what you're in for – which is more than most people do! She says she has no intention of remarrying – which means she's actively looking for her next husband. Step right up, my boy – but don't fool yourself you'll be the one who can control her –'

'Don't worry. What's left of the lozenge will do that.'

'Where is the disgusting evidence?'

'It's safe.'

'*Where*, Lusius?'

'I'm not an idiot. Nobody can get at it.'

'If you ever tell her where it is, you're a dead man!'

Lusius patted my shoulder. He had a quiet confidence that almost frightened me. 'I've arranged perfect protection, Falco: If I'm a dead man before I'm ready to go, my executors will find the evidence, together with the doctor's sworn statement, and an explanatory note.'

A true lawyer's clerk!

'Now I'm going in,' he said. 'Wish me luck!'

'I don't believe in luck.'

'Neither do I really,' admitted Lusius.

'Then I'll tell you this: I met a fortune-teller, who told me the next husband Severina fastens on will live to a ripe old age . . . it depends if you believe in fortune-tellers, I suppose. Have you got a nest egg?'

'I might have,' answered Lusius warily.

'Don't tell her.'

Lusius laughed. 'I was not intending to!'

I stepped away from the porch; he lined up to bang the bell.

'I still think you ought to tell me where you have put the fatal jujube.'

He decided it might be useful for someone else to know: 'Corvinus deposited his will in the House of the Vestals recently.' Standard procedure for a senator. 'He let me put mine in with it. If anything happens to me, Falco, my executors will find that my testament has a rather intriguing seal . . .'

He was right: he was no idiot. No one, not even the Emperor, could get hold of a will without proper sanction, once it had been given for safekeeping into the Vestal Virgins' charge.

'Satisfied?' he asked me, smiling.

It was brilliant. I loved it. If he hadn't had such a ghastly taste in women, Lusius and I could have been real friends.

I even thought, with just the slightest tinge of jealousy, that it was possible Severina Zotica might at last have met her match.

XLVII

The Senator was sitting in his courtyard garden, talking to his wife. In fact they looked as if they had been wandering round and round some subject until they were both tired of it: probably me. But Camillus Verus had a cluster of grapes in his hand and continued pulling off the fruit in an easy manner even after he saw me, while Julia Justa – whose dark hair in the dusk made her startlingly like Helena – made no move to breach the peace.

'Good evening, sir – Julia Justa! I hoped I might find your daughter here.'

'She comes,' grumbled her father. 'Borrows my books; uses up the hot water; raids the wine cellar! Her mother usually manages some snatch of conversation; I count myself lucky if I glimpse her heel disappearing round a doorframe.' I started to grin. He was a man, sitting in his garden among the moths and flower scents, allowing himself the privilege of sounding off against his young. '. . . I brought her up; I blame myself – she's mine . . .'

'True!' said his wife.

'She has been here tonight?' I butted in to ask her mother, with a smile.

'Oh yes!' her father burst out rowdily. 'I hear your house fell down?'

'One of those things, sir! Lucky we were out . . .'

He waved me to a stone bench with a flourish. 'Your house fell down; so Helena Justina had to ask me how to replace the deeds for her Aunt Valeria's legacy; Helena came to raid her old room for dresses; Helena wanted me to tell *you* that she would see you later –'

'Is she all right?' I managed to squeeze in, turning again to her mama in hope of sense.

'Oh, she seemed her usual self,' Julia Justa commented.

The Senator had run out of jokes; a silence fell.

I braced myself. 'I should have come before.'

Helena's parents exchanged a glance. 'Why bother?' shrugged Camillus. 'It's pretty clear what's going on –'

'I should have explained.'

'Is that an apology?'

'I love her. I won't apologise for that.' Julia Justa must have moved abruptly for I heard her ear-rings shivering and the flounce on her stole swished against the stonework with a scratch of embroidery.

The silence stretched again. I stood up. 'I'd better go and find her.'

Camillus laughed. 'Can I assume you know where to look, or should we get up a search party?'

'I think I know where she is.'

Tired as I was, I walked. I approached my old lair over the high crest of the Aventine; I came to it with dragging feet, thinking about the handsome houses rich people own, and the awful holes where they then expect the poor to live.

I entered the Twelfth district. Home smells assaulted my nose. A wolf whistle, without violence, followed me in the darkness as I took the lane.

Fountain Court.

Of all the groaning tenements in all the sordid city alleyways, the most degrading must be Fountain Court . . .

Outside the barber's, Rodan and Asiacus lifted their gladiatorial frames from a bench where they were chatting; then they sank down again. They could find another day to batter me. At the laundry I heard convivial strains from where Lenia must be entertaining her sordid betrothed. Rome was full of women planning how to fleece their men; grinning, I wondered if she had managed to persuade him yet to name a day.

A door opened. Outlined against the light behind I glimpsed a disorderly lump, topped by a few scrags of hair: Smaractus!

I was all paid up until November; no point stopping to insult him. It would keep. I could exercise my rhetoric some other day. Pretending not to notice him, I tightened my cloak and pulled down my hat so I could pass by like some sinister wraith, enveloped in black. He knew it was me; but he stepped back.

I steeled my legs, then warmed by nostalgia for familiar aggravation, I broached the first of those depressing six flights of stairs.

273

LXVIII

The place was a dump.

An amphora, nobbled from the Senator's mansion, stood leaning against what passed for a table. The bung was out. So this was what went on here when I was off elsewhere, struggling with a case . . . Two pastry doves, oozing with raisin juice, were standing in an old chipped dish, beak to beak like battered lovebirds. One still managed to look sleek enough, but the other had a tired droop to his tail – like me.

The glamorous piece who pretended to take in messages was sitting on the balcony with a beaker of wine, reading one of my private waxed tablets. Probably the one I would have ordered her not to read. The poetry.

She had left a spare cup on the table in case anyone happened along who liked decent wine. I poured myself a drink. Then I leaned against the folding door and rapped with my signet ring. She appeared to take no notice, but her eyelashes ruffled slightly so I reckoned that my manly presence had registered.

'Falco live here?'

'When he feels like it.'

'I've got a message.'

'Better give it to me.'

'You're beautiful.'

Her eyes lifted. 'Hello, Marcus.'

I gave her my masterful grin. 'Hello, fruit! It's all over. Gone as far as I could.'

'Will you convict her?'

'No.'

Helena laid aside my poetry. Alongside her on the bench was a small pyramid of published works. She was wearing one of my more disreputable tunics and her feet were pushed into a pair of crumpled old slippers, also mine. I said, 'Trust me to pick a girl who pinches my clothes and raids my library!'

274

'These came from Uncle Publius –' She gestured to the scrolls. I knew the Senator had a brother who died earlier that year, *"lost at sea"* (made a bad mistake in politics). 'His house had jumble going back to the province where he served as a young man –'

'You read all those this evening?' I asked, afraid it would be an expensive business keeping this quick reader stoked.

'Just skipping.'

'Skipped anything good?'

'I've been reading about King Juba. He married Cleopatra Silene, the daughter of Mark Antony. He seems quite an interesting person – for a king. One of those eccentric private scholars who write detailed notes on curious subjects – a treatise on Spurge, for example.'

'Good old Juba!'

'Are you familiar with Spurge?'

'Naturally.' I sounded as if I were thinking *What in Hades is Spurge?* I grinned. 'Spurge is that green plant, all the same sickly colour: spear-shaped leaves and bitty flowers –'

Helena Justina brought her two strong eyebrows together, then went quiet in a way that meant *How does this idiot know about Spurge?* I heard a warm gurgle: the laugh, full of delight, which she reserved for teasing me. 'Oh you're a market gardener's grandson!'

'And full of surprises!' I said defensively.

'You're clever,' Helena replied, giving me a soft look.

'I like to show an interest. I can read. I read everything I can lay my hands on. If you leave those scrolls around the house, I'll be an expert on King Juba by the end of the week.' I was feeling sore; due to failing in the case maybe. 'I'm not an Aventine lout. Wherever I go I notice things. I pay attention to the Forum news. When people talk I listen properly –' Helena's patient silence stopped my bitter, boisterous flow. 'I know, for instance, that you, my darling, have something particular to say to me about Spurge.'

She smiled. I loved Helena's smile. 'It can be used in medicine. King Juba named one kind Euphorbia, after his physician. Euphorbus employed it as a purgative. Mind you,' declared my darling caustically, 'I wouldn't allow Euphorbus to spoon a dollop into me!'

'Why not?'

'The dose has to be exactly right. Spurge has another use.'

'Tell me,' I murmured, leaning forwards expectantly at the glint in her bonny eyes.

'In King Juba's province archers use it to paint on arrowheads. Spurge is also highly poisonous.'

275

'Poisoned arrows usually work by causing rapid paralysis . . . so where,' I asked, to give her the pleasure of telling me even though I already knew, 'is this province your uncle once served in, which had the famous and scholarly king?'

'Mauretania,' said Helena.

I closed my eyes.

Helena stood up and wrapped her arms round me. She spoke in the quiet, reasoned way she used when we were unravelling a case. 'Of course, this proves nothing. A jurist might deny it was even evidence. But if a prosecution lawyer read out an excerpt from King Juba's treatise, then you told the court about the scroll you saw in Severina's house, then – if the barrister was persuasive and you managed to look more sensible than usual – this is the kind of colourful detail which might condemn.'

I opened my eyes. 'The plants have a milky sap; I remember from weeding. Probably tastes bitter. She may have mixed the juice with honey so Novus would lap it up greedily . . .'

Helena found a way to hold me even closer; I coloured but met her, as they say, halfway. 'Have you worked out how she applied it?' she asked.

'We both knew that some time ago –' Helena nodded. 'She spread the poison on that silver dish, the one used at the dinner party for the cakes. Then she fixed it with her egg-white glaze, so none of the poison touched the cakes. Minnius sent seven; so when Severina failed to attend the dinner, if everybody was polite – as I was told they were – one last cake must have stayed on the dish. All through the business conference Hortensius Novus must have had his eye on it. When the party broke up and he disappeared, he had dashed back into the dining room. He gobbled up the remaining pastry. Then –'

I stopped.

'Then,' Helena completed for me, 'Hortensius Novus licked the plate!'

Would it convict? Only circumstantially. But all evidence is circumstantial in some way. A defence lawyer would be keen to point that out.

Was there any point going on? The gold-digger had made her fortune. She might reform now; she might be reformed by Lusius. I had a personal reason for denouncing Severina, but an even stronger

276

motive for attacking my ex-landlord Novus. If Severina had not murdered Novus for me, I would be a murderer tonight myself.

'Marcus, you're exhausted. I wish I had never told you. You did enough; now let go!'

'No client,' I said. 'No reason to do anything . . . No justice!' I exclaimed.

Justice was for people who could afford it. I was a poor man, with myself and a decent woman to support, on an income that would hardly stretch to let me breathe, let alone save.

Justice never paid a poor man's bills.

I freed myself and walked out to the edge of my balcony, looking over towards the dark shadow of the Janiculan. That was a place to live; good homes with delightful hillside gardens and wonderful views. Close to the Tiber, yet set apart by the river from the jostling of the city, and its noise, dirt and intensity. Some day, when I had money, the Janiculan might be somewhere to look for a home.

Helena came up behind me, nuzzling against my back.

'I saw a house today that I'll buy for you, if ever we're rich,' I said.

'What was it like?'

'Worth waiting for . . .'

We went to bed. The bed here was as horrible as I remembered it, but felt better once Helena was in my arms. It was still the Kalends of September; only this morning I had promised to pay my lady some attention. I was falling asleep. She would wait for me. Tomorrow morning we would wake up together with nothing to do but enjoy ourselves. Now the case was over, I could stay in bed for a week.

I lay there, still thinking about what had happened today. When Helena thought I had fallen asleep, she stroked my hair. Pretending that I *was* asleep, I began caressing her.

Then both of us decided not to wait until tomorrow after all.

FIC
DAV   Davis, Lindsey   28163

Venus in Copper

DATE DUE

AUG 1 0 1992	MAR 2 6 1993			
SEP 0 1 1992				
SEP 1 5 1992	APR 1 7 1993			
OCT 1 0 1992	OCT 1 6 1996			
OCT 2 7 1992	SEP 1 2 1998			
NOV 2 7 1992	SEP 0 5 2001			
DEC 2 2 1992	OCT 0 3 2001			
JAN 1 8 1993	JUN 0 8 2002			
FEB 1 7 1993	IH 10/27/04			
MAR - 8 1993				

DEMCO 38-301